TAKE CARE,
Sara

USA TODAY BETSELLING AUTHOR

LINDY ZART

Take Care, Sara
Published by Lindy Zart
Copyright 2013 Lindy Zart
All rights reserved.
Cover Art by Sprinkles On Top Studios
Formatting by Inkstain Interior Book Designing
Author Photography by Kelley C. Hanson Photography

ACKNOWLEDGEMENTS

MANY, MANY THANKS to my awesome beta readers: Tawnya Peltonen, Kim Drake, Tiffany Alfson, Migdalia Gerena, Shane Lucas, Judith Frazee, Ana Love, Melissa Yoder, Kendra Gaither, and Robin Nichols. Thanks so much for all your input. You are greatly appreciated.

Thanks to Lauren Marie Sloan for the name inspiration of Cole Walker and Jessica Ryba for the name inspiration of Mason Wells.

Special thanks to Cassie Chavez.

I don't know if I would have finished this without urging from you. I know I wouldn't have finished it this soon.

Thank you!

This is dedicated to Tawnya Peltonen and Judith Frazee for the simple reason you are exceptional, humorous, wonderful ladies that I am so glad I had the fortune to never meet. You know what I mean.

And that really isn't a "simple" reason at all.

Again, you know what I mean.

TAKE CARE,
Sara

CHAPTER 1

HE ASKED HER name and smiled.

It wasn't the blueness of his eyes or the crinkles around them when he grinned. The brown softness of his hair or the way it curled on the nape of his neck didn't come close. The masculine beauty of his face; plain, but so much more, and yet nothing more than average, wasn't it either. It wasn't any of those things that made her pause and pretend her heart didn't speed up, though the blush of her skin proved otherwise.

He asked her name and smiled. It was all of that and as little as that.

Sara blinked and drew in a ragged breath. Her eyes took in her surroundings, a reminder of where she was and what she was about to do. The park was empty, which was just as well. The wind was picking up, caressing her dark brown hair and sweeping it up and around her head.

She had realized something over recent months. It didn't matter who you were or what you'd accomplished in life—none of that mattered when tragedy struck. You had no pull, no power. You had no choice. There was nothing to gamble with, nothing to do to put the odds in your favor. You were there and then you were gone, leaving those around you to realize how insignificant they all really were. Leaving them to try to pick up the destroyed pieces. Sara knew now.

No one mattered, not really.

The sun, making a brief appearance moments ago, was once again behind the clouds, and it was fitting somehow. Why should the sun shine on this day, as though to applaud her actions? Sara's flesh was bumpy and tingly and her teeth lightly chattered together. She looked down and reflexively jerked back. It had seemed so simple earlier, so very easy. Now that she was about to do it, it wasn't as uncomplicated as she had thought.

"Don't," she told herself, "don't you dare be a coward."

Sara squeezed her eyes tight against the burning wetness. It trickled past the closed eyelids and made jagged trails down her cold cheeks. He always loved her eyes and said they were like warm chocolate. Sara let out a shaky laugh. He wouldn't think they were so lovable right now, would he? The laughter abruptly cut off and she forced her eyes open. It registered in her mind that she was clutching her midsection, as though to hold the pain in, and she let her arms drop to her sides. Inhaling slowly, she stepped toward her destination. Leaves crackled under her shoes and a sob escaped her.

"Leaves make their own music. Listen once. You'll see what I mean," he'd told her with a wink and a sweet smile.

She stared straight ahead at the mountain on the other side of the vast river. The mountainside was trees and rocks, and a covering of fog kept it out of focus. A bird's cry startled her and she jumped, flinging her arms out to steady herself. Her eyes traveled downward, focusing on the choppy water below as she watched the waves lower and rise, over and over. The river was wide and deep and brown and cold—she knew it would be so cold.

He came home every night from work and before anything else, before he took off his coat or boots or baseball cap, he pulled her into his arms and held her close. He kissed her forehead and told her he missed her and he smelled so good, so familiar, like sunshine and warmth. Like home. He told her once that if anything ever happened to her, there wouldn't be enough tears in the world for him to cry.

Sara placed a hand to her mouth as pain wracked her frame. It was strange how much a body could physically hurt from one's emotions. The same could be said for memories. If she focused really hard, she could almost feel his arms, smell the scent of him—that addicting combination of man and soap—or taste his lips of cherry-flavored Carmex and coffee.

She took a step forward.

Sometimes, when she was really silent and still, she thought she could hear his deep laughter and his low voice. He always sounded far away and faint and Sara had to strain her ears to make out his words. If she thought too hard about it, his voice disappeared, and she was left feeling empty, hollow.

Another step.

They bought their first house together. It wasn't much, just a little two bedroom ranch, but it was theirs. She planted flowers along the front of it, red and pink and yellow ones. Sara kept forgetting to water them and they died. He teased her about her green thumb and then he bought her a fake plant to put outside on the porch.

"This one can't die 'cause it ain't alive," he drawled in that slow country boy way of his. That twang had always been an enigma to Sara, since he had lived in Wisconsin his whole life.

Sara lined the toes of her scuffed tennis shoes an inch away from the edge of Wyalusing State Park. The side of the bluff was jagged rocks and bent trees and dirt. She tried not to look at it. She didn't want to think about the landing and she didn't want to think about where that landing might be.

She didn't want to think. Period.

"I'm sorry," she whispered, wondering if he could somehow hear her.

Closing her eyes, she inhaled slowly, and let her body fall forward.

"Hey!"

The unexpected shout caused Sara to snap her eyes open and flail her arms, which in turn propelled her backward and away from danger. Before she could land on the hard ground, vice-like arms were wrapped around her and pulling her farther and farther away from where she wanted to be. Sara didn't like the arms around her. She didn't like what she knew instinctively to be a man holding her that way—the way he held her. No one else could hold her that way.

"Get away! Let me go!" she shrieked, kicking her legs out and slapping at the warm flesh.

With a grunt, the arms were suddenly gone. Sara landed on her side in the leaves, the crisp sound of them agonizing to her. She stumbled to her feet, shaking, and turned to face her unwanted rescuer. She didn't see features or eye or hair color, she didn't see anything but a person who had thwarted her plan, a plan it had taken every ounce of her courage to put into motion.

The man asked something. Sara saw his lips move, but there was a buzzing in her ears, blocking out the sound of his voice. She felt numb, like all the energy it had taken to get to that ledge had drained her. Sara looked at him, not really seeing him at all, and turned away, back to her car, back to her unnecessary life.

"Hey! Lady! Do you need help?"

Sara walked the short distance to her car, a red four door Pontiac Grand Prix, opened the door, and got in. She sat with her hand on the keys, looking out the window. She could drive her car over the ledge. A vision of her in her vehicle falling, falling, falling into the icy cold water shot through her mind. She saw the car filling up with murky water, she saw herself struggling to get out, to breathe. Sara shuddered. No. Not today.

A knock on the window had her turning her head. Her brown eyes met amber ones. The man motioned for her to roll down her window. She shook her head. He mouthed, "Are you okay? Can I help you?"

Sara stared at him for a long time. He stared back, his eyebrows lowering. She slowly faced forward, turned the key in the ignition, and put the car in reverse.

As SHE SLICED a tomato, her eyes were fixated on the long, serrated blade. She looked at her right wrist, at the way the veins formed an 'H'. The veins of her left wrist wove a jagged line to her palm. She carefully set the knife down on the counter and turned her attention to her salad.

She sat at the table and forced two bites down her throat, her body unconsciously turning toward the chair he'd always taken. Sara's appetite disintegrated as she watched the empty spot, waiting for him to appear and tease her about eating 'rabbit food'. Abruptly standing up, Sara threw away the salad. Her eyes skimmed across the kitchen walls, looking through the pale blue wall paint and decorative pieces and white cupboards and remembering him.

"Why do they call them cupboards?" he asked, standing with one lean hip against the counter.

Sara gave him a quizzical look. "Why do they call a door a door? Who knows?"

Cole followed her into the living room to continue the conversation. "But...they're not boards, not really, and there's more than just cups in there, so why cupboards? Why not...dinnerware holders? And another thing—why is it spelled like that? 'Cause when you say it, it comes out like 'cubberd', not cup and board together. You see what I'm saying?" he asked, plopping down beside her on the couch and flinging his arm around her shoulders.

"I know you're saying something, but I'm not sure what."

To which he responded to by grabbing her face and kissing her breathless. "You know what I'm saying and you know I'm right 'cause I'm always right."

"I know you think you're always right."

He shrugged. "Same difference."

"In your mind."

"That's right, darling, and that's all that matters. As long as I make sense in my own head, everything's okay."

"You're delusional."

Cole grinned, showing off white teeth that were slightly crooked and completely endearing. "And you love it."

"I must be delusional," she said, smiling.

"And I love it."

Sara took a staggering breath and rubbed her eyes. She was standing in front of the garbage can, an empty plate and fork next to her on the counter. She quickly washed the supper dishes and dried them, carefully putting them in their proper places.

A long, almost unbearably hot shower soothed her and she thought maybe, just maybe, this one time she wasn't crying. But when the water stopped and the wetness continued to trickle down her face, she knew otherwise. Wrapped in a towel, she combed her long hair and brushed her teeth. When she looked in the mirror, the face she saw was close to unrecognizable. It was too pale and the bone structure was overly prominent. The red and puffy eyes couldn't be hers. But who else's could they be? The life had been sucked from her brown eyes, leaving them dead, and her brown hair was limp and hung past her shoulders.

Never one to consider herself beautiful, or even that pretty, Sara had always found it odd that he told her she was on an almost daily basis. She was average. Average in height, in weight, in looks, and yet he'd looked at her like she was incomparable to anyone, like she was *more than*. The way her nose upturned at the end had forever been a recipient of his kisses. The fullness of her upper lip had repeatedly drawn his finger to it to trace and receive her kiss.

He wouldn't like seeing you like this, a voice told her. Sara blinked and turned away.

She quickly dressed in a pink nightshirt and left the bedroom before too many memories ensnared her thoughts. A look at the clock told her it was eight. Sara grabbed a blanket and a pillow from the closet in the bedroom and set up her bed on the couch, as she did every night. As she lay in the darkness, looking at a ceiling she couldn't see, she held her hands together to pray, the act so ingrained in her she almost did so without thought, but caught herself in time. Prayers hadn't helped before. Why would they help now? And what exactly would she pray for?

Restless, she got up and turned the light back on, her agitated fingers continuously twisting the silver-banded ring with the lone diamond it. Around and around it went over her bony finger too small for the ring to properly fit on anymore. Remembering the wedding proposal brought a fleeting smile to her lips. He'd put the ring around a single red rose and presented it to her with an achingly honest speech.

The walls of the living room were ivory and bare, but she still saw the framed photographs that used to grace the walls. Their first picture taken together. The engagement photo. Christmas. Their wedding. A photograph of them making silly faces at the camera. It had been too painful to look at them, day after day, mocking her. Reminding her of what she had lost. Sara had taken them down and put them in a box and in the garage they now resided.

Her eyes landed on the pale green recliner that had been his. He complained about the girly color at first, but it hadn't been long before it was his favorite place to sit. Sara ran a trembling hand along the back of it, leaning down to sniff its scent. Pain, sharp and immobilizing, shot through her. It didn't smell like him anymore. When had his scent disappeared? It was one more thing she'd lost of him, and the knowledge was too much to bear. Sara grabbed the blanket from the couch and climbed onto the recliner, pretending his arms were around her, holding her close. She curled into a ball, huddled beneath the cover, and wept until she fell into a fitful sleep.

The nightmares began with a flourish, as they did almost every night. Her mind replayed the otherworldliness of it—how it had started in slow-motion and still somehow ended before she knew what had happened. In Sara's mind she saw the smile that had mutated to horror, the instant pain, the smell of blood, and the heat. It ended with the screech of heavy metal crashing and the eerie silence that had followed.

She awoke screaming, tangled in the blanket. She struggled to free herself, to sit upright. Covered in sweat and shaking, her heart slammed against her chest. And of course, there were the tears. They streamed down her cheeks, warm and unwanted, and dropped onto her lap. Sara covered her face with her hands and rocked forward and backward, trying to remove the images from her mind. She would cut them out if she could.

A kaleidoscope of that final moment with him raced through her brain. His smile she loved, the striking blue of his eyes, warm with love and happiness, his hand on her shoulder. Sara squeezed her eyes shut, but it didn't block the remembrance of his grip tightening painfully, and then jerking away, as though something wrenched him from her. The shouts ripped from his lips. The fear on his face. But not for him—for her.

Always for her.

She found it strange the way she remembered it all, as though she had watched it from afar and her eyes had seen him and nothing else. Nothing but him had registered. Which made it that much more terrible. Because that's what she remembered, what she relived, every single day.

Him.

In fine detail.

Dying.

"You have to move on."

Sara looked at her clasped hands. "I can't."

"You *have* to. It's not a matter of can or will, it's *have* to."

"He'll come back."

"He won't."

"You don't know that."

"I do."

Sara pressed her lips together and watched her fingers go white in her lap. "This is all a dream."

"This is reality. He's gone, you're not. Live, Sara."

"He's not gone, not really."

"Yes. He is."

She bit her lower lip to keep it from trembling. "No."

"He wouldn't want this."

The tears, her ever-present companion, showed themselves. "I know," she whispered.

"It's been over a year."

Her eyelids slowly closed against the pain those words evoked. One year. Had it been so long? Had it been so short? "I know."

"Sara."

She stopped rocking in her chair, and then wondered how long she'd been rocking without knowing it.

"Sara."

Her eyes opened. Sara jumped to her feet and looked around the room. It was empty. Her house was empty, like it should be, like it always was. She frowned and rubbed her pounding forehead. Her hands were shaking. It was happening again. Not again. She was losing her mind, she had to be losing her mind. There was no one there. On top of everything else, she was mad. But if she was insane, she wouldn't realize it, right? So maybe she was okay.

The phone rang and she jumped. Sara grabbed it from the wall. *Please be whoever was just talking to me, please don't let that all be in my head. We were talking on the phone and we somehow got disconnected and I sat down to wait for you to call again.*

"Hello?"

"Mrs. Walker?"

Sara squeezed her eyes shut and mutely shook her head. *You're not who I wanted to be calling me—who my sanity needs to be calling me.*

"Hi," she managed to get out. She sank into a chair at the kitchen table and held her head in one hand.

"Is everything okay?"

"Of course."

"You haven't visited in a long time."

"I've...I've been busy," she lied, holding the phone so tight against her ear it hurt.

"You missed your last two appointments."

"Yeah, sorry, I was working."

A pause. "On your artwork?"

"Yes." Sara's eyes slid to the right. There was a door there, and beyond that door, was her career, dusty with disuse. She hurriedly looked away, as if by looking in that direction she was announcing the massive untruth.

"And how is it coming along?"

"Great."

"What are you working on?"

Her leg shook a frenzied beat as her teeth gnawed on the skin around her thumb. "Uh...listen, Doc, I gotta go."

"Can we set up a time to meet?"

"I don't—"

"It's imperative that I see you. You have to know this."

Her shoulders slumped. A whispered, "I know," left her.

"How's Tuesday, the 29th? At ten in the morning."

Tuesday. When was it Tuesday the 29th? What day was today? Sara massaged a circle into the middle of her forehead. Tuesday the 29th. Only a little over three weeks away. It was too soon. Panic seized her. That Tuesday was too soon.

"Sara?"

"Yes?"

"Great. See you then."

No! Sara's mouth opened, but there was no point in arguing when all that would hear her was a dial tone. She hung up the phone. She'd been acknowledging that she was listening, not that she was agreeing to see him, and she knew he knew that. She lurched to her feet. She couldn't do it, couldn't go there, couldn't see him, couldn't talk to him. Sara couldn't even look at him. No. She'd been putting it off for so long and he knew it. Yet it was still too soon. She wasn't ready. Sara would never be ready.

SARA HAD BEEN an only child. She'd grown up in a big house in Iowa with a loving mother and father who both passed away from this world far too soon. They'd tried for years to conceive and had given up when she came into the picture. Older than they'd thought they'd be as first time parents, they'd done all the activities parents decades younger than them would have and more. They didn't want her to miss out on anything. They didn't want her childhood to be lacking in any way. Her throat tightened and she leaned back on the couch, rubbing her face and wiping her stinging eyes.

Her mother was a kindergarten teacher and her father was an electrician. Jim Cunningham had a heart attack at the age of sixty-one—one he didn't recover from. Darcy Cunningham died not long after that at the age of fifty-nine. The doctors said she had a stroke, but Sara knew what she'd really died from. It was a broken heart. They were both seemingly healthy and both taken from Sara when she was only twenty years old.

It had been hard to accept one of their deaths, but both of them had been smothering. She literally hadn't been able to breathe for short amounts of time for weeks after her mother's passing. Sara had had to force air into her lungs when all she'd wanted to do was *not* breathe. Breathing had hurt. Breathing had meant she'd lived while her parents no longer did. It was like her body had wanted to stop living because it couldn't deal with the pain of losing them.

Sara had thrown herself into her schooling and her artwork and lived, but not like before, never the same as she'd lived before their deaths. She'd existed in a numb state for months. She closed her eyes. It was nothing like what she felt now. It hurt whether she breathed or not. And the one thing that stung the most was knowing her parents' love had been so true and pure that one had not been able to live without the other, and yet, here she sat, without her love, still living, still breathing.

No matter how many times Sara loved, she lost. She longed for it all to *stop.*

CHAPTER 2

EVERY ROOM IN the house was spotless. It had a perpetual lemon and bleach smell to it Sara didn't think would ever go away. The scent had seeped into the walls and carpet and floor of every room, a blaring testimony to Sara's obsessive housework. It was amazing how such menial work could distract one's thoughts. Sara spent most of every day cleaning and when it was nice out, she did yard work. A look outside told her there would soon be snow on the ground and then the shoveling would begin. But for now, she occupied herself with a complete scrub down of the bathroom.

She was on her hands and knees, inhaling chemicals and sweating.

"That's not good for you, ya know."

Sara blinked and looked behind her. He stood in the doorway with one broad shoulder propped against it, grinning at her. She could have cried at the sight of his tall and lanky form, the rugged tan of his skin. His ice blue eyes were full of love and mischief.

She frowned, confused. He couldn't be here, could he? Not really.

"Did you hear me?"

Sara sat back on her heels and stared. "What?"

He took a step into the bathroom, his shoes almost touching her. She looked at his shoes, reached out to touch him, any part of him. "All those chemicals going into your pretty little head. It's not good for you."

"How are you here?" she whispered.

He laughed; a wonderful sound Sara hadn't heard in over a year. Her ears stung from the sweet sound of it. "Come on, babe, don't you think the house is clean enough already? Let's go have some fun. It's a beautiful day out. You and me. The beach. And your sexy bikini." He wiggled his eyebrows up and down.

Sara inhaled sharply, blinked, and came back to reality. It wasn't beautiful out. It was cold and dark. She looked to the place he'd been standing. He wasn't there. A memory or something her mind unconsciously manifested was all it had been. She swiped an arm across her face and went back to cleaning the bathroom, drops of sweat and tears mingling on the floor.

The phone rang. Sara ignored it. She scrubbed the inside of the toilet with a toilet brush, kept scrubbing even after it sparkled. Her hands shook and toilet water and cleaner splashed up on her. Sobs wracked her body so hard she jerked from them. *So pathetic. Can't even clean a toilet without crying. Weak. I'm weak. He was the strong one. He should be here. Not me.* Something hot and ugly formed inside of her. *Why wasn't it me? Why him? Why?* Sara let out a scream of anguish and whipped the toilet brush across the room. It hit the shower curtain with a wet smack and dropped to the floor.

The phone still rang; the shrill sound making her teeth clench together and a headache form. She slapped her hands on the tiled floor, welcoming the sting to her flesh. It brought her back to the brink of lucidity, if only minutely. She stayed there, on her knees, until control came back. Sara got to her feet, swiped a hand across her sweaty, tear-stained face, and answered the phone. No one was there. She slammed the phone back in place. Sara stood there shaking, unable to move. Had the phone even actually rung, or had that been in her head as well?

On the verge of losing it completely, Sara picked the phone up and dialed a number.

"Hello?" The voice was deep, familiar. It reminded her of him, and though it hurt to hear it, it helped a little too. She sank against the wall, slid down it, and cradled the phone to her ear. Sara closed her eyes and waited for the respite to come.

When she remained silent, the person on the other end of the line began to talk softly. "Bad day, huh?" He made a sound of derision. "Not that any day is spectacular. I had one a couple days ago. It didn't make any sense, not really. I was at work, fixing a leak in a roof, when I remembered a time we went fishing. Nothing significant happened that day we went fishing, nothing to make me remember it, or to think of it at that moment. But, well, does it ever have to make sense?

"We were ten and twelve that summer. We grabbed our fishing poles and headed to the creek. I carried the bucket of worms. Because I was younger, he said. We sat in the grass at that creek all day. We didn't catch a single thing and it was so hot out. The sun burned our skin. Bugs had a meal out of us. It smelled like sweat and grass and fish."

Sara felt herself begin to relax. She took a deep, calming breath.

"But it was just us, there wasn't another soul out when we first got there. Probably because it was six in the morning on a Saturday. And later, because it was too hot out for any smart person to roast away under the sun." He laughed.

Sara closed her eyes at the sound and let the sad, but musical notes wash over her.

"Only thing we heard was the sound of rushing water from the stream and my voice whenever I tried to talk, which wasn't much, since he kept telling me to shut up. We stayed there all day. We ditched the poles in the late afternoon and jumped in the water. Needless to say, we forgot to mention to our parents where we were going or what we were doing that day.

"So when we finally showed up at home, wet and sunburned, it was to find police cars and frantic adults in the yard. They grounded us. For the rest of the summer. And it was only the beginning of June. That summer sucked." He laughed softly. A long pause. "I hope that helped." Then a sigh. "Take care, Sara."

She turned the phone off and sat there, her back flush against the hard wall and beginning to twinge in discomfort from her position. Sara didn't care, her thoughts on the phone call. He always ended their one-sided conversation the same. The longer she sat the more the sense of tranquility fell away from her and sorrow once more cocooned her. But for one small period of time she'd been at peace. Sara clung to that for as long as she could and when it finally left her, her heart ached at the absence of it.

THERE WERE FRIENDS, or rather, there used to be friends, but Sara had alienated them. Friends of his, mostly. Sara had always kept to herself; most comfortable in small social groups and with her family. She'd had a few friends growing up, but none close. Any friends she'd acquired since her marriage had been his first and remained his before hers. It wasn't that she didn't like people, but she was easily flustered around strangers and wasn't very outgoing. Basically, she preferred her own company to others. He'd been the friendly, outgoing one.

His friends came by at first after it happened, offering their support. Some would cry, others would stumble through awkward conversations, and some even took it upon themselves to try to get a smile or a laugh out of her—all failing. They would give her advice she didn't want to hear, they would say they'd been in a similar situation, they would say they knew how she felt. They told her it would get better. It wasn't long before only an infrequent straggler would stop by out of a feeling of obligation.

Sara had enough sense to realize that her gloomy demeanor chased them all away. She couldn't pretend things were okay when they weren't. She couldn't laugh when she wanted to cry. She couldn't talk about it, and everyone wanted to talk about nothing but it. Her soul had been ripped out; what was the point in pretending it hadn't been?

So she was shocked when there was a knock on the door and she came face to face with Spencer Johnson. He'd been a good friend of her husband's, one of the last to give up on her. It had been at least a month, maybe two, since she'd last seen him. Time had no meaning for Sara, other than to mock her with its endless sorrow. Spencer looked the same—big and dark-haired and dark-eyed.

He shifted his feet and shoved his hands in his brown leather coat pockets. "Hey, Sara," he said, shoulders hunched.

"Uh, hi." Sara pushed hair out of her face and waited.

Spencer met her eyes and faintly smiled. "Can I come in?"

With a hot face, Sara opened the door wider. "Yes, of course. Sorry."

He ambled by and stopped in the kitchen, did a slow circle, and faced her. "Place looks the same," he commented.

She closed the door and pulled at the hem of her shirt, eyes downcast.

"Clean," he continued.

Sara glanced up and caught his grin. She looked away as she answered, "It keeps me busy."

"Right." He nodded. "So what's new?"

Sara swept past him and began to fiddle around the kitchen. "Nothing. Would you like something to eat? Drink?" She had a carrot cake on the counter and coffee going before he had a chance to answer.

"Sure."

Manners and small talk were not something one had to worry about by oneself and Sara found herself struggling to act human. "Um...sit," she commanded and pointed at a chair. Spencer gave her a look of surprise and she modified her drill sergeant tone. "I mean, please sit." She gestured toward the table.

Spencer pulled a chair out and slowly sat down. "How are you doing?"

The coffee stopped percolating and Sara kept a sigh inside as she turned her back to Spencer. It was easier to lie that way. "Fine. Everything's fine." She grabbed two mugs from the cupboard, recognized one as his, and put it back and chose a different one. She knew without looking Spencer was watching her and was glad when he made no comment.

"Are you doing any painting?"

Coffee sloshed over the rim of the mug and onto her hand. Sara yelped. Spencer was instantly by her side, pulling her toward the sink. He quickly ran cold water over the angry-colored flesh of her hand.

"Coffee's sneaky that way," he murmured, still holding her hand. They both went still, studying the slim pale fingers of her hand within his larger, darker one. Sara snatched her hand away and moved to put distance between them.

Spencer acted like he didn't notice and said, "Why don't you sit and I'll get the coffee? Still take it black?"

Sara nodded, realized he wasn't looking at her, and answered, "Yes. Thank you."

He set the coffee mugs on the table and slid one over to Sara.

"Thank you," she said again.

"No need to thank me for your own coffee," he told her, opening another cupboard and removing two plates.

"I don't..." she began, but stopped at his lethal stare.

"Yes. You do. You're skin and bones."

Sara held the cup between her hands and looked into the black depths. "I'm fine."

Spencer went about the task of getting them each a piece of cake, making no comment. He sat down, immediately digging into the cake with a fork. "Mmm, this is good. You make this?"

Sara nodded.

He squinted his eyes at her. "Yet you don't eat it?"

She shook her head.

"Why do you make it?"

Sara rubbed her finger over a line in the wood of the table. "For something to do."

"What do you do with it?"

With a shrug, Sara responded, "Give it away."

"To whom?"

"Neighbors."

"Eat," he said, pointing his fork at her untouched slice of cake.

Sara took a small bite to pacify him.

"I'll have to move into the neighborhood. Or stop by more often," he added.

Sara didn't respond. She didn't want or need someone checking up on her, least of all Spencer, regardless of his good intentions. She searched her mind for something to talk about. "How's Gracie?"

Spencer paused with the mug of coffee close to his lips. He set it down without taking a drink. "Gracie and I broke up." He finished the last bite of his cake and sat back in his chair.

Sara jerked, startled. "Oh. I'm sorry." She was, in that place deep inside of her that still felt things like empathy.

He shrugged with a little smile on his lips. "It was months ago."

She met his eyes, and then slid her gaze away. "You didn't mention it the last time I saw you."

"You were preoccupied."

Sara hung her head, wanting to forget the last time he'd made an impromptu visit. She'd been in the throes of a binge of destruction and rage and pain; smashing and breaking anything she'd laid eyes on reminiscent of her husband. Spencer had shown up in the middle of it, calmed her down, and listened to her terrible sobbing. He'd held her in his arms and rocked her like a baby, and then he'd even helped her right the house. And then she'd thrown him out.

She was still mortified over the incident. Of her lack of control, of her weakness, of allowing him to hold her and offer comfort. Sara was especially remorseful over her rudeness. Spencer had only meant to help. At the same time, she wished he'd stayed away; she wished he wasn't here now.

"It's okay, Sara," he said softly, with conviction.

She refused to raise her head. She knew what she'd see in his eyes. Pity, sympathy. She blinked her eyes against the stinging in them and took a deep breath, composing herself. *Say something. Ask something. Don't just sit there and try not to cry.*

"You went out a long time, right? You and Gracie?"

"Yeah. Five years."

Five years. One more year than she'd had with her husband before the accident. "Why'd you break up?"

Spencer shrugged as he got up to refill his cup and plate. "She decided she didn't like my career, even though I'd had the same one since I met her. Too dangerous. Want some?" He motioned to the coffee pot and cake pan.

Sara shook her head. "Gracie was nice."

Spencer got a slightly wistful look on his face. "That she was."

"I'm sorry," she repeated.

He sat down and took a bite of cake. Spencer met her eyes, looking sheepish. "I skipped lunch."

Sara waved his comment away. "Eat as much as you want."

"We still talk. I'm over it, she's over it. We actually get along better as friends than we ever did dating."

"That's good then," was the best reply she could think of.

A long silence ensued.

Spencer sipped his coffee, his eyes on her. "You done any hiking lately?"

Sara went still. "No. Why?"

"You haven't been to Wyalusing?"

"That's not what you asked," she said stiffly.

"So you have been there?"

She got to her feet. "Why are you asking me this?"

Spencer sighed and stood. "Friend of mine was there, Sara."

She backed away, toward the counter. "So?"

The sad look on Spencer's face was too much. Sara looked down.

"So I know what happened."

"No, you don't."

Spencer slammed his fingers through his hair, messing it up. "Really? Maybe you should explain it to me then. From what my friend said, a woman looked like she was ready to...to *kill* herself, jump off the damn cliff, for shit's sake."

She flinched, but remained silent.

"He had me run the plates, Sara, and imagine my shock when I realized the car belonged to you."

She couldn't talk, because if she did, she would cry. So she stood there, silent and still and on the verge of weeping, and willed him to leave. Sara wanted him to go away and stay away and leave her alone.

"Tell me he was wrong. Tell me it wasn't you," Spencer pleaded, his gaze locked on her.

Sara glanced up, surprised to find Spencer close, and that he looked so very earnest.

"Talk to me. I lost Co—"

"Don't say his name!" she shrieked. Spencer flinched. "Don't say his name," she repeated, in a calmer tone.

"Why?" he demanded, hands on hips.

"Because," Sara whispered, tears trickling down her cheeks.

"Because why?" he asked, sweeping the wetness from her cheeks with his thumb.

She moved her head away from his touch. She hated anyone touching her. It seemed like a betrayal to him, even with the most innocent of intentions. She didn't deserve to be comforted; she didn't deserve anyone's sympathy.

"Why are you doing this?" He ran a hand over his face. "Why are you living this way, Sara? You can't keep doing this. You can't keep living like this. You need to stop. If you can't talk to me, talk to *someone*. Talk to Lincoln."

Sara looked at him then, flinching at the sound of her brother-in-law's name. "Don't you think I know that? That's why I was there, to stop living this way! Your stupid friend ruined it!" She suddenly let out a weary breath. "And Lincoln can't help me. No one can help me. I'd be better off—better off dead." She swallowed thickly.

He jerked his head back as though he'd been slapped. "You can't be serious."

Her chin notched up.

"You think the answer is to kill yourself?" Spencer asked in a low voice, looking incredulous and furious at the same time.

She closed her eyes and sank to the floor. She was tired, so tired. She rested her head on her knees and closed her eyes. "Then I don't have to hurt, then I don't have to wonder, then I don't have to worry about any of it."

"You think this is what he'd want?"

She opened her eyes to find Spencer kneeling beside her. "Maybe."

"Why? You can't possibly blame yourself for what happened."

Sara didn't answer, just looked at him.

"It wasn't your fault," he said slowly.

Sara blinked her eyes, but the wetness continued to come forth. "Wasn't it?"

THERE WERE TIMES, split seconds of a minute, when she forgot that he was no longer there, times when she could stare out at the night, like tonight, and simply take in the beauty of the moment without the constant ache. The peace was fleeting, almost to the point where she barely acknowledged it before the pain was back. But for just a moment, she breathed easier as she closed her eyes against the star-strewn night. In these rare and brief moments, she was almost normal.

She opened her eyes and huddled under the fleece blanket, her feet sliding against the porch floor where they hung down from the swing. It was cold out, the breeze causing a chill through her. It was late October and they were lucky it wasn't colder than it was by now, but the scent of winter was in the air. . She should go inside, but she couldn't seem to find the energy to move.

There was a void, a hole within her only he could fill. She felt like half a person; bereft, lost. Nothing was as bright as it used to be, nothing smelled as good. Everything was dimmed, even Sara.

You're losing yourself, Spencer had said.

It was true. She didn't recognize herself from the person she'd once been; the person he'd met that fall day.

It was autumn in southwest Wisconsin and it was beautiful, more beautiful than any fall she'd previously witnessed. Sara gazed at the changing colors of the trees; the many shades of reds and oranges and yellows breathtaking to behold. She loved it here, so thankful she'd decided to relocate after finishing college in Iowa. She inhaled the crisp air, held her arms out at her sides, and twirled in a circle. The fallen leaves crunched under her boots as she spun and spun. She laughed, dizzy and happy.

"You know you're trespassing." The voice was soft and deep and spoke in a slow drawl.

She gasped and whirled around, almost falling in her unbalanced state. She lurched to a stop with her mouth open. Before her stood a man; a tall, rangy man. He wore faded jeans that hugged his muscular thighs, boots, and a brown sweatshirt. A baseball cap was low over his eyes and she had to squint to make out his features. What she found most disturbing of all was the ax he held in his hands.

"I, uh, I didn't know that. Actually," she stuttered, eyeing his possible weapon.

He nodded. "You are."

Sara self-consciously pushed her hair out of her eyes and mouth and looked around the countryside. She'd decided to go for a mid-morning walk and hadn't realized how far she'd gone from town until nothing but woods surrounded her. Not exactly a reassuring setup with a strange man holding an ax and informing her she was where she wasn't wanted.

She turned back to the stranger. "Can you, uh, put down the ax?"

He looked down, as though surprised to find himself holding it, and dropped it. The man pulled the hat from his head, revealing a finely chiseled face, piercing blue eyes, and light brown hair. He rubbed his head and resituated the hat. "Shit, I'm sorry. You're probably wondering if I'm some ax murderer or something, ain't you?"

"Well, I did hear Ed Gein and Jeffrey Dahmer were from Wisconsin. If that says anything about the state." Just the names passing her lips caused a shiver through her.

He threw back his head and laughed; the sound deep and booming and a little scary, given the situation. Because didn't crazy people laugh at things that weren't funny? Like her mentioning serial killers. Who on earth would find that humorous?

"You're not from around here, are you?" His eyes flashed with humor.

She inched back a step, preparing to run if she had to. "No. But my family visits me often, like, every day. Plus they know I go for walks, around here, right here, actually. And if anything happened to me, this is the first place they'd look," she babbled.

"You better get going then, before you have to find out if there are any more serial killers here in Wisconsin," he told her, nodding beyond her to the endless forest.

She just about peed herself at that response. Instead Sara spun around, intent on taking flight. She'd run track in high school, and though it had been a while since she'd tested her long ago skill, she was thinking she'd give him a run for his money in a mad dash, especially if it meant her survival.

"Hey," he commanded.

Sara stopped, her stomach dipping, and looked over her shoulder.

He smiled at her, a beatific transformation of the lips and face that caught her breath. That smile turned his average features into something extraordinary. It was in that instant that Sara knew she was in trouble. And not the kind of trouble she'd been prepared to sprint from moments ago. That smile, those eyes—they did something to her.

With laughter on his lips and in his eyes, he asked, "What's your name?"

Sara dashed a hand at her leaky eyes, abruptly brought back to the present by the sounds of neighborhood children playing in the leaves. She turned her head to watch them under the blanket of twilight. They were the Niles children; George at age 6 and Ramona at age 9. Their peals of laughter were bittersweet to her; a reminder of something she had wanted, almost had, and now would never have again.

Isn't it a little dark for them to be playing outside?

Just as she thought this, the mother—a slim, attractive lady named Tracie, opened the front door and called them inside. She paused, her eyes on Sara, and gave a little wave. She raised her hand in greeting. The door closed, shutting the warmth and joy of the kids inside with their parents.

She sighed, rubbing her face. It was time to go inside for the night.

CHAPTER 3

SARA GREW UP going to Sunday school and church. She said her nightly prayers. Her family gave thanks at mealtime. She spoke to God in her mind on an almost daily basis. If she was scared at night in the dark, she asked Him to watch over her and only then could she sleep. She'd believed so steadfastly in Him, in His wonder and omnipotence, in her certainty that He would always look out for her and keep her safe. She had been so unfailingly devoted. She'd felt sorry for people who didn't have faith, for those who chose not to believe, for those who doubted.

She had always wondered how it was okay for them to tell their children to believe in Santa Claus and the Easter bunny and all those other mythical beings, but not in the one true solidarity, the one true Being. She'd known bad things happened to good people, but in the back of her mind, she'd always rationalized that if you were truly good, you would be salvaged and nothing too horrible would afflict you and yours.

She had been wrong. Unequivocally wrong. Her faith hadn't saved her husband. It hadn't kept him with her. Her faith had done nothing to heal her pain and it had done nothing to ease her guilt. Sara had found no peace. It had been like a weight of deception on her shoulders, like she had been kidding herself her whole life, and finally, she saw the truth. He'd never helped her. He hadn't saved the person she loved above all others. In fact, He wasn't real. He didn't exist.

And then...she just...gave up.

She tightened the tie of her old blue robe and glanced at the clock in the living room. It was church time. A look out the window showed her the Niles', her neighbors with the two kids, were on their way to worship God, as they did every Sunday. She turned away and sat on the couch, staring at a blank television screen. She no longer had satellite service. When she'd forgotten to pay the bill three consecutive months in a row, it had been canceled. It had taken her another few months to figure that out. She had her laptop and the internet—both of which she rarely used—a cordless phone in the kitchen, and a cell phone she never turned on. That was it. Even having those seemed pointless. She was all alone, but that was how she wanted to be and how she *needed* to be. Sara felt like poison. Anyone who came too close to her died.

She turned her gaze to the closed bathroom door. A shower determined how her day was going to be. If she got enough ambition to take a shower, then she normally got enough drive to do other things. Those days were easier to get through. It was such a small, simple task and yet its act had monumental power over her state of mind. On the days she couldn't get enough energy to shower—those were bad days. Today was going to be a bad day. Not that any day was good, but some were easier to take than others.

The knock at the door startled her. Sara froze, not wanting to answer the door. She waited for whoever it was to go away. Instead the banging turned persistent.

"Sara. Open up." The voice was muffled, but distinctly Spencer's. No one else's growled like that. Funny how she'd forgotten that about him.

She didn't want to see him. He couldn't badger her into feeling a certain way. He couldn't make her think something she didn't just by being an insistent pest.

"I'm not leaving, Sara. And unless you want my impending pneumonia on your conscience, you'll open up, 'cause it's colder than...cold out here."

With a sigh, she unlocked the door and flung it open. Her eyes blinked at the stinging sunlight and she shivered against the blast of icy air. "What do you want, Spencer?"

She quickly deduced Spencer wasn't alone. A man stood next to him. They were dressed similarly in jeans and brown jackets. He was shorter than Spencer, which wasn't saying much since Spencer was close to six and a half feet tall, and had dark blond hair and unusual colored eyes.

Sara turned away from his penetrating gaze, feeling uncomfortable. Those eyes seemed to be able to see into her soul. It was disconcerting and she didn't like it. She looked at Spencer. "What's going on?"

"Colder than cold?" the man asked Spencer.

"Can we come in? Please?"

She wanted to say no. She wanted to close the door and never open it again, to have the world outside her house disappear. *She* wanted to disappear. Sara didn't want useless conversations from people who meant well but had no clue. She was about to say so when something clicked inside her head. Her eyes flew to the stranger. He watched her, expressionless.

Sara felt something like betrayal as she looked at Spencer. "What are you doing?"

"He can help. Please. Just talk to him." Spencer gave her a beseeching look.

"No offense, but I don't want to talk to you," she told the man. Even with being shorter than Spencer, he was still half a foot taller than Sara and she had to look up to meet his eyes. They were the color of wine and revealed nothing.

"None taken." He stepped forward until Sara had to move back or be sandwiched against him. She moved.

Spencer gave her an apologetic look as he followed the guy into her house. Sara closed the door, stunned at the man's audacity.

"We never got the chance to be properly introduced the other day," he said, turning to face Sara.

The featureless man from Wyalusing State Park now had a face. It was sharply angled with a long nose and thin lips. It wasn't handsome, but it was arresting.

"Who are you?" She tore her eyes from his and frowned at Spencer. Spencer wouldn't meet her eyes. Why had he done this? All he was going to accomplish by this spectacle was her embarrassment and resentment.

The man moved in a slow circle, his eyes studying the bare walls. Sara wanted to hide from the knowing look on his face. His expression said he knew her secrets and he knew why she had them. Her pain was hers alone and he had no right to act like he understood it.

"I was just about to get to that." He stopped, giving her his full attention. "My name is Mason Wells and I'm a grief counselor."

Sara stiffened, her face turning hot. "I don't need a counselor."

"Lucky for you I'm on vacation for the next month. So technically I'm not a counselor right now."

"I want you to leave." She looked at Spencer. "Both of you."

"Sara, you need to talk to someone. Mason can help you. Just talk to him. *Please?*"

She shook her head, crossing her arms and uncrossing them. Sara wouldn't look at either of them. They'd invaded her home, her privacy, and she wanted them gone. She wouldn't forgive Spencer for this, not ever. He'd crossed a line, good intentions or not.

"I went to Wyalusing State Park to commit suicide once."

Sara's head snapped up and her eyes shot to Mason.

"It wasn't the first time I'd attempted it. Actually, it wasn't the last either. It's so convenient—rocky cliffs, choppy waters below. Imminent death." He shoved his hands into his jeans pockets. "I hated myself for a long time. Carried guilt around like a blanket I couldn't remove. I didn't want to remove it. If I let go of the guilt, it was like saying what had happened was okay, and it wasn't. It would never be okay. So I had to keep that blanket on, I had to feed the guilt, I had to hate myself, I had to never forget as penance."

Her eyes burned and she swallowed thickly. She'd hated herself for a long time now. And the guilt...she didn't think that would ever go away. "Never forget...what?" Sara whispered.

The door softly clicked and she looked up, surprised to find that Spencer had left, leaving Mason alone with her. She tensed. She didn't know this man. He was a stranger in her home. So what if Spencer knew him? So what if he was Spencer's friend? Sara didn't know him and he wasn't her friend.

"I think you should leave," she told him, backing toward the bathroom, her fingers tightly gripping the tie on the robe.

Amusement lit up his wine-colored eyes. "I will. In one hour. That's how long our sessions will run."

"We're not—we're not having sessions. You can't just...come in here, into my house, and—and boss me around," she stuttered, disbelief raising her voice.

Ignoring her, Mason said, "My brother died four years ago. Snowmobile accident. We were making jumps. He went first and didn't make it all the way across. I didn't know it and drove over him, killing him." He paused. "I killed my brother."

Her stomach clenched as she looked at Mason. He was staring at his boots. When his tortured eyes found hers, she felt sick. She'd seen that look before—she saw it every time she looked in the mirror.

"Derek was younger, smarter, better-looking, pretty much better in every way imaginable. He had his whole life ahead of him. He was going to be a lawyer. He was engaged to a girl who loved him like I'd never seen anyone love anyone." Mason sucked in a sharp breath. "No matter how much Annie, his fiancée, hated me, she never could hate me as much as I hated myself."

Sara felt something warm and wet on her cheeks, and was surprised to find she was crying. Why that surprised her, she had no idea. Maybe because this time, the first time in a long time, her tears were for someone else, and not herself.

"I'm sorry," she whispered, fisting her trembling hands under her crossed arms.

"Everyone's sorry, aren't they, Sara?" Mason's eyes drilled into hers. "Everyone's sorry, but does it really do anything? Does it bring them back? Does it bring my brother back? How about your husband? Does it make you feel better? Is there really any point to it? Why do people say it, Sara?"

"I don't...I don't know." She swallowed.

"Then why did you say it?"

Sara stared at him, flustered and confused. "Because—"

"Because why?" he interrupted, his expression stern.

"Because I wanted to help!" she cried, agitated from his berating of her.

Mason smiled briefly. "Spencer wants to help. I want to help. Talk to me. Let me help."

Sara walked toward the kitchen, stopped, and turned back to Mason. "What good will talking do? It won't bring him back. It won't make what happened go away. It's a waste of time, a waste of words. Just like saying you're sorry. Right?"

"Spencer told me you're an artist. Show me your artwork."

Sara's body jerked, her mind unable to keep up with Mason's. "No."

Mason moved to sit down on the recliner that was his and Sara lurched forward, throwing her body between him and the chair. She trembled as she met his eyes and her breathing was too rapid, her heart pounding. "You can't sit here."

His eyes narrowed, but Mason moved away, into the kitchen. Sara wanted him to leave. She opened her mouth to demand it when he directed his gaze toward her. There was stark pain there, so vivid Sara's mouth went dry. It contorted Mason's features into a mask of anguish.

"I did a lot of drugs. I'd always had a tendency to drink too much, experiment with illegal drugs, but after Derek's death, I became dependent on them to function. They dulled the pain, but never for long enough. It was never enough. The pain always came back. The memories. The guilt."

Mason tapped his fingers on the table, watching his hand. "You don't have to talk, Sara. You can just listen. I'll do the talking for now, and when you're ready, you can talk. Whatever you do, though, don't do anything stupid." He looked up, freezing her where she stood with the directness of his gaze. "Don't do something you can't forgive yourself for doing."

"I already have," she choked out, her eyes burning with tears.

"No. Not yet. That wasn't your fault." Yes, it was. It was Sara's fault. It would forever be her fault and nothing would or could change that.

"So that wasn't my fault, but what happened with your brother, it was yours?"

"I was drinking. I'd smoked marijuana that night. I think it's safe to say it was my fault."

"It could have happened regardless."

"Only it didn't."

A tense silence ensued. Sara finally broke it, curiosity driving her to ask, "What got you to stop? The drugs and alcohol, I mean."

"I had to find something to make me want to live. I had to find something that was bigger than the guilt and pain I carried around."

"And you did?"

Mason's eyes softened. "I did."

She almost envied that, that Mason had been able to find peace when it continued to elude her for any length of notable time.

A knock came at the door, followed by Spencer. He looked from the kitchen where Mason stood to the living room where Sara was. "Do you hate me now?" he asked Sara.

Sara rubbed her face. Of course she didn't hate him. She wasn't especially happy with him at the moment, but she didn't hate him. That emotion was reserved for herself.

When she didn't answer, Spencer sighed. "Ready, Mason?"

"I'll be back next week, Sara. Sunday. At nine." He didn't ask, he told. "Be dressed next time. Showered. Oh, and have coffee ready too. I like Dunkin' Donuts. Spencer said you bake?"

Sara's face heated at his demanding tone. "You're bossy."

He smiled. "Derek tells me that every day."

She frowned, wondering what he meant. His brother Derek was dead. How could he talk to him every day? Was he loonier than she was? Sara sometimes thought she saw and heard her husband, but she didn't hear his voice in her head on a daily basis. Not yet.

Spencer paused at the door. "I really did just want to help you, Sara. I hate seeing you like this."

She hesitated. Spencer was almost out the door. "Spencer." He stopped, looking over his broad shoulder at her. "I..." Sara blew out a noisy breath. "I know you meant well." It was as close to a thank you as she could get.

He gave a brusque nod and left, the door closing with loud finality.

The quiet was too quiet. It usually didn't bother her, but today, for whatever reason, she couldn't stand it. Maybe because in the silence her thoughts morphed into one mass of questions and remembrances she couldn't deal with. You always thought they'd be there, day after day; alive, whole. Sara had thought he'd always be there. She'd imagined years and years of them together, growing old together, having children and grandchildren, and then when it was time, dying together. In her mind it had always been them as a couple; not her without him. If only she'd known. If only she'd known he would be taken from her. She would have done things so differently. But that was the thing about life—no one ever really knew when it would end.

STANDING JUST INSIDE the door, she stared at him, watching his black tee shirt tighten over his strong back as he held a nail to the wall with one hand and raised a hammer with the other.

"I'm pregnant."

Cole dropped the hammer on his foot, cursing. He straightened, turning those magnetic blue eyes on her. "What did you say?"

Sara inhaled slowly, shakily. Stomach in knots and alive with wild fluttering she knew had nothing to do with the life already growing inside her, she fought for a calm she did not feel. "I'm pregnant."

She didn't look at him; she couldn't. It hadn't been planned. Babies were in the future, sure, but not yet. They weren't ready. They weren't ready, but she was. Of course she was. Already she could feel the love for her unborn baby inside, already she couldn't wait to hold her child; their child.

He slammed his hands on his lean hips, inhaling sharply. "What—?" Cole looked down and swallowed. "What was that? One more time. Did you say—did you say you're pregnant?" His eyes met hers, brighter than normal and focused intently on her.

Nodding, eyes stinging with happy tears, Sara smiled. "Yes. Tell me you're okay with this."

Cole exhaled noisily, averting his face. His posture was stiff and he hadn't moved his hands from his hips. He seemed to be struggling. Sara felt her joy dim. It was scary and new; they didn't have a clue how to raise a baby, but they'd learn. No one was ever really ready to have one, mentally or financially. If Cole was completely against this, Sara didn't know what she would do. She couldn't take that.

"Cole? Are you not glad about this?" she whispered, dropping her purse to the floor. She rubbed her arms, cold in the stillness of his response. "I know it's unexpected and business has been a little slow and..." Sara trailed off as he strode toward her, his eyes on fire and his jaw tight.

"How can you ask such a thing?" he said harshly, stopping before her. Cole's body heat radiated off him, warming her with his nearness.

She swallowed against a suddenly dry throat. "You're not saying anything. What am I supposed to think?"

"I am so happy," he said slowly, cupping her face in his rough palms. "So happy. You have no idea how happy I am." He took a shuddering breath, pressing his cherry-flavored Carmex lips to her forehead. "So happy," he whispered.

Sara cried, loving Cole more in the moment he knelt before her and pressed his cheek to her flat stomach than in any other moment she could remember. "Love you, baby."

"Love you too." She brushed his soft hair back from his forehead, loving the texture of it, loving him.

He looked up at her. "I was talking to the baby. You know, love you, baby."

With a snort, she pulled away. "Of course you were. What were you attempting to hang up when I walked through the door?"

Cole stood, rubbing the back of his neck. "Nothing." He looked guilty.

Sara sighed, moving toward the living room. "What is it?"

"I won it," he announced, a slight scowl on his face.

Eyebrows lifted, she looked at the 10 X 13 picture resting on the couch. "So everything you win must go up on the wall?"

"No. Just the cool stuff."

The 'cool stuff' was a close-up photo of a vintage red Ford truck from the fifties or sixties. It sat in a field of grass, shining with the glint of sunlight on it and blue skies behind it. The body was rounded in a way the newer trucks had gotten away from.

"I thought you were a Dodge boy?"

"Well. Yeah. But look at it! And I won it."

Sara smiled at him. "I like it. Not above the couch, but I like it."

"So you're saying I should put the wedding picture back up?" He laughed at the look on her face, grabbing her wrist and spinning her into his arms. He kissed her nose, saying, "We are going to be the coolest parents ever."

Sara blinked her eyes and the sink full of dishwater came into view; a sink full of water and dish soap for two plates, one cup, and a fork and spoon. The soap smelled like apples and the bubbles made a fizzing sound. She would give anything to have a sink full of dirty dishes if it meant he was still in her life. With a sigh, she quickly washed them and set them in the strainer, wondering how such a small task could so completely wear her out. But then, the effort it took to get through each day wore her out.

CHAPTER 4

IT WAS TUESDAY. **Three weeks exactly from Tuesday the 29th of November.** That was the date she'd been told to be there, to talk to Dr. Henderson, to do what had been chosen for her to do. It was a countdown of dread for Sara. She would never be ready to talk about what he wanted to talk about. It was unequivocally impossible for her to do what had been designated as her duty long ago.

Her feet unconsciously moved in the direction of the art room she hadn't entered in months. Sara stopped by it, running a hand over the rough wood, closing her eyes at an onslaught of sorrow. She couldn't bring herself to open the door. It reminded her of him. Everything in this house did. But she couldn't forget. She didn't want to forget. Maybe part of the reason she couldn't let go, the reason Sara refused to let go, was because if she did, she feared she'd lose him as well. She couldn't say goodbye to him.

She touched her forehead to the door, hot tears pooling in her eyes and dropping to her cheeks. She closed her eyes as shuddering breaths wracked her body. Her mind formed the image of his laughing face with the crinkles around his pale blue eyes and she couldn't move from the pain that came along with it.

She missed his eyes the most. They'd been electrifying, charged with life and passion, able to see every part of Sara there was to see and those she'd rather weren't seen. The thought of them never being open again, the thought of never staring into them and getting lost in the blue ocean that was her husband's eyes—it was heart wrenching. Unbearable.

He used to watch her paint. He'd sit in a chair in a corner of the room and watch her for hours. He said it soothed him to watch her work. A sob was torn from her and Sara slapped her palm against the door. She wanted him back. She wanted to feel his arms around her; she wanted to have his scent cocoon her. This emptiness inside of her—it was killing her.

"Don't cry, Sara."

She inhaled sharply, spinning around. Her eyes scanned the kitchen, looking for a body and face to put with the voice. There was no one. *I'm losing my mind.* She slumped against the door, putting a shaking hand to her temples, and closed her eyes.

"He wouldn't want you to cry for him. It's okay to be sad. It's okay to hurt. But you still have to live. You have to go on."

She kept her eyes closed. The voice seemed to leave only when she tried to find it. "I can't go on without him. He's supposed to be here, with me." Pain tightened her throat, made it almost impossible to swallow.

"He is. He'll always be with you."

With a hand over her mouth and an arm across her stomach, Sara leaned over, trying to shrink in and away from the hurt that never went away. It had wrapped its arms around her and held her tightly within its grasp. She had to get away, from the pain, from the voice that wasn't really there.

She lurched forward, toward the phone. One voice could ground her. One voice could give her relief. She punched in the numbers, pacing in front of the refrigerator, jittery and sick feeling. One ring. Two. Three. Sara whimpered, beginning to pull the phone from her ear.

"Must be one of those days again, huh?"

She closed her eyes, immediate relief dropping her shoulders. She leaned her back against the fridge as she listened.

"First time he talked about you I knew you were it for him. There was this look on his face. It's hard to explain, even now. It was shock and joy rolled into one. The look of love. I teased him about it and he punched me in the gut, so I knew it was true. He fell for you fast and hard."

He went silent. Sara wiped her eyes with the back of her hand, waiting.

His voice was softer when he spoke again. "He said you were the most beautiful thing he'd ever seen. More beautiful than the sun or a flower or any kind of scenery I could imagine. That's what he said, Sara. He said when he looked at you he couldn't breathe and his stomach went all crazy. He said when he looked at you he was home."

A sob escaped her and the phone dropped from her hand, clattering as it hit the floor. Sara went to her hands and knees next to it, her head dropping forward. It hurt too much. The pain swept through her, wracking her body with tremors. *Make it go away. Please. Make it go away.*

She pulled herself to her feet, eyes trained on a drawer next to the sink. She was pulled to it by an invisible force, her fingers locking on the top of it. Once it was open, Sara stared at the collection of knives in all their different shapes and sizes. She closed her eyes, jumping when someone pounded on the front door. Her eyes went back to the knives. The door burst open and Sara reflexively slammed the drawer shut, whirling around to face the intruder, her pulse racing. How had he gotten there so fast?

They looked nothing alike. Lincoln Walker was bigger, taller, with gray eyes and dark hair. But when Sara looked at him, she saw his brother. It was in the perpetually lowered eyebrows, the square jaw, and the stance. Lincoln was the moodier, easier to anger brother while her husband had been the more amiable, if slightly wild brother. Nothing alike in personalities or looks and yet she saw her husband in Lincoln. Maybe because she wanted to.

"What are you doing?" he demanded.

"I'm—what are *you* doing?" she shot back.

"You look guilty." Lincoln strode for her, not stopping until he was inches from her and looming over her.

She had to crane her neck back to meet his eyes, and when she did, she saw they were red-rimmed and bloodshot. She took in the dark stubble of his jaw and the unkempt, shaggy hair he used to always keep short. She'd never noticed before how it waved up around his ears on the nape of his neck. Brackets had taken a place around his mouth and he seemed thinner than she remembered. It was wearing on him too.

"You can't just barge into my house." She backed up a step and he followed.

He had on a gray hooded sweatshirt and faded jeans and brought the citrus and mint scent of soap and toothpaste with him. It was all wrong. Wrong man, wrong scent, wrong everything.

"Yeah, I can, 'cause technically, it's my brother's house too. You look like shit. When's the last time you showered or ate a decent meal?"

Lincoln had always been blunt, something Sara had admired. Now, though, she really wished he wasn't. This was why she had been avoiding him as much as she could. Because she knew he'd do this. He thought he had to look out for her, he thought it was his responsibility to take care of her for his brother. On the phone he could talk to her and not expect anything, because he knew he wouldn't get anything; not even a response, but in person, Lincoln agitated and pushed her and made demands. He always had. They'd used to argue as a form of communication, something that had forever irritated her husband.

"You're one to talk. You don't look much better."

He opened his mouth, and then closed it. "What happened on the phone? You were there and then you weren't." Lincoln's eyes went to the floor and he leaned down to pick up the beeping phone. He turned it off and resituated it on the wall before narrowing his flint-colored eyes on her. "I miss him too, but at least I work. At least I *try* to be normal. I don't hide in my house and push everyone away. You lost your husband, but I lost my *brother*."

Those words pierced her with overwhelming anguish. "Why don't you hate me?" she asked raggedly.

Lincoln slammed his fingers through his hair, messing it up more. One lock went to rest against his forehead. "I think you hate yourself enough for the both of us." He pointed a finger in the direction of the living room. "Go take a shower. Now."

She shook her head. "No."

He shifted his jaw back and forth, determination darkening his features. "You get in that shower now or I'll put you in it myself."

A trickle of fear went down her back, but she didn't really believe he would do that. But the look on his face said he would. "I'm fine. I just...I dropped the phone and..."

"Don't lie to me. Believe me, I've said it all before myself. Maybe instead of wallowing away in self-pity, you should think of how Cole would feel knowing you're like this. Is it your goal to end up like him? Is that it?"

Sara recoiled at the use of his name, sucking in a sharp breath and turning away from Lincoln. He kept talking, but she couldn't hear him over the roar in her ears. She fought for every breath she took, wanting to drop to her knees. Hearing his name was too much. It hurt too much to hear it, to say it, to even *think* it. So she didn't.

The tears streamed down her cheeks, dropping to the white and gray linoleum floor. She braced a hand against the fridge and hung her head. She felt his warmth like he was behind her, holding her. Only it wasn't him. It would never be him again. Lincoln touched her shoulder and Sara jerked away, stumbling back and bumping into the stove. "Don't touch me."

His jaw clenched. "Why? What happens when someone touches you? Do you melt?"

"You're an ass," she told him in a voice that shook.

"I've been gentle with you, but no more. This has gone on long enough. Now get in the shower and get dressed. We're going to go see him."

She mutely shook her head. No. She couldn't. Sara couldn't go to that place. She couldn't see him. It wasn't him. It wasn't her husband. She wrapped her arms around herself and hunched over, trying to make the hollowness go away, trying to make the unrelenting sick feeling disappear. She was dying on the inside, losing herself, turning into a pulsating mass of pain and nothing else. That was all she was now. Sara didn't know how to make it stop.

Lincoln grabbed her arms and pulled her up and toward him.

"I said don't touch me!" she shrieked, trying to tug her arms from his grasp, but he only tightened his grip. "Lincoln, let *go* of me. Let go of me!" Sara moved to slap him, to push him away.

He brought her body against his. Panic made her fight harder. No one's arms but his should be around her. Not ever. She lurched away, wanting his hands off her. Not letting her get away, Lincoln pulled her to him again and rested his chin on the crown of her head; large, resilient, and unmovable. Sara made puny, pitiful attempts to remove his touch, but it wasn't going anywhere. He was too strong and she was too weak.

"Lincoln, please," she whispered, unable to stand the touch of another man. It felt like disloyalty to him.

He didn't answer—he just kept holding her.

Shaking, spent, she finally went still. Her arms were wedged between them and of their own accord her palms rested on his hard, warm chest. His heart pounded beneath her hand. *Bu-bum...bu-bum...bu-bum.* Sara turned her attention to that, her breaths slowing, and her body relaxing the longer she concentrated on the steady, strong beat.

The minutes they stayed like that were endless. For the first time in a long time she felt not quite so alone. Relief washed over her in the safety of his arms. Lincoln knew her pain. He knew what she was going through. He was going through it himself. He'd lost him too. The catastrophic difference between them, though, was that it wasn't his fault. It was hers. It was a glaring truth she couldn't ignore or forget. Sara stiffened as the remorse came back in full attack, punching her in the stomach and taking her breath away.

"What are you doing to yourself?" he murmured.

She had no response. When she tried to pull away, Lincoln held her nearer. She closed her eyes, exhaling deeply.

"*Stop* doing it." His hands moved to the sides of her head and he smoothed her tangled hair from her face, leaning down so their eyes met. "You're not alone. Don't ever feel like you're alone. You know that, right?"

Sara stared at the gold flecks in his eyes, swallowing thickly. His eyes were silver and gold. She jerked her head in a semblance of a nod.

He sighed deeply and dropped his hands. "Go. I'll wait here."

She blinked her eyes against the tears, but they kept coming. "Lincoln, I...I can't. I can't go there." Sara took a shaky breath, moving to put the table between them.

He looked at her for a long time. "But you will take a shower?" he finally asked.

"Yes."

"I'll take it." He nodded his head in the direction of the bathroom, one eyebrow lifted.

Sara slowly walked toward the bathroom. "What will you do?" she asked when she reached it.

"I'll be right here." He patted the back of the cream-colored couch.

Once inside the bathroom, Sara fell against the closed door, struggling to get air into her lungs. She went to the mirror. A hollow-eyed, haunted face stared back. Her eyes had always been big, but now they almost looked cartoonish. Large and dark in a white face. She gripped the counter and leaned over it, staring down at the sink. A drop of water dripped from the faucet, disappearing down the drain into the dark unknown. That's what she felt like—she was being sucked into a black hole of nothingness, and once that happened, she would disappear. She would cease to exist.

"How's that shower going?"

She jumped at the sound of Lincoln's voice on the other side of the door. She wanted him to go away and leave her alone. She wanted the world to go away. Sara sighed. That wouldn't be happening. And she knew him well enough to know once his mind was set, there was no changing it. He wouldn't be going anywhere either.

She rubbed her face and turned on the faucet in the shower, the small tan-walled room quickly steaming up with moisture and heat. Sara untied her robe and let it drop to the floor. The worn and ratty robe had been a gift from him and taking it off was the same as shedding a security blanket. It was removing a piece of him from her and doing so for even a short period of time was painful to her. She practically lived in the thing. Its frayed and unraveled fabric was proof of that. She removed the rest of her clothes and got into the shower.

AFTER QUICKLY THROWING on an old UW-Platteville sweatshirt of his and jeans that almost hung on her, she hurried from the room too many memories lived in, and walked into the kitchen. The scent of coffee hit her along with fried eggs and toast. She looked from the table where a steaming mug of coffee and a glass of orange juice sat with a plate of one egg and two slices of toast over to where Lincoln leaned with his elbows against the counter, his eyes on her.

Sundays had been their breakfast days. They'd sleep in late and make a mess out of the kitchen preparing a midday feast. Sara had been in charge of the eggs and potatoes and he'd always prepared the pancakes and bacon. He'd made the best pancakes. She hadn't had pancakes in over a year, not since the last time he'd made them. A lot of things had stopped with him—her, for one.

She inhaled sharply, looking away from his intent stare. It didn't matter. She still felt the heat of his eyes on her. Those stormy gray eyes were studying, judging. Those eyes were not happy. "I should have stopped by sooner. I didn't realize you'd gotten this bad."

Sara tucked wet, limp hair behind her ears. "I'm fine."

"You're not fine. I really wish you'd quit saying you're fine when you are so obviously *not* fine." He straightened and walked to the table, pulling out a chair. "Sit. Eat."

"Aren't you supposed to be working today?"

"Yeah. I was."

He was until she'd called. Lincoln didn't have to say the words, but she knew that's what had happened. Sara swallowed as guilt heated her skin. "I'm sorry."

"Stop being sorry. Please."

She grabbed the back of a chair and lowered herself into it, staring down at the plate. The thought of food made her stomach turn. "How...how are things going? At work?"

He poured himself a cup of coffee, sitting down across from her at the table. "Work is work." The room shrank with him inside it—he was big and towering and intense. It made Sara nervous. She'd never realized how large of a presence he had nor how commanding it was.

Lincoln and he had owned a carpentry business together: Walker Building. They'd done everything from roofs to siding to interior renovation—other than plumbing. *That* they didn't do. Now Lincoln ran it by himself; the lone brother where there should be two. More work, more stress, less help, because of her. He was without a lot of things these days, because of her.

She took a piece of toast. He had cut the toast in triangles for her. Why was he so nice to her when it was her fault his brother wasn't around? She would never understand that. How Lincoln could be so forgiving. He was the one person she had *expected* to loathe her, above all others, and he was the one person she'd been so wrong about.

"Did I cut it wrong?"

She looked up, the toast still in her hand. "No. You cut it right."

He paused with the mug to his lips. "Good to know."

The toast was dry and Sara choked down half of one slice to appease Lincoln. She drank the juice and sipped at the coffee. The silence was drawn out to the point of uncomfortable. She repeatedly opened her mouth to tell him about the phone conversation with Dr. Henderson, but she held back. It was her burden alone. And when he did find out, what then? She didn't want to tell him until she had no choice. But he had a right to know. Sara knew that. It still wasn't enough of an incentive for her to tell him. Not yet. She needed more time.

It was cowardly of her, but that was inconsequential when she thought of the alternative. Would he turn his back on her when she found out? Would he no longer look at her with compassion, but with detestation? And why did the thought make her stomach clench? *Because he's all I have left of him.* Startled by the thought, she unconsciously jerked, her hand hitting the coffee mug. It didn't tip. Lincoln reached over and grabbed it before it did. He slowly slid the mug to her right, far enough away that there was no chance of her accidentally bumping it.

"How long has it been since you've gone there?"

She stiffened, knowing exactly where he was talking about. There was no pretending she didn't. "A few weeks." Two. It had been two weeks and two days.

At first she had gone every day to the place where her husband rested, for hours and hours at a time. But the longer she'd gone to that place and stared down at what was supposed to be her husband and wasn't, the harder it had been. She didn't want to remember him that way; Sara wanted to remember him as he had been alive. She feared all her old memories of him would fade away and be replaced with the nothingness he now was.

Sara hid away in her house that used to be *their* house and tried to ignore reality. It was stupid of her to think such a thing was possible. The pain was alive in *her* and there was no way to escape it as long as she drew air into her lungs. She hated herself for staying away as long as she had, and yet she continued to stay away.

The last time she'd seen him had been the day she'd gone to Wyalusing State Park. The day it all had been too much. The day she'd been unable to exist with the constant ache anymore. When the pain had been too much, when she'd looked at what was supposed to be her husband and hated herself more than she'd ever thought possible. *That* was the day she'd wanted to end it all, the day she'd yearned for a way to stop the regret and longing. Her existence was a bitter toxin. Too weak to live; too weak to die.

"How can you stay away?" he demanded, breaking through her bleary reverie.

Her eyes flew to his face. She saw the anger in it, the hurt, and she looked away. That's what Sara did. She looked away from things that hurt, she pretended they didn't exist, she avoided. It was agony going to that place, seeing what he was, knowing what he would never be again. It wasn't *him*. It wasn't her husband. Sometimes Sara could almost convince herself he was on a trip, a really long trip, and someday soon he'd return. Sometimes she almost believed it. But then the pain came back, the memories, the profound sense of loss, the emptiness and the guilt, and she couldn't pretend any longer.

"Don't you think you at least owe it to him to visit?"

Sara lurched back in her chair, pain wracking through her as she stared at Lincoln.

He pressed his lips together, his brows furrowing. "Shit. That's not—I didn't mean it like that." Lincoln rubbed his face, sighing. "That wasn't what I meant. I only meant...he's your husband. You should go there, be with him, see him."

"It isn't him," she choked out, blinking away tears that continued to wet her eyelashes.

He shot to his feet, causing Sara's stomach to spasm, and stated, "Get your coat. We're going for a drive."

"*No.* I'm not going there. I'm not ready," she said, shrinking away from him as he advanced on her.

He stopped by her chair. "Not ready? For what?"

She swallowed, avoiding his eyes. *Not ready to accept what he is instead of what he was.* She was a coward. Not strong enough to see him, not strong enough to live. When had she turned into this person she didn't recognize? *It happened on a warm summer night when my heart was ripped apart and flung in a million unrecoverable directions.*

"We're not going there, but we are going somewhere. You need to get out of here. *I* need to get out of here. And this is what we're going to do—we're not going to talk about anything that makes us sad. Deal?"

Lincoln offered a hand. It was large and long-fingered with callouses over callouses on it. It was a hand that swung a hammer on a daily basis. Sara hesitantly put her hand in his. His swallowed hers whole as he pulled her to her feet.

"Don't you need to go back to work?"

He headed for the closet near the door. "I'm the boss. I don't have to work if I don't want to work. It's pretty much the best thing about having my own company." He flashed a grin as he pulled a purple jacket from the closet and tossed it at her. Reflexes slow, it hit Sara before she even raised her hands in preparation. He laughed a little. "I see your athletic abilities haven't improved with time."

The only thing she'd ever been able to do was run. Any sports where hand and eye coordination and teamwork were needed she was a liability more than anything. She almost smiled. Sara felt her lips muscles begin to lift and instead frowned.

Lincoln's laughter broke off and he shook his head. He strode for the door, muttering, "It's okay to smile, Sara."

It wasn't.

CHAPTER 5

THE AIR WAS cold and sharp. It went through her coat and jeans, layering her body with an uncomfortable chill she couldn't shake. Sara shivered as she took in the gray-tinged day, knowing snow was in the forecast. It would come. That was the one thing that never changed—the world kept moving, even when a life stopped.

The smoky wood smell of a wood burning stove filled her nostrils as she followed Lincoln to his silver Dodge truck. The Walker boys had always loved their Dodges with the diesel engines. The street was quiet as most people were at work and their children were either in school or at daycare. Houses of different shapes and sizes lined the streets; most small, but nice. An occasional shabby house stood out among the more pleasant ones.

Boscobel, Wisconsin was a modest town with a population in the three thousands. It had a correctional institution on the outskirts of it and boasted to be the 'turkey hunting capital of Wisconsin'. Everyone knew everyone's business in Boscobel, which sometimes was a good thing, but usually wasn't. People knew things about people the person in question didn't even know about themselves. Sara was pretty sure she didn't want to know what was being said about her.

There was Subway, A&W, and Dairy Queen to pick from for fast food restaurants. Three gas stations strategically placed—one at one end of town, one in the middle, and the other on the other side of town—so no matter which direction you went, you were sure to find a reminder to fill up your tank.

The big hot spot of the town was the old movie theater that had been open since 1935. It played one movie at a time and had inexpensive ticket and snack food prices, bringing in a large portion of the town on a regular basis. There was also the Civil War reenactment that took place every August, rain or shine. Cannons could be heard going off from the battlefield and people in 1800s garb roamed the streets.

"Where are we going?" She hauled herself into the cab and put on her seat belt. It smelled like spearmint in the truck and the interior was clean. Lincoln had always been particular about his belongings, making sure his bedroom, truck, house, and everything else he owned were always clean and tidy. Opposites—he and his brother.

Riding in vehicles with people didn't bother her and driving her own car didn't bother her, but Sara had yet to drive with a passenger in her car. The thought made her tremble and feel clammy. She didn't care what happened to her, but she wouldn't be responsible for another's life. Never again.

Lincoln started it up and the truck vibrated as the diesel engine rumbled to life. He grabbed a battered black baseball cap from the dash and situated it low on his head so that his hair winged up around it, putting the vehicle in drive as he answered, "I'm not sure. Wherever the truck takes us."

He glanced over with a grin and Sara blinked at how it transformed his face. When had his features gotten so sharp and masculine? She remembered him as a baby-faced young man of twenty-two who teased and badgered her the first time they'd met, and pretty much every day after that. She'd always thought of him as being younger than she, though he was actually a few months older. That was the image her mind brought up whenever she thought of Lincoln. Only it didn't fit anymore. Sara saw that now. This was Lincoln; this leaner, more angular-featured man whose shoulders slumped a little more than they should, whose face showed strain and weariness from too much sorrow. She'd done that to him. Indirectly, but what did it matter?

She turned away, a fresh wave of remorse slamming into her. She was drowning from all the guilt she had inside her. Sinking, disappearing. She tightly clasped her cold hands together in her lap and stared out the window, not really seeing anything as the truck led them out of town and in the direction of Fennimore. The truck was quickly warming up, but it seemed to bypass her somehow. She couldn't get warm.

Lincoln found a song on the radio and cranked the volume up. The bass was loud, the beat fast. It thrummed through Sara's body, pulsating with musical life, demanding attention, demanding to be felt. She'd always loved music. She had loved to sing, loved to dance. She hadn't done either since the accident. Each song had a story to tell, each song was a small, but significant tale. It had manipulated her art to be either ethereal or angry or simply bold. A good song had the power to change someone's whole outlook in so many ways.

He began to sing along, completely off key, which Sara knew was on purpose. Out of the two brothers, Lincoln was the one gifted with a musical voice. When he chose to use it. Sara looked at him. He caught her eye and winked, bellowing out the next verse. He made his voice really high, so high it cracked, and her lips unconsciously curved. She bit her lip to stop the smile from completely forming, but when he changed the words to ridicule himself, a snort left her.

Sara clapped a hand over her mouth, widening her eyes. Lincoln took in her expression and laughed long and hard. In that moment, she forgot everything. She was her old self. The person she'd been before the pain had overtaken everything and warped her into what she now was. She giggled, her eyes on Lincoln.

"Come on, Sara, help me out." Another song started and Lincoln mutilated that one as well, doing a neck roll and upper body dance as he drove the truck up the hill to Fennimore.

She shook her head. "No way. I'm not adding to the horrible sound coming out of your mouth."

"What was that song we sang at karaoke that one time?"

"The song you *forced* me to sing even though I didn't know it?"

"Yeah. That one. You learned it soon enough. What was the name of it?"

"'Love Shack'." Sara swallowed thickly. It was supposed to have been a double date, but Lincoln's girlfriend dumped him right before it was time to go and as he had gotten stuck finishing up a company project it had ended up being Sara and Lincoln. In spite of all that, it had been a fun night.

"That would be it. We should do that again." Lincoln pulled the truck into a gas station parking lot and put it in park. "Let's get some bad coffee. You game?"

"You go. I'll wait here."

He hopped out of the truck and turned back to her. "If you don't go inside with me, I'll be forced to stand on the sidewalk and sing at the top of my lungs. Loudly. And badly. Promise."

"Why does it matter if I go in or not?"

"It doesn't. To me. But I think it matters to you. Let's go."

She glared at him. He was right. Every normal act she'd used to do without thought took great effort from her to accomplish these days, even getting out of a vehicle and going into a gas station to get a cup of lousy coffee. Even getting into the truck. Showering. Getting dressed. All of those things wore her out and some days she couldn't even get them done. Even eating was a chore lately.

One of Lincoln's eyebrows lifted as he intently gazed at her, his eyes never leaving her. With a sigh, Sara opened the door and slid down from the cab, huddling in her coat and tucking her chin under the collar of it to keep as much cold away from her skin as she could. It didn't help much.

He met her on the sidewalk, smiling, bumping her shoulder with his arm as they walked inside. She knew she was being paranoid, but she felt like everyone was watching her, like everyone knew what she was responsible for and they all hated her because of it. He was the only one she didn't imagine looking at her like that and Sara's eyes continued to drift to Lincoln because of it. He was her rock. That scared her, knowing she'd come to rely on him so much, because she knew that would change in weeks to come.

It smelled like pizza and coffee and doughnuts in the convenience store; an odd mixture that was somehow enticing all tossed in together as it was. They stood side by side, looking at the different kinds of coffee. Sara and Lincoln looked at each other at the same time and when he smiled, she felt her lips turn up in response.

"They all sound terrible."

"They probably all *are* terrible," she murmured, eyes back on the coffee selection.

"Here goes," he said, reaching for a cup and pouring 'Jamaican Me Crazy' into it.

Sara watched his face as he sipped it. His face went perfectly blank, revealing nothing. "Good?"

"Mmm-hmm," was all he said, lifting his cup in a salute. He methodically raised the cup to his lips and took another drink.

She fought laughter and lost, surprising herself and him. He went still, blinking at her. Sara turned away as the laughter abruptly cut off, flustered. She fumbled with the coffee cups, knocking a stack of them over and onto the floor. When she reached down to pick them up, Lincoln was there with her, taking them from her shaking hands, and then taking her hands in his. She stared at their joined hands, not able to move. His hands were rougher and larger and tanner than hers. The nails were short and blunt, but clean. They were strong hands, hands that worked.

"You don't have to feel bad for living," he said slowly.

She snatched her hands back, grabbing the cups off the floor and standing. Without looking at the kind it was, Sara quickly poured coffee into a cup. "I'm ready."

It was a silent drive back to Boscobel. After a few sips of the bitter, stale coffee, she gave up on it and set it in the cup holder. Lincoln did the same.

"It really was horrible."

She looked at his profile and saw that he was grinning. "Yes. It really was," she said.

Lincoln pulled the truck up to the curb by the small white ranch-style house, putting the vehicle in park. He twisted his body so that he faced her, the bill of his cap hiding his eyes in the gloomy light. "We're going to change some things."

She stiffened, but didn't respond.

"We're going to do things we don't want to do, we're going to socialize, we're even going to hang out together weekly. I know, once a week just isn't enough. Fine. We'll try to make it a couple times a week. We're going to laugh and smile. We're going to *live*. Understand? This is what Cole would want. He would freak out if he saw the way you're living now. You know it too. This is stopping. Now. You can get mad at me and you can try to push me away, but guess what? I'm not going anywhere."

Her eyes filled with wetness. There was a lump in her throat that wouldn't go away no matter how many times she swallowed. He was so nice now, but soon, he would hate her. Maybe she should just tell him and get it over with.

"Lincoln..." she began.

"I'm removing your free will from this subject. You have no say in this," he said firmly, resituating his hat so that his face was partially shadowed.

Sara sucked in a sharp breath as she watched him fiddle with his cap until he had it just right. Lincoln did it just like him. She'd never noticed that before. It made sense. They'd grown up together, only two years apart in age. Of course he would have some of the same mannerisms as his brother.

"Sara? What is it?" Lincoln leaned closer, a frown on his face.

"Nothing." She turned away, grabbed the door handle, and jumped down from the truck. It had begun to snow and her shoes slid on the cement.

He met her at the front of the truck, reaching for her arm, and she jerked back, not wanting him to touch her. "What's going on?"

"Nothing," she muttered again, hurrying toward the house and away from Lincoln. Only he followed.

He grabbed her arm and swung her around, his eyes like stormy gray clouds. "You need to talk. You need to tell me what's going on *right now*. Or I'm not leaving." His hand dropped from her arm, but his eyes never left her face. Those were stronger than his hands would ever be; they had the power to hold her in place with their intensity. "You know...every time that phone rings and no one talks and I know it's you, I get this pressure in my chest. Every time I hang up that phone knowing you're on the other end of it, that pressure builds until it just...*aches*. I worry about you. I worry about you a lot. *Talk to me.*"

She stared at his unrelenting face, tripping over her words. "You just—you remind me of him, okay? Sometimes you do or say something just the way he would have. And it hurts. Being around you hurts sometimes." Snowflakes fell harder, blanketing them in a layer of cold whiteness and wetting Sara's face along with the warm tears that never really went away. They were always there, below the surface, waiting to be unleashed in all their sorrow and anguish.

Lincoln stared at her. His lips pressed together and Sara looked down, wrapping her arms around herself. She was so cold. Always so cold. As though he heard her thoughts, he pulled her to him and cocooned her against his chest, his arms warm and strong around her.

Her first impulse was to move away. She knew it would do no good, she knew he wouldn't let her go. Sara inhaled a ragged breath, lowering her head as his heat seeped into her, finally warming her. For once, she wasn't so cold. But it felt wrong. It shouldn't be him holding her. Sara stepped back and Lincoln let her go.

She didn't say anything. She didn't even look at him. She kept her eyes lowered as she walked to the door, quietly opened it, and shut him out. She didn't move away from the door until she heard the loud engine roar and the truck barrel down the street. Only then did she exhale. Only then was she able to get her legs to move.

"WHAT ARE YOU thinking, Sara?"

She set the yellow fleece blanket on the dresser and turned. Lincoln stood in the doorway of the partially painted nursery, arms crossed, eyes directed at her. His hair was messy in a way only a hand repeatedly run through it could accomplish.

"Where's Cole?"

"Outside. Where else? What are you thinking?" he repeated.

"Nothing. Why?"

He straightened. "Bull shit. You might be able to fool Cole because he's too thick-headed to see the strain on your face, or he's too deliriously happy to want to think you're not the same, but I'm not like that. I see you, even when you don't want anyone to. You're pale. You're not eating. Your eyes are red and you're subdued. What gives? Are you not happy about the baby?"

Inhaling slowly, she said softly, "Of course I'm happy." But her voice cracked and there was a tremble to it. "I'm pregnant. I'm supposed to be pale and not able to eat and whatever else you said."

"Hormonal. That one I forgot."

She gave him a look.

Lincoln flashed a quick grin before becoming serious again. "This is more than that."

Sara didn't answer. He was right.

With a sigh, he put his hands on her shoulders and lowered his head so they were at eye level. His hands were warm and he smelled like citrusy soap. It didn't repel her, like most scents did lately. It was familiar, welcome, like Lincoln. "Talk to me."

"I'm scared," she admitted, blinking her eyes against tears.

"You wouldn't be normal if you weren't. What are you scared about?"

"What if something happens? To me or the baby. I can't say any of this to Cole. I can't worry him."

"He should be worried," Lincoln said grimly "He's your husband, he's the father. He should be worried."

She shook her head. "No. He's so happy. I want him to be happy."

"You want him to be happy while you're miserable? That doesn't sound fair. If anything, you should both be miserable together, worrying about things you have no control over, losing hair, losing sleep, looking...you look terrible. Where's your glow?"

Scowling, Sara slapped his arm and moved away. "I haven't found it yet."

"Well, until you do, I'll be miserable with you. How's that? Cole can be blissfully unaware of reality and I'll sympathize with you. You have a worry, a complaint, some disgusting tidbit to share, I'll be here for you to dump your problems on. You can traumatize my brain and ears with all your pregnancy woes. I'm a man, I can take it. Deal?"

Sara looked at her brother-in-law, thinking she couldn't have asked for a better one. But she had to ask, "Why?"

"I want you to be happy, and if you're not happy, I can't be," he said simply.

IT WAS SUNDAY. Sara had her portable bed put away and was showered and dressed long before the time Mason had threatened to reappear.

She'd even made a pot of coffee, but she defiantly did *not* bake anything. Part of her wondered if he'd even show up, but in the pit of her stomach, where it churned and flipped all around, she knew he would.

The knock sounded at exactly nine in the morning, startling her even though she was waiting for it. She swallowed, opening the door to cold air, a snow-covered street, and Mason. His amber eyes flickered over her, approval in them. He rubbed snow from his dirty blond head, stepping inside and taking off his leather jacket to reveal a black sweater. He handed a small white bag to her, the scent of cinnamon and sugar teasing her senses. Sara took it, looking at it and then at him.

"I figured the baking comment was probably pushing it."

"You were right."

Mason smiled and bent down to take his boots off.

"Where's Spencer?"

He paused, glancing up. "Spencer isn't part of the sessions."

She moved to the kitchen, careful not to look at him. Her pulse picked up at those words and her chest squeezed. Spencer she knew. Spencer she trusted. This guy was an enigma and she wasn't sure how to read or take him. Sara didn't particularly like him either. She set the bag down.

"I didn't ask for your help."

"The ones that don't ask for it are usually the ones that need it the most."

"I don't want it."

"But you need it."

"Philosopher on top of grief counselor. Multi-talented." Sara poured two mugs of coffee.

"That's me." He took the mug she offered, blowing on it before taking a sip.

"Do you have any credentials? Anything to show me you're not a hoax?"

One eyebrow lifted. "Spencer's a cop. It'd be pretty dumb of me to masquerade as something I'm not when one of my good friends could have me checked out at any time."

"You never said you were smart."

He choked on his coffee, setting it down on the table and wiping a hand across his lips. Amusement, fleeting but intense, blazed over his features. "Tell me about yourself."

She wrapped both hands around her cup, slowly raising it to her lips. It hovered there, brushing her lips as she said, "I'm twenty-seven, I'm an unemployed artist, and I'm responsible for my husband's death."

Mason acted like she'd never spoken, his facial expression perfectly blank. "What's this room?" he asked, walking toward the room she used as her art studio.

"Don't go in there," she said, panic making her voice harsh. Sara thumped her coffee cup to the counter, hot dark brown liquid sloshing over the rim as she hurried for the door. He was already opening it when she reached him. "Mason! Don't!" she gasped, her heart thundering and her breaths leaving her in short, panicky bursts.

Cool air swept over her in an icy hug of sorrow as the door swung open and she closed her eyes against it. It cocooned her in longing and unforgettable loss. Whispers of the past tingled through her scalp and under her skin, chilling her. He was in there, waiting for her, waiting to crash her world around her with images, scents, and sounds of everything she missed, wanted, and would never have again. Sara couldn't open her eyes. If she did, she'd see him.

"Open your eyes. Face it. You have to face what hurts you. That's the only way you're going to cope. Open your eyes and see. It's just a room."

Mason knew nothing. It wasn't just a room. It was where they'd spent hours and hours together in quiet harmony. It was where she'd created with her hands what she wouldn't have been able to had he not been there with her. It was where they'd laughed and smiled and simply *were*— existing and together.

He said, "Look at me. Tell me what you see."

"What do you see when you see me?" he asked, eyes intent on her.

Sara set her paintbrush down, turning her attention to him. "What do you mean?"

He motioned to her half-finished project. "I see you glancing at me, and then you paint something. What you're painting looks nothing like me." He leaned closer in his chair to get a better look. "In fact, it doesn't even look human. Or like anything else, for that matter. What is it?"

She stared at the blues and greens she'd swirled together. They meshed, pulled apart, and went off in their own elegant tendrils. She cocked her head. She didn't know what it was. But it signified how she felt about him.

"It's the blue of your eyes. See here?" She pointed. "That's the same shade as your eye color. It's...serenity and peace and wholeness. It's you and how you make me feel." Sara shrugged. "I don't know how else to explain it."

"You know what color a painting of you would be?"

She caught the teasing glint in his eyes and smiled. "What?"

"Red hot. Fiery," he murmured, his eyes darkening.

He reached for her and the artwork was forgotten. He was able to wipe her mind clean of all thoughts other than ones of him. His arms wrapped around her, his scent enveloping her, as he pulled her to him and kissed her like it was their last kiss.

It had been one of their last kisses.

"Sara?" Her eyelids flew open and wine-colored eyes met hers instead of blue. "Where were you just now?"

She tried not to look at anything in the room, every single part of the room reminding her of him, but it was no use. Her eyes were drawn to all that had a piece of him to them. He lingered in the room. She thought she could smell him even. Coffee and cherry-flavored Carmex.

There was the rocking chair he would sit in and read as she painted. Pressure formed on her chest, pushing down, making it hard to breathe. There was the easel that still held her last painting, the one with the greens and blues. The pressure built. The walls they'd painted a cheery yellow, getting almost as much paint on each other as they did the walls. Her throat tightened painfully. Vision blurred with wetness, she stumbled from the room.

"I don't want to do this," she said in a shaking voice. "I want you to leave and I don't want you to come back. This isn't helping. It won't help. You can't just make me get over him. I can't get over him. I'll never get over him."

Mason stood near the door and she had to look away. He was out of place. He didn't belong here, in her house, standing where her husband used to stand.

"What makes you think I'm trying to make you *get over* anyone? I'm just trying to get you to stop hiding from everything, from yourself, from the world, from your emotions. There's a difference. It's been over a year. What are you waiting for?"

Her face crumpled and she hung her head. Staring at her purple-socked feet, she said quietly, "Do you know what happened?"

"Yes. Spencer told me."

"Then you know why I am the way I am."

"I'm no one to judge. I'm nowhere near an example of how to be. Derek died four years ago. I spent the first year hating myself and living in self-pity, doing every kind of drug I could get my hands on. It's amazing I'm even alive, actually. I overdosed a couple times, had my stomach pumped. I have scars from other dumb things I did." Mason held up his arm and slid the sleeve of his sweater back, revealing a jagged, raised line of skin pinker and paler than the rest of his arm.

She swallowed, tearing her eyes away. She crossed her arms, hiding the veins she'd studied so carefully more than one time.

"You and me, Sara, we're two peas in a pod," he said in a low voice. "But you...you have it better than me. Derek died instantly, without me having a chance to say I was sorry or goodbye or anything. Without me being able to tell him how much I loved him and admired him. You have that chance. Embrace it. Don't hide away until it's too late."

"It is too late. He died a year ago. I keep...thinking he'll come back. I know it's crazy, but that's what I keep thinking. Only I know he really won't." She blinked her tear-filled eyes. "Please, Mason, just go. I don't want to do this anymore."

His eyes searched the kitchen, pausing on the fridge. He grabbed the magnetic pen and paper pad from it, jotting something down. "Here's my cell phone number. Call me anytime. I'll be back next Sunday. Sorry." He didn't sound sorry. "I have a task for you. Open up your art room and *work*. Create something. Anything. See you in a week."

After he left, she stared into the room, the door now open. She took a hesitant step toward it, and another, until she hovered in the doorway. Sara hugged herself, imagining it was him hugging her, but it wasn't the same. It wasn't even close. She let her arms drop away and walked to the painting. She trailed a finger along the clumpy surface, seeing his face, seeing his eyes. This time, though, they weren't laughing or shining. This time, they were dim, unseeing. They were as they had been the last time they'd been open.

THE PHONE WAS hard and cold, quickly warming from the heat of her ear against it. They were like a drug—these one-sided conversations with Lincoln. The soothing pull of his deep voice was an addiction, the peace Sara felt as she listened to him was unable to be imitated in any other way. She could hear the television in the background as she stared at the empty blackness of hers, almost able to see herself sitting beside Lincoln as he talked, watching the same rerun of 'King of Queens' right along with him. Absently twirling a strand of her long hair around a finger, Sara silently devoured his words.

"Remember that painting you made of the forest outside the house that Cole lost? I have a confession to make. I stole it. It's in my bedroom, on the wall above my bed. I think he knew. I mean, he had to have seen it, right? I'm sure he was in my bedroom at least once since you painted it. Never said anything. Maybe he thought I needed it more than he did. I don't know why I took it. I suppose I could have just asked for it. But where would the fun have been in that? You're so talented, Sara. You could paint a nondescript ball of nothing and it would be amazing. You know that, right?"

She closed her eyes at his kind words, not really believing them, but thankful for them just the same.

Lincoln sighed, sounding tired when he said, "No, I suppose you don't. You always think less of yourself than is warranted. I always hated that about you, probably the only thing. You never thought you were smart enough, pretty enough, talented enough, strong enough. But you are. You always have been. You're so much stronger than you give yourself credit for. I mean it."

How did he know her so well? She had always had an insurmountable mountain of insecurities, no matter how she wished otherwise. But Lincoln, Lincoln always seemed to know them all and denied each and every one as well. Sometimes Sara thought he knew her even better than her own husband, which was ridiculous. Warmed by his words, she had hope that maybe it wouldn't be so hard to fall asleep now after hearing his voice. Before she'd called him, it had been futile.

"I got an early start tomorrow, so I'm signing off for the night. I'll be seeing you soon. Good night. Take care, Sara."

CHAPTER 6

AS THE DAYS came and went, pulling her closer to that fated day marked on the calendar, the nightmares didn't remain during the nighttime like they should. Sara saw the pain in his eyes at the collision. She felt his hand tighten on her in fear. The immediate loss as his touch was wrenched from her. She saw it all, whether her eyes were open or closed.

The hollowness was growing inside her. At times she looked down, expecting to see a round circle of emptiness where her stomach should be. A gashing wound where her heart was. Time healed all wounds was the saying. That saying was a lie. Time made the wounds deepen, it made them grow. It was her enemy and it was winning the battle against her soul. Time was ruining her, dissolving her, destroying her. It was all she had and everything she hated. Time mocked her in vivid detail of that final moment.

The time it had taken for the car to crash, time as it had slowed down and sped up. The last minutes she'd had with him, the seconds his eyes had filled with anguish and disbelief and the seconds it had taken for the light to fade from them. The hours she'd sat in the hospital, hoping and praying. The days and months she'd had to exist without him. It was all about time. And it was killing her.

Sara clutched the phone to her chest, her first impulse to call Lincoln and confess everything. Instead she set the phone down, grabbed keys off the hook by the door, and braced herself against the cold and snow as she walked to the short driveway. The icy wind snapped at her, his worn sweatshirt not enough to keep her warm against the frigid air. White, fluffy snow seeped through the soles of her old shoes, making her toes stiff and her feet uncomfortably wet.

She tried not to think about what she was doing or where she was going. She sat in the car, shivering as she started it up. Her breath was visible in puffs of misty air as she inhaled and exhaled. She drove down the street, taking a left and heading out of town. Five miles outside of Boscobel, she parked the car and turned it off. Her eyes swept over the snow-covered scene. It looked different. Everything did now. Nothing was as beautiful. Nothing was as peaceful. The haze of pain covering her eyes had darkened the world to her. The trees were tall and spindly, their leaves gone. It saddened Sara, seeing them in their dilapidated state. It was as though they wept for him too. They cried as Sara cried, each lost leaf a teardrop for him.

Sara got out of the car and stood there, envisioning him the second time she'd seen him. He'd stood just a few steps to the right from where she now stood. Sara could feel his warmth, she could smell his scent. She could feel the sunshine beat down on her as it had that day, masking the bitter cold of the present.

She'd been walking, careful to stay near the road and out of the woods. Part of her had wondered if the mysterious man would be there again. Part of her had been excited by the thought, especially when she'd thought of his smile.

His back had been to her, broad and muscular through the long-sleeved red Henley shirt he'd worn, his faded jeans tight against his defined backside and legs. His physique had made her mouth go dry, especially watching his muscles clench and bunch as he worked. He had a chainsaw in his hands, the engine loud and grating to her eardrums as he'd cut fallen tree limbs in half.

She walked past, eyes on him the whole time. Sara had known the exact moment he sensed her. The engine had abruptly cut off and a deep, raspy voice called out, "Aren't you worried about serial killers with chainsaw fetishes?"

Her heartbeats picked up as well as her breathing. Sara had spun around, blinking at the sight of him. His tall body lounged against the back of a blue Dodge Ram, one elbow on the tailgate. His eyes had been hidden below the bill of a dirty gray baseball cap, but she'd known they were watching her raptly. Sara felt them on her, going up and down the length of her, searing in their intensity. He stripped away her clothes with that look, visualized himself and her naked together, writhing on a bed, or maybe against the wall, intertwined. She'd known it and it hadn't bothered her one bit.

"Wrong state," she called back.

He tipped his head back and laughed. "I think you've watched too many horror movies," he drawled, removing his cap to wipe a hand across his forehead before tugging it back down in place. In that brief moment he'd been hatless, his electric blue eyes had zapped her, her body unconsciously jerking in response.

"Maybe," Sara said, slowly moving toward him. She'd been scared. She'd been scared and it had had nothing to do with serial killers. Sara had been scared because she'd never been so instantly attracted to any man before.

"So...Sara...Cunningham, is it?" She nodded. "Miss Cunningham, I do believe you are a thrill seeker."

"You think so?"

"I do." He straightened as she drew nearer, naturally looming over her at his height of somewhere around six feet tall. "Why else would you have shown up here a second time?"

"I like the scenery?"

His lips had formed into a slow smile and her stomach had dipped at the facial transformation from sharply angled features to rugged handsomeness. "Which scenery?"

Oh boy, she'd thought, I'm in trouble.

"I think I should take you out," he said before she had a chance to form a reply.

"Take me out where?" she asked, arching an eyebrow. She had been almost to him, close enough to know the top of her head *might* have reached his chest if she were to test it out.

"How about a movie? What are you in the mood for? Some 'Texas Chainsaw Massacre'?"

She laughed and he grinned and a date had been set.

Sara shook her head, pushing the image away. Only he didn't fade away. She inhaled raggedly, closing her eyes against the tall form walking toward her. It was a ghost, an illusion. It wasn't real. He wasn't really there.

"Sara? What are you doing here?"

She opened her eyes, her racing heart slowing. It was real. But it wasn't him. Lincoln made his way to her, his features becoming more defined the closer he got. He had on jeans, boots, a red flannel jacket with the hood of a gray sweatshirt sticking out the back of it, and leather work gloves. He pulled his gloves off as he reached her, shoving them into the back pocket of his jeans.

"I'm..." Her teeth chattered together, making it almost impossible to form words. She hadn't realized it was so cold, lost as she'd been in her memories.

"How long have you been standing out here?" Lincoln exclaimed as he moved closer, briskly rubbing her arms to bring some life back to them.

"I don't...know."

"Come here." He enfolded her between his arms, his clean smell mixing with the scent of the wood burning stove from the house nestled back in the woods. "Why didn't you tell me you were coming?"

She couldn't speak or move. She wanted to pull away, but couldn't gather the strength to. She felt safe, safer than she had since her world had been destroyed.

"Come on. I'll drive your car over to the house. What were you thinking, coming out here without a coat or boots or anything?"

"I...wasn't thinking," she stuttered, following him to the red Pontiac Grand Prix.

"That much is obvious." He opened the door for her, shutting it after she was in the car.

"What were you doing?" Sara asked as Lincoln started the car.

"Looks like I was rescuing you from being frozen alive." He pulled the car onto the road and drove the two miles it took to reach the house he'd grown up in. It was a two-story log-sided cabin, almost disappearing into the trees cocooning it to become part of the background. Smoke curled up from the chimney, lights shone through the windows in the gloomy-skied day.

Will the sun ever shine again?

Sara walked up the steps that led to the large deck, nostalgia hitting her. She went still, thinking she heard his laughter on the wind, picturing him standing at the now-covered grill, flipping burgers, a beer in his hand. She would have been sitting at the black wrought iron patio set, eyes repeatedly pulled to him as though a magnet connected her to him.

"You okay?" Lincoln asked, watching her, one hand on the doorknob.

She nodded, shifting her gaze from his. This was the house he and Lincoln had been raised in, and after their parents moved to Florida to retire, the house they'd shared as bachelors until she'd come along and changed all that. What if she hadn't gone for a walk that day? Would he still be alive, living his life with some other woman?

She hadn't been to the house since before the accident. She inhaled deeply, the scent of coffee enveloping her as she stepped inside, the heat of the interior quickly warming her. Her eyes went to the black leather couch to the left, where they'd sit and watch movies. He'd play with her hair, his arm around her, his lips smiling against her cheek as he kissed her.

"Coffee?"

She blinked at Lincoln. He'd removed his jacket and hat and stood by the coffeemaker in the kitchen area to the right. He looked back expectantly. His features changed, altered, and she was staring at her husband. She closed her eyes, inhaling deeply, and when she opened them, he was Lincoln again.

"Yes. Please."

"I was walking."

She frowned at him. He set a mug of coffee on the black marble counter top and pulled out a bar stool across from her. Sara did the same, sitting and wrapping her frozen fingers around the hot cup.

"In the woods. I was walking. I didn't have much to do today for work with the snow and all, so I went for a walk. Some days are great, others kind of get to me. Today is one of the latter days. I thought some fresh air might help clear my head."

"Did it?"

He gave a short bark of laughter. "Nah."

"What does help?" Sara sipped her coffee, hoping he had some magic answer that she could try. She knew she was wishing for things that could never be before he even answered. There was no quick fix, there was no solution to eradicate the guilt and sorrow she carried around.

He tapped the fingers of one hand on the counter. "You know, I don't really know. If I'm kept busy I don't dwell on things too much. I guess work helps."

Mason's demand that she work on her art flashed through her mind. She didn't know how to do that without being overwhelmed by the past. How would that be helpful? It wouldn't. His next visit was only a few days away. She sighed, rubbing her forehead.

"What is it?"

"Have you talked to Spencer lately?" she blurted, and then wished she hadn't.

"Not for a few weeks. Why?"

"Uh..." Sara fidgeted. "He..." She blew out a noisy breath. "He brought this grief counselor over and the guy is completely whacked. Completely." *Like me.*

"Really? Who is it? I might know him."

"Mason Wells."

"Nope." He shook his head. "He must not be from around here. Why did Spencer bring him over? Not that I don't think it was a good idea."

Sara's face heated up. She wasn't going to tell Lincoln about Wyalusing State Park. He would look at her differently and she couldn't bear it. Not yet. Not before it was unavoidable.

"He thought I needed to talk to someone," she mumbled.

"Clearly he doesn't know what he's talking about."

She looked up, almost smiling at his carefully blank expression. "Clearly."

"Without a doubt."

"Without question."

"What defines him as being loony?"

She sat back, agitated and flushed. "I don't know. He just...he demands things and is bossy and...and he made a comment about his brother telling him something all the time, like in the present tense." She paused. "His brother is dead."

Lincoln flinched and she immediately felt bad. She reached over without thought, touching his rough hand. "I'm sorry, Lincoln. I didn't think of what I was saying before I said it."

His fingers curled around hers, anchoring them to one another. Sara stared at their interlaced fingers, her heart beating much too fast. She looked up, confused by the force of his gray eyes. His features were tight with held-in emotion and she instinctively knew it was because there was something he didn't want her to see.

She tugged her hand away, fumbling with the bar stool and almost knocking it over in her haste to get to her feet. She was going to pretend whatever had just happened hadn't happened. From the closed look on Lincoln's face, he had decided to go the same route. Nothing *had* happened. Maybe that was what bothered her so much. That frozen space of time when their hands had touched and their eyes had met and everything had gone still.

"This guy...Mason...what exactly is he having you do that you don't want to do?" Lincoln was turned sideways from her, head averted, coffee mug clasped between his white-knuckled fingers.

She opened her mouth, but her throat was too tight, and nothing came out. *Keep it normal.* What was normal? She closed her mouth, swallowed, and tried again. "He wants me to paint."

His brows lowered as his head lifted. "And that's bad?"

She shifted her feet. "Yes. No. Not exactly."

Humor briefly lit up his eyes, lightening them to a slate gray. "Well, which is it? Yes? No? Or not exactly?"

"I haven't painted since...since before. I can't. I have no ambition or inspiration to, and even if I wanted to, everything would be of him. Somehow. Even if I didn't mean it to be. It would hurt too much," she ended softly.

"Maybe it would be cathartic."

"Maybe it wouldn't be," she shot back.

"You won't know unless you try."

"Trying is overrated."

Lincoln snorted, getting to his feet. "There's a movie I've been meaning to watch. Come on, you can be my date." He stiffened at the same time she did, quick to add, "I didn't mean it like that."

"I know."

His expression cleared. "Still take your popcorn smothered in ranch seasoning and oil?"

She hadn't had popcorn in too long. It was her favorite snack. Well, it had been, when she used to eat regularly and enjoy food. Now it was something she did as an afterthought. "I do."

He smiled. "Good. I'll get it started and *you* can put the movie in."

"What is it?" she asked, curious.

His back was to her as he opened and closed cupboards, rounding up the essentials to popcorn-making 'Lincoln Walker style'. "A funny movie. I was planning on watching it today. It's already in the DVD player. Just get it ready to go."

Sara turned toward the living room. The whole house was wood walls and black accents. It was very rustic and it was clear funds hadn't been an issue during its design. She'd always loved this house. Their parents had it built after they'd married. The upstairs had three bedrooms and a bathroom, the outline of the structure was basic with spacial open rooms. The walls were imbedded with him, the air around her lingering with his touch.

She reached the flat screen television, seeing his reflection in the black monitor. "Sara," was whispered near her ear. She spun around, a choking sound leaving her.

Lincoln was to her before she had a chance to completely freak out. "What is it? What's wrong?" He clutched her arms, watching her face.

She searched the room with her eyes, looking for him. She shook uncontrollably, jerking with the force of it. He was gone. It was disturbing how upset she was that she couldn't find him again. Not for the first time, Sara thought maybe she was losing her mind. Then she thought, would that be such a bad thing? At least then she'd think he was with her and it wouldn't matter if he really was or not, because in *her* mind, he would be.

She turned pained eyes to Lincoln.

He inhaled sharply as he gazed at her face.

"Lincoln, there's something wrong with me," she whispered.

His lips thinned. "There is absolutely nothing wrong with you."

"Yes, there is. There *is*. I..." Did she really want to tell him? She did. Sara had to tell someone. "I think I see him. I think I hear him. Voices talk to me in my head."

He lowered his head until his lips were close to her ear, his breath fanning the side of her face and neck as he murmured, "He's like my conscience, telling me what to do and say, what *not* to do and say. I feel him all around me. Sometimes...sometimes I even think he *is* me, inside of me, part of me. He badgers me into doing things I don't want to do. He tells me to stop being stupid. He warns me against doing things I shouldn't. So, no, Sara, I don't think something is wrong with you, and if there is, well, then, there's something wrong with me too."

She moved back from his too-close face. She felt strange. Connected. Sara felt like she hadn't felt in a long time. There was nothing romantic about it, but still guilt washed over her at the link to another man other than her husband. Lincoln's eyes darkened as she drew away, shaky and confused. Why did she sometimes think she saw things in his expression, in his eyes, that shouldn't be there?

He straightened, messing up her hair, looking like the normal Lincoln, a teasing grin in place. "Got that movie ready yet?"

She worked to keep her voice steady when she replied, but it shook regardless. "Got that popcorn ready yet?"

That was apparently the queue for the popcorn seeds to start popping, filling the room with the scent of roasted kernels. The *pop pop pop* became louder and frenzied, the seeds in a race to see which could be popped the fastest. Lincoln left to concentrate on the popcorn and she turned the television and DVD player on, letting the previews play as she waited. A framed photograph on the shelved bookcase along the wall caught her eye. She slowly walked to it, her breath catching.

It was them, on their wedding day.

Sara's dark hair was upswept to the side so that it waved down over one shoulder. She was smiling, her eyes sparkling, and her skin healthy and glowing. A strapless cream-toned dress in a simple design fit to her slim body. The backdrop was the woods outside the house she now stood in, green and abundant with life.

She stared at herself, wanting that Sara back. Her eyes slowly went to him, the sight of him stabbing her in overwhelming grief, so strong she couldn't breathe for a moment. She trailed a finger over his grinning face, closing her eyes as recollections whispered through her mind.

"*Do you have any idea how much I love you?*" *His face was close to hers, his eyes trained on Sara's. His fingers sifted through her hair, cupping the nape of her neck.* "*If anything ever happened to you, there wouldn't be enough tears in the world for me to cry. That's how much I love you.*"

"Popcorn's ready."

She started, turning away from the photograph. Lincoln sat on the couch, popcorn bowl on the coffee table with two sodas next to it. He lifted an eyebrow at her and she hesitated, the intimacy of sitting next to him locking her in place.

"Do you want your own bowl so you don't have to sit next to me?" he asked dryly.

"No." Sara rubbed her arms as she made her way to the couch, sitting on the edge of the couch, stiff-backed.

A long pause ensued.

"Are you going to push play?"

"Are you going to stop acting like you're afraid of me?"

She sat back, eyes on the television screen. "Better?"

"It'll do."

The movie began.

SARA BURST OUT *laughing as he ambled toward her, neon orange speedo in place. Not that his physique was anything to laugh at. Not in the least. He was all toned agile muscles and rangy build. Her fiancé had the body of a man who worked outside seven days a week with his broad shoulders, narrow waist, tanned skin, and athletic legs. She laughed only because he wore a speedo, and an orange one at that.*

"*Where did you come from?*"

"*Got done fishing early. Thought I'd surprise you.*"

"*You did. Believe me. What are you doing in...that?*" *Sara set a folded shirt on the duffel bag and turned to face him, hands on hips.*

Her small bedroom was covered in clothes, ready to be packed. They were on the dresser, on the floor, all over the bed. She wanted to make sure everything was perfect for their honeymoon, even her clothes. Apparently her fiancé did not have the same idea.

"I'm getting ready for Hawaii." He struck a pose in the doorway of the bedroom, flexing his arm muscles above his head. In spite of his goofy ensemble, Sara's mouth went dry and her body responded. He always had that effect on her. Always would.

"You are not wearing that in Hawaii. Where did you get that from?"

"Early wedding gift from Lincoln."

Sara rolled her eyes and grabbed her white and pink striped two-piece off the bed, shoving it into the bag. "Figures. Shouldn't you be home? Packing?"

"Now why would I want to be there when my favorite thing is here?"

"I don't know, so you're ready for the honeymoon?"

"That's not for seven days. Plenty of time."

"Procrastinator," she mumbled.

"Anal retentive."

He moved behind her, his scent and warmth making Sara crazy. He smelled like sunshine and deodorant and man—an intoxicating combination. She went still as his hands moved up and down her arms, his head bent so his hair tickled her ear and his breath fell across her neck and shoulder. "What have we here?" he murmured, slowly reaching around her.

Sara's heart thundered and she gasped as his body came flush with hers, causing her pulse to ascend on a maddening course to Heart Attack Central. Two years. Two years they'd been together and every day was like the first day she'd known she loved him. It hadn't taken long. Days, really. Or maybe minutes.

He snagged the two-piece around one long finger and twirled it in front of her face. "Looks like you got some modeling of your own to perform, now, doesn't it?"

She made a grab for the garment, but he was quicker, moving his arm out of her reach. "Uh uh uh. You get this back on one condition. You know what it is."

Sara spun around, her chest heaving with the force of her breaths as her eyes swept up and down his body that was perfection to her. She wanted him. She always wanted him.

His eyes darkened in response, narrowing into slits. His nostrils flared as he said in a low voice that made a shiver go down her back, "Come on, Sara, help a guy out."

The innuendo was blatant, especially when her eyes drifted down. She had no choice in the matter, not really. None. It had never been just sex between them. It had been more. Always. Sometimes it was frenzied and rough—others slow and sensual—but every time it was potent, consuming. The way their bodies came together, his hardness against her softness, the feelings inside her. The way they moved together in perfect sync. It was so much more than sex.

It was completeness.

THE CANVAS WAS blank. It stared at Sara in judgment, berating her for neglecting it. The scent of paint lingered in the cool room, though none had been used in it in over a year. Maybe it was all in her head. Memories had a funny way of inducing scents and sometimes even sounds. The past never seemed to fully leave a room—just as memories kept one's history alive as well. That was where he lived—in her memories. Good and bad, Sara couldn't escape them. She wasn't even sure if she *wanted* to.

The room was on the small side, but the large windows that allowed sunshine in made up for that. The white trim and wood floor made the sunny yellow walls pop out. The sun shone today and that was a small gift. It beat down on her arm and half her face, warming her skin. Sara sat before the empty project, willing inspiration to hit. Instead she saw him. She supposed that made sense, as he had been her inspiration more than anything else. She glanced at the empty chair in the corner to the left of her, thinking if she looked hard enough, he'd materialize, offer a sweet smile and a wink. Only no matter how long or hard she stared, he didn't. Sara had hope he would come back to her, somehow, someway, even if it was ludicrous and close to insane. She thought it was a little insane.

Shaking her head, she grabbed a paintbrush and mashed the bristles against her fingers, the softness of it gently prickling her skin. She randomly picked a color without looking, popped the goopy lid, and slammed the brush into it, blobs of paint splattering her face and hands. Only when the brush hit the canvas did the color become known. Blue. Her chest tightened. Of course it would be blue, like his eyes.

The strokes were angry, hard, and it showed on the splotches and streaks left on the painting. The acrylic scent assaulted her nostrils in a biting yet soothingly familiar way. The image turned into a deep blue circle, uneven and bold. The longer she mindlessly worked at it, the surer her hand became, the calmer the brushstrokes, and when her hand finally fell to her lap, she stared at the door she'd created. Sara tilted her head as she examined it, wondering why, out of everything she could have made, that was what her mind had told her hand to produce.

The phone rang, startling her, and the wet paintbrush fell from her hand, making a picture of its own on the wood floor. She let out a curse, hurrying to get up without knocking anything else over, and moved for the kitchen.

The shrill sound of the phone ringing caused her to wince as she reached for the phone. "Hello?"

"Sara? Hey. It's Spencer. How ya been?" The nervous undertone in his voice was not lost on her.

"I'm painting."

"Really? That's great. I'm really glad. Mason must be helping—"

"I'm painting because he ordered me to," she interrupted, swiping hair out of her eyes with her forearm.

"Oh." Something like a snicker came over the line. "Sorry. At least you're painting. You could have always said no."

"I did. It didn't work."

"Mason can be intimidating, but everything he does he does with good intentions. Honestly. I wouldn't have sent him your way if I didn't believe that."

She leaned against the fridge, rubbing her paint-covered fingers together. "Yeah."

"Is it helping?" he asked after a pause.

"Maybe." She didn't know. Surprisingly, painting had ended up being therapeutic for her, although the start had been rocky.

"I hope it is." When she didn't respond, he continued, "So, uh, I was wondering...Gracie and I, we're seeing each other again and we're kind of having a party and I thought maybe you would want to come? I mean, Mason will be there...Lincoln, some other people. Not really a party. Well, kind of. It's more of a get-together. For my birthday. Anyway, I thought you might want to come."

Sara felt awful that the first thing she felt was envy and bitterness toward Spencer and Gracie for being able to rekindle their relationship. It wasn't their fault she couldn't be with the only person she wanted to be with. Her throat closed and she couldn't utter a word.

"I mean, if it's too soon...I just thought maybe you'd like to get out, socialize, try to have some fun."

"Having fun isn't exactly on my to-do list," she said softly, the phone pressed hard against her ear.

"Sara...come on," he gently coaxed. "Please? If you can't deal, then someone will take you home. Just try. Please."

"Okay," she whispered. As soon as the word left her, her stomach rebelled.

"I'll tell Lincoln to pick you up on his way over. It's this Friday at seven. See you soon."

The hand that held the phone went limp at her side. Her brows furrowed at the thought of Lincoln picking her up. She knew it meant nothing. She knew it wasn't a date in any way. It wasn't cheating. It wasn't being unfaithful. It wasn't a betrayal. No one could replace him, not even his brother. No one ever would. She *knew* all of that. So why did she feel so weird, so awkward, about it?

She remembered the spilled paint and grabbed a dishcloth off the side of the sink, wetting it with warm water. The rag fell from her hand with a heavy *splat* when she entered the art room and looked down. It was ragged and bent, but the blue paint was unmistakably in the form of a 'C'. She stumbled back, blindly feeling behind her for something to brace herself against before she fell.

Sara landed against the wall, shaking. She blinked at it, but it didn't disappear and it didn't transform into a normal splotch of paint. A whimper left her as she dropped to her knees beside it, tracing it with a trembling finger. She hung her head, tears burning her eyes, and quickly cleaned it up, feeling as though she was wiping a part of him away from her soul, hating every swipe of the wet cloth against the paint.

CHAPTER 7

SHE WAS NERVOUS and she had no reason to be. Sara chewed on her thumbnail as she paced the living room floor. There was no one to impress, no one she had to look good for, and even if there had been, he'd been the only one she'd ever wanted to impress and he'd liked the way she'd looked no matter what she'd worn or how she'd looked.

It was the thought of trying to pretend to be normal. They would expect things out of her. Like conversation. And smiles. They would expect her to laugh and joke and be the old Sara. Only she couldn't be the old Sara because that person was gone. That Sara wasn't ever coming back. She knew that as surely as she'd known she was going to be a painter the first time she'd picked up a paintbrush at the age of four.

She'd unseeingly grabbed a pair of jeans and a top out of the dresser and now wore a hot pink buttoned-down shirt with a black buttoned vest over it and a pair of dark blue jeans, and a pair of knee-high black boots on. She'd applied perfume and just as quickly wiped it off. She had tried to hide the paleness of her face and the darkness from under her eyes with makeup, but it had been a useless attempt. Her hair needed a decent cut and not knowing what to do with it, she'd twisted it into a low ponytail at the nape of her neck.

The flash of headlights in the window alerted her to Lincoln's arrival. Sara grabbed her purse, made sure all the lights were off in the house, and locked the door behind her. The temperature hovered somewhere between the forties and fifties and the scent of rain was in the air. Most of the snow from less than a week ago had melted. Wisconsin could never make up its mind which way it wanted to go as far as the weather went.

Sick feeling and jittery, she walked down the sidewalk with the *click click* of her boots in tempo with her heartbeats. Every step taken toward Lincoln was a step Sara fought an intense urge to turn around, race back into the house, and stay there. Indefinitely. *Be normal, Sara. For once, for tonight, just try to be normal.*

She paused near the curb, gathering her strength. The sound of a door opening and closing made her flinch, and there Lincoln was, striding toward her, a tall shadow with no features under the glow of a streetlamp. He didn't say anything, stopping before her, watching her in the dark.

"Hi," she squeaked.

He nodded, silently opening the door for her. Sara frowned, wondering at his quietness. She moved past him to get into the truck, his scent going with her. It had a hint of citrus to it. She sat down and looked ahead as the door shut.

As soon as he entered his side of the truck, she went at him. "What's your problem?"

Lincoln flipped a light on in the truck. She blinked, but it wasn't from the sudden light—it was from Lincoln's appearance. His hair was shorter, making his flinty eyes sharper and more noticeable. He wore a gray sweater the same shade as his eyes and faded black jeans. His cologne or body wash wafted through the small enclosed space. She quickly averted her face, her pulse too fast. What was wrong with her?

"I wanted to tell you how nice you look," he said slowly.

Her head jerked up as her eyes went to his face, her brows lowering.

"Only I didn't want to upset you. Seems like everything I do or say comes out wrong lately, so I decided to keep quiet. But you do, Sara. You look really nice." He faced forward, turning off the light, blanketing them in black, and putting the truck in drive.

The silence was tense between them and it took a few attempts to say it, but she eventually got out a soft, "Thank you."

He gave an almost unnoticeable nod of his head, messing with the radio as he drove. Lincoln found a hard rock station and drums and guitar took over the quiet. It took less than five minutes to get to Spencer's house located at the edge of town. Sara sat there, staring at the red two-story house, inhaling and exhaling deeply. It would be all wrong in there. Everyone would be the same except for him—he would be the missing link that should be there and wasn't. Would their eyes be full of judgment, full of contempt? Would they shun her? Or would it be even worse than that; would she see pity in each pair of eyes that met hers?

"Breathe, Sara," he murmured.

She glanced at him under the cover of night, knowing his gaze was trained on her. She couldn't see it, but she felt it like a warm caress of understanding. She jerked her head up and down and reached for the doorknob.

They met at the front of the truck and when he wordlessly reached his hand out to her, Sara looked down at it for one heartfelt moment, feeling as though she was making an unknown decision of some kind. She clasped it and his fingers wrapped around her smaller ones. Just his hand around hers gave her strength to make her legs move, gave her courage to walk through the front door and into a scene from her past minus one. The most important one. Her throat thickened and she blinked under the bright lights of the entryway.

Music played from a stereo system in the living room. It smelled like a variety of appetizers dunked in fragrant sauces. Conversations were loud and laughter rang out through different rooms of the downstairs of the house. A card game was going on at a table to the right and people were strewn about the furniture in the living room to the left of her. The interior of Spencer's house was simple and uncluttered. Every room had the same theme. The walls were beige, the floors wood, and the furniture a forest green.

Sara became flushed as her eyes glanced over person after person. There were so many people. She felt dizzy, like she was suffocating. Lincoln squeezed her hand, his fingers interlaced with hers, and moved toward the kitchen, never once loosening his grip from her hand. She stared at his broad-shouldered back as she followed him, focusing on that.

"Lincoln!" Spencer jerked her anchor from her, causing his fingers to slide through hers and away. He slapped a hand on Lincoln's back. "You made it. Where's Sara?"

"Probably hiding behind me."

Spencer's head popped around Lincoln's arm. His eyes were unfocused and bright, his face red. "Sara!" She was enveloped in a tight hug and panic threatened to kick in. The only other man to hold her other than her husband that hadn't completely driven her crazy was Lincoln. "I'm so glad you're here."

Her eyes found Lincoln's and he immediately pulled Spencer from her. "Sara's glad you're here too, aren't you, Sara?" He grinned at her and she could breathe again. "I thought this was going to be a small get-together?" he asked Spencer.

"Well..." was all he came up with, shrugging.

"I'm glad things are working out for you and Gracie," she said. She was happy, but she was also sad. She wanted that second chance with her husband too and she'd never get it.

Spencer blinked. "Oh. Yeah. Me too. Where is she anyway?" He turned and swayed to the left, catching himself with a hand against the kitchen counter. "I'll be back. I'm going to find her. I know she wanted to see you, Sara." He walked off.

She looked at Lincoln.

He shrugged. "Want a drink?"

She opened her mouth to say no, but then something grabbed a hold of her, something rebellious. Something that wanted to tell the pain and self-loathing to suck it. Maybe, for one night, she could forget it all. At any rate, she could try. The thought oozed into her brain, taking over all the rational reasons why she shouldn't drink, and guided her into saying, "Sure. Why not?"

He hesitated, obviously seeing something in her expression. "Are you sure? You don't have to."

"For tonight, Lincoln, I'm going to pretend."

"Pretend what?"

She watched the people around her having a good time and looked at him. "I'm going to pretend everything is okay."

He moved closer, leaning down so that they were at eye level. "You don't have to do this. You don't have to pretend. There's no shame in being sad. We can go. Right now. I'll take you home. We can hang out, watch a movie. We can stare at a wall. Hell, I don't know. Don't feel pressured to do anything. This is me. Not giving you any pressure." He lifted his hands, palms out, and nodded at his hands. "See? Pressure free."

Warmth trickled over her scalp and down her back as she gazed at Lincoln, feeling a little lost at the wonder of him. She had never noticed him before, not like this. Had he always been like this? Maybe he had. Or maybe circumstances had matured him, changed him.

She broke their stare, her face heating up. "If I need to go, I'll tell you," she said in a soft voice, playing with a button on the bottom of her vest.

"Promise?"

"I promise."

He slowly nodded. "All right. I'll be right back."

She watched people interact as she waited, her eyes landing on, and going back to, Mason Wells. Even though Spencer had mentioned him being there, she was still surprised to see him. He stood with his profile to her, talking to a pretty blonde leaning against the wall near the bathroom. In his hand he held a glass containing clear liquid, sipping from it as he talked.

As though feeling her gaze on him, he looked up, catching her eye, and saluted her with his glass before continuing his conversation with the woman he was with. The lady laughed and Mason leaned down to kiss her. Sara swallowed, feeling...something. It wasn't jealousy. Maybe envy? He'd moved on enough to be normal, something there was no logical way for her to accomplish. Well—she cocked her head as she watched him brush hair out of the woman's eye—she wasn't sure how normal he was; given the fact he talked to his deceased brother on a regular basis, but at least he'd managed to move on.

She turned away, feeling intrusive, feeling like she had no room to talk. The things Sara thought she heard and saw clearly made her no one to judge someone's lucidity. The pull of the woman's tinkling laughter was too much to ignore and she found herself staring at them once more. Was she it? The reason Mason had had to get past the guilt and pain and drugs. Would Sara's redemption not be something, but someone, as well?

"What's got you frowning so intently?"

Sara glanced at Lincoln. "That's Mason. Over there." She nodded toward the pair.

"The evil grief counselor?" Lincoln handed her an uncapped Leinenkugel Berry Weiss. The bottle was cold and had a layer of perspiration on it, chilling her hands.

She turned away from Mason, not wanting to think about her reality. The temptation to lose her truth in a haze of falsehood, if only briefly, was strong. Maybe one night of reprieve wasn't too much to hope for.

"Yep. I don't want to talk about him. Or any of it."

"Then we won't."

She raised the bottle to her lips. The cold beer with a hint of fruit washed over her taste buds, and she was surprised by how good it tasted.

Lincoln watched her, saying after a while, "You aren't going to get drunk and pass out from one beer and make me carry you out of here, are you? 'Cause, I don't know, you look pretty heavy."

"Or, I don't know, you're weak," she retorted, gulping down the beer. "It tastes good."

"Touché. What do you want to do?"

Sara watched the card games and people interacting around them as she finished her beer. They stood in the middle of it all and yet were somehow on the outside of it. A horrible sound came from the direction of the living room and she realized someone had turned on the karaoke machine and was doing their version of singing.

Her eyes collided with his.

Lincoln's face lit up and he laughed, nodding. "Yeah. That's what we need to do. You wanna?"

She swallowed, taking in the way his gray eyes crinkled at the corners, the flash of straight, even teeth, the deep timbre of his laughter slamming into her like a bolt of life. He was becoming alive to her when no one else had since that night. Why? Why *him*? She frowned, averting her eyes from where they continually seemed to want to go.

He paused and she glanced up to catch the smile falling from his lips. "Sara? You okay?"

With a jerk of her head, she said, "Yes. No. Uh...can I get another beer?"

Lincoln took the empty bottle from her hand. "I'm only going to ask this one more time and then I'll shut up about it, I promise." He touched her cheek, bringing her eyes to his. "Are you sure?"

Animation shot through her, or maybe it was the beer hitting her already, but Sara's body hummed with anticipation and her skin heated. She nodded. She was sure. Maybe she would regret it tomorrow, or even in an hour, but right now, she couldn't regret wanting a piece of normalcy back in her upturned world.

They sang '(I've Had) The Time of My Life'. She stumbled a little at first, but then Lincoln grabbed her shoulder and turned her to face him, and when he sang each and every word in his clear deep voice with his eyes locked on hers, she relaxed and had fun. She even laughed and didn't feel bad about it. *Why Lincoln?* was in the back of her mind, hovering, trying to ruin it for her, but she continually shoved it away until it was gone.

The applause and catcalls at the finish of it burned her cheeks with exhilaration and joy. She hadn't felt so alive in so long. Sara set the microphone down on the coffee table and looked at Lincoln. He had this grin on his face that gave him a boyish, endearing look and made his eyes sparkle. He spontaneously grabbed her and spun her around. She tossed her head back and closed her eyes, laughing. She was dizzy, and maybe a little sick feeling, but she was *feeling*.

When he stopped, they swayed as they caught their balance. Sara looked up, smiling. Lincoln intently studied her face, causing her to stiffen. He lowered his forehead to hers, his heart thundering under her palm. She quickly pulled away and tucked hair that had fallen from her ponytail behind her ear, averting her face from his gaze. Her throat was dry and her pulse chaotic.

"I, uh..." she began, needing to get away, to regroup from the things she couldn't understand or accept, the things she didn't want to or *couldn't* see.

"Sara! Yoo-hoo!" Spencer waved from the couch, his arm slung around a pretty redhead's shoulders. "Come here. Gracie wants to say hi."

Gracie gave a small smile, looking exasperated with her intoxicated boyfriend. She had pale skin, freckles, and large green eyes. She had always been nice to Sara, but as she approached the couple, she wondered if she still would be. Spencer stood and tugged his girlfriend to her feet, almost knocking them both over.

She rolled her eyes at Sara as she righted them. "Hello, Sara. It's been a long time."

Since the accident. She hadn't seen her since the night of the accident.

She had trouble speaking. "Yes. Hi," She finally choked out.

"How've you been?"

There was that look. That sympathetic, pitying look she hated. Without meaning to, she took a step away, as though that would somehow block her from Gracie's expression. She bumped into the coffee table and when she would have fallen, Lincoln caught her. He raised his eyebrows at her in a silent question.

"I'm fine," she muttered, whatever semblance of fun she'd been having completely evaporated. This had been a bad idea. She'd *known* better.

"Sara needs to get out more," Spencer slurred. "Have fun. Forget about stuff."

She stared at him, stunned at what she was hearing, her hands fisting at her sides. She wanted to shout at him to keep his stupid opinions and useless words to himself. He didn't understand anything. He didn't know what it was like.

"Forget, Spencer?" Lincoln asked in a low voice, his entire body taut beside her. "We should just forget about it all and move on? Pretend it never happened? Pretend he never existed? Is that right?"

Spencer blinked his eyes, swaying a little. "No, man, that's not what I meant. You know that. He was my best friend."

He slowly nodded, his jaw clenched. "Was. Not is. Right. I get it."

"Lincoln," Sara murmured, placing a hand on his forearm. The muscles tensed beneath her fingers, holding fury, just barely, at bay. "He's drunk. Let's go, okay?"

"I didn't mean anything!" Spencer called after them, sounding miserable, as Lincoln stormed toward the door, Sara following. She glanced back as Gracie put her hands to Spencer's face, drawing his gaze to hers as she spoke to him. Her heart squeezed and she turned away.

Mason stood up from the card table as she passed, wedging himself between her and the exit. "Everything okay?"

The door banged shut after Lincoln. Sara glanced at Mason, the urge to race after Lincoln impossible to ignore. "Spencer's drunk and said something that upset Lincoln."

His eyes narrowed as he looked through the window of the front door. "Are you sure it's safe to ride with him?"

Instant heat shot through her and she gritted her teeth. "That's my husband's brother. Of course I'm safe."

"I meant since he's been drinking."

"He had one beer." The silence grew and she gestured impatiently. "I need to go."

"Right. See you Sunday." Mason turned away, back to his card game.

She bit back a retort in the negative to his comment, its importance absolutely *nothing* compared to getting to Lincoln. Sara was out the door before he'd completely sat down.

It was raining. Cold, large drops of wetness soaked through her clothes even before she was to the darkened truck. The air was crisp with the scent of it. Where was he? She swiped a hand across her face and blinked her eyes through the sky's shower. She peered into the truck. It was empty. Panic grabbed her chest and clenched. Sara whirled around, searching the surroundings for Lincoln.

The house glowed with lights, music and conversation floating out to her. Scraggly trees loomed in the yard, cloaking the scene with a layer of foreboding. It was silly to be worried about him, really. Obviously he hadn't driven off in a rage. Lincoln would never abandon her. *You thought the same about him.* Sara flinched, refusing to dwell on that too much. He hadn't meant to leave her; he'd had no choice. That's what she told herself.

She turned in a slow circle, wondering where he could have gone to. Then she saw him. He stood on the other side of the truck, near the tailgate, facing away from her. He was hunched over, his back rigid. She slowly walked to him, her boots sinking into the soft ground, each step filling her with something. Relief. And something more, something Sara couldn't put a name to, not yet. Her hand trembled as it reached up, just barely grazing his hard shoulder.

Lincoln whirled around, his face cast in shadow, but not enough to hide the way his eyes zeroed in on her face and locked there, as if she had the power to ground him, as if she could heal what wounded him. His eyes were tortured and Sara's heart hurt seeing that look in them. He hid it better than she, but he was hurting just as much as she was. A tick in his jaw pulled her gaze to it. She focused on that, her breaths short and hurried. They were changing—she and Lincoln. She felt it, and it scared her. It terrified her. She didn't know how or why it was happening, and that scared her more.

"I miss him."

Her eyes jerked to Lincoln's.

"I want my brother back," he said in a ragged voice.

She nodded. "I know."

"But he's not coming back."

Sara wanted to deny his words, but logically, how could she? She looked down at her rain-covered boots, saying nothing.

He sighed loudly. "Come on. I'll take you home."

The drive was silent and awkward. When the truck pulled up to the house, Sara stared at the dark structure, thinking even in the daytime it was still dark. His light was gone from it, tossed away from one mistake it had taken a second to act out, and a lifetime to relive. She grabbed the door handle and pushed.

Lincoln's hand grabbed her arm, his touch like fire on her skin, stopping her. She looked back, his features obscured in the dark. His hand fell away. "Good night, Sara."

Her held breath left her in an exhalation. "Good night, Lincoln."

CHAPTER 8

GUILT WAS HER companion when she awoke. Sara sleepily opened her eyes with a creak in her neck as she sat up in the recliner, flipping the blanket off her. Her head hurt and she winced at the bright sunlight streaming in through a window. She'd laughed and smiled and had fun without him, in spite of the situation. How could she have done that? She covered her face with her hands as the night's events came back in a wave of regret. She had no right to live, to enjoy anything, not when he was where he was and she where she was. It should have been her. Why hadn't it been her?

"There's a reason for everything."

She went still, dropping her hands from her face, and slowly raised her head. The room was empty. She really was losing her mind. Was that what grief did? Made a person go insane if they couldn't deal with it?

"Sometimes you can't see it and it doesn't make sense, but eventually, in time, it does. Even when it hurts. Even when it's bad. Something good happens because of it."

She shot to her feet as a sob left her, whirling around in a circle, searching for the face that went along with the voice she heard. Sara grabbed her hair and pulled, the sharp pain bringing tears to her eyes. Or maybe they'd already been there. They always seemed to be. Her eyes were overworking waterfalls of grief.

Her hands shook and she stumbled into the kitchen, grabbing the phone off the wall and clutching it to her. *Don't call him.* She had to call him. *You're becoming too dependent on him.* Sara slammed the phone back, her attention drawn to the scrawled handwriting on a Post-It stuck to the fridge.

The phone rang, making her jump. Sara swallowed, staring at it, her heart pounding. Her hand slowly reached out to pick it up. "Hello?" left her in a choked whisper.

"Hello, is this Sara Walker? This is Georgia from Dish Network calling to see if you'd like to reactivate your account with us."

Her shoulders slumped and a sigh of relief left her. "No. Thank you."

"Now—"

She hung up the phone, resting with her back against the cold fridge. Sara didn't understand how everything in the house reminded her of him when she'd removed everything she'd thought would do so as a way to deal with the pain. Didn't matter—he was in the woodwork, the air, *her*. She couldn't escape him. She couldn't escape the ache that had made a home inside her chest. That ache was him, *for him*, and would never leave, not while she had a breath left in her body. It wasn't that Sara wanted to forget him, never that, she just wanted it to not hurt every time she thought of him.

She tried not to think about it, and sometimes, Sara forgot. It made her feel terrible that the escape from the past was like a blessing. She'd lost him and she'd lost a part of him before that in the death of their unborn child. Was Sara not meant to have any of him? Her eyes went to the room down the hall and a barrage of memories hit her, one after another, bringing her to her knees. And along with the remembrances came him. Always.

"We'll have more babies, Sara. We'll have a houseful of little munchkins that will drive us absolutely bat shit crazy and we'll be worn down and exhausted to the point of never wanting to have sex again. We won't speak—we'll grunt. Talking will require too much energy. Your legs will be hairy and your hair a matted mess and I'll get a gut and have dark circles under my eyes and we'll be so unbelievably happy it won't matter." His voice cracked and he paused, exhaling deeply, his hands tight on her face, holding her gaze with his.

"Don't cry. Okay, cry if you want to, but know that that baby knew you, if only for a moment. That baby knew you loved him or her, and that baby is loving you even now. And we'll have more babies and they'll love

you too. So cry if you have to and be sad." He swallowed. *"But don't lose hope. Don't give up. Don't hate yourself. And don't forget what I just said."*

Tears streamed down her face and her feet moved in the direction of the closed door. So many closed doors. What did she think she was accomplishing? Did she really think she could close away the memories and the hurt inside a room? It wasn't working, if that's what her subconscious was trying to do. Sara's hand reached for the doorknob and turned.

They'd painted the walls celery green. The curtains were blue with yellow stripes. In the middle of the room sat an unused crib made out of pale wood. A cream and pale green checked comforter rested on the sheeted mattress, never to know the feel of a soft little being or be snuggled in a tiny hand. It smelled like baby powder in the room and Sara inhaled deeply. She tweaked the teddy bear mobile and watched as it gently swayed back and forth. It had been too soon to know what sex the baby was, but they'd been excited and hadn't wanted to wait to decorate, so everything had been made neutral.

It began with cramps, then blood, then the reality that had to be a lie and wasn't. She remembered him holding her, crying with her, his grip painful, his arms the only thing keeping her upright. Sara remembered the hollowness, the disbelief, the hope that somehow, it was wrong, and somehow, everything was still okay. Then the blackness as consciousness left her and still the blackness when consciousness returned. The pain in her stomach, the pain in her heart, the pain that had never fully left her.

Her chest ached and she unconsciously rubbed a hand to it. After she'd lost the baby, Sara would find herself in the room, just staring, not really seeing. He'd come and get her, wrap her in his arms, and bring her back from the brink of nothingness that had threatened to erase all she was. He wasn't here to do it this time. He wasn't here to do it this time because *he* was the one she'd lost and mourned. Sara wondered who, if anyone, would save her this time. Maybe she wasn't savable.

Maybe she was already gone—like her baby, like her parents, like her husband.

"WELL?"

Mason gave her a pointed look Sara ignored. She poured herself a mug of coffee after handing him one. "Well what?"

"Show me your creation."

He was irritating and bossy, but at least he didn't hide things. Sara had to respect that about him. He didn't try to avoid the world, like her. Still, she wasn't ready to talk, not about herself, not about her husband.

"That woman...at Spencer's, was she the reason you found to move on? To live?" She fiddled with the hem of her shirt as she waited for him to answer.

"Nope."

"Then who was?"

"I'll tell you, after you show me your painting."

Sara swallowed as her gaze went to the closed door. It was only a piece of canvas. It was only a piece of canvas that symbolized her whole world and all she'd lost, all she'd had at one time and no longer did.

"How did you and Spencer meet?" she hedged.

Half of Mason's mouth quirked. "He arrested me."

"I'm not really surprised to hear that," she muttered.

"I'm not really surprised to hear you say that either."

Her lips tried to smile at his dry tone and she bit the inside of her lower lip to halt it. He didn't need to know she found him a little amusing. Then he'd probably never go away.

"What did he arrest you for?"

Mason sighed, rubbing his face. "I really don't think it's necessary for you to know."

"That bad, huh?"

His hands dropped from his face. "It was in my, quote unquote, bad stage. I was drunk. I peed in public. On Main Street, actually. Right in front of the cop shop."

Sara snorted. "Nice."

"Oh yes. It was my way of sticking it to the man and all that."

"Sounds like it was counterproductive."

"Maybe. Slightly." He grinned, and then sobered. "Just so you know, Spencer feels bad about the other night. He said he called Lincoln."

Sara hadn't seen Lincoln since Friday night. He'd stopped by yesterday and she'd sat in the dark until he'd driven away. Not that she hadn't already been sitting in the dark, wallowing in stifling emotions she never fully escaped. Or if she did escape them, they came back even worse. The phone had rung intermittently and she'd let it. She hadn't had the strength to do much of anything. Yesterday had been a bad day, to summarize.

"That's good," she mumbled, picking at the jagged edge of an uneven nail on her thumb, thoughts locked on Lincoln.

She'd wanted to open the door. She'd forced herself not to pick up the phone. Sara felt awful about the way she'd avoided him, but not awful enough to call him back or go see him. Lincoln needed to stay away from her. He was better off by himself and he'd hate her before too long anyway. It was best to distance herself from him. Sara wondered if he'd let her.

Mason rubbed his forehead, letting out a sigh. "Look, I know you don't want me here. I know you want to be alone so you can hate yourself in peace, but...that's not going to happen. You have people that care about you. You have people that are worried about you. Humor them. Talk to me. Open up. Did you paint?"

She swallowed, giving an almost imperceptible nod.

"Did you feel better afterward?"

She thought of how the urge to create had taken over, how she'd been mindless with the need to paint and hadn't felt or thought anything for joyous minutes. Then she remembered the letter she'd seen on the floor after dropping the paintbrush.

Sara looked up, meeting his eyes. "No. I felt crazy."

He frowned. "Why?"

She pushed herself out of the chair and stared out the kitchen window above the sink, not really seeing anything. "You want to know what I'm thinking? You want me to open up to you?"

"It doesn't have to be me. Talk to *someone*. Talk to Lincoln if you're the most comfortable with him. You two seem close. Just don't keep it all inside. It'll ravage you from the inside out if you let it."

It already had. It had torn her up. She was a bloody, throbbing mess of pain, a wound that never healed.

"Can you do something for me?" Mason stood and walked toward the door, pulling his coat on and then his boots.

"What?"

"Can you try to forgive yourself?"

Her answer was immediate and needed no thought. It was a resounding, "No."

He sighed, opening the door. "Well, that right there is your first mistake. See you next week," he mocked, shutting the door behind him.

"WHY DIDN'T YOU answer the door or phone?" his voice immediately demanded, gruff with annoyance.

Sara inhaled deeply, something as close to peace as she was allowed trickling over her at the sound of his deep voice, even if he didn't sound happy with her. Didn't matter. Her breathing evened, her pulse steadied. All from that one sentence.

"So you're going to do that again, are you? Avoid me? Not talk to me? Fine. Try it. I'll keep calling and I'll keep showing up. Next time you pull something like that I'm not leaving, Sara. It was too cold yesterday to hang around outside, but next time, I'll be prepared." Lincoln paused, picking up steam as he went. "Next time, I'll wear my snowmobile garb. Doesn't matter if I haven't worn it since high school and it doesn't fit me anymore and I'm in dire need of new gear. I'll still wear it. So you'll make me look ridiculous on top of it all. Is any of this sinking in?"

A small smile started to manipulate her lips. She rested her elbows on the table and held her forehead in one hand, the other holding the phone to her ear.

"And FYI, you're coming with me tomorrow to pick out a Christmas tree. Be at my house at nine. Wear a coat this time. And a smile. Those are my rules. Don't even try not to be there. I'll hunt you down, Sara, I swear. Are you going to say anything?" He blew out a noisy breath full of irritation. When she remained silent, Lincoln sighed and said, "Anyway, hope you're okay. Take care, Sara."

She set the phone down, feeling lighter than she had been before she'd placed the phone call. Sara didn't like feeling the way she did most days, but the thought of being anything else caused guilt to overrun all other emotions. She was stuck. Trapped. But every time she began to fade completely away, Lincoln somehow managed to find her, just a sliver of her, but it was something.

It was enough.

She got up from the table, her eyes traveling along the bare walls that whispered of her past. She turned in a circle, remembering the photo they'd taken of each other the day they'd danced by the creek. It used to reside on the refrigerator, held there with a heart magnet. Longing and euphoria washed over her, trickling down her scalp in shivers, his scent and touch coming with it.

They danced. Around and around they twirled, eyes locked on each other's world. The sun beat down on them, heating their skin. When the sun touched his face, it made his features shine and sparkle, his rugged beauty amplified and breathtaking, his eyes blue gems in a sun-kissed face. The creak trickled beside them as nature's lyrical music and grass poked the bottoms of her bare feet.

Sara let her head fall back and closed her eyes. She'd never been so centered, so whole, as she'd been since that day he'd smiled and asked her name. She opened her eyes, lifting her head, and caught his soft smile. Emotions overwhelmed her, brought tears to her eyes. She'd never thought it could be like this with another person. She never thought she could be so happy, especially after losing her parents. It scared her and thrilled her and made her sick and she never wanted it to end.

"What are you thinking?" he murmured close to her ear, his clean scent, the tickle of his breath on her skin, the sound of his voice, him, making Sara melt. One look and she melted.

"I'm thinking I love you and I'll always love you, even when you're old and wrinkly."

"Ditto," he said, spinning her around until she was dizzy.

"I will never be old and wrinkly, just so you know," she said, laughing when he dipped her.

"You will most definitely be old and wrinkly, but you'll still be beautiful and I'll still love you. I'll always love you, even after I'm dead and gone and am nothing. My love will linger on. It's that awesome, that strong, that real. Have no doubt of that, Sara Walker." His eyes held her

in place, the conviction in them, the set of his jaw, telling her he spoke the truth. He straightened then, pulling her up with him, his chest noticeably rising and lowering as his lips pressed together.

"What is it, Cole?"

"I just...I love you so damn much, Sara. It makes me weak and stronger at the same time and drives me absolutely mad and I wouldn't change it for the world, not for nothing."

"Ditto," she whispered, her throat tightening.

He pulled her to him, one hand on her back, the other gripping the side of her face as he turned those lips that spoke so passionately to wreak havoc on her mouth. Her stomach dipped, her body reacted as it always did, and she kissed him back, telling him with her mouth what she couldn't find the words to say with her lips. All she wanted, all she ever needed, was right before her.

"WHAT ARE YOU doing?" she asked, staring at his gloved hands packing snow into a round, firm ball. Sara's breaths were visible and she crossed her arms in an attempt to keep some of her body's warmth from leaving her.

Lincoln glanced up at her, his eyes shining silver against the white atmosphere. "I'm making a snowball." The sun glowed behind him, making him appear haloed all around.

She slowly backed away. "I thought we were finding you a Christmas tree."

"We are." He straightened, a flash of white teeth showing as he grinned. A dark blue stocking cap covered his head and he wore a brown coat and gloves that had been a birthday present from her and his brother one year. His breath left him in frosty puffs of air and he looked like an ad for an outdoorsy magazine.

"What—" The snow smacked her chest, cold chunks of winter flying up and hitting her neck, face, and going down the front of her jacket. Sara sucked in a sharp breath at the icy sting of it against the heat of her skin. She stood there, disbelief holding her immobile.

Lincoln laughed, bending down again.

Panic set in and she searched for cover, her eyes zooming in on the trees closest to her. She knew he wouldn't really throw another snowball at her and yet her pulse began to race. Then he looked at her, his facial expression telling her, yes, he would.

"Don't you—" An involuntary cry left her as the second snowball whirred through the air and made contact with her face. Sara gasped, stunned to find her upper body encrusted in slush.

His head tipped back as his laughter filled the woods around them, loud and deep. Birds chirped in response, their chatter taking the place of Lincoln's mirth. It was a beautiful sound and Sara went still as it washed over her. The trees, the snow, nature—it was close to perfect. She hadn't enjoyed anything so simple and significant in too long.

"Come on, Sara. Fight back." Lincoln opened his arms wide, a grin on his face. "Hit me with your best shot."

She shook her head. "No."

With narrowed eyes, he purposely crouched and grabbed a handful of now. "Sure?"

"This is not Christmas tree searching," she pointed out, her voice a little shrill.

The snowball hit her leg. "Lincoln—" Another one smacked her arm. Sara gritted her teeth, determination snapping through her. "Fine. You asked for it."

"Oh, I'm scared. Look, Sara. I'm *terrified*." He raised his eyebrows, clearly unimpressed by her declaration.

"You're gonna be terrified," she muttered as she firmly packed snow into a misshapen ball.

"What was that?" he asked, one hand behind his ear.

She straightened and whipped the snowball toward him as hard as she could. It flew over his head and splattered against a tree behind him.

"Really?" He gave her a disappointed look.

Scowl in place, she quickly scooped up more snow and flung it at him. Lincoln ducked and it hit the ground to the left of him.

"You suck."

Flushed, her breath leaving her in pants, Sara went to make another snowball.

"I think you should stop before you embarrass yourself anymore."

She chucked the partially made snowball to the ground and glared at him. When he laughed, a cry of frustration burst from her and Sara took off toward him, the look of surprise on his face when she clothes-lined him across the chest one she would never forget. He stumbled back, hanging onto her. Sara lost her balance and fell on her face in the snow, Lincoln on his back beside her, clutching her arm.

Her shoulders shook and gasps left her as she fought to breathe. She laid there, the front of her lodged in a mound of snow, and laughed, inhaling the icy particles and not caring how wet and cold she was getting. She couldn't remember the last time she'd laughed and it surged from her, loud and close to hysterical. The laughter soon turned into a sob and then she was tugged to the left.

Lincoln pulled her into his arms and held her, shielding her upper half from the snow with his body. He rested his chin on the crown of her head as she wept, not speaking, just holding, and Sara was so grateful for that. His arms were warm and tight around her back, his body heat trying to block out the shivers that were taking over her body. The side of her face was pressed against his cold jacket that smelled like winter and laundry detergent.

"I think," he began slowly, "what you need to find is a way to not feel bad about living." She stiffened and tried to pull away. He only tightened his hold on her. "*And* I'm going to help you find it."

"Why?" she choked out.

He sat up, taking her with him. He tipped her chin up so their gazes locked. "Because stupid people try to do things on their own and smart people realize no one can do anything on their own. And you're smart." He smiled and Sara swallowed. "Even when you don't act like it. Let's find our tree."

They spent close to an hour roaming the woods, searching for the perfect tree. Lincoln let her pick and Sara was drawn to the most straggly, uneven, imperfect tree. It was her. Surviving, but in no way striving.

There was no better tree.

"You're kidding." He gave the tree a dubious look.

She touched a bent limb. The tree was only as tall as she. "I'm not."

He watched her for a long, silent moment. He finally nodded. "Okay. I get it. We'll have a Charlie Brown Christmas tree."

Her eyes burned at his easy acceptance of her wishes, no matter how strange he thought they might be. "Thank you."

He tied a red ribbon to the tree to mark it. "Don't thank me yet. This tree is going to need some serious decorating to make it acceptable. You're in charge of that. I'll be back later to cut it. You're shivering. Let's go warm up." Lincoln nudged her. "I'll even make you hot chocolate with a peppermint candy cane."

Her throat tightened. "Stop being so nice to me."

Lincoln began to walk, shaking his head as he went. "Stop being so hard on yourself."

She hurried to catch up, stumbling over a fallen tree limb. He turned, catching her before she fell. His brows furrowed as he stared down at her, his eyes searching her face. Her heart picked up its pace and Sara pulled away, confused by her body's reaction to Lincoln. She looked at her brown snow-covered boots, wanting to escape all the things she didn't understand.

"Sara." He said it quietly, but there was so much emotion in the way he said it. Why did he do that? Say her name like it meant something, like it was a benediction or prayer?

She could try to pretend it wasn't there, and maybe for a while it would work, but eventually it would be inescapable, like life. *Don't think about it. You're imagining things.* Maybe she could use avoidance for a little while longer. Through the five years she'd known him, there had been instances where Sara had thought Lincoln had said something a certain way, looked at her a certain way, but she'd always brushed it aside, like she would now. With a frown on her face, she met his eyes, willing him to keep his secrets.

He hesitated, and then said, "You have a leaf in your hair."

He pulled it from her tangled hair and showed her, letting it drop to the ground, her eyes going with it. It lay there, torn and wrinkled and dead. It looked so beaten, so sad. She blinked her wet eyes, thinking of her husband and thinking of her and wanting to not think at all.

"I got a joke," he announced, slinging an arm around her shoulders and pulling her along with him as he herded them toward the house.

She squinted her eyes against the glare of the sun as it flickered through the tree branches, periodically blinding her as it played peek-a-boo with the earth. "I'm sure it's good."

"Are you saying my jokes usually aren't?"

"Of course not. I wouldn't be that rude."

Lincoln snorted. "There's a blonde, a Russian, and an American talking. The Russian says, "We were the first to enter outer space." The American comes back with, "Yeah, well, we were the first on the moon." The blonde says, "My friends and I are going to the sun." Russian says, "You idiot. You'll burn up halfway there." Blonde goes, "Duh. We're going at night.""

Sara giggled.

"Good, right?"

"I don't know about that."

His arm tightened around her shoulders. "You know I'm outstandingly funny. It's okay to admit it."

She smiled softly as the house came into view. The smile fell from her lips, the fleeting serenity she'd had with it. She ceased moving and Lincoln dropped his arm from her shoulders, stopping beside her.

"It's just a house."

Just a house filled with him in every way imaginable. That was all. What did Lincoln think and feel every time he walked inside the door?

"Is it just a house to you?" she asked softly.

Their eyes met and in his, Sara saw pain, and she felt horrible. It was always about her. Lincoln was always trying to make her feel better, always trying to drag her away from the edge of desolation. What about *him*? He'd lost his best friend, the older brother he'd looked up to growing up, because of her. She owed it to him to let him know his brother's wishes. Sara owed him so much.

"What is it?"

She opened her mouth to confess the secret locked inside her. Her pulse was careening madly, her heart pounded so fast and hard she felt faint. "Your...I..." She stared at him in helplessness and misery.

His features tightened and then his face closed. It went completely blank. "Tell me."

"He—"

"Say his name," Lincoln interrupted sharply. "He's a person, your husband, say his fucking name."

She flinched at his harsh tone and words, stumbling back a step. If he'd slapped her she wouldn't have felt the sting more.

He cursed again, yanking his gloves from his hands and flinging them to the ground. "I'm sorry, but...this is over. You can't pretend anymore. I'm not letting you. So say his name, and stop acting like your world has fallen apart and mine *hasn't* and...*fuck.*"

Lincoln turned away, showing her his granite profile. "Just say his name, all right?" His throat convulsed as he swallowed.

"I'm sorry," she whispered, her eyes stinging with unshed tears. Sara reached for his arm and he shrugged her off. "I'm doing what Spencer did, only in a different way. I didn't...I didn't realize. And I know better. I'm so sorry, Lincoln." A wave of sorrow hit her, but this time it wasn't for her or her husband. This time, it was for Lincoln.

He whirled around, his jaw clenched. "I don't want you to be sorry. I want you to *live.* I want you to stop blaming yourself and acting like a martyr waiting for her execution. I want you to smile and laugh and not give up. Because I'm not giving up and Cole wouldn't want you to give up. Do you know how *pissed* he would be, right now, if he knew the way you're living? He would be *furious.*" He glared down at her, his hands fisted at his sides.

She was suffocating. Sara gasped for air that didn't come. She had to tell him. She had to tell Lincoln and face his wrath. "You don't understand, Lincoln. I don't know how. I *can't.*" The pressure built, in her chest, in her throat.

Lincoln strode toward her, his gaze locked on her. He stopped when only an inch separated them. "Find a way."

"He wrote a living will," she blurted out. Her words ran together until they were jumbled and hard to understand. But once Sara started, she couldn't stop. "He wrote a will stating that if he was ever put on life support, that once a year had come with no change in his health, he...the machine is supposed to be shut off." Saying it out loud made it true and she sucked in a ragged breath, pain lacerating her heart.

Lincoln's face—his face was stone as he stared at her, saying nothing.

She swallowed thickly, the words like cement in her throat. It was too late to stop. She had to finish, she had to get them all out. "I'm supposed to approve it. He stated in the will I'm to approve it. I have....they want me to sign the papers. It's been over a year, Lincoln."

Everything in her dimmed, shut done, as she studied his expression. It was dead. His eyes were dead. Those stormy gray eyes usually so full of life were flat. He didn't move. He didn't appear to breathe. He just stared at her, as though he hadn't heard her words or couldn't accept them. The world turned gray, listless, it disappeared as she watched him stand there, too hurt to even move;, and she wanted to erase his sorrow. Sara would take it from him if she could.

She was back in time, back to that horrible day the doctors told them the prognosis wasn't good. The day they were told the head trauma he suffered from was most likely irrevocable and unfixable. His brain was damaged too much. Sara was back to that day when Lincoln was broken right along with her. He'd had the same look on his face then as he did now. Only then there'd been reason to have a little hope and now there was none. And yet a small part of her continued to hope anyway.

When Lincoln spoke, she knew it was the same for him.

"Maybe..." He swallowed. "Maybe he'll be okay." His voice was rough, his eyes downcast.

"Maybe," she agreed, nodding her head as she reached for him. It felt like a lie and that caused an ache in her chest. Sara cupped Lincoln's face with her hands. He looked at her, his brows lowered, his jaw tight. His unshaven jaw shifted against her palms, gently abrading the sensitive flesh.

She smiled. She smiled for Lincoln and she hugged him, knowing in that place inside a person where the truth was always heard, no matter how hard it didn't want to be, that she was lying to him, they were lying to each other, but a lie was all she could handle at the moment. Lincoln too.

His arms slowly enclosed her, stiff and loose at first, but eventually squeezing her so close and hard it was an effort for Sara to suck air through her lungs, but she didn't mind. At least she was breathing, for a little while. His warmth cocooned her along with his arms, his scent of mint and lemon filling her with peace, the sound of his stable, strong heart soothing. She let her eyes close, and though her heart was torn and possibly irreparable, like Lincoln's, with the two ruined pieces there was one whole heart.

CHAPTER 9

"HE TAUGHT ME how to ride a bike. How to tie my shoes. How to bait a hook." Lincoln laughed gruffly. "He taught me a lot of things."

Sara sipped from the red and blue striped coffee mug, the mint and chocolate mix coating her tongue with pleasure. The mug heated her cold fingers. They sat on opposite sides of the couch with their bodies turned toward one another. The room was dim with only one lamp on to offer light. A fire crackled in the fireplace across the room, the yellows and oranges hypnotic as they flickered and danced.

"Like what?"

"I'm sure you've heard this all before." He set his mug down on an end table and rubbed his face. He looked tired and worn down, his features tight with repressed pain. Lincoln's shoulders were slouched with the grief he tried to keep inside. That barrier he kept up would crack one day, and Sara wanted to be there for him when it did, like he'd been there for her countless times. If he'd let her.

"Tell me again," she offered softly, knowing he needed to talk about his brother. He needed to relive their shared history, make him real again so he didn't completely fade. Seeing him in that bed, it was a punch to the senses. That wasn't him. It shouldn't be him. Yet it was.

He glanced at her. "Cole didn't have to say a lot to get his point across. Me, I was always the more belligerent, loud-mouthed one. It wasn't that he was shy; he just said what he had to say and then shut up. He didn't have the time to waste on words. He said so himself." Lincoln grinned, sadness tingeing it.

"He had better things to do than talk," she agreed.

"Yeah." He stared at the fire, showing her his profile. "I got in a fight with a kid at school. I was fifteen. He was making fun of another kid and I intervened. Then he started making fun of me. Of course I got pissed and gave it back to him, even punching him when he wouldn't back down. I got three days out of school for that. Cole reamed me for it. Told me only a dumbass lets another dumbass get to him like that. Only it hadn't seemed right not to stick up for the kid. When I told him that, he said that wasn't what he'd meant. I asked him what he had meant then and he told me to figure it out for myself." Lincoln shook his head and offered her a quick smile.

That was her husband—honorable, gruff, and to the point. It was unbearable how much she missed him. She set the mug down on the coffee table, the taste in her mouth going from good to bad.

"This doesn't seem real."

She stiffened at the quietly spoken words. She looked up and saw Lincoln gazing into the crackling fire, his mind somewhere else.

"None of it. This past year or so, it all seems like a bad dream. Some days I wake up and forget, but then reality always slams me over the head and tells me what a fool I am to try to pretend, even for a second, that my brother is going to show up at the work site and hand me a gas station coffee."

"I know. I keep thinking he's going to come home from work or from a fishing trip. I know he's not, but..." She took a shuddering breath, clasping her chilled hands together in her lap. "It's not easy to accept. Seeing him like that, wondering..." She swallowed, unable to finish the sentence.

Lincoln jumped to his feet, startling her. "I'm going to the hospital. I don't know what else to do. This...this is..." His voice trailed off and his throat bobbed as he repeatedly tried to swallow. "I feel like bawling my fucking eyes out," he confessed roughly.

She stared up at him, tears filling her eyes. She wordlessly nodded.

"Will you..." He paused and tried again. "Will you go with me?"

Her lips trembled as she whispered, "Of course."

He offered his hand and Sara slowly placed hers in his, the connection of their hands locking them together. On their own, they were weak, but together, they seemed to be able to cope. Lincoln pulled her to her feet and into his arms, and this time, he was the one that needed to be comforted, this time, he was the one whose heart was breaking. His head dipped forward as his arms held her to him and she pressed her cheek to his soft hair, closing her eyes as she felt his body shake. He was so much stronger than she, so much larger, and so much more fragile right now.

"I don't want this to be real," he said against her neck, his breath causing her skin to pebble.

She tightened her hold on him, trying to heal his inner pain with her embrace. As if Sara could take it away with her touch—as if she had that power. She knew she was deluding herself, but maybe she eased it a little, like he was able to do for her.

Lincoln pulled away, grim-faced and red-eyed. Their eyes locked. *So much pain in his eyes,* she thought. Sara wanted to make it fade away.

His eyes darkened, something shifted in his expression, and he moved away, running his fingers through his wavy hair. "Let's go."

THE COLD PRICKLED her skin as hot tears burned her eyes. She stared down at the place he rested, not seeing her husband. It was hard for Sara to come to this place, to see what he'd become. It was turning into an obligation and that made her nauseous. She tried to tell herself it was because it wasn't really him, that he was in some other place and what she was staring down at was not her husband. It wasn't him, but it *was* him. She was holding on to what he used to be, not what he was now.

It had been too long, she knew that, logically. Her heart couldn't accept it. Over a year she'd been coming to this place, looking at what remained of the man she loved, and it killed her, and she hated it. She hated herself. She loathed feeling the way she did. Because, in the deepest part of her mind and heart, the place she tried to ignore and pretended didn't exist, something was telling her he wasn't coming back, not ever.

Guilt consumed her, telling her what a horrible person she was. It was her fault he was here. Sara would forever be to blame and she had to bear that burden. It was hers alone. With each day that passed and she didn't come here, with each memory she tried to escape because it hurt too much, with each breath she breathed that was hers and his he didn't breathe, she was to blame.

She sucked in a sharp breath, trailing a hand over his cool forehead. Words never came to her at these visits, not anymore. There was nothing more to say. She had said it all. She'd pleaded, wept, begged, and none of it had changed a thing. Sara even hated him a little for not waking up, for not coming back to her, for not fighting to be with her. She hated herself for what she'd done to him. She hated herself for hating him.

Everything about this place made her skin crawl—the smell, the beeping of the monitor, the whooshing sound of oxygen being forced into his lungs, the tubes running to and from him. It wasn't any way to live. It *wasn't* living, it was existing.

"How long?"

They stood on either side of him, Sara wanting to look way from the wrecked being that had once been whole and resilient, and unable to. Her eyes hurt to see him and for once she was grateful for the tears that blurred her vision, made his image altered from what it truly was. She loathed the relief she felt when she turned her gaze away from him. What she hated the most was wondering if she would feel a tiny sliver of reprieve when it was all finally over as well. It was destroying her—seeing him, not seeing him, wanting him to live, and wanting it done.

"Less than two weeks," she choked out.

Lincoln's features tightened and the slump to his broad shoulders deepened. He softly swore, slamming fingers through already mussed hair. He turned so his back faced the bed where his brother was, every muscle in his body tense, to deal with his pain away from her eyes.

The room had that chalky medicinal smell that made her stomach roil. The lights were dimmed in the white-walled room. It was cooler than Sara thought comfortable, but of course it didn't matter to him. In fact, he'd always liked it colder in the house than she did. So maybe it wouldn't matter even if he was awake. He'd liked his snow in the winter and snowmobiling. All things outdoors in the fall, summer, and spring appealed to him too.

Sara looked down at his gray, sunken face. He'd always had sculpted cheekbones, but now they stood out as sharp blades of bone. His body was dying, his brain didn't want to or couldn't wake up, and he was stealing breaths that weren't his. There was no way to make this situation acceptable. *That's why you gave us the time limit, isn't it?* She resented him for giving them a figurative clock on the days he had left. But she was also grateful and she resented *herself* for that. What kind of wife dreaded and longed for something at the same time? This wasn't a way to live, she knew that. He'd known that. But to not have him live at all...it was unfathomable.

Seeing him this way was too much. Did he sleep? Did he hear things? Was his mind completely shut off or did he know she was near? The not knowing was the hardest—that was what was tearing Sara up. Was her husband in there somewhere or was he simply gone? Had he left a long time ago, at the wreck? If she only knew, maybe then she could cope.

She didn't realize she was crying until a broken sob left her. "I never got to say goodbye," she wept as Lincoln strode across the room and scooped her into his arms. Tears flowed like miniature waterfalls from her eyes and down her face. "I can't say goodbye. How do I say goodbye?"

"You don't have to say goodbye."

She stiffened in his arms, slowly lifting her eyes to his. That hadn't been his voice. "What did you say?" she asked, breathless, her heart pounding.

Lincoln's eyebrows lowered. "I said you don't have to say goodbye."

She moved away, putting a shaking hand to her forehead. "But that wasn't...you..." She couldn't voice her thoughts. She would sound crazy if she did. Was she crazy? She had wondered that a lot since the accident.

"What?"

"Nothing. I..." Her face crumpled as she turned her gaze to the bed. He was unmoving, his chest lifting and lowering with artificial life. It couldn't have been him. Why had it sounded like his voice and not Lincoln's?

"You don't have to say goodbye because I'll always be with you, Sara," the gruff voice drawled through the air, soft and full of conviction.

She whipped her head toward Lincoln. "What?"

"I said, he'll always be with you." He frowned, tapping his fingers on the metal railing of the bed. "What's going on, Sara? Are you okay?"

A laugh that sounded much too close to hysterical burst from her. "No." She shook her head. "I'm not okay." She staggered back, toward the door, bumping into a metal stand and sending it toppling over. "I'm going...to go...I'm going to go outside. Get some air. I'll be back...to say...I'll be back."

When she bent to right the stand, Lincoln was there, ceasing her movements with his hands on hers. "I'll get it. I'm going to talk to him a bit and then I'll be out." He crouched by her, looking worried. "Will you be okay?"

She tugged her hands away and stood. "What else can I be?" Her eyes slid from Lincoln's to the bed. Pain welled in her heart, expanded, and wiped all other emotions out. *Am I losing my mind?*

As Sara walked out of the room on weak legs, she wondered if that would really be such a bad thing.

"I BROUGHT YOU something." Mason held out a red notebook and a single #2 pencil. He stood near the door, boots and coat removed, waiting for her to take it.

She frowned, hovering near the kitchen counter. "What is that for?"

"Whatever you're thinking or feeling, write it down. If you're not ready to paint, or don't want to, or simply don't want me to see what you're painting, I'm cool with that. But you need a release. Keep a journal. Write. Or sketch even. Do whatever you want. Write down a memory, one page at a time. Only don't throw this away." He lifted an eyebrow as he approached her, motioning for her to take it.

She did, quickly setting it down on the counter as if it would burn her. "I don't need it." Sara stared into the half-full coffee mug between her hands, the dark brown liquid endless and free, nothing to tether it, nothing to keep it from gently lapping against the sides of the mug.

"You know how small towns are."

"Meaning?" She glanced up, noting how the brown of Mason's sweater made his eyes seem closer to burgundy than amber.

He sighed and leaned his hips against the counter, crossing his arms, his gaze locked on her. "I know about the will."

She flinched, her elbow bumping into the cup.

Mason scooped it from the counter and raised it to his lips, sipping it. "Thanks for the coffee."

"That was mine."

He shrugged.

"I drank from it."

Mason lowered the cup, still not speaking, his expression telling her he didn't care. "How do you feel about that?"

"Not happy. It was the only cup. Now I have to make another pot of coffee."

"Sara."

She averted her face, pulling out a chair and sinking into it. "How do I feel?" Like death would be welcome. But he probably already knew that. She clasped her hands together and stared at the uneven nail of her left pinky finger. "Guilty. Betrayed. Angry. Sad. Horrible."

"Horrible?" He pulled out the chair opposite to her, placing his arms on the table as he scrutinized her face, drinking her coffee. "Why horrible?"

"Do you really have to ask that?"

"Yes."

She leaned back in her chair and leveled her eyes on him. She couldn't answer that. Not right now. "Do you hear your brother in your head? Think he's talking to you?"

Mason set the coffee mug down on the table, his gaze on the cup. "Why do you ask?"

"Because you said something about Derek talking to you and..." Her face burned and she lowered her eyes to the table. "I hear him sometimes."

"Who?"

"My husband. And sometimes...I think I see stuff." She looked up, pain forming in her chest. Her eyes pleaded with him to tell her she wasn't crazy, or maybe that she was. She just wanted to know, either way.

"Stuff?"

"I don't know. It's...nothing. Never mind."

Mason didn't say anything for a long time, finally breaking the silence to say, "I think that's normal. It's how we cope."

"You don't think I'm losing my mind? Imagining things? Seeing and hearing things that aren't real?"

"Is it real in your head?"

"Yes."

"Then it's real and that's all that matters."

"And you're not concerned that maybe I'm losing my mind?"

"If you were, you wouldn't know it."

"Thanks."

He chuckled. "Anytime."

"I used to hear a voice, but sometimes, now, it seems like it's *his* voice." Sara fisted her trembling hands.

"Sara."

She looked up.

His features were etched in somberness. "You're not crazy. You're not losing your mind. You're grieving. Your mind only gives you what you can accept, what you can deal with, and maybe that's what you have to see and hear right now to accept what's going on. You're fine."

"Promise?" she joked weakly.

"I do."

She saw how serious he was and gave a slight nod, looking at the table. "I go over all these scenarios in my head," she began softly. "What if we'd left a minute earlier or later. What if we'd gone another night? What if he'd driven instead of me? Would he still be here? I'm tormented by the what ifs."

"It's normal. I went through it. Everyone goes through it. It does no good, hurting yourself like that. It doesn't change anything. That's the thing about what ifs—they don't matter. They don't change anything. All they do is make it unable for you to heal. You have to find a way to get past them."

She exhaled loudly, her breath quivering as she released it. "Right." Sara rubbed her forehead, nodding. "Okay. I'll write in the notebook."

"Sara." Her eyes met his. "Sometimes when you think you have nothing, you realize you have yourself, and that's something. That's enough. I know you don't think you are, but you're strong. You're strong enough to get through this. You're stronger than you realize." He paused. "You wouldn't have jumped."

Her eyes burned and Sara blinked them. "How do you know?"

"Because you already would have by then if you were going to."

THE THREE OF them sat at her kitchen table, untouched cups of coffee before them. They wouldn't meet her eyes. She looked from his mother to his father, feeling their blame pointed at her like a loaded shotgun, the trigger already pulled, the damage irrevocably done.

Henry and Ramona Walker had changed since she'd seen them last, although she couldn't remember when that had been. The time since he'd left her was a blur—days and months meshing together until she couldn't remember one from the other. The first six months she'd existed and that was all. She was honest enough with herself to admit she hadn't progressed very far since then.

Their skin was tanned from the Florida sun, but it somehow had an unhealthy, pale look to it at the same time. Heartache did that to you. It did as much damage on the inside as it did on the outside. They visited their sons from time to time, but never for long, and never her. She knew they held her responsible.

"I didn't...I don't know how...to do this. I didn't want this," she said softly, knotting her fingers together in her lap, her eyes down.

When she looked at his father, an older version of him, she saw his blue, blue eyes gazing back at her with accusation, the same look she imagined she would see in his eyes if he ever opened them again. She wanted to be angry at Lincoln for calling them, but that would be wrong of her. They had a right to know even if he hadn't wanted them to know. Sara wished it was their decision to make and not hers. They were his parents—she was just the wife. They'd made him, she'd destroyed him.

Lincoln stood with his hips against the counter, his arms crossed over his chest. "But Cole did. This is what he wanted."

His name stung her heart and she lowered her head.

"I don't know what to say," Ramona said quietly, her throat convulsing as she swallowed. She was a smaller, more feminine version of Lincoln.

"Were you going to tell us? Or were you just going to let them pull the plug and let us think he'd died on his own?" Henry demanded in a harsh voice.

Pain swept over her, making it impossible for her to speak.

"Dad, that's enough." He straightened from the counter and moved to stand beside her. His nearness made it a little easier for her to breathe and she was grateful. "Sara didn't have to tell you. In fact, Cole didn't want her to."

"She *didn't* tell us. You did." Those pale blue eyes drilled into hers, unwilling to let her look away. "You can't do this. I refuse to let you do this to my son."

"Henry," Ramona said, reaching over to put a hand on his arm.

"It's what he wanted, Dad."

"Haven't you done enough?" Henry snapped.

"*Dad,*" Lincoln warned.

Her throat closed and she had to get away. She jumped to her feet, the chair scraping against the floor. "I..." Dizziness hit her and she grabbed the edge of the table.

"You were driving that car. You weren't paying attention. *You did this,*" he continued, his voice vibrating.

The room began to spin.

"That's *enough,*" Lincoln shouted, slamming a hand against the tabletop.

Ramona began to cry, covering her face with her hands. Her frail shoulders shook with each sob.

Henry shot to his feet, looking at his youngest son like he was a stranger. "How can you defend her? How can you stand to look at her, knowing she's responsible? My son is *gone* because of her."

Nausea hit her and her grip fell away from the table. Each word out of his mouth was a knife wound to her soul. Sara couldn't stand to hear them. They hurt. Her soul was ravaged by them—clawed and mutilated. She stumbled back, her equilibrium off. A ringing began in her ears.

"I'm about two seconds from throwing you out of here, Dad. I mean that." His voice was low, even.

Father and son stared each other down and Sara just wanted them to stop. She wanted it all to stop. The animosity was stifling, making it hard for her to breathe. She didn't want them fighting, especially over her.

"You know what I say is true."

"No. I *don't*. Sara isn't responsible. She was driving the car, yes, but she wasn't the one that crossed the center line. She wasn't the one drinking. She didn't do this to your son. You *know* that."

He was wrong. It was her fault. He didn't know. The room was starting to fade, their angry voices becoming background noise. She shook her head, but only made herself woozier.

She started to fall.

"What do you want do when we get home?" she asked, glancing at him with a smile on her face.

The wind swept in through the open windows of the black Grand Am, playing with his light brown hair and sending his scent she loved over to her. The sun caught his eyes just right and they glowed with blue heat. A lazy smile turned his lips up. Sara laughed.

"I think you know how the birthday celebration is supposed to continue once we get home."

She nodded, her eyes on the road. "I do, yes."

"Explain it to me, so I know we're on the same page."

"Hmm. Okay. You're going to get naked..."

"Mmm-hmm. I'm liking this."

"You're going to straddle me."

"Oh, yeah."

"And give me a full body massage."

"Uh-uh. You had it up till then." He reached over to play with her hair and her insides sighed. "Thanks for dinner, babe. It was good."

"Welcome."

"You always spoil me."

"You need to be spoiled now and then."

"Want to spoil me some more and go fishing with me tomorrow, feed some fishies?"

Sara smiled. "Sure."

She liked to go fishing for the peacefulness of it, but she abhorred the worm and hook part of it and the actual catching of fish part of it. She liked to feed them and let him do all the rest.

"It's a date." His fingers moved from her hair to caress her earlobe and then down to massage her shoulder.

"That feels good," she murmured, briefly closing her eyes.

"Sara." His hand painfully squeezed.

Her eyes flew open to see a red truck in their lane, heading directly for them. She tensed, watching it like it was on a movie screen and not really before her. It swerved back and forth, making it impossible for her to guess its destination. She couldn't think. What do I do? What do I do? It was getting closer and closer. Sara wrenched the steering wheel, fear and panic overtaking logic.

"Sara, look out! Sara!"

The car spun, its side colliding with the much larger truck once, twice. There were horrible, crunching, shattering sounds drilling through the car, through her ears. He doesn't have a seatbelt on, she dimly thought. Why doesn't he have his seatbelt on? His hand was torn away from her on impact, his body slamming against her, then the side of the car the truck hit, only a layer of metal between him and the other vehicle.

Sara's heart died as she watched his body thrown forward, then backward, and then he didn't move at all. The airbag went off, crashing his already ruined body. She screamed, reaching for him. Blood trickled from his head and he still wasn't moving, his eyes halfway open, staring, but not seeing anything.

She tried to unbuckle her seatbelt, but her fingers were shaking and slick, and the pain—the pain was everywhere. Not for her, but for him. Dying. She was dying. If he was dying, Sara was dying. She couldn't get to him. There was this terrible pressure on her chest, so heavy with foreboding, so thick with finality. It was killing her.

She screamed in helpless impotence. "Cole! Cole!" she shrieked, her voice high and unnatural. Over and over she called his name, willing him to respond.

He didn't move. Why didn't he move? Tears burned her eyes and cheeks, blurring her vision. Sirens blared in the distance, getting louder. Still he didn't move. Still his eyes remained in that partial place of not really closed and not really opened.

"Don't you die on me, Cole, don't you die on me," she pleaded, straining against her seatbelt to touch the fingers of his hand. Hers grazed his, just barely, choking sobs leaving her lips. A crack in her heart formed, grew, became her, as she stared at her broken husband she knew couldn't be repaired. *She died on the inside, dimmed, as she watched him, waiting for the impossible.*

Sara's eyes slowly opened. *His eyes never opened.* She'd waited and waited and they'd never opened. Months, a year, over a year she'd waited for him to open his eyes and come back to her. He'd given himself that time limit to come back to her as well and he hadn't done it. *He isn't coming back.*

Tears formed, slowly sliding down her cheeks. She became aware of another presence beneath her, around her, cocooning her as though to protect her from the world, maybe from herself even. For one bittersweet instant she thought it was him and that the past year had all been a horrible, unimaginable dream, but then the piercing pain came back and she couldn't pretend. A heart steadily pounded by her ear, an arm locked her against a warm, hard chest.

She stiffened, but didn't immediately pull away. "What happened?"

"You passed out."

"Where are your parents?"

"They left. They're going to say goodbye to him now and go back to Florida. I don't know if they'll be back. They can't...they can't accept it. It's not your fault and it has nothing to do with you. I hope you realize that. I'm sorry my dad was being such a dick. It's just...it's really hard for them. But that's not an excuse for his behavior. There is none."

She pulled away, sitting up on the couch. Her head was pounding and she went still until the dizziness faded. She angled her body away from him and Lincoln's hand dropped away as he straightened. "Why were you holding me?"

He sighed and when she glanced at him, it was to see his elbows on his knees and his hands holding his head. Lincoln rubbed his hair and dropped his hands, looking at her. He looked beaten, ravaged. "I don't know. Because you just...you looked like you needed to be held. That's all."

She jumped to her feet, angry and confused and so disgustingly sad. Sara was *sick* of feeling the way she did. She was sick of having no control over her life, her emotions, *anything*. She was sick of being weak. She was sick of the lies. Her body shook with the need to release all she kept hidden, locked away in a dark place.

Lincoln's eyes narrowed as he looked at her. "What is it?"

She looked at him, sitting on the couch, the one person who was always there for her, whether she wanted him to be or not. Sara didn't deserve his unflinching support. She didn't want it. Her lips pressed together, the words forcing their way out. If she said them, it would be over. She would be lost. Lincoln would be done. But the relief...it would set her free.

"I closed my eyes."

He blinked. "What?"

Her body was trembling and her stomach kept swooping, over and over, until she felt sick. She walked to his recliner, staring down at it, wishing he was sitting in it. "That night, the night of the wreck, I closed my eyes while I was driving, just for a second, but it was enough."

Lincoln didn't speak. Everything went still as she waited, dreading his reaction. She didn't want to see the expression on his face, but her eyes drifted to it anyway. It was blank. Perfectly, carefully blank. She swallowed, pressing an arm across her midsection.

When he slowly stood and walked the few steps it took to reach her, his body heat and lemony scent gently waving over her like a caress, Sara averted her face. If she saw in Lincoln's eyes what she'd seen in his father's and what she imagined she'd see in her husband's if he was ever to open them again, she'd shatter. It would be the end of her. *Isn't that what you want?* a voice mocked.

But then he raised his hand and touched her cheek, his rough fingers gently pushing her face in his direction so that she couldn't avoid his eyes. What would she see in them? What *did* she see in them? Her eyebrows furrowed as she tried to define it. Lincoln's eyes were stark, full, immersed in a strong emotion, but it was one Sara couldn't describe. He studied her, seeing her, looking past her barriers and into her pain-filled world. Lincoln *saw* her.

One word. One softly whispered word left his lips. "*Don't.*"

She should have been immune to them by now, but watery drops of sorrow fell from her eyes anyway. She moved away from him, turning to stare out the living room window at the snow-filled scene. The snowflakes fell in wispy feathers of winter, trickling from the sky in slow motion. She clenched her jaw and blinked her eyes to keep a sob within, but it made its way from her in spite of her efforts to keep it in. She wrapped her arms around herself and hung her head, her shoulders shaking from the force of her weeping.

"Stop *blaming* yourself. You closed your eyes for one second? Big *deal*. It's not your fault. One second of not looking at the road does not put you at fault. The other driver was *drunk* and *crossed into your lane*. How the hell is that your fault? Cole wasn't wearing a seatbelt. Was that your fault too?"

"Stop it!" She whirled around, pinning Lincoln in place with the look on her face. She clenched her fists at her sides, her body convulsing with anger. "Just stop it. Stop being my personal support team. Stop trying to make me feel better. Stop trying to do whatever it is you're doing. I don't want you to try to make me feel better. I don't need you to. What I need, what I *want*, is for you to leave me alone."

It was a lie. It was a lie and it tasted like a lie—bitter with injustice— on her tongue. Sara almost took it back. When she saw the look on Lincoln's face, she yearned to take it back. It closed. His face, the life in it, it shut down. She tried to look away, but something wouldn't let her. Her conscience, maybe. *Look at what you've done, see what you've done to him, the only person who really understands, who really cares about you. Are you happy?*

"That's the way you want it?" A tick under his eye drew her attention to it. It pulsated there—anger in his veins even.

"Yes," she croaked, finally able to look away. Her gaze fell to the empty recliner and her throat tightened. *Go away, Lincoln, go away and leave me with my pain.*

"That's too bad."

Her head shot up.

"I'm not going anywhere. Deal with it. And on that day you sign the papers, I'll be right there with you. And on that day Cole takes his last breath, I'll be there too. I'll be around, even when he's gone. I'm not going anywhere. I'm not leaving you." His eyes flashed as he leaned his face close to hers. "You don't get to tell me to leave you alone. I'll never leave you alone. I'll never abandon you. That's my promise to Cole and that's my promise to you."

Lincoln left, and with him went a little of her fear. Sara stared at his truck as it pulled away from the curb, and even with the distance between them, she could see his profile was stiff, unmovable. Why did he have so much faith, so much belief, in her? She was undeserving and at the same time so very grateful. She closed her eyes and inhaled deeply, some of the guilt disintegrating with his words echoing through her head.

CHAPTER 10

SHE WANTED TO remember him the way he'd been before the accident. She had to keep a piece of her real husband in her memories and it wasn't who was in the hospital room. As she lay on the couch in the dark, staring in the direction of where heaven was supposed to be, her thoughts instead went to God. He wasn't supposed to be designated to some place in the sky. He was supposed to be all around her, always. She'd told herself she no longer believed, yet she was thinking of Him at the time when she'd soon be losing her husband for the second time, for the final time. So maybe some part of her still had faith, still had hope. But if God was all around her, did that mean he would be all around her too, still with her somehow for always, if he was with God? Maybe that was what she needed to choose to believe.

She shook her thoughts away, too tired to think of such things. She hugged the ratty robe to her, burying her face in it, wetting the fabric with her sorrow. She hadn't had enough time with him. The years had been happy and fast and now time did nothing but drag. Except that day—that fateful day loomed overhead, approaching much too quickly.

Warmth swept over her, an unknown trickle of air caressing her hair, that forever elusive sense of peace finally taking pity on her and teasing her for a bit with tranquility. Sara sighed, slumber tugging at her, pulling her into the darkness and away from reality. She welcomed it. She pretended it was his arms keeping her warm instead of a blanket, she pretended it was his chest she clutched to her instead of his robe. She pretended she wasn't alone, she wasn't lost, and she wasn't without him.

She fell asleep, knowing it might be her last night of serenity for a long, long time.

IT WAS SNOWING again. She stood in her yard, the flakes covering her and the ground. Sara held her black-gloved hand out, watching as they dropped to her palm and melted. So quickly their existence was over. They fell from the sky and ended.

The low rumble of a diesel engine getting louder and louder drew her attention to the street. The engine cut off and silence surrounded her once more. Sara waited, watching as Lincoln approached. The bill of his olive green baseball cap shielded his eyes, but she knew they never left her as he walked toward her. She was always the center of his attention, without fail. He had on a brown coat with jeans and boots. His hands were shoved into his coat pockets.

Lincoln stopped when he was almost to her, his expression unreadable. He loomed over her, his presence eradicating all others in the vicinity. "We have a tree to decorate."

She blinked. "What?" She wasn't sure what she'd expected him to say, but that wasn't it.

"You and me. Charlie Brown Christmas tree. Let's go." He didn't wait for an answer. He turned and strode back to the truck, opening the passenger door for her. One dark eyebrow lifted. "I'm waiting."

Exasperated, Sara walked toward him. "You're obnoxious," she told him as she got into the warm truck.

"Thank you." He slammed the door shut and jogged around to his side. "Here's the deal," he said, starting the engine. "We're each going to only say positive things the whole time we decorate the tree and drink hot chocolate and eat popcorn."

"We have to do all that?"

"Yeah. We do. We're going to be *festive*." Lincoln shot her an annoyed look, driving the truck out of town.

"I don't feel like being festive."

He made a growling sound. "I don't *care*. Christmas is less than a month away."

Less than a week away was the deadline given to Sara papers. She briefly closed her eyes at the ache in her chest that brought. Not that she'd forgotten. It was always there, in the back mind, coating everything in misery. *Don't think about it.*

"When does it start?"

"When does *what* start?"

"The festivities and positive comments and all that."

"I...it starts now. *Now.*"

"How long does it last?"

Lincoln glowered at her and she wanted to laugh. "The *whole time.*"

"*You're* not being very positive."

He opened his mouth as he glanced at her, quickly snapping his mouth shut as words failed him. A minute later, Lincoln said in a rough voice, "Cole made a damn good steak."

The urge to laugh died, her small smile with it.

"Your turn."

Sara shook her head, crossing her arms, and stared at the forest of snow-encrusted trees outside her window.

The truck lurched to a stop and he slammed the shifter into park, the engine going quiet. "You're not being maudlin anymore. We have one week, *one week*, to honor him, and we're going to fucking do it. No crying, no sad faces. In fact, we're not even going to think about next week. We're going to think of him the way he was before the accident. I *demand* it."

She faced him. Sara couldn't even get angry at him for his rude tone, not after she looked at his face. His eyes were flashing with pain and his jaw was stiff, but his expression was fierce. He meant it. There was no denying Lincoln this. She wouldn't even try.

"Okay, Lincoln," she whispered. She nodded, swallowing against the tightening of her throat.

"Okay." He blew out a noisy breath. "Okay. Come on."

Once inside his house, she gazed at the pitiful tree missing patches of pine needles and slightly drooping over. He'd set it up in front of the bay windows by the table. The tree looked so weak, but still it was persisting. Maybe strength wasn't decided by what you could do, but by what you

stared at it, feeling a kinship to the pathetic tree
It was stronger than her even. It *wanted* to live.
think it will survive?"

vive for as long as it needs to."

. "Or as long as it wants to?"

"No. What you need and what you want are rarely
the same things. It'll hang on until it's ready to go, until it needs to go."
Lincoln's words made her think of the still form lying in a hospital bed.
Was he staying because he wanted to, or because he needed to? Or
because *Sara* needed him to?

He set a box of ornaments on the table, moving to stand beside her.
"I do have to say, though, that that is the saddest tree I've ever seen. Just
so you know."

"In case I didn't already know?"

He nudged her shoulder with his arm. "I'm all about informing
people."

"Yeah. Bossy." She gave him a small smile.

Lincoln blinked. "Holy fuck. You just smiled."

She nervously tucked hair behind her ear, looking away from him. It
didn't make sense to smile with what was to come, but she would try, for
Lincoln, for him.

Clearing his throat, he said, "Coffee or hot chocolate?"

"Coffee, please."

"I'll make some. You can start making it pretty." He grinned. "Good
luck."

She opened the dusty box, wiping her hands on her jeans as she gazed
into it. The first ornament to catch her eye was a pale blue crystal angel.
Her stomach dipped and her hand trembled as she reached for it. It was
the same shade as his eyes. His eyes she longed to see again—wondered
if she'd ever see again.

"What's that?"

Sara started, almost dropping the ornament. She fumbled with it,
setting it safely away from her on the table. "An angel."

He picked it up, perusing it. "It was Cole's. From Grandma Lena. She
passed away when we were kids."

"Did you get one?"

"Nah. She didn't like me as much as she liked Cole. She told me so every time I saw her."

"That's—that's terrible."

He laughed, shrugging. "At least she was honest."

"Did she ever say why?"

Lincoln shoved his hands in his jean pockets, looking at the tree. He snorted. "Very simply put: I talked too much. She liked Cole because he was quiet and I, unfortunately, never shut up."

"Poor Lincoln." She patted his shoulder, feeling sorry for the little boy whose grandmother hadn't like him. "I would have liked you."

He looked at her, a half-smile on his lips. "Thanks. Too bad I didn't know you then. You could have been my only friend."

A twinge in her chest propelled her to ask, "You didn't have any friends either? What was wrong with you?"

He laughed shortly. "What was wrong with me?" Lincoln tweaked a limb of the tree and a few pine needles fell to the floor. "I had a little too much energy. I liked to fight. I was mouthy and always getting into trouble." He shrugged. "I wasn't Cole."

She swallowed, her brows furrowing. "I never knew...I'm sorry."

"It's not a big deal."

But it was. Sara could see it was. He wouldn't look at her and he *always* looked at her. Her heart ached for the misunderstood child Lincoln had been. She opened her mouth, but he was walking away.

"This is supposed to be a happy day, I said so, and here I am getting depressing. I'll be right back." He crossed the room and took the stairs two at a time.

She found a pile of tangled hooks at the bottom of the box, pricking her finger with one. She put the angel on one of the sturdier looking limbs and watched as it bent way down, looking close to the point of snapping. Sara stared at the angel appearing to fall from the sky, too heavy to fly, and sadness hit her.

"Here you go."

A red sweater was dangled in front of her face. "What's this?" She looked up, blinking, and then laughed. "What are you wearing?"

A brown fleece sweater a size too small formed to his fit frame. Rudolph, red nose and all, stared back at her. She grinned at Lincoln and hewent still, his eyes on her, a strange expression on his face.

"Why are you looking at me like that?" she asked, the grin fading.

He shook his head and the look was gone. "It's nothing. Put this on."

She took the sweater, holding it up before her. A candy cane with a green bow was on the front of it. "Whose is this?"

"Does it matter?"

"A little, yes."

"Grandma Lena's. Do it justice."

She touched Rudolph's red nose. "And whose is this?"

"Grandma Lena's."

She laughed. "And are you doing it justice?"

"I'm trying."

She nodded, her eyes meeting his. "That's all you can do."

Lincoln leaned toward her, his lips close to hers as he said, "Exactly."

Her pulse quickened at his nearness and Sara hastily moved away, bumping into the table. Why did he do that? And why was she all flustered? She clutched the sweater to her chest, keeping her eyes downcast. "I'll just...go put this on."

"Please."

THE TREE HAD candy canes, gold tinsel, red garland, and as many of the Christmas ornaments as would fit on it. It was ghastly and garish. Sara loved it. She stood beside Lincoln, both of them looking at the decorated tree. The scents of melting cheese, Italian herbs, and red sauce floated over to them from the oven in the nearby kitchen and it was pleasantly warm in the house. She felt almost normal, close to happy.

"That is the ugliest Christmas tree I've ever seen, Sara. And I mean that."

"It has character."

Lincoln glanced at her. "Is that what they call it?"

Sara tugged at the neck of the itchy sweater. "Yeah. Like these sweaters have a *lot* of character."

"At least you're not a guy wearing a woman's sweater."

"No one made you." She gave him a pointed look.

"Pizza's ready. What do you want to drink?"

"How do you know the pizza's ready?"

"Because I have no witty comeback to your comment, so that means the pizza's ready. Drink?"

"Water. I'll get it." She moved before Lincoln did and bumped into him, his hands reaching out to steady her. Wariness shot through her as her eyes met his. His were intense, focused. Lincoln's nostrils slightly flared as he stared down at her.

"Why do you always look at me like that?" she blurted before she could stop herself.

"Like what?" he asked cautiously.

"I don't know. Like...*that*." She gestured to his face, perplexed by him, by her reaction to him. Sara didn't understand any of it.

Lincoln's hands dropped from her arms and he moved away. "Because it's all I can do."

"What does that *mean*?" she demanded, following him into the kitchen.

The oven beeped as he turned it off. He swung around, stopping her with his gaze. "Do you really want to have this conversation?"

She helplessly lifted her hands, palms up. "I don't know what's going on. I don't even know what conversation we're having. I'm confused."

With a sigh, he grabbed oven mitts from the counter and took the pizza from the oven. "Confused is good. Stay confused. Easier that way," he muttered.

With a frown on her face, Sara leaned her hips against the counter, crossing her arms, and watched as Lincoln meticulously cut the half cheese, half pepperoni pizza into eight pieces. His fingers were long-boned and lean, covered in callouses and small cuts, but still graceful in a way she wouldn't think a carpenter's fingers could be, or maybe that was backwards—maybe they were exactly as a carpenter's should be.

"Gonna get your water?" he abruptly asked, glancing over his shoulder at her.

"Yeah." Caught staring, Sara quickly moved beside him and opened a cupboard door, reaching up and grabbing a blue cup. "You want one?" She looked over and found his eyes on her, a pained expression on his face. "All right." She slammed the cup down on the counter. "What's going on?"

He straightened, dropping the pizza cutter to the stove. "You really have to ask that?"

"I—"

"What do you think is going on?"

Her face began to heat up. "I think you're purposely being an ass."

"Really? That's what you think?" Lincoln moved closer, those silver with gold-flecked eyes narrowed and locked on her.

Sara backed up, bumping into the counter. "What's your problem? Why are you acting like this? Why are you always pushing me lately, testing me? What's the purpose of it?"

"I want you to live," he said in a voice low with emotion.

"I am." *I don't want to be, but I am.*

Shaking his head, he said, "No. You're not. You're *pretending* to live. It's not the same."

"It's the only way...I can endure this," she said in a quaking voice.

He closed the distance between them, bracing an arm on either side of her, locking her between his arms and the counter. He lowered his head until his lips were close to her ear. Sara tried to swallow and couldn't. She was scared to move, scared to breathe, scared to think.

"I know. I'm sorry. I'm sorry I'm so screwed up in the head," he whispered raggedly, his breath tickling her ear. "So *unbelievably* fucked up." Lincoln's shoulders slumped and his head dipped lower, his forehead grazing her shoulder. "I thought I was okay. I thought I could do this. But I'm cracking, unraveling. I'm being an asshole and I want to stop and I just...*can't.*" The pain in his voice was like a laceration against her soul, bringing with it hot agony that grew instead of lessening.

"I don't understand what you're saying. I don't understand any of it." Her voice was high, breathless.

He pulled back so that he could look at her. "Just...let me talk, okay? Just let me talk." Lincoln drew in a ragged breath, his body tightly coiled and yet trembling all the same. "I don't even know what I'm trying to say. I'm just...I'm angry and I'm sad and I just...I want to forget. I wish I could forget. Forget him, forget you, forget it all. I'm sick of feeling the way I do. I'm twisted inside. Knotted."

He gently touched his forehead to hers. "I want to stop being this way. But I can't. Because only one thing can make it better and it's the one thing I can't have. And I'm sorry. I'm so sorry, Sara." The misery, the self-loathing she heard in the tremble of his voice—it was aching to hear. Her ears would bleed from the pain of it if they could.

She didn't know what he was talking about, or maybe she did, but she didn't want to know. Her pulse raced at an uncontrollable speed. This Lincoln was different. This Lincoln wasn't the one she'd known for years. He was altered, changed. He felt more, hurt more. Could it be *this* was the real Lincoln and she was only now seeing him?

Had that teasing young man with the easy grin been an illusion and was she now seeing past the illusion to the real man? And who was Lincoln then? She'd thought she'd known him, but maybe she hadn't really known him at all. The thought made her stomach knot up. Sara studied the face she knew almost as well as her husband's, yet was so very different from his; the high forehead, the angular cheekbones, the square jaw. There was beauty and strength in that face and mysteries stared at her from stormy gray eyes. What truths did Lincoln keep locked inside, for him alone to know?

"Who are you?" she whispered. What was she asking him? She didn't even know.

Lincoln stared at her, his long eyelashes lowering to hide his eyes from her as he answered, "I'm me, Sara."

But who are you?

"I've always been me," he continued.

The air was thick with unspoken truths and enigmas. It was riddled with shadows and murkiness. Sara felt like she wasn't seeing something. There was something glaring her right in the face and she couldn't see it. Her eyes were veiled—because they had to be. She opened her mouth to tell him to move, but he was already dropping his arms and turning away. She exhaled loudly, her nerves jumbled and shaken. Her eyes refused to go to him. She couldn't see his face, not now.

"I think...maybe I should go," she said, her mouth and throat dry. Sara grabbed the cup and filled it with water from the faucet. She gulped it down so fast it hurt her throat.

He stilled. "Do you want to?"

She looked at him then. One look at Lincoln's face and the answer she was going to say disappeared and was replaced with another. He looked lost, young. He stood tall and proud, and yet there was frailty to him she'd never noticed before.

"No," unconsciously fell from her lips, surprising her. Didn't she? Why didn't she want to go?

He tried to hide the relief on his face from her by looking away, but she caught it, something inside her twisting at the vulnerability he didn't want her to see. "All right. I got 'National Lampoon's Christmas Vacation' queued up. Sound good?"

"Perfect," she said, trying to smile. The tension was still there, though she was trying her hardest to pretend it wasn't.

"I'm zero for two." Lincoln got two plates out of a cupboard and loaded them with pizza.

She gave him a quizzical look, taking the plate with four slices of cheese pizza on it. Sara would maybe eat half of that.

"This was my idea. I said we had to talk about happy stuff. I screwed it up twice now," he said as he walked into the living room, turning on a lamp. Days were shortening now and dusk was already approaching, turning the inside of the house dark, even though it wasn't even four in the afternoon yet.

Sara sat down on the couch, setting her plate on the coffee table. "You can't make yourself feel how you don't. Pretending only makes things worse. I guess not knowing how you feel about something is normal too. You can love someone and hate them at the same time. You can want something and not want it too. Sometimes lies are all you have and sometimes you have to tell yourself them just to be able to breathe." She clasped her hands and looked at them in her lap.

"Is that would you do? Lie to yourself? Of course you do," he answered for her, not sounding judgmental, only matter-of-fact. "We're all guilty of it. Sometimes you have to pretend, just to survive. Isn't that how you make it through each day? Pretending? Sometimes that's all you can do or you'll break, Sara. You'll ruin everything by *not* pretending. Believe me, I know."

She looked at him, but he was readying the movie on the TV. She was missing an astronomical piece of information and until she grasped it, nothing would fit. *And when you figure it out, what then?* Unease trickled through her veins, chilling her.

"Remember how he used to buy Peeps by the armful at Easter time?" Lincoln grabbed his plate of pizza as he sat down on the couch, setting it on his lap.

Sara smiled softly. "Yeah. Those things are disgusting. I can't believe he didn't have tons of cavities. I tried a Peep once. Never again." She shuddered.

He laughed, consuming half a piece of pizza in one bite.

He would have eaten chocolate every day if he could have, and actually, he probably had. After every meal, his dessert was a Snickers or a Kit Kat or some other kind of candy bar. Snacks consisted of Hershey's Kisses and miniature Reese's Peanut Butter Cups. Good genetics and physical labor had kept him cavity-free and his body lean and hard.

That restless energy he'd had had kept him moving, never able to sit down or be still for too long. She had admired that about him at the same time it had annoyed her. Some days she'd just wanted to sit and watch a movie and he hadn't even been able to do that. His knees would bounce, he'd tap his fingers on the armrest of the couch, he'd get up and move around, decide he needed to call someone. Even on her husband's days off he was working. Come to think of it, all that sugar consumption could have been a large part of his inability to relax for any length of time.

"Don't forget his orange soda." Lincoln shuddered this time.

Laughter fell from her lips. "He liked his sweet stuff."

"And baseball."

"And snowmobiling."

"Beer."

"Grilling out." She tried to smile, but instead her face crumpled.

She could see him clearly, the sunny summer scene playing out in her mind. His blue fire eyes, his teasing grin—the dirt on him from work he had yet to wash off. She took a deep breath and the image faded. Sara rubbed her eyes, not wanting Lincoln to see her tears.

The movie began, already forgotten before it had even started. Neither of them spoke, lost in their thoughts. Her mind was stuck on the words Lincoln had revealed in the kitchen. What had they *meant?* Would she ever know? Did she *want* to know? Some secrets were too painful to unravel.

When she looked over, he was watching her, his expression indecipherable. The only indication he felt anything at all was the tick in his strong jaw. He wordlessly reached for her and Sara fell into his arms, holding him as he held her. It felt right to be in his arms, it felt right to let him hold her when no one else felt right doing so. He alone loved him the same as she. She didn't understand Lincoln. She didn't know what he was trying to tell her or not tell her with his words, spoken and unspoken, but in regard to her husband and his brother, they were in accordance.

They would remember him together and they would love him together, just as they would mourn him together.

"HOW ARE YOU dealing with everything?"

Pushing the almost empty coffee mug back and forth between her hands, Sara focused on a red stripe on the cup as she answered, "Terribly."

As was customary, they sat at the table in her kitchen. Mason had brought caramel rolls, scenting the air with them. She'd eaten almost half of hers, to his surprise. She almost thought she'd forced that much down just to prove to herself she could. Her stomach was *not* happy with her.

"It's to be expected. I know I said you were lucky to be able to say goodbye, but it has to be hard knowing there's a set date. Or maybe that's a blessing instead of indefinitely wondering when his final day will be."

She looked up with a frown.

He sipped from his cup, eyebrows lifted, waiting for her response.

"You do realize you say a bunch of nothing almost every time your mouth opens?"

Half of his mouth quirked. "Depends on how you choose to interpret what I say. If you want to hear nothing, then nothing you shall hear. If you want to get something out of what I say, then you will."

"There you go again," she muttered.

He laughed, opening the crinkled white bag to pull out a second caramel roll. Mason took a bite, licking icing from his thumb.

"I thought these sessions were only going to last a month?"

"I don't remember saying that."

"You said—"

"What I *said* was," he interrupted smoothly, "I was on vacation for a month, so technically I wasn't here as a grief counselor. I never said the sessions would only last that long. People always hear what they want to hear, even if it isn't the same as what someone *says*. Clearly you needed me for longer than a month. It's okay. I get that I'm your favorite person." He winked.

She blinked at him.

"How long have you known Lincoln?"

Sara froze, not wanting to think about him. Not that that mattered, because he seemed to be *all* she thought of. It was unnerving and worrisome how *much* she was thinking of him lately. And she wondered what he was thinking. Sometimes she even turned to ask him his opinion on something, so used to his company now, almost *longing* for it when he wasn't around.

"Sara," he prompted.

Taking a sip of cold coffee, she used the time it took her to swallow to gather her scattered nerves. "I met him a few days after I met my husband."

"Do you know him well?"

"As well as I know myself," she answered without thinking. She blinked as her words registered in her head, looking at Mason. He'd caught them.

His face was blank, but his eyes were narrowed on her. "Interesting."

Face red, she shifted in her seat. "What is?"

He set his cup of coffee down, splaying his long-fingered hands on the table. "You said you know him as well as you know yourself, not your husband. I find that interesting."

"You would," she retorted, but she wouldn't meet his eyes and her skin was abnormally flushed.

"I would. Yes." He stood, carrying his plate and cup to the counter. "I'll see you soon," he said as he walked to the door to get his coat and boots on.

"That's it?" She got to her feet, rooted to the place beside the table. "You're leaving?"

Mason tilted his head and studied her. "Yes. I'm leaving. But first, I want you to tell me something about Lincoln."

She shifted her feet, looking anywhere but at him. "Like what?"

"Anything."

Sara thought of Lincoln, picturing his stormy eyes and stiff jaw and the way his lips curved up, softened, when he smiled. "He..." A smile captured her lips. "He has this habit of nodding his head to music, even when he isn't aware of it. His body moves too. It's like he has to restrain himself not to bust out dancing. It's funny watching him, and most times, he can't help but sing. Lincoln loves music, always has. It's...endearing. Sweet." She exhaled deeply, looking at him.

Mason didn't speak for a long time, finally saying, "I realized something just now."

One eyebrow lifted. "Oh?"

"It wasn't anything you said, but it was what you *didn't* say."

She frowned. "*What? What does that even mean?*"

"You, talking about Lincoln. It's not the words you use, but how you look as you say them. Your face softens, you smile. You *glow*, Sara. Lincoln is it."

"Again with the nonsense? Lincoln is *what?*" she said, exasperated.

Smiling as he shrugged into his leather coat, Mason gently mocked, "Open your eyes. You won't be able to see until you do." He left, leaving a reeling Sara behind him.

SARA WIPED SWEATY hair from her face with her arm and leaned back on her heels. The kitchen floor was gleaming clean. Somehow housework did what painting used to do for her, but now couldn't. It was therapeutic. Maybe she should change her career from painter to housekeeper. She snorted. Sooner or later she would have to figure out what she was going to do about that. She had made enough money from her artwork in the past that she was stable for now, even though there was no new income coming in from that. They'd saved a lot too. And of course there was the monthly compensation she received from the accident. Those were in a messy stack in the junk drawer, none cashed.

Lincoln was heavy on her mind, not that he was ever far from it. She was confused and upset by his behavior. She didn't know how to read him. It was more than sorrow for his brother. He seemed tormented by something, something he couldn't, or wouldn't, tell her about. Or maybe he just couldn't take it anymore. She understood how that could happen. Maybe it was simply too much for him and she understood that as well.

Lincoln is the key. She shook her head. Mason and his crazy ideas. She never knew what he was saying and he always acted like it was because of *her* that his words made *absolutely no sense at all.* Saying that about Lincoln just proved it. He wasn't the key to anything except maybe Sara's constant aggravation lately. She frowned. That wasn't fair. Everything Lincoln did he did with her in mind. She knew that. But what was *with* him recently?

She had never seen his moods alter so much like that. What was hurting him so much he had to lash out like he had? And later, the way he'd held her; as though he was holding her up as much as she was him. She didn't know how to help him and she wanted to. Part of her thought maybe she *couldn't.* Maybe *she* was what was tearing him up like that. She didn't want to be responsible for his pain, for anyone's pain. *Only you already are.*

The whirring sound of a motor, getting louder and closer, gave her pause and made her heart rate escalate. In her cracked mind, Sara knew it was him, finally returning. He'd been on a long snowmobiling trip and he was back. The sane part of her mind receded, letting her have her false reality for a time. She jumped to her feet, racing to the door. She flung it open, her pulse crazy, her heart thundering. Biting air snapped at her and her bare feet turned to ice on the cold step outside the door. The rider turned the engine off on the red and black Polaris snowmobile. He took off his gloves and set them on the snowmobile console. His hands reached up to grip the helmet and Sara couldn't breathe. Whose face would she see?

The black-garbed rider stood and strode toward her as he pulled the helmet from his face, holding it against his side as he reached the porch. It was Lincoln. Sorrow and relief punched her in the stomach and Sara sucked in a sharp breath, unable to look too closely at that response. His hair was matted against his head, but still managed to wave up in spots.

His jaw was unshaven, giving him a rough appearance and making him even more handsome.

Open your eyes, Sara, Mason had said. She inwardly shook her head, knowing she would never truly understand Mason Wells.

"I thought you outgrew your snowmobile gear?" was the first thing she thought of saying.

"I lied. Ready for a ride?" He grinned, his gray eyes flashing with silver.

She looked down at her dirty, stained yellow shirt and ripped jeans, wondering why her heart rate hadn't slowed down any. "No. I'm cleaning."

"O...M...G, Sara," Lincoln said, rolling his eyes. "That house is clean enough to eat meals off the floor, even when you haven't cleaned it for weeks. You clean over clean. Get your stuff on. We're going."

She crossed her arms, getting tired of his bossiness and wanting to laugh at him at the same time. "Stop trying to run my life."

"Really? Stop trying to run your life? If I were trying to run your life, it'd be all kinds of different. Trust me. It's day two. Let's go."

Heat warmed her cheeks. "You can't do this."

"Do what?" he asked, moving forward so she had to backtrack into the house.

"Make me do things. Make me...make me..." Her throat closed on the words and she blinked her wet eyes.

He shut the door behind him. "Make you forget? Make you have fun? Make you live?" He leaned forward, his cold nose bumping hers. "Yes...I...can." Lincoln straightened. "Hurry up. I'm getting snow all over your clean floor. You might have to, like, mop it again or something." He widened his eyes at her, clearly making fun of her.

She wordlessly shook her head. Sara couldn't think straight with all of his ups and downs.

He sighed, crossing his arms, the material of his snowmobile jacket sliding together as he moved. "If you can't do these things for yourself, then you're going to do them for him. Think of Cole. Do it for him. Stop fighting me and just *do it.*"

Her brows furrowed as she stared at him. He looked back, eyes steady and clear. Lincoln was like a rock, standing tall in the wake of a tsunami, unbending and unbreakable. She spontaneously hugged him, his jacket cold against her skin. His arms rose and his hands held her against him, somehow warming her through the chilled material of his snowmobile garb.

"What was that for?"

"For being you," she said, pulling back.

His eyes narrowed and his lips pressed together. He shifted his gaze away as he said, "We're both hurting. Instead of wallowing in it and letting it take over, you, and I, need to find things to keep the pain at bay. We need to *live*. We need to do all the things Cole can't and we need to be grateful for every breath we get to breathe on our own that he doesn't. Understand?"

She inhaled deeply, taking in his unflinching gaze. "You're better at it than I am."

Lincoln flashed a quick grin. "I'm better at a lot of things than you are."

"Thanks."

"I'm sorry about the other night. About the way I've been acting lately."

"It's okay."

"It's not okay." He sighed and then gently bumped his forehead to hers and stepped back. "Get your stuff on. I'll be outside waiting."

Sara walked toward the closet as Lincoln went outside. Her heart was hurting, not because of that hated date getting closer every day, but for another reason. Lincoln was shoving life back into her, in spite of what she thought she wanted, in spite of her wishes. She could continue to fight it, but she knew it was pointless. Lincoln was...Lincoln. She was so thankful for him, even as aggravating as he was. He managed to put everything into perspective, he managed to make her see what she couldn't see on her own. *What about what he doesn't want you to see?*

IT WAS LOUD. The engine was fast and high-pitched and so loud she could barely hear her own thoughts, which was a blessing. She held on to Lincoln, her arms wrapped around his waist, trees and hills passing them by in a blur. Sara closed her eyes, feeling the snowmobile's power underneath her,

Lincoln's solid back against her front, the way her legs straddled the sides of his. The windshield of the helmet fogged every now and then, showing how cold it was outside her snowmobile geared body, but it quickly dispersed, once again giving her a view of fluffy snow and countryside.

Lincoln and he had always liked their toys—be they motorcycles or boats or snowmobiles. In that way they were as one. She had never understood that need to disconnect from the world with speed and what she'd considered unnecessary wildness, but now, she kind of did. It was liberating, to go so fast, to forget about obligations and reality and just *feel*.

The trail was narrow and rough, and at times she knocked into Lincoln, her helmet clunking against his. Up and up the hill they climbed, Sara adjusting her body to his, moving with him around turns and corners. Then they were wide open, nothing but space on either side of them. He cranked on the accelerator and they were soaring. She laughed, tipping her head back. Free. She felt free. She wanted to bottle the feeling up and take it with her. She hadn't felt so guiltless, so alive, in a long time.

She didn't know she'd loosened her grip until they hit a bump and the snowmobile went up and slammed down, dumping her off the sled and into a snow bank. Sara landed on her back, the air knocked from her lungs. She lay there, wondering if she was okay or not, wondering if it really mattered. Nothing hurt. She flipped the windshield up and stared at a blue sky, mirth bubbling up her throat.

That's how Lincoln found her—lying on her back, laughing.

He jumped off the snowmobile before it was completely stopped, sprinting for her, snow flying up behind him. He fell to his knees in the snow beside her. "What the *hell*, Sara? Are you trying to get yourself killed?" he shouted through his helmet, the windshield of it flipped up.

She looked at the wild, panicked look in his eyes and laughed harder. She didn't know why. It seemed the sensible thing to do.

"*Fuck!* Are you hurt?" He grabbed her shoulders and shook. "Would you stop laughing and say something? Are you okay? *Sara.*" He fumbled with strap under her chin and yanked the helmet from her head, cupping the back of her neck with his gloved hands. "Are you okay, Sara?" Lincoln asked slowly, his voice shaking.

She went quiet, the smile fading from her lips, when she saw, *really* saw, what Lincoln couldn't or wouldn't hide. He was scared. For her. And not just scared, but *out of his mind* scared. His lips were pressed into a thin, white line and his eyes had a haunted cast to them.

"I'm okay, Lincoln," she said softly.

The relief on his face hit her hard, the tension leaving his body as he pulled her close. Lincoln was trembling. He muttered something, using one hand to tear his helmet off, tossing it into the snow, the other hand never releasing her. "I thought you were hurt. You were just lying there. I thought you'd broken something or were seriously injured. What *happened?*" he said into her hair, clutching her to his chest.

Cold air stung her cheeks, snow from Lincoln's gloves brushed against her neck, chilling her. "I'm fine. I'm sorry. I just...I wasn't holding on tight enough." She gently pushed at his chest and he let her go.

He swallowed. "Promise me something, Sara."

Her eyes collided with his, her lips parting at the intensity of his charcoal gaze.

"You hold on tight from now on, so tight it hurts. Got it? Don't let go of me, not ever. Don't worry about hurting me, don't worry about suffocating me, don't worry about holding on too tight. You hold on and you never let go. You'll only hurt me, I'll only suffocate, if you let go. Promise." Silver flames sparked in his eyes and Lincoln's jaw was clenched as he stared her down.

She was burning up from the heat of his gaze. It swept up her body and neck and into her face, warming her. He wasn't talking about snowmobiling. She knew that. What *was* Lincoln talking about? She lowered her eyes, conflicted by the way she was responding to him lately, confused by *him*. She never knew what he was saying to her anymore.

"*Promise.*"

She swallowed, nodding her head. "I promise, Lincoln."

He blew out a noisy breath, running his fingers through his hair, rumpling it more. "All right." He stood, offering her a hand. "You ready to head back or do you want to keep going?"

She took his hand and he hauled her to her feet. *You ready to head back or do you want to keep going?* turned into *Do you want to live in the past or do you want to move forward?* She stood there, flummoxed.

"Sara?"

"I..." She turned toward the way they were going. It was clear and straight and limitless. She turned back to the way they'd come from. It was rough and narrow and littered with possible barriers. Sara faced Lincoln. He stood in the middle of it all, quizzically watching her, waiting for her answer. Go back, go forward. Stay with him, come with me. Was that *really* what he was asking?

"You want to go back, don't you?" His tone was flat, as though he was disappointed, but not surprised.

She squinted her eyes from the sun, turning her gaze to the glistening snow as spots formed before her eyes. "No. Let's keep going."

"You sure?"

Taking a deep breath, she nodded. "I'm sure."

Lincoln grinned, his teeth flashing white. "Don't let go this time."

"I won't," she promised.

As she got back on the snowmobile behind him, she wondered what or who she was promising she wouldn't let go of. The past, her husband, or Lincoln?

CHAPTER 11

SHE WAS SLEEPING, dreaming of blue eyes and warm lips, when the pounding on the door started. She sat up on the couch, flinging the blanket off her. It took a moment for the dream to fade, and along with it, the peace she'd found in sleep—a peace Sara was never truly able to find while awake. She blinked at the door, her eyes unfocused and her brain not completely awake. She slowly got to her feet, rubbing her matted head of hair. One side was sticking up and the other was mashed to her head. She tightened the tie on the old robe as she shuffled to the door. Fighting a yawn, she unlocked the door and opened it, her eyes shying from the sun-filled day.

Lincoln grinned at her, a cup of coffee in each hand. "Rise and shine, sunshine."

"Don't you ever work anymore?" she grumbled, moving back to allow him in. She was *happy* to see him. She didn't want to be happy to see him.

"I took the week off. I can do that. I'm the boss."

"Slacker."

"Don't be crabby."

"What time is it?"

"Seven-ish", he said, shrugging his jacket off and bending down to remove his boots.

"I'm allowed to be crabby at seven-ish in the morning."

He stood and Sara caught a whiff of his scent. She backed away, moving to the couch. He tugged down his dark blue long-sleeved tee shirt, covering the band of tanned flesh momentarily exposed. Sara flushed, quickly looking away.

He messed his hair up more than it already was with his hand and eyed her sleeping arrangement. "What's that?" Lincoln asked, pointing to the pillow and blanket.

"A couch."

"What's *on* the couch?" He frowned. "And what are you wearing?"

She self-consciously fingered the knotted tie at her waist. "A robe."

"Are you sure? 'Cause it looks like a dead animal dyed blue hanging off you. You don't sleep in your bedroom?"

She stiffened. "It's none of your business and if you just came over here to badger me, you can leave."

"Oh, no. Uh-uh. It's day three." Lincoln crossed the room to her, softly touching her cheek. "Look at you with your sad brown eyes. I want to take the sadness from them. Let me today." His face cleared and his hand fell away. "But first, you need to shower. Your hair looks like rodents could get lost in it."

Sara took a shuddering breath, remembering she needed air. "I..." Her brain wasn't cooperating. "What are we doing?"

"Good question."

She waited, sighing loudly when she realized he wasn't going to tell her.

"You. Shower. Make yourself pretty."

She glared at him as she walked to the bathroom, shutting the door a little too exuberantly behind her. She brushed her teeth, fuming as she stared at her flushed face. His brother had never talked to her like this, had never bossed her around. *Stop comparing them.* She wasn't trying to. It was involuntary, like breathing when you thought you no longer could. It just happened. Sara grabbed her hair with one hand as she finished up brushing her teeth, and spit in the sink. Her mouth was fresh and cool with spearmint and she inhaled deeply, her attention turned toward the shower.

Sometimes she wondered what she was holding on to. That cruel replica of her husband lying in the hospital bed was not the man she loved. What exactly did Sara cling to? Memories were like ghosts that never went away, always there to haunt her. Is that what she loved? A memory? Steam filled the immediate air around her, making it hard for her to breathe, though of course she still managed to.

Sara quickly washed up, wondering how much longer she would cling to memories she'd be better off forgetting. She winced at the pain that thought caused, shutting the water off. She grabbed a towel, shivering, her skin pebbling from the shock of going from warm to cold. There was nothing she could do but continue to love a man who'd left her with a car crash, to let ghosts haunt her so she remembered that love. She had to hurt to feel something other than hurt and still she hurt anyway.

Dried and dressed in jeans and a long-sleeved black top, Sara loosely braided her brown hair so it rested over one shoulder and pulled on a pair of black boots. She met Lincoln in the kitchen, where he was sipping from a Styrofoam cup and staring in the direction of the nursery.

"Gas station coffee?" she guessed, wrinkling her nose. She didn't want to know what he was thinking, not as he looked at that closed door.

"Nah. From home." Lincoln handed the other cup to her.

"Thanks."

"You look nice. Smell good, like vanilla."

She blushed. "Thank you." He watched her take a drink from the cup. The coffee was smooth and the perfect temperature. "What? Why are you staring at me?"

"You don't know what day it is, do you?"

She searched her brain. "Wednesday?"

Lincoln snorted. "Yeah. It's that."

"Oh. Tomorrow's Thanksgiving. What are you...what are you doing for Thanksgiving?" He was probably going to spend it with his parents, like he should. They were still in town, as far as she knew, waiting.

"It's your birthday," he said, sounding exasperated.

She gasped. "I forgot your birthday! I'm so sorry. I didn't...I wasn't...I'm sorry, Lincoln."

He shook his head, a wry grin on his face. "I don't care about *my* birthday. And you didn't forget. You called me. You don't remember?"

She touched a hand to her forehead, shaking her head. "No. I was...out of it. More than usual," she added at his look.

"You called. You didn't say anything. I talked. But, hey, you called."

"I'm sorry," she whispered.

Lincoln grabbed her shoulders, dipping his head so they were at eye level. "Sara. I don't care about my birthday."

"But you care about mine?"

"Yes."

"Why?"

He dropped his hands from her shoulders and turned away. His back was tense and his hands fisted at his sides. "You know how sometimes you wanna say something, but it isn't the right thing to say? Or it isn't the right time? Or if you did say it, you'd wish you could take it back?"

"Yes."

"Good. Ready?" He shrugged into his jacket and tugged his boots on.

"That's it? That wasn't an answer."

Lincoln paused and lifted his head. "Yeah it was. Enough of one. Wrong thing to say, wrong time to say it. Let's go." He straightened, lifting one dark eyebrow. "Coming?"

Sara opened the closet, grabbed a gray jacket and pulled it on, all the while scowling at him.

He laughed, shrugging.

"You're so annoying. Did anyone ever tell you that?"

"I seem to recall you telling me that once in a while. Only one ever to say that, just so you know."

She snorted, following him outside. The wind was fierce and biting cold. She shivered, wishing she'd grabbed her gloves and scarf. Sara slung her purse over her shoulder and shoved her hands in her coat pockets as she walked to the truck. Snow crunched under her boots and she was already wishing it was spring and winter hadn't even really started yet.

Ever chivalrous, he opened the door for her, closing it after her. Sara huddled into her coat, lowering her face under the collar to try to warm it up. "Where are we going?"

"It's a surprise." He started the engine and the truck rumbled to life, cool air blowing from the vents.

"I hate surprises," she reminded him.

"If you could go anywhere, right now, where would it be?"

"Texas," she answered immediately.

"Oh yeah. I guess I knew that. Okay, I'm talking internationally. Anywhere in the world. Where would it be?"

"Texas."

Lincoln sighed. "Way to be adventurous."

"Are you taking me to Texas?"

He laughed. "No. Sorry. Not this trip."

The cool air warmed and Sara sat up straighter, poking her face out from behind the collar of her coat. "Way to be adventurous. You won't even take me to Texas."

"Touché."

"What are you working on anyway? I mean, when you actually work." She laughed when he shot her a look as he turned the truck toward Fennimore.

"Shed over by Blue River. Framework and siding and roof are done, but there's a lot to do inside yet."

"Is that what you want to do for the rest of your life?"

Sara had asked her husband a similar question. He'd said it was all he knew how to do. He'd trained under a guy he knew over the summer when high school was done, somehow going to school full-time too in the fall as well as working full-time. Then he'd graduated and started up his own business, Lincoln joining him later. She'd always wondered how it was possible to be so happy with something so simple—to not dream and want more than an everyday life.

Clearly he *had* been happy as a carpenter. Sara had always wanted to be something more, to have her name known for creating something out of nothing, and she had found that in her artwork. But that drive— that inner voice telling her anything ordinary was unacceptable—where had it come from? Why did some people have it and others not?

"No. It's not. For now it's fine. I make good money. But..." He shrugged. "Do I want to be doing it for the rest of my life? No. I want to be able to walk when I'm in my fifties. I want to be able to keep my knees and hips and not have to have back surgery when I'm older. Construction work is hard on a body."

Sara knew. He'd come home with his knees bothering him and his back aching more times than he hadn't. Construction work made young men old.

"Plus, there's always the chance of falling off a roof."

She glanced at him. "Yeah. I know."

"Don't even bring it up," he warned, sipping from one of the cups he'd carried to the truck.

"I didn't. You did. That was horrible. I'd never seen him so scared."

You'd never seen him so scared except for the night of the car wreck, just before he lost consciousness. Then you never saw him look anything at all after that. Sara clamped her mouth shut, wishing there was a way to turn off her thoughts at will. Mindless, numb, unable to feel—what a reprieve that would be.

"It's not like I meant to fall off the roof. I slipped."

"You shouldn't have been up there in the rain anyway. Duh you." She remembered the phone call from his parents, the fear in his eyes, the dread that had filled her, and the dread that had stayed with her until they were at the hospital and she saw Lincoln was okay.

"It was leaking," he said, like that made it all justified.

"Stupid man," she said softly.

Lincoln glanced at her, the faintest of smiles on his lips. "That I am."

"You're lucky all you got was a sprained ankle and scraped up."

"I don't need luck. I got skills."

"Clearly." Her eyes met his again and she laughed, Lincoln joining in.

They reached Fennimore. It was located on top of a hill, Fennimore Hill, as it was called by locals, and had a population under three thousand. It was a pretty, scenic town with a nice library Sara liked to frequent, or used to, when she read. She couldn't remember the last time she'd lost herself in a story.

"Coffee?" Lincoln asked as the truck went by the busiest gas station of the town, his lips twitching.

"I'll pass."

The truck veered to the left by another gas station, taking them in the direction of Dodgeville. Lincoln tapped his fingers on the steering wheel in tune to a Nine Inch Nails song.

"You never said what you want to do later."

"I know."

"So...are you going to tell me?"

He grabbed a black baseball cap from the dash, repeatedly adjusting it on his head. "Nope."

She crossed her arms. "I don't understand why you're so elusive all the time lately."

"Especially today?"

"Yes. Especially today."

"All in good time. The best things in life come to those who wait. Patience is a virtue. You—"

"Lincoln."

"Yes?"

"Shut up."

His deep laughter filled the cab of the truck, and something close to, or maybe even, happiness warmed Sara at the sound of it.

SHE STARED AT the counter full of tins and other various containers of flavored popcorn. Lincoln had basically bought the small Montfort Rural Route 1 store out of stock. She could smell the butter and popcorn scent through the boxes.

"Is it overwhelming?" he asked, popping some cheese popcorn into his mouth.

"It's..." Her eyes watered. "It's perfect. Thank you. I had fun today."

"Day's not over." He grabbed a paper towel from the holder on the counter and wiped his hands on it, tossing the used paper towel into the garbage. "Be right back."

Sara rubbed her face, a fresh wave of sadness hitting her in Lincoln's absence. She didn't even know why. It was a different kind of sadness from what she normally felt and she couldn't determine the cause of it. Loneliness maybe, or the loss of warmth, the fading of light and the impending submergence back into darkness.

Lincoln carried in a pizza with a Papa Murphy's label on it. He set it on the table. The pepperonis spelled out 'Happy 28 Years, Sara'.

She stared at it, her eyes burning with tears. She looked at Lincoln and he tilted his head to the side.

"You're gonna cry over pizza? Don't be such a girl," he gently teased, wiping his thumb under her eyes and taking her tears away.

She sobbed and laughed at the same time, wiping her eyes.

"I got one more thing."

"Don't you dare. You've done too much already."

"It's your special day," was all he said, leaving her once more.

Sara rubbed her aching chest as her eyes lingered on the words spelled out with pepperonis. It was corny and sweet and she loved it. He had always had a giving nature, but this, this was too much. She didn't deserve it. She didn't deserve his friendship. Friendship. It didn't feel like the right word. It was more than that—a kinship of two lost souls struggling to live under the loss of substantial grief.

She flat-out bawled when he carried in a large hope chest made out of cherry wood. Butterflies and vines were carved into the lid of it. Sara loved butterflies. She hadn't known Lincoln knew that. Or maybe she had and she'd forgotten—everything was a jumbled mess in her head most of the time.

"You're not supposed to cry," he chided gently, stroking her hair as she sobbed onto his shirt, wetting it with her tears.

"You're not supposed to make me cry," she wailed, his shirt fisted between her hands.

"Trust me, that was not my intention. Do you like it?"

"I love it."

"It's my first project. Well, the first I've actually finished. I've been working on it for months."

She stiffened, slowly moving back so she could see his face. "You made that yourself?"

"Yeah." Lincoln rubbed the back of his neck, avoiding her eyes. "That's what I want to do. I want to make stuff. Woodworking." He looked at her. "Do you think I'm lame?"

She wiped her eyes, sniffling. "I think you're brilliant." Sara thought of the time and hours it must have taken to make that for her and her chest squeezed.

His eyes lit up and he grinned. "You haven't seen all of it. Here, I'll open it for you."

They knelt beside it, her arm and leg brushing his as he explained the making of the piece of furniture to her in great detail. She listened, in awe. He was excited, animated as he went on about things Sara didn't understand. It didn't matter, though, because she could have listened to him all night. His eyes sparkled with life and Lincoln's hands repeatedly gestured as he talked. The gift that he'd made for her couldn't outweigh the gift of him sharing his dream with her.

"How did you learn how to do this?" She slowly trailed a hand along the smooth wood, touched beyond words by his thoughtfulness. He'd gotten a one-sided conversation from her for his birthday and she'd gotten more than she could have imagined.

"You'll laugh."

Sara turned her head at the same time Lincoln did. Their faces were only inches apart. "No, I won't."

"YouTube and I checked out some books from the Fennimore library."

"YouTube is very informative," she deadpanned.

He smiled, touching his forehead to hers. "That it is."

"This is flawless. You have a real talent, Lincoln." She had a hard time looking away from it. It would go perfect at the foot of the bed, the bed she never slept in. Sara shoved the thought away.

He shifted his position. "Yeah, well, I got a lot to learn yet too."

"I can't believe I never knew you liked to do this kind of stuff."

"You know guys. Macho and all that. Can't tell people about stuff like this. What if I got made fun of?" He widened his eyes.

"You'd probably just punch whoever made fun of you."

"You're probably right."

"Did…" She stopped herself and tried to find different words from the ones she was about to say. Sara had been about to ask if he knew about it. "As a child…did you do stuff like this?"

"I tried carving pieces of wood. I sucked."

She laughed at his admission. "Everyone gets better at everything with practice."

"Think so?" he murmured, his penetrating gaze holding her captive.

"If they want to, yes," she said breathlessly, her pulse picking up for no reason; no reason she could explain to herself anyway.

He smiled, but there was sadness to it. "There it is in a nutshell." He got to his feet and offered her his hand. "Hungry? I'm starving."

"Isn't pizza what we ate the last time we were together?" she asked.

"Not even comparable. This is *Papa Murphy's*. In case you didn't know."

She stood, releasing his hand. "Right. Incomparable to all other pizzas."

"Exactly."

"Where are my twenty-eight candles?" She innocently blinked her eyes at Lincoln.

"You want a pizza or a torch?"

Sara laughed. "Smart ass."

SHE WOKE UP with a smile on her face, forgetting about him and instead thinking of the day before spent with Lincoln. It had been a good day. The smile slid from her face as the heaviness in her heart grew. How could she have forgotten, even for a moment, even in sleep? She sat up, staring at the blank TV she hadn't turned on in months. Everything had stopped, paused, on that day over a year ago. Especially her.

Was it really happening? Was he really in that hospital bed, waiting to die? While she pretended her life was fine and laughed with his brother and he rotted away in a sterile room. Sara hung her head as warm tears trickled from the corners of her eyes. He'd been gone for a while, but where it really mattered he'd left her so very long ago. It *didn't matter*. He was still her husband and he was still her burden or joy to bear.

She got up, unable to take herself in the direction of the bathroom and into the shower. Her mouth tasted like stale popcorn and pizza and she was sure she didn't smell the greatest. Sara didn't care. She wandered around the house in her robe, making a pot of coffee, and staring at all the closed doors.

"One day you have to open them."

She clutched the edge of the kitchen counter, closing her eyes. She had been wondering when the voice would show up again to torment her. Shivers went up and down her body and her scalp prickled.

"You're not real. Whoever, whatever you are, you're not real," she whispered. Sara opened her eyes, forcing herself to turn around and confront air.

She took a deep breath, reaching into the cupboard for a cup. She pulled his favorite one down, resting her forehead against it and closing her eyes. It was pale blue with white letters that read: Addicted to Caffeine. It was tacky, but he'd loved it. It was silly to feel closer to him by using his favorite coffee mug, and yet Sara did. It was a connection to him, however small.

She sat at the table, misery adding a slump to her shoulders, grief pulling her head down. She sipped the coffee, not really tasting it. It was hot, warming her body, but other than that, it might as well have been water. Thoughts went to Lincoln and she wanted him to not come over to pull her from herself, not this day. This day belonged to her melancholy.

She knew he'd come regardless of what she wanted and she knew he'd make her laugh and make her feel something other than pain and she wanted to resent him for it, but couldn't. When she was with him, she felt closer to normal. Sara felt closer to alive. Even if it was an illusion, even if it never lasted for long.

All those dreams they'd had together—the house, the children, the life they'd planned on living together—all of it had been a lie. An unknown one, but a lie just the same.

"Why did you leave me?" she whispered to the emptiness of her house, knowing because she wanted an answer, this time there would be none.

The knock came. She ignored it, staring into the black depths of her coffee. *Go away, Lincoln. You make it worse by giving me joy only for it to be snatched away as soon as you go.*

Her head began to pound along with the door and Sara finally gave in, unlocking and opening the door to see a furious Lincoln staring back at her. A tick throbbed in his jaw as he glared down at her with his stormy eyes. "Why...didn't you...answer...the door?" he ground out between clenched teeth.

She didn't say anything, simply turning and walking away to let him enter.

He followed her inside, shutting the door harder than he needed to. "You can't just not answer the door. I need to know...I need to know you're okay."

"I'm okay," she said, crossing her arms defensively. "What are you doing here? Don't you have Thanksgiving with your parents or something?"

"No."

"Why not?" she asked, curious.

"Don't worry about it. Going back to feeling sorry for yourself, are you?" He whipped the stocking cap from his head, tugging his gloves off next. Lincoln slapped them onto an end table beside the recliner. His movements were jerky, restrained.

"Don't worry about it," she tossed back at him, moving to sit on the couch.

He tore his jacket off, his boots thudding to the floor next. "I see you still got your little bed all set up too." He jabbed a finger in the direction of the couch.

She grabbed the blanket and held it to her as though it would protect her from the onslaught of his words. When Lincoln sat down in the recliner she lurched to her feet before she knew she even was.

"You can't sit there. You know that," she gasped out, her pulse racing.

He lifted one eyebrow, his expression carefully blank. "I can't? Clearly I can, because I *am*."

Sara wrung her hands, wanting to literally remove Lincoln from his chair. "This isn't...fair. This...you...Lincoln," she pleaded, unable to form words over the panic she felt. It was crushing, insurmountable in its entirety.

"You know what? You're right. I don't feel like sitting. I'm kind of tired, actually." He stood and walked toward the bedroom door.

She didn't think—she lunged. She grabbed his arm, tugging. "No, Lincoln. Don't. Please don't."

He couldn't go into her bedroom. He couldn't put his touch on the room, mask the room's scent with his. Lincoln would change it. He would take over it, like he did with everything. She could see it happening. Lincoln was sweeping all that was him away and replacing it with himself, whether it was his intention or not.

He swung his head around to pierce her with his gaze as her hands slowly fell away from his arm. "You didn't die. You're not dying. You don't get to die, Sara," he ground out. "Start *living*." Lincoln grabbed the door handle and swung the door open.

She didn't know what she expected to happen when he opened the door. Her breath hiccupped at the view of the room. It was normal, nothing to mark it as a room filled with ghosts. It smelled faintly of the vanilla lotion Sara favored. The room was cast in shadows. The king-sized bed was to the left, under a set of windows. The dressers were against the wall and a full-length mirror was along another wall. The walls were painted a marshmallow white and the bedding was lavender with brown accents.

He walked inside and Sara's heart cried a little. Lincoln stood in the middle of the room, his back to her. The seconds ticked by, turning into minutes. She hovered by the door, unable to walk into the room, not with him in it.

"You moved it in already."

She frowned, not knowing what he meant. She followed the direction he looked and saw the hope chest at the foot of the bed. "Yes."

"You walked into the room you never sleep in to put the chest I made you in front of the bed."

"Yes."

"Why?" he demanded, his broad shoulders tense.

She stared at the back of his head, scrutinizing a wayward lock of hair that curled up on the nape of his neck. His shaggier, unkempt hairstyle fit him better than the shorter one had.

"It had to have been hard to move it. Why do all that?" He turned, his features swathed in nothingness. His face was perfectly neutral.

"Because..." She searched her brain for the right words.

"Because?"

"Because..." Sara looked at the bed she hadn't slept in for over a year. "Because the room isn't so lonely with it in here. It's not so sad, with that...with what you made me in here. I know that sounds dumb, but..." She shrugged.

Lincoln approached her, the blank expression shattering and sadness and ferocity bursting through the shield he tried so hard to keep erected. "It doesn't sound dumb. It sounds..." He swallowed, looking like he was struggling for words. "It sounds fucking beautiful." He rubbed his eyes, sighing. "I can't believe I just said that. I swear I'm turning wimpier the longer I hang out with you."

"Adding the swear word made it sound more masculine."

He dropped his hands from his eyes, a grin forming on his lips. "Ya think?"

"Definitely."

"Good 'cause that's what I was aiming for."

"Spot on," she murmured.

He laughed and Sara realized no one had laughed in this room since him, the night of the accident. He said her name and her head jerked up, a question in her eyes. He held out his hand and motioned her forward.

"No."

"Come on, Sara. I'll help you. You know I will. Take my hand. Take it."

She blinked her eyes, turning away.

"You'll never heal if you don't face what hurts you."

She whirled around. "How can I heal when I know he's about to die, Lincoln?" Sara hissed, storming toward him. "I can't heal from that. It's like he's dying all over again, *twice*."

His eyes darkened with grief and anger. "He left a long time ago. You know that." A muscle jumped under Lincoln's eye. "It pisses me off that he did what he did."

She jerked back. "What?"

"It wasn't fair what he did, giving you a countdown, dragging it out for a year. You're stuck in limbo. You can't go back, you can't go forward. And...there he lies on that bed, a shell of himself, a piece of who he used to be, but not him. It's not him."

"He did it—" Teardrops fell from her eyes and her throat tightened, making it hard to talk. "He did it to give us time, to give him a chance to come back."

"But he hasn't. And he's not." Lincoln's eyes watered and he took a ragged breath. "Nothing's changed. Nothing's gotten better. He would have shown improvement by now if he was going to. I understand why Cole had his will set up that way. I understand the hope he had that if anything like this would happen, he would somehow recover. But it wasn't fair of him to do that to you. It was selfish of him, making you wait, making you watch him die. You can't heal from the loss of him when he's lingering, not really alive, and not really dead. And you have to heal. You can't live like this. You're...you're..." He closed his eyes, rubbing his face.

"I'm in the room," she whispered. It was unbearable to see Lincoln in such pain. He usually hid it so well. *Take it away, somehow take it away.*

He opened his eyes, showing her his sorrow even when he smiled faintly. "That you are," Lincoln said quietly, not reaching out a hand this time.

Sara reached for his instead, linking them. The room wasn't so overwhelming with Lincoln in it. The world wasn't so tragic with him before her, holding her hands. She even thought maybe she could get through anything if he was with her. Their eyes connected, and in the strength of his gaze, she found hers.

"What has the last few days been like?" he asked.

"I don't know. Why?"

"Yes, you do. Tell me. Did you have fun at all?"

"I guess."

"Did you forget to be sad, did you laugh, did you smile?"

"Maybe."

One dark eyebrow rose. "You can still miss him, you can still mourn him, without giving up your life. You just have to have a reason to keep going."

She stared at him, her brows furrowing at the truth of his words, at the fact that *Lincoln* was the reason she had to not give up. She turned away, not wanting it to be true and unable to deny it. He was it for her. It was Lincoln. How had that happened? Maybe it couldn't have been anyone else, or any other way. Maybe it *had* to be him.

"Sara?"

"Thank you," she said quietly, facing him once more.

He looked down. "I'd do anything for you." Lincoln's head lifted. "You have to know that."

She did. Sara closed her eyes, nodding. "I know."

"I'll always be here for you, no matter what. Even when you don't want me to be. Even when you don't think you need me to be, or you don't think you deserve me to be. I'll still be here."

She touched a wayward lock of his, surprised by how soft his hair was. He went still, his gaze locked with hers. She didn't say anything. She couldn't. But Sara smiled.

"Come here," Lincoln said in a gruff voice, moving toward the bed.

"What are you doing?" she asked warily, watching him as he sat down on the bed.

"I'm not trying to seduce you, if that's what you think. As much as your blue rag turns me on, I will somehow manage to restrain myself." He patted the bed, his eyebrows raised.

"I don't—I can't..." She shook her head, her chest tightening painfully. Lincoln on their bed was all wrong. It would be even more wrong if she joined him on it.

"Just come here. Please."

Sara closed her eyes, took a deep breath, and gingerly sat down on the bed as far away from him as she could get without falling off it.

"See? Not so bad, right?" He stretched his long-limbed body out and put his hands behind his head. "Your turn."

It was too intimate. She couldn't do it. She couldn't even lie down on the bed by herself, let alone with a man other than her husband next to her.

"Sara."

"You're evil," she muttered, lying down on the bed, her hands on either side of her body. Her arms and legs were stiff, immobile, like she was frozen by some kind of tragic spell.

"Close your eyes." Lincoln's voice was low, hypnotic.

"No."

"Do it."

She obliged, her teeth clenched, her body hot with annoyance. "What is the point of this?"

"You're reacquainting yourself with your bed. It's such a small thing, sleeping in your bed, and yet it holds such power over you," he mused. "You have to realize you're stronger than the pain and the sorrow."

"I'm not," she choked out, squeezing her eyes tightly shut.

"You are," he said with conviction.

"You know I'm just going to go back to the couch at bedtime, right?"

"That's fine. At least I got you here now." Lincoln paused. "Every memory I have of my childhood includes Cole. He was such a major part of my life, being the big brother and all. It's hard going each day without him being a part of it. You know what helps me get through it?"

She shook her head, eyes still closed.

"At first I thought by not thinking about him, I'd be okay. But I wasn't. Instead I made myself think of him and it hurt, a lot, but the more I

thought of him, the easier it got. The more I did things I
do, the more able I was to function without bawling m
daily basis. The more I remembered him, the more I cou
with happiness instead of sorrow."

Her limbs loosened a little under the influence of his soothing tone.

"I mean, yeah, it still hurts. It always will. Cole's my brother. I love
him. I also hate him, just a little. But I love him more. You don't have to
accept what's happened to him, but you have to find a way to live with it.
Know what I mean?"

Tears leaked from the corners of her eyes. A hand, warm and
calloused and strong, clasped its fingers around hers and squeezed. Sara
held Lincoln's hand, both of them silent, and felt oddly at peace for the
moment.

CHAPTER 12

IT WAS TIME. How could he have put such a burden on her? How could he have thought it was right to ask such a thing of her? She couldn't decide such a thing. It was like she was killing him all over again, for a second time. And still she had to do it. Sara had done it. Dr. Henderson had sadly smiled as she'd signed her husband's life away, offering no words of sympathy. Maybe he realized none would be sufficient enough. The antiseptic smell of the room made her stomach roil and though she wanted to run from the room, her feet remained rooted in place.

"No one else can do it."

Her head shot up and she looked around the room, her eyes taking in the white walls, the beeping monitor, the hospital equipment, and finally, slowly, slowly going to his still form. His skin was waxen and gray-tinged. He looked unreal, like one of those celebrity replicas found in a wax museum. Tubes ran in and out of his body, giving him an inhuman, robotic quality. She hated the thought just as she hated the truth of it. His chest rose and lowered with air that wasn't his, stolen breaths of life that kept him alive, but not living.

His light brown hair was thick and waved around his head. She lifted a hand to touch it and let it fall back to her side. His body was shrunken in size, the muscle and tan gone from his form. Sara closed her eyes, not wanting this to be him, unable to accept him this way, seeing him this way. He should be laughing, smiling, spending his days working and loving and *living*. How could she have signed his death warrant?

"No one else could do it, Sara. It had to be you."

She slapped a hand to her mouth, eyes stinging with tears. Sara stared down at him, her pulse jumping in incomprehension. It had sounded like his voice. He was silent and unmoving on the hospital bed before her. It wasn't him talking, but for the first time, Sara realized it had always been his voice talking to her. She just hadn't heard it as his before—she hadn't been able to accept it was his voice in her mind. Chills went up and down her arms, encasing her in icy revelation. How could that be?

"You have to say goodbye now. It's the only way you'll be able to move on. It's time for you to move on."

"I just...I just want to see your blue eyes, just one last time. Please," she whispered brokenly, hot tears of sorrow making jagged tracks down her cheeks. "*Cole.*"

Whatever had been keeping her together, sheer will maybe, finally abandoned her when his name fell from her lips. It was the first time she'd spoken it since the accident. It was real. Saying his name made it real. It hurt so much. A sob left her, broken and weak, like Sara. She hung her head as the tears made a river out of her face, her throat painfully tight. She wrapped her arms around herself, pretending they were his.

She couldn't do this. How could she do this? He was her husband, her love. He was her life. Sara couldn't say goodbye. She refused to say goodbye. Her shoulders shook and she held her head between her hands, trying to hide from the terrible act she'd set into motion with a signature.

The air shifted behind her and two arms overlapped hers, warm and strong and alive, and for a second, she let herself pretend they were his. Sara turned into the embrace with her eyes closed, not wanting reality to creep back in yet, inhaling his citrus scent, and just like that, the spell was broken. She opened her eyes, moving away from Lincoln and closer to him.

An unknown emotion flickered in Lincoln's eyes. "Dr. Henderson and the nurses are ready. They're waiting outside."

Resignation and defeat warred with a hopeless faith that maybe he'd come back to her. He'd open his eyes and be miraculously healed in all ways. He'd be hers again. Sara took his cold hand in hers and brought it to her lips, softly kissing the stiff fingers, her tears falling to his hand. *I need magic tears to bring you back to life, Cole. You've been sleeping so long and all I wanted was for you to wake up. Why wouldn't you wake up for me? Why wasn't I enough to bring you back?*

Lincoln was on the other side of him, blank-faced as he stared down at the shell that was now his brother. "It's not him," he said in a raspy voice, eyes downcast. "He left a long time ago. This isn't him. This is just a way for us to say goodbye."

"But you said—"

"Forget what I said. I was pissed. I mean, I meant it, don't get me wrong, but...I'm choosing to believe this." He inhaled deeply and lifted red-rimmed eyes to hers. "From this day on I'm choosing to believe he held on for this, for us to come to terms with everything, for us to be able to let him go. And I don't care what you think or say, what anyone else thinks or says. This is what I know to be true. This is *my* truth."

She felt her face crumple and her vision blurred with tears. Lincoln's expression turned pained and he rapidly blinked his eyes, swiping an arm across his face. She'd done this. She'd taken his brother from him. Now she was taking him away again, for the last time.

"Don't you look at me like that," he warned in a menacing tone.

Sara looked down, unable to speak.

"I'm sick of you blaming yourself for something out of your control. This is what we're gonna do now. We're going to respectfully say our goodbyes to my brother and your husband. There's no room for guilt in this room, not today. You got that, Sara? You take all that guilt and you shove it away. I mean it." As if he thought he could will the culpability away, he glared at her, tight-lipped and stony.

To be so sure of something, to have such faith when you had no reason to—Sara envied that about him. She inhaled deeply, briefly closing her eyes. *Be strong. If you can't be strong for you, be strong for Lincoln. Lie to him without saying a word.* She opened her eyes and gave a stiff nod just as a knock came at the door.

IT WAS ALL so anticlimactic. She didn't know what she'd expected, but it hadn't been the quiet, somberness of all those around her as the mask was removed from his face. She stared down at him, not recognizing the still being on the bed as her husband. Maybe Lincoln was right. Maybe he had left a long time ago. The doctor and nursing staff were silent and still—this was just another regrettable task they were designated to perform within the course of their workday.

His heartbeats didn't quicken like she'd hoped. His chest didn't continue to lift up and down as she'd told herself it would. Lincoln held one hand and she the other, the two of them trying to force life into him from theirs. His parents stood behind Lincoln, his father stoic and his mother quietly weeping. There were some things that couldn't heal, no matter how long the wrong had been committed. She knew her relationship with her husband's parents was one of those things. Their connection was cracked beyond repair. It didn't matter, not now.

She looked up at the same time Lincoln did, saw him breaking on the inside though he remained impassive on the outside. It was in his eyes. His gray eyes were shattered. She had to look away before she shattered as well.

Sara leaned forward and rested her forehead against his cool one. "I love you, Cole. I always will. Be at peace," she whispered, teardrops falling from her eyes and landing on his expressionless face. She watched one tear trickle down his forehead and touch the corner of his eye before moving on to rest on his too prominent cheekbone. It was as though he cried as well.

For the merest of seconds, his face was as she remembered it. The piercing blueness of his eyes, his lips lifting into a smile; it blinded her and tore her breath from her lungs like he'd sucked it away and back into himself for one stolen minute of life before all existence was gone. Sara saw him as he'd been before the wreck, and then once again, she saw him as he really was.

The beats lessened, slowly trailing off and ending. Her breaths became quicker as his became nothing. Sara was trying to breathe enough for the both of them, but it was pointless. The countdown until he was officially pronounced dead had run its course. She was frozen, her eyes glued to his face. *Move. Make a sound. Come back.*

Nothing. There was nothing.

The monitor stopped with one terrible, never-ending *beeeeeep.* Sara's entire body jerked with the pain of her heart being severed and ripped from her as the realization that he was truly gone and would never come back slammed through her. Someone unplugged the machine, a faceless being registered with her peripheral vision.

"I'm messy and a slob and I like beer a little too much. I work long hours and I like to be outside more than inside. I'm restless and reckless, and yes, I admit, a pervert. Upon occasion. But I love you. I've never loved anyone like I love you, Sara. Never will. I want to be with you until I take my last breath, and even when I take my last breath, I want it to be next to you. Please. Redeem my selfish soul and make it better, make me better. Say you'll be my wife."

The last breath was a sigh, an unspoken final goodbye, and the world stopped. No one moved and the silence became intolerable. The quiet was filled with pain so thick to utter a single word would destroy her, him, all of them. Sara watched him, willing him to breathe on his own, to make his heart start again, willing him to *open his eyes*. The minutes dragged on, the profound loss unbearable to her. She pressed a lingering kiss to his stiff, cold lips, saying a silent farewell. She pulled back, unable to look away from the soulless shell that no longer housed her husband. *Come back.* Sara knew he wouldn't, but it didn't stop her from wishing it anyway. He was gone. He wasn't coming back. Never again.

She unconsciously cried out and fell back against a desk, close to collapsing. She wanted to lie down, close her eyes, curl up in a ball, and become dust, nothing, *erased.* Instead Sara turned and blindly fled from the room, bumping into a nurse on her way out. Her heart pounded so hard inside her chest she thought it was going to slam right through her body. She couldn't see. She didn't know where she was going. She only knew she had to escape.

There was a buzzing in her ears, getting louder and louder, so loud she wanted to scream just to hear something other than it. *Never again.* She stumbled, almost falling over as a wave of pain hit her, slashing into her midsection with a knife of agony. She bent at the waist, trying to shield herself from the inward ache there was no relief from.

"Sara!"

She shoved her shoulder against the metal door that led to the stairs, jarring it upon impact. She rushed forward and swayed at the edge of the winding steps, almost tumbling down them. For an instant she contemplated letting herself go, but instead her hand reached out for the railing. *Never again.* A sob was torn from her lips, grating to her ears. She was falling again—falling on the inside, falling on the outside.

The world swayed and Sara sank to the cool floor, shaking and dizzy. Her eyes wouldn't focus, the buzzing in her ears was now a roar, and she thought she was going to vomit. She leaned her head forward and a flash of his lifeless face greeted her. Sara whimpered, covering her face with her hands and rocking forward and backward.

She sat there, images and words and emotions hitting her one after another, overlapping and melding into a collage of him that was heartbreaking to endure. The way his laugh had made her laugh. His eyes that had always looked at her so intently, so focused on her and nothing else. His arms, warm and sure, enveloping her within them, making her feel safe. The way his kisses had taken her breath and given her life at the same time.

Never again.

The arms wrapped around her from behind, two muscled thighs cocooned her frame. Sara stiffened. Her first inclination was to move away, but she couldn't, not this time. She needed to feel a connection with another human and she knew Lincoln needed it as well. It fit, somehow, that they should mourn together. Her hands gripped his forearms of their own accord, and when he rested his chin on her shoulder, she felt the tears from his eyes dampen her skin through her thin shirt. His scent was familiar and welcomed, the feel of his soft hair against her cheek a caress of empathy. She slowly relaxed, her eyelids sliding shut. His chest trembled against her back and she cried for Lincoln as much as she cried for herself and for him.

Time ticked by, slow and painful—that horrible thing inescapable no matter how much she wanted to. They quietly grieved him and each other. He was gone, and so was a part of her, and so was a part of Lincoln. She inhaled and exhaled, gently pulling away. She moved down a step, still sitting with her back to him, but not touching.

"He always wanted to be more like you. He said you had all the brains and talent and he just had the brawn. He said it annoyed the piss out of him because he was the older brother and you were supposed to look up to him, not the other way around," she said softly, staring at the white wall.

A long pause ensued before Lincoln said brokenly, "I looked up to him."

She nodded, blinking her eyes against the endless tears. "He knew you did. He loved you so much, Lincoln. If we..." Sara swallowed as a fresh wave of pain washed over her; a different kind of pain, but just as profound as the pain of losing him. The pain of a lost child never held, never seen. "If we'd had a baby, he said he hoped he or she took after you more than him. He said, of course, he or she could take after me however much they wanted." Her voice cracked.

He didn't say anything for a long time. She knew why. If he tried to talk, he would break down, lose control. She'd been there. She was there now.

His voice was strained when he finally said, "Come on. Let's get a cup of coffee. Or not. I don't care. As long as we leave here. I don't want you to be alone. And I don't want to be alone either."

She heard and felt him move behind her and a hand appeared before her face. She looked up, flinching at the damaged look of Lincoln. His shoulders were hunched as though to protect himself against unfathomable anguish and there were brackets around his lips. Without thought, she stood and grabbed him, pulling his stiff body to her. He slowly hugged her back and when he did, it was crushing, but essential. Both of them were struggling. It was real. How could it be real?

"I don't want to be alone," she whispered. If she was alone, she feared she'd disappear and never come back. She'd lose herself and be trapped within herself, like him. Sara would disintegrate.

She began to walk down the steps, her legs stiff, her movements jerky. The walls and stairs moved around her, shrinking and growing before her, and she paused as a wave of dizziness plowed into her. *He's gone.* Sara closed her eyes, swaying back and into Lincoln. His hands gripped her shoulders and steadied her. Nausea formed in her stomach and she stumbled down the rest of the stairs and outside, falling to her knees and retching in the bushes beside the hospital.

She dry-heaved long after the small amount of food in her stomach was gone. An acidic taste in her mouth and over her teeth and tongue, she grimaced. The cold chilled her more than she already was, biting and unforgiveable. It jabbed at her, stabbing its hatred toward her into the sensitive skin of her flesh. Even the wind blamed her. *You just killed your husband*, it shrieked. Her body jerked from the icy air, from the guilt. It registered in her head that Lincoln was behind her, holding her hair away from her face. It was too much. She hung her head, the pain building and building and rupturing from her in broken sobs.

"Come on, Sara, let's take you home." He let her hair fall through his fingers and reached for her.

Sara let him help her, let him escort her to his truck. Her teeth chattered. The ice was crawling up her legs, entering her heart, and freezing it over. When he buckled her in, she wept harder. She was dying, dimming, fracturing. Lincoln stood by the door, saying nothing. He didn't have to. Finally he shut the door and got in on the other side of the truck.

THE THOUGHT OF going into their house, knowing with an aching finality he would never be in it again, was something she couldn't deal with. Lincoln somehow knew that and had wordlessly driven to his house instead of hers. How long they'd sat in the unmoving and quiet truck, she had no recollection.

She stared straight ahead, seeing him standing on the deck, adjusting his baseball cap, laughing. She could smell the dirt layered on him from work, the somehow sweet taste of beer on his lips. He turned and winked at her, his blue eyes promising he'd love her in all forms once they got home. She sucked in a painful breath, bending over from the agony of it. It was happening. She was finally crumbling, splintering into so many pieces she'd never be able to be put back together again.

"Sara?"

Lincoln's fingers grazed her arm as she fumbled with the door handle, falling out of the truck and landing on the cold ground. She stayed that way, crouching, wanting to sink completely into the ground. Sara's fingers clawed through the icy slush; her nails finding grass and dirt beneath it. Choked sounds of pain left her and she crawled, head down, out of her mind with grief. She wanted to be where he was, and if he was nowhere, that's where she wanted to be. *Let me die. Let me close my eyes and not wake up. Let me be with him. Please. I never asked You for anything. Just this one time I'm asking You. Let me be with him!* She flung her head back and screamed and screamed with all the agony living inside her. It wasn't enough. It still hurt. She was full of anguish, would never be able to get rid of it all.

Strong hands grabbed her under her arms, pulling her up and away from the cold, hard ground. Sara fought. She didn't know why. She just knew she had to. He would thwart her plan. Lincoln would keep her away from what she wanted. Death. She wanted to die. She wanted to be with her husband. She kicked her legs and slapped at him, tortured gasps and cries bursting from her. She was hot, she was on fire, why didn't she burn up and melt? Pieces of her were chipping, falling away, leaving her. What was she? Who was she? Ugly. Sara was ugly. She was ugly without him.

"Let me go!" she shrieked, turning around and shoving him.

Lincoln stumbled back, his chest heaving, tears streaming down his chiseled features.

"I killed him! This is my fault. I killed him. He's *dead.* Because of me. He's dead." Sara couldn't breathe, she continued to breathe, she wanted to stop breathing. In and out, in and out, still she breathed. She breathed too fast, she breathed too heavily, but she still breathed. Her lungs were on fire, her body scorching, her throat dry flint ready for the littlest of sparks. And then she could burn up and die.

"Stop this," he pleaded in a low voice, a voice she barely heard over the roar of the flames burning her from the inside out.

Sara tried to speak and only mewing sounds found their way out. The flames licked at her soul, turning it to ash. She was numb. Nothing was left inside her. It was all gone. Burned up. Dead. Ashes. Dust.

Lincoln opened his arms, his head slightly tilted. He waited. If she went to him, he'd burn up with her too.

"I killed him."

He shook his head, not speaking, arms still open. Waiting. Always waiting for her.

"I want to die," she confessed. "I've tried...I want to die, Lincoln."

Lincoln's face distorted. "Don't you fucking say that, Sara!" he thundered, storming toward her. "You don't *ever* say that again, you understand?" His voice shook. "Stop saying it, stop *thinking* it." His fingers dug into her arms, showing her she wasn't dead, not yet.

"I'm lost. I'm lost and you can't save me." She stared up into his pained eyes, caressing his features with her gaze. He was always trying to save her.

His jaw clenched and his grip turned painful. "Yes. I can. I *will*. I just lost my brother. I'm not losing you too. I'm never losing you, Sara, *never*. I'm *not* letting you go. *Ever*. Your life is worth living. You don't get the right to throw that away."

The conviction of his words, the way his eyes were locked on hers, nearly made her believe he could, that Lincoln had the power to save her, to hold on to her tight enough that she wouldn't be lost, wouldn't fade into nothing, wouldn't burn up and disintegrate. She almost hated him for it.

EVERYWHERE SHE LOOKED she was hit with something that reminded her of him. She sat on the couch, an untouched cup of coffee cooling between her fingers. It was heavy and she set it down on the coffee table. Lincoln was in the bedroom that used to be his parents', fixing it up for her to sleep in. They had gotten a hotel room, refusing to stay in the house full of him. She understood. This house was close to being as unbearable to be in as hers was.

The meltdown outside was a locked subject. Hours ago, it still replayed over and over in her head. The look on Lincoln's face, the fierceness in his tone, the overwhelming despondency that was with her now even. He'd brought her back from the brink once again. But he wouldn't always be around. Lincoln wasn't responsible for her. He thought he was, but he wasn't.

Her eyes shied from the framed photographs hanging on the walls of Lincoln and him growing up, and then went back to them anyway. Her breath shuddered as her throat tightened. She covered her face with her hands, unable to cry, which should have been a relief, but it wasn't because she was overflowing with grief and had no way to release it.

How could he be gone? Agony had wrapped its arms of heartache around her and wouldn't let her go. Sara understood how her mother had died of a broken heart. Why wasn't she worthy of the same? She didn't want to live without him. She didn't want to exist when he didn't.

The stairs creaked, alerting her Lincoln was near. Sara dropped her hands from her face. Seeing his grief-stricken eyes pulled a choking sound from her. He didn't speak for a long time. And when he did, Lincoln's voice was gruff with emotion.

"I got the bed ready."

She nodded, her throat tightening.

He blinked his eyes, angling his body and face away from her. "I sat in his room for a while." He inhaled sharply. "I remember one time when I was five, I had a bad dream. I woke up screaming, scared. Cole came in, told me a story about baseball until I wasn't afraid anymore. He always did stuff like that. He always looked out for me." His hands fisted and opened, fisted and opened.

"Lincoln—"

"A part of me is gone. A part of my childhood, a part of my world is just...gone." He stared at her, not really seeing her, but maybe seeing enough. "I thought he would get better, at first. How stupid is that? I really thought he would get better. Why wasn't he strong enough to get better? And then...and then I knew he wouldn't and I was so pissed at him. I was so *angry* at him."

Sara slowly rose to her feet. "I'm sorry."

His eyes narrowed as his lips thinned. "It's not your fault. I never said it was your fault. I never *hinted* it was your fault. *It's not your fault, Sara!*" Lincoln slammed a fist into the wall beside him, knocking a picture loose and causing her to flinch. The glass shattered as it hit the wood floor. "*Fuck.*"

Lincoln fell to his knees, hanging his head. She looked down at him, feeling helpless. He was so strong and so fragile at the same time. She had to do something. Seeing him like this, it hurt. Lincoln's pain on top of her pain was devastating. She went to her knees beside him, staring in misery at the toothless gray-eyed boy grinning at her from a picture with shattered glass over it. That boy was gone, that boy would never come back. She put her hand on his back, feeling the muscles tremble beneath her fingers. Lincoln turned to her, burying his face in the crook between her neck and chin, wetness trickling from his eyes to dampen her shirt.

She wrapped her arms around his shaking frame, her cheek coming to rest on his soft hair that smelled like lemons. She let her eyelids slide shut, listening to Lincoln's pain, wishing there was no reason for it, wishing she could somehow remove it from him. His hands grabbed fistfuls of her shirt near her back and clenched, holding her, clutching her, as though afraid she would disappear if he let her go. Chances were she would. It was impossible for her to disappear with Lincoln holding her. He seemed to know that.

SOMETIME DURING THE night, Sara awoke, sweaty and trembling. She couldn't remember the dream that had awakened her. She could only remember the agonizing sense of loss that stayed with her, but *that* was real and could never be imagined—not loss that profound or inescapable. She sat up in the bed, wrapping her arms around her knees and placing her hot cheek to them. She closed her eyes, trying to steady her breathing. Moments ticked by and still her heart pounded and her pulse raced. The room was suffocating and too warm.

Before she was aware of it, she was walking from the room. The hallway was dark with only the glow of a nightlight to offer respite from total blackness. It cast a dim radiance to the area, giving it a surreal, dream-like state. *Am I still dreaming?* she wondered, hesitating near the door to her in-laws' bedroom. Sara shoved her hair from her face and inwardly warred with herself.

Not that she thought Lincoln would think more into it than there was, but still, would it be *right?* She was hurting, she was destroyed. So was he. She wanted a night of peaceful sleep and she was so alone—so alone that she thought if she disappeared she wouldn't even notice it. She thought maybe Lincoln would understand. He always seemed to know her, even when she didn't know herself. Her bare feet silently moved along the wood floor, the bottoms of them chilled by the coolness of it. She didn't understand how the air could be so hot and the floor still so cold.

He was waiting for her, sitting up in his bed. A lamp was on next to the bed, turning his features into shadows and light. His eyes didn't need the lamp to be seen because even in the semi-dark they were bright, intent on her. A closed book rested on the bed next to his blanketed legs. She tried not to stare at his unclothed chest, but it was well-muscled and deserved to be admired, even if only clinically.

"Can't sleep?" his voice rumbled, low and quiet.

She tore her eyes from his chest, face heating up, and met his eyes. "I— no. I mean, I *was* sleeping, but then I woke up. Bad dream," she ended lamely.

Lincoln set the book on the nightstand. "I can't sleep." He ran a hand through his already rumpled hair and sighed. "I can't stop thinking about him. I tried to read. That didn't happen. I've been sitting here, for hours, just...thinking."

She tentatively walked closer to the bed, hugging herself with her arms. "I want to sleep."

His eyes were red, sad. He nodded. "Me too."

They stared at each other, neither speaking. She took a shaky breath, seeing all the suffering she felt mirrored in him. "Can I—? I mean, it wouldn't..." She blushed, not knowing how to continue.

Lincoln wordless scooted over, making room for her. He waited, eyes downcast, his body held stiffly. Sara slowly got in beside him, not looking at him. The bed was warm, imprinted with his body and smell. Almost immediately, she relaxed a miniscule amount, but not enough to be completely at ease. Neither moved, neither spoke. A clock ticked off two minutes.

"It doesn't—"

"I *know*, Sara," he cut in. "It doesn't for me either. You don't have to say anything or explain anything, not to yourself or to me. Let's just try to sleep, okay?"

She wanted that peacefulness only he was able to provide, almost greedy for it. Sara tried not to feel guilty about that. Reaching over, she turned off the lamp, allowing darkness to blanket them. She reclined on the bed, her body straight and rigid. She focused on Lincoln's breathing from where he lay a short foot away. Her eyelids began to droop. The sheet gently rustled and a hand found hers in the dark. Warm, familiar. Sighing, close to content, she let slumber take over.

CHAPTER 13

THE SUN SHONE on the day he was buried. Sara didn't understand that. It should have been gray, overcast, and cold. It was a day to mourn, not rejoice. She wanted to grab that sun out of the sky and fling it far, far away. It shone, but somehow managed to miss her. A cloud of despair hovered over her, shielding her, keeping the sun and all it stood for out of her reach. That was the way she wanted it. Lincoln stood next her, stoic and grim. His parents kept their distance and that was fine. She couldn't make herself care. She was empty, numb. So many people came to pay their respects, so many people started to approach her and then backtracked. Only Lincoln didn't stay away.

With the canvas tarp over the burial site, it seemed circus-like, surreal. She looked at the people around her, not seeing them. None of them registered. They were just things that took up space, like her. Sara swayed and Lincoln grabbed her arm, steadying her.

"Are you okay?" he murmured into her ear.

She didn't respond, didn't acknowledge him in any way. He knew better. Why did he ask such a stupid question? She wasn't okay. Lincoln wasn't okay. Neither of them was and they never would be again. His hand dropped from her, leaving her even colder than she'd thought possible.

The ground was covered in a fine layer of snow, and though she wore black boots, gloves, and a thick gray winter coat, it did nothing to keep the chill away. She was so cold. Today was the day she died with her husband. She closed her eyes, her eyelashes miniature icicles against her cheeks.

How she'd sat through the service she had no idea. Lincoln had given an eulogy. His mother had cried. Sara had sat there, stiff-backed, frozen. His words might as well have been spoken in a different language. None of it had sunken in. It had been a closed casket wake and ceremony. Even in death he was elusive. She kept trying to tell herself it wasn't real, that it was a bad dream, but the gouged out part of her wouldn't let her lie to herself, not anymore. It was growing, taking over her being, turning her into a pulsating entity of anguish. That was all she was now. She was brittle, ready to snap from it all. Dead. *Let me die too.*

"Sara?" Lincoln whispered close to her. "Talk to me."

The pastor droned on about God and how her husband was now with Him and it angered her. Her cheeks flushed and her hands fisted at her sides. She didn't want to talk to Lincoln. Sara couldn't speak. If she said one single word, she'd collapse, break. But as the pastor kept talking like he'd known her husband, like he knew God on a personal level and had tea with Him and knew, one hundred percent, that her husband would also be having tea with Him for all time henceforth, she bit her tongue to keep in a scream and tasted blood.

Lincoln put his arm around her shoulders, his scent coming with it, and said into her hair, "If you need to leave, we'll leave."

Her lip began to wobble. She was cracking. *Stop talking, Lincoln.* The fury seeped out of her as quickly as it had appeared and the splinter deepened.

"Everyone will understand if you need to leave and if they don't, too bad for them. Say the word, and I'll take you away from this. Cole would understand."

Why didn't he stop talking? Dizziness hit her and she stumbled back, Lincoln catching her before she landed. The pastor paused as he looked at her, his lips almost immediately moving again. He was a kind-faced man with balding black hair and glasses. She tried to focus on him and what he was saying—anything to center her, but his voice was muffled and far away. She shook her head and another wave of lightheadedness struck her.

"Talk to me," he repeated in a voice low with urgency.

Their eyes met, his glazed with concern. She had to stay. For him. She owed her husband that. Sara opened her mouth, trying to talk around the dryness of her throat, trying not to break in front of everyone. His eyebrows lowered as he waited, never taking his eyes from her face.

"I'll...stay. I need to," she whispered, her face burning as eyes turned her way.

"Sure?"

She nodded.

Lincoln kept her plastered to his side, his arm strong and steady and enough to keep her standing. Somehow she got through it. Somehow she didn't scream or break or collapse. Sara's body trembled as the casket covered in white roses was lowered into the ground, her eyes filling with hot tears. She blinked and they fell to her cool cheeks, warming them.

People were leaving. She watched, bleary-eyed, as Lincoln's father finally pulled his wife away and headed for their vehicle. She stared at the hole in the ground that held her husband's body and would be his home from now on. Searing hot pain lashed through her heart, a fiery whip of devastation. What if she crawled into the hole with him? She would if it meant she'd be closer to him. She could close her eyes and forever sleep.

"You lied to me," she whispered, dashing a hand across her face to make room for more tears. "You said you'd never leave me." Her voice cracked. "But you did. You left me."

A movement caught her eye and she looked up from the black hole. Lincoln stood on the other side of it, tight-jawed. He wore a gray suit that matched the shade of his eyes and a red tie. His hair was in need of another cut, the waves taking over and unruly once more. One lock of dark brown hair hung on his forehead, giving him a boyish look.

As she stared at him, he morphed into her husband. His build turned rangier, he shortened a few inches in height, and his eyes were a piercing blue. "I didn't lie to you, Sara."

She inhaled sharply as she lost her balance, careening dangerously close to the edge of earth that led to the grave. Lincoln swore and raced toward her, gathering her in his arms and roughly pulling her back.

"What the hell is wrong with you?" he demanded.

She studied his features. It was Lincoln. Gray eyes, sharp features, wavy hair. Relief and disappointment warred inside her, and she went weak in his arms. "What did you say? When you were over there?"

"I didn't say anything. I watched you almost fall into a grave and thought I'd better rescue you."

She waited for him to admit he'd spoken the words she'd heard and seen her deceased husband say. Only he didn't.

"I'm losing my mind," she said softly.

"I won't argue with you there."

Sara gave him a sharp look.

The smile that flashed across his lips was thin and didn't reach his eyes. "We're all a little crazy at times. Sometimes that's the only way to deal with life."

He began to walk away, his back stiff, his strides precise as he took himself farther and farther away from where his brother's body would reside for all eternity.

THE UNWANTED GUESTS with their sad eyes and words of condolences that mimicked every single other person were finally gone. Lincoln helped clean up even though she'd told him to go. His suit jacket was slung over the back of the recliner and her eyes kept going to it, wanting to remove it so his scent didn't replace his.

Her husband would be honored by all that had attended the services. He'd had a cocky and sometimes arrogant demeanor that had made people think he'd thought he was better than others at times, but that hadn't been it at all. He'd actually thought he was less than. She'd never understood why. Sara knew that wall of self-confidence had hid the insecurities of a man who'd wondered if he was all that good time and again.

She had seen it. She'd known the true soul of the man who'd acted one way and had really been another. He'd always thought he had to prove something to someone—that he was good enough, or maybe he'd needed to prove that just to himself. But knowing all those people cared for him and mourned the loss of his life would have eased some of that.

She hoped it would have anyway. Not that it mattered, because he'd never know.

She looked at his brother. He'd always gone the other way. He really *didn't* care what people thought. They'd grown up in the same house and they'd been raised by the same people and they were nothing alike. How did that happen? He was so pale. Lincoln's shirt sleeves were rolled up to his elbows and his shirt and tie were rumpled. He looked tired, his mouth bracketed in sadness, an impossible weight dragging his shoulders down from their normal proud stance.

The scent of dish soap mixed with the turkey and dressing sandwiches from the local deli and Sara's stomach roiled. She picked up Styrofoam cups and paper plates, putting them in the garbage. They hadn't said a lot since his parents had left close to an hour ago. Every time their gazes met, she had to look away from the pain she saw in his.

"Any more dishes?"

Sara flinched at the sound of his deep voice. "No. Thank you. I can finish up," she said, motioning to the dishes he was dutifully washing and setting in the strainer next to the sink.

He rinsed a dish off, it gently clanging against other dishes as he set it down to dry. "Yeah. You told me that. But I'm not going anywhere."

Her breath hiccupped. "What?"

His expression was stern as he faced her. "I'm not going anywhere. Not tonight. I don't think you should be left alone."

Heat shot through her, flushing her cheeks. "I don't care what you think. It's my house and if I want to be alone, I get to be alone."

Half his mouth quirked up. "Any other time, sure. But tonight..." Lincoln shook his head. "No."

"Get out, Lincoln."

"*No.*"

Sara made a sound of frustration, flinging her hands in the air. "You can't babysit me forever."

He straightened and moved toward her. "What makes you think I'm babysitting you? Maybe I don't want to be alone either. Ever think of that? Maybe the thought of going to my house, the house Cole and I grew up in, the place he'll never come back to, is too much for me right now."

She swallowed, slowly nodding. "Okay."

He frowned and then said, "Okay. I'll finish the dishes. You go relax. Or try to relax."

"I can't relax."

"I said *try*," he said, an annoyed look on his face.

She left him to do the dishes, stopping outside the closed door to her bedroom. The house was full of all the many closed doors. She thought of the painting of the door and wondered what it symbolized. It probably wasn't that hard to figure out. She just didn't have the energy to try to decipher its hidden meaning.

"What is it?"

"I just…" She rubbed her forehead, glancing over her shoulder at him. "Do you believe in God?"

He let the dishrag splash into the sink. "Why do you ask? Do you not?"

She slowly shook her head, turning so she faced him more. "I don't know. I did. I mean…I always have, but…" She briefly closed her eyes. "I've lost so many. My dad, my mom, my…our…baby and…" She swallowed, trying to say his name. It lodged in her throat.

Lincoln crossed his arms over his chest and leveled his gaze on her. "So what you're wondering is, if God *does* exist, why does he hate you so much?"

She flinched, her eyes watering. Tears dropped from her face. "I just— why do so many good people have to die? What's the point of that? Why does He let it happen?"

He straightened. "What makes you think He lets it happen?" he said slowly. "How do you know He's not crying right along with you?"

She looked away, her throat closing with pain.

"He gave us life. All the rest of it…that's part of living. I don't think He randomly picks people to lose more than others or that He decided He didn't like you so He's making you suffer. I don't think He has any control over any of that. It's all about free will, right? We're given life and what we decide to do with that life and what happens to that life is out of His hands. I could be wrong. I am a lot." He rubbed his head, sighing. "Anyway, that's what I think. Maybe it's stupid."

"No." She crossed the room to him. "It's not stupid. Thank you, Lincoln." She touched his cheek, emotions choking her into silence. She wanted to say more—she thought she should, but she couldn't.

Lincoln stilled, carefully breathing in and out, his hand lifting to hold hers against his face. His silvery eyes stabbed her with their directness, somehow clear even with all the shadows in them. She abruptly backed away, her hand falling from his face. Without speaking, he turned his back to her and returned to washing the dishes.

SARA WAS FALLING into a swirling vortex of misery and darkness. It was sucking her soul away, ripping it from her, and along with it, him. It was agony, having him severed from her. She didn't know herself without him. She'd been so lost before she'd found him and now she was lost again. She already felt it happening—the disappearance of her soul. So she clutched him to her; his image, his voice, the smell of him, and yet he was still taken from her.

She walked through the house in a daze, haunted by him, longing for him, hurting so much she wondered how she was still alive from all the pain. She felt it in the tightness of her chest, she felt it in the pressure that never left her. No matter how hard she fought or tried to stop, it was winning. The abyss was pulling her down, removing everything that made up Sara, and leaving her empty. Hollow.

She was turning into the man she'd thought she'd be with until her last breath was taken, the man that had been her universe, her soul, and was now nothing. He was stolen from her, and with him, she was stolen from herself. He was dead. She was dead. Sara thought maybe she should let it happen. Then they could be nothing together.

The bottle of prescription painkillers mocked her from its perch on the bathroom counter. One week. It had been one week and two days since he'd been buried. Sometimes Sara pictured him waking up, finally, in the ground, trying to breathe, scratching at the lid of the casket, forever trapped. He screamed for her, using his final breath to shout her name, like he had in reality. She had nightmares of it when she slept, which wasn't often. It didn't matter, though, because they followed her, tormented her, even when she was awake. There was no reprieve.

It was so much worse than when he'd been in a coma in the hospital. At least then she could see him, even if he wasn't *him*. Now he was just...gone. It really happened. He really died. She fell to her knees and hung her head, weeping into her hands. She screamed her rage and anguish, slamming her palms to the cold, hard floor and shoving herself to her feet. Shaking and chilled all the way to her marrow, Sara looked up and stared at the bottle with longing. She could end it. The pain, the nightmares, the memories—*all of it. Weak people give up; strong people keep going.* She was weak and she didn't care. If being strong meant suffering, then she'd rather be weak.

"You don't mean that."

"I do," she moaned, covering her face with her hands and leaning her back against the bathroom counter.

"Lincoln needs you."

"No, he doesn't. He's stronger than me."

"Not strong enough to survive the loss of your life. It would crush him."

"And your death didn't?"

"Suicide is a sin."

"In whose eyes?" she demanded.

"In all eyes."

"Just go away," Sara whispered, tucking her legs close to her chest and resting her head on her knees. If she closed her eyes, maybe the voice would go away.

"I can't. Not yet. I need you to live for me, Sara."

She growled, jumping to her feet and whirling around. Grabbing fistfuls of her hair, she shrieked, "*Stop fucking with my head!*" Heart pounding, her whole body a quivering mass of agony, she searched the house for her aggravator, storming through the rooms with closed doors, swinging each one open, mindless with devastation, intent on finding him, anything, *something*, to let her know she wasn't crazy.

"You wouldn't wake up when you could have. You wouldn't come back to me, but you're going to fucking *haunt* me?" Her voice was shrill, unnatural. She was losing it, control was completely slipping away.

She tore into the bedroom, slamming the closet doors open. "Where are you?"

She shoved clothes around on the hangers, knocking shirts and dresses to the floor. Some hit her in the face, landing on her, and Sara retaliated by yanking the clothes from the hangers and tossing them behind her. On and on, her breath leaving her in gasping sobs, she destroyed the perfectly ordered closet.

When Sara spun around to see what she could upheave next, sunlight streamed through the window, landing on the hope chest, making it glow. She dropped to her knees, resting her head on the hard wood, and let the wretched tears take over.

"How could you leave me?" she moaned to the vacant room.

"Sara?"

She froze, wiping her eyes, thinking she was hearing things again.

"Oh, Sara, what are you doing?" Warm hands grabbed her, turned her around. Lincoln's sad eyes slammed into her. "Did you decide to redecorate?"

Sara snorted, it turning into a half-laugh, half-sob.

He pulled her to him, rocking her, making her feel safe and taking the loneliness away. "You're not alone. You don't have to be alone. You can't do this on your own. You don't have to. That's why I'm here."

"You left." She closed her eyes, inhaling his scent, and becoming centered once more.

"Only for a little bit. I came back. I'll always come back." She stiffened in his arms and Lincoln said, "I'm not him. I'll always come back. I promise."

She pulled away, searching his tight-lipped expression, seeing the fierce gleam in his eyes. "You don't know that."

"Yeah. I do. I'm not leaving you. Not ever. Not *ever*." His fingers dug into her shoulders, keeping her anchored to reality. "I swear to you, Sara, ain't nothing taking me away."

It was a lie, but it was a lie she needed to hear. She let herself believe it. *Lincoln needs you*, whispered through her head and she shivered at the truth of it.

"YOU'RE STRONG ENOUGH to get through this."

She shook her head. "I'm not strong. I don't even want to try to be. I'm just...struggling to not want to die, and the thought of living...it really holds no appeal to me. So I *exist*."

"I know you lost your parents and I know you lost a baby. Now Cole." Mason crossed his arms and leaned against the kitchen counter. "You look surprised. You really shouldn't be. Spencer's talked about you and Cole often enough, even before I met you that fateful day at Wyalusing. What I'm saying is...you got through all of that and you can get through this too."

Swallowing, she played with her wedding ring. Her hair was pulled back in a messy ponytail and she'd thrown on an old yellow shirt of his and black leggings. She looked like an oversized bee. Mason had said as much.

"You make it sound so simple."

"Not at all. But it's not unattainable and you act like it is. *That's* what you need to change. The way you think about things. About yourself."

"Don't you think there comes a point when it's all too much? When you cave, give in from all the pain and all the loss? Maybe that's where I'm at."

He smiled. "Nah. If you were at that point, you wouldn't be standing here, talking with me."

"You *make* me," she pointed out.

"Truly? You're going to do me like that?" He looked disappointed in her, but she knew him well enough to know he wasn't, not really. "You could have not answered the door that first Sunday, or even the second one, or even today, but you did. You want help. You want to move on. You just don't know how. But that's part of it, finding out how to handle the things in life you can't change."

"You either know way too much or not enough," she mumbled, rubbing her forehead. She was tired, so tired.

"Have you seen Lincoln lately?"

Her stomach twisted at the mention of his name. "Yes," she answered breathlessly. "Why?"

He shrugged. "No reason. Keep seeing him."

"I don't think he would let me stay away even if I tried," she said dryly, the hint of a smile on her lips.

"Ah, see? In all of this sorrow and pain you feel, you just smiled. You had a reason to smile, and it was Lincoln. That's what it's all about, Sara, finding reasons to smile. It gets easier, it gets less painful, and then it doesn't hurt so much. You don't have to *hurt* to mourn someone. Do you understand what I mean?"

She drew in a shaky breath, briefly closing her eyes as she nodded. "I think so. Yes."

Mason walked to her, grasping her cold hands in his warm ones. "You're strong enough. Know that. *Believe* it." He squeezed her hands before releasing them.

"Why are you so adamant about helping me? It's not like I'm paying you and I know I'm not exactly your idea of fun."

"You remind me of me, only more melodramatic." He winked, moving toward the door.

"*I'm* melodramatic?" she demanded, incredulous.

He paused, his hand on the door handle. "Yes. I think that's what I said, didn't I?" He nodded. "Yes. I did say that. You *define* melodrama, Sara dear. You should have been an actress. See you next week."

Mason had rendered her speechless.

SARA MARKED EACH day off on the calendar next to the refrigerator, wondering when that elusive day would come when she would be healed, when the pain and guilt would be gone. One month. It had been over thirty days since his body was lowered into the ground.

She set the black marker down on the counter, staring at the bold X on January 2nd. Another day down and still no relief. Sara ran a hand through her stringy hair, not even sure when she'd last washed it. She shuffled toward the phone, staring at it. She hadn't heard from Lincoln or seen him in almost a week. Maybe he'd finally given up on her. Maybe he finally blamed her.

She had been waiting, the thought always in her mind, no matter how far away she tried to shove it, that the day would come when he realized everything he'd lost was because of her. It would kill her, losing Lincoln on top of losing her husband. It would take what was left of her life and end it. She swallowed painfully and turned away from the phone. Staring at it wouldn't make it ring. Thinking of him wouldn't make him appear. Just like remembering her husband wouldn't make him alive.

The knock at the door was soft and she almost didn't hear it. She paused, her head tilted, as the faint knock came again. Sara moved toward the door, not sure who it would be, and almost hoping it would be no one. Her nerves came to life at a name that slithered through her mind: *Lincoln.* A glance at the clock showed her it was close to eight, late enough to try to shut the world out.

She hesitated with her hand on the doorknob. She could ignore it, lie down, and pretend no one had ever been on the other side of the front door. Only she couldn't, because she knew who it was. Somehow she could feel him, feel his body heat even with a door between them. Even if he hated her, Sara didn't have the power to ignore Lincoln. She'd rather deal with his loathing than his absence.

And so she opened the door.

Flint-colored eyes set in a face pale with strain stared at her from the shadows of night. It had only been days since she had last seen him, but his cheekbones seemed more prominent, his jaw more angular than square. Stubble covered his jawline and his dark waves were long again, giving him a disheveled look. The death of his brother was physically ravaging him, stripping him down to someone Sara didn't know. Or maybe she did. He was her.

"You look horrible," he said in a gruff voice.

She couldn't get mad. She knew it was true.

"Can I come in?"

She nodded, not moving. Her stomach was churning as she imagined all the hateful words about to leave his lips. One dark eyebrow lifted and Sara flushed, backpedaling into the house to give him room to enter. He inhaled deeply, his eyes trailing over the kitchen to the right and the living room they stood in. She wondered if he saw his brother in the smallest of details, like she did.

He looked at her, his features impassive, shoving his hands into the pockets of his green hooded sweatshirt. Wisconsinite through and through, Lincoln rarely wore a jacket, even on the coldest of days.

"How've you been?" Lincoln muttered something and glanced away. "Don't answer that. Stupid question."

"Are you okay?" she forced out, immediately regretting her words. Of course he wasn't okay.

"No. I'm not okay. You're not either."

She shook her head, looking at the floor.

"My parents left yesterday." Her head jerked up and her eyes searched Lincoln's face. "They wanted to hang around until after Christmas." His mouth turned down. "It was awful. Christmas. My mom cried, like usual. My dad barely said anything. And the whole time, all I could think about, was you. If you even knew it was Christmas. If you even cared. What you were doing. If you were alone. I hated the thought of you being alone."

"It's—it's okay," she whispered, turning toward the couch. She hadn't realized it was Christmas until it was the day after. She was glad she hadn't known. Christmas had always been with the Walker family. A stab of pain in her chest acknowledged that that was no longer the case.

"They don't blame you."

"Don't lie" she said wearily.

"They're just grieving and aren't doing a very good job of it. That's all. I just...I don't want you to think they hate you."

"It doesn't matter."

Lincoln rubbed his head and sighed, casting a bleary-eyed look her way. "It does matter. It matters to me, okay? I hate the thought of you hurting any more than you already are."

"Why?"

His jaw tightened. "Because I—" Lincoln cut himself off, snapping his mouth shut.

"What? What is it?"

He shook his head. "Here. This is for you." He dug into the pocket of his sweatshirt, pulling something blue and twinkling from it.

She took it, her eyes watering as she clutched the angel ornament to her chest. It was smooth and warm from being inside Lincoln's pocket. She tried to say thank you, but her throat was tight with pain.

"Merry Christmas, Sara," he said in a low voice, reaching out to gently touch her cheek.

Sara looked up, wanting to say something, anything, but Lincoln was already leaving, taking his warmth with him. *Don't leave me*, she inwardly pleaded, but said nothing. He wasn't hers to keep. Her fingers tightened on the smooth crystal ornament, holding it to her chest. This was, though. This she could keep.

THE HOUSE WAS a mausoleum—a gravesite for him and their baby and the love they'd had. Sara felt trapped within its walls at the same time she felt strangely safe in the past. But today the walls were closing in on her and she had to escape, just for a little bit, until the outside world became too much and she had to retreat back to the house full of ghosts that somehow felt right when everything else felt wrong.

It was the middle of February and it showed outside. The streets were slush, the yards white with packed snow. She wrapped a heavy scarf around her neck and put on gloves and a coat. She shivered and her breath frosting as she exhaled. It wasn't exactly great weather for a walk, but it didn't matter. The thought of being inside any longer was maddening.

She was numb on the outside like she normally was on the inside. When had the house begun to feel more like a jail than a refuge? He was always on her mind, but something had changed and now it was like everything was distanced from her, distorted. Her thoughts, her feelings, the memories—they all seemed to be someone else's and Sara was watching them on a movie projector. She was a bystander. When had that happened? *Why* had that happened?

She did the usual things, but in a haze of unreality. She bought groceries without seeing people, without remembering if she said a word to anyone while in the store. She drove places, not remembering the drive to them. Sara did what was required of her to survive, but that was all. She'd lost more weight and even she could tell it was to the point of unhealthy. She had no desire to do anything other than what was absolutely necessary. Even that was a chore. It didn't matter what Mason or Spencer or anyone else said to her. Nothing and no one was getting through to her.

Except Lincoln.

He was the one person able to pierce the layer of emotionlessness wrapped tightly around her. When he was near he forced her to feel things, to *live*. Why didn't he just give up on her? *Because you need him and he needs you.* Sara hated that voice. She didn't know if it was hers, or his, or God's, but she wished it would go away.

She'd spent almost as much time with Lincoln as she had her husband; while they were dating, and even later, after they were married. He'd been at their house more than his own. They'd had their own form of communication, riddled with good-natured arguing and sarcasm. He'd been her buddy, the person she laughed with the most, especially since her husband didn't get most of their humor. But she hadn't *needed* him, not like now. She couldn't breathe unless he was with her and that scared her. When had he gone from her husband's brother to her very *air?*

She crossed the street and walked along the shoveled sidewalk, waving at an elderly man when he called out a greeting. Sara didn't really know her neighbors. She'd never been too social, and after everything happened, she'd turned into a recluse. Going out in public made her nauseous. It seemed like everywhere she went people were watching her, judging her. They knew her secrets, they knew what she did. They knew the life she'd indirectly taken.

She lowered her head as she hurried her pace, eyes on her boots as she walked. There was no destination in mind. If there was a literal place that could remove the agony in her soul, or even her soul and somehow heal it before putting it back, that was where she would walk to. She blinked at the edge of the sidewalk, surprised to find herself across the street from the Dollar General store. The parking lot was busy, cars going in and out of it. The building was pale stone with the signature yellow and black Dollar General sign above the door.

"Sara!"

She looked to the left of the store. Gracie, Spencer's girlfriend, waved from where she stood next to a tan Buick. She smiled and beckoned to her. Her legs froze along with the rest of her. When Sara just looked at her, too scared to move, her smile fell from her face and she looked away. When she looked up again, determination was etched into her pretty features. She began to walk. Cold seeped through her clothes as Sara waited with apprehension. Gracie's fiery hair haloed her pretty face, her eyes wide and fixated on her. Her stride was purposeful. She wore a green jacket the same shade as her eyes and jeans.

Gracie stopped before Sara, searching her face for something. She fought the urge to look away. "I'm not going to ask how you're doing because I imagine you're pretty miserable, and frankly, I would be too. I'm not going to give my condolences because I know you're tired of hearing those from people. I'm not even going to judge you for your apparent lack of manners. All I'm going to do is invite you to have a cup of coffee with me. Would you like to do that?"

Sara blinked, not sure what she'd been expecting to hear from her. That had not been it. She didn't know what to say. "I…"

"I'm your friend. Maybe not a close friend, maybe not a friend you've had all that long, but a friend just the same."

Her chest tightened at the honest, earnest look on Gracie's face. Gracie considered her a friend? She blew out a noisy breath. "Sure. Yes. That would be nice."

She smiled. "Great! I'll drive."

"I didn't mean to be rude," Sara told her as they walked.

"I know. I'd be a bitch on wheels in your position. I'd pretty much hate the world. Like I said, I don't judge. I can't imagine how you feel. I won't even try."

She got into the car, feeling awkward. It smelled like cinnamon and yellow Dollar General shopping bags littered the back.

"Timbers okay?"

Sara nodded. The coffee shop had once been a bar that had been renovated into the character-filled establishment it was today. It had vaulted tin ceilings and an eclectic, but stylish collection of furniture. Its coffee was robust and full of flavor—much better than gas station coffee. The drive from the store to the coffee shop was a short one, but even so, it seemed to drag. She didn't know Gracie that well. She didn't know what to say to her. Sara searched her brain for conversation starters and drew a blank. Luckily Gracie seemed to have an overflowing database of information to discuss.

"Spencer has this crazy camping idea for summer," she stated as she pulled the car into an empty parking spot.

"Oh?"

"Yeah. He wants to get everyone together. Lincoln, Mason, you, whoever else, and go to River of Lakes in Bagley for a week. Or maybe just a weekend. You still have your camper?"

"I call it Love Bug. Can you guess why?" His eyes twinkled at her.

Sara looked around the compact, but fairly new camper. The furniture, curtains, and carpet were cream and tan. It had a clean linen smell to it. "It's full of bugs?"

"No. You and I are going to fill it with love."

"So why the bug part? And why do you insist on naming everything?"

He grinned, his pale blue eyes flashing, darkening. "Like Tater and Tot?" He gave her chest a pointed look.

She crossed her arms, rolling her eyes. "Yeah. Like that."

"They're endearments. And bug and love rhyme. A little. Let's break in the couch."

"Let's not." Her body warmed up, a pulse of need forming inside her, silently calling her a liar.

"Do you like it?" he asked, wrapping his arms around her so Sara's back was flush with his hard chest. Her heart began to pound, her palms turned damp with want.

"I do. Let the camping adventures begin," she said, her voice breathless.

"Soon enough. But first..." He spun her around, his lips finding hers, seducing and manipulating them.

"Sara?"

She blinked and looked up. "What?"

Gracie stared at her, her brows drawn quizzically. "Where were you just now?"

Stuck in the past, like almost always. She wordlessly shook her head. "Nowhere."

She turned the key and the engine shut off. "So do you still have it?" At Sara's confused look, she added, "The camper."

Her chest tightened. "Yes. I still have it." He'd surprised her with it one spring day, saying it would be their summer home away from home. They'd camped a lot with the 2008 Mallard. Sara thought if she entered the camper the remembrances would entangle her in their never agains and keep her there forever.

"Awesome. That would be fun, I think." Gracie opened the door and got out.

She couldn't think of the upcoming summer, of months from the day she was currently on. It was hard to get past the present and have any desire to think of the future. She got out of the car and followed Gracie into the coffee shop, the strong scent of it teasing her senses as soon as the door opened. Gracie chattered as they placed their orders and continued when they took their seats at a small table along the wall.

"You and Spencer are doing well?" she asked, searching for something to talk about.

She smiled, her eyes sparkling. "Yes. We can't seem to stay away from one another for too long. It's—Oh, hey! There's Lincoln."

Her head jerked to the side fast, her eyes immediately scanning the inhabitants of the business. Something pulsed through her, something intense and unknown and scary. When her eyes found him, and it didn't take long—seconds, really—the unnamed feeling grew, stole her breath, and forced her pulse into overdrive. His back was to them, broad-shouldered and clad in a brown jacket with an outline of a hammer and the company name on it: Walker Building. Her eyes tripped over him, noting his messy hair and the slight hunch to his shoulders. Even from behind, he looked tired, worn down. She wanted to wrap her arms around him and never let go.

"Lincoln! Over here!"

He turned, his chiseled features drawn. His eyes went from Gracie to Sara and they flashed, darkened, with emotion as they landed on her. His gaze lingered on her, the longer he stared at her the more uncomfortable she became. She shifted in her chair, wanting to look away, but something was keeping her from being able to do so. He finally broke eye contact, grabbing his coffee off the counter.

"What was that?" Gracie asked slowly, eyes fixated on Sara.

With a burning face, she took a sip of her coffee, the temperature scalding. Sara quickly gulped it down, gasping, "What was what?"

"The way he looked at you. It was—I don't know—*intense*."

"It was nothing. I don't know what you're talking about," she mumbled quickly. It wasn't a lie. She had no idea what was or wasn't between them. Nothing. There was nothing. Yet that didn't seem entirely true either.

A chair scraped against the wood floor and Lincoln was beside her, elbows on the table, hands cupping a to-go cup of coffee. The heat of his eyes on her was hotter than the coffee she'd just choked down. She inhaled his scent, felt a sliver of peace wisp its way through her.

"Sworn off the gas station coffee?"

She smiled faintly. "You too, apparently."

"My guts couldn't take it anymore." He turned to Gracie. "How's it going, Gracie?"

"Good. Sara and I were just talking about camping."

"Really? What about it?"

She tucked hair behind her ear as she said, "Spencer wanted to get everyone together to go camping this summer. You up for it?"

Sara glanced at Lincoln out of the corner of her eye, knowing his gaze was on her again. Their eyes collided and broke apart. "You know me. Always up for a good time." Even his voice was exhausted.

"How's work?" she blurted, struggling for normalcy.

"Annoying. Wanna come be annoyed with me?"

Sara gave a short laugh, shaking her head. When he didn't say anything else, she looked at him. "You're serious?"

He shrugged. "Why not? I'm measuring a couple houses this afternoon. You can take notes for me."

"You're measuring houses in the snow?"

"Yep," he said cheerfully. "Best time *ever*."

"You should go, Sara," Gracie urged.

She frowned. "Why?"

"Might be good for you."

"To freeze?"

"To not be home. Alone."

"Come on, Sara, all the cool kids are doing it," Lincoln said quietly, mockingly.

She looked from Gracie's encouraging expression to Lincoln's shuttered one. "Okay." She shrugged. "Why not?"

"We should get together again. Maybe go to a movie or something?"

She stood up at the same time Lincoln did, looking at Gracie. She looked hopeful, her expression twisting something inside her. "I would like that," she answered honestly, emotion closing her throat a little.

Gracie smiled brightly, getting up as well. "Great. I'll call you. Have fun." She waved and walked off, leaving Sara and Lincoln.

"Let's go, partner," he said, slinging an arm around her shoulders and aiming them toward the door. It was probably wrong of her to enjoy the feel of even just his arm around her so much, but she did. It was a little bit of completeness in the broken shards of her life.

When they got to the silver truck, he said one word, "Drive."

She jerked back from the truck, shaking her head. "No," she said faintly. Her hands began to tremble around the to-go cup she held and she stepped away from the curb, closer to the coffee shop.

The streets were busy with traffic, the sounds of tires slugging through wet snow loud in her ears. The coffee taste in her mouth went bitter as Lincoln studied her, a determined set to his jaw.

"The house I have to measure is two miles outside of town," he said softly. He had one hand braced on the hood of the truck, the other held his coffee. His body was angled toward her, as though he thought she could gather strength from him. Usually she could. Not this time.

"I can't. I haven't—I haven't driven with someone with me since... since..." Nausea rolled through her and she swallowed back bile. Her skin was clammy, her heart beating too fast. Sara tossed the coffee cup in a nearby garbage can, the thought of drinking it making her feel worse.

"I know." He nodded, straightening as he set his coffee on the hood of the truck. He moved away from the truck and closer to her. The sidewalk gave her a little height on him so that they were almost at eye level. Still she had to crane her neck back to clearly see his features. Lincoln's face was closed, revealing nothing of what he was feeling. "It's two miles. Not so far."

"It's *too* far. It's too far. What if something happened? I can't. No." Sara shook her head, hair sticking to her mouth. She brushed it away, turning her face from his intense gaze. "What if you got hurt? *No.*"

Lincoln touched her chin with his free hand, the fingers cool and calloused, turning her face toward him. "I'll make you a deal. You drive us to the edge of town and then I'll take over. Okay?"

She exhaled loudly, muttering, "Why do you make me do these things?"

"I make you do them for you," he said, his eyes serious.

"Why?"

Instead of answering, he pulled a set of keys from his pocket and tossed them to her. They jangled as they connected with her hand. She held them to her chest, watching as Lincoln bent his tall frame into the passenger side of the truck. Her stomach flipped as she slowly walked to the driver's side. She paused by the door, touching a hand to her damp forehead. *It's just through town.*

Lincoln stared back, eyebrows lifted, waiting. She inhaled slowly, opening the door to the truck. The interior was still warm, though the truck was off. It smelled like Lincoln, his scent a security blanket as she got behind the wheel. Her hand shook as she tried to put the key in the ignition and she almost dropped the keys. She gritted her teeth, ignoring the horrible swirling sensation in her stomach, and finally got the key in the ignition. She wouldn't look at him—she couldn't. She felt him, felt his eyes on her, felt his confidence in her, and her eyes stung because of it. To have such unwavering faith in her was humbling.

"Is your seatbelt on?" she asked in a low voice, clicking hers into place.

"Of course."

She gave him a look.

"I don't want to get a ticket," he added.

The truck slowly, jerkily, backed out into traffic, her knuckles white from gripping the steering wheel so tightly. She forced air in and out of her lungs, trying to focus on that instead of how hard her heart was pounding. It wasn't such a big deal. Sara drove herself where she needed to go all the time and was okay with it. She knew it was irrational to have such a fear, especially when it was only through Boscobel, but that didn't stop the apprehension from turning her into a trembling mess of nerves. This was different—she wasn't alone this time.

"Remember the day on the river when we went tubing a few summers back?"

Sara shifted the gear from reverse to forward, eyes darting over cars and trucks in the immediate vicinity. "Yes. What about it?" She stalled at the stop sign, not wanting to go at the same time another vehicle intended to. A horn honked and she jumped, glancing in the rearview mirror at the large white truck behind her.

"I think it's your turn to go," he said dryly.

The truck crept forward. Lincoln laughed, which caused her face to burn, but Sara ignored him, concentrating on driving.

"Remember how Cole was determined to knock us off the tube?"

The sun was burning down on them. The inner tube bobbed up and down in the small waves made by other boats, splashing warm brown river water on her. Sara smelled seaweed and sand, the faint scent of fish in the air. She was on her stomach, one arm under Lincoln's hard chest, the other pulled toward her with her and Lincoln's arms crisscrossed over each other's, both hands locked on the handles. Her lifejacket dug into her ribs, slightly raised over her shoulders from the way she was laying.

Water glistened down his face as he turned his head to grin at her, his gray eyes sparkling silver in the sunlight. "Ready?"

Sara glanced up at the white and green pontoon boat and saw Cole watching her with a certain gleam in his crystal blue eyes. His light brown hair was streaked with gold from the sun, his body tanned and toned from working outdoors on an almost daily basis. A slow smile curved his lips, turning her into a fiery ball of need. Her eyes stayed locked with his, promises communicated back and forth. He winked at her.

"You know he's going to try to dump us, don't you?"

"I told him not to." She glanced at Lincoln, saw his eyes were on her.

"He still will. You know that, right?"

She locked her jaw, nodding. "I do."

Cole laughed, raising his bottle of water in a salute and turning to the seat behind the dashboard of the boat.

"Wrap your leg around mine."

She shot him a look.

The boat started, a low purr filling the air.

He rolled his eyes. "I know you'd like any excuse to touch me and I really shouldn't encourage your behavior, but unless you want to take a bath in the not so clean Mississippi, you'll wrap your leg around mine."

The boat started to move, gaining speed as it went.

"Sara." Without thinking, she edged closer to Lincoln, his muscled leg twining around hers. "Hang on," he shouted as the boat slammed forward, the tube gliding along the river after it.

"You can pull over now."

She blinked. Trees and rolling hills loomed ahead. They were almost in the country. Sara shook her head. "No. I'm okay."

"Sure?"

"Yes. Just tell me where to go."

He didn't speak for a time, and then said, "Okay."

"Why'd you bring that up?"

"What?"

"The river. Tubing."

"It was the first thing I could think of to take your mind off driving. Did it help?"

She nodded, taking a slow breath. "Yes."

"Good. Turn left up here. The first house on the right. It's blue. See it?"

"I see it."

"And we're here."

She turned the key and the engine went silent. Her taut nerves were slightly relaxed, her breathing close to normal. She let her hands drop to her lap, staring at the red barn to the left of the house. A chicken darted past as she watched.

"Way to go, Sara Lynne." He gently slugged her shoulder with his fist.

She turned to him. "Why *that* memory?"

He shrugged, but he wouldn't meet her eyes. "I told you—"

"He dumped us. He dumped us and then I hit the water and was sucked down. My lifejacket got stuck on a limb underwater. I couldn't get it loose and I was fighting to undo the lifejacket. I even thought maybe I would die." She was breathing fast, the words stumbling from her lips.

"Sara—"

"You found me. Somehow. You got the lifejacket off me and you pulled me from the water. The boat was coming back around. Your arms were locked around me tight. You had to be tired, but you never let me go. He was frantic, hauling me up first, hugging me, kissing me, telling me he was sorry. You got into the boat, you spun him around, and you punched him in the face. Spencer and Gracie were there, on the boat. Spencer had to pull you off him. You shouted things." She suddenly stopped, a lump in her throat. She couldn't say anymore.

"I told him he was an idiot."

Other things. You said other things too. But all she said was, "Right."

"Ready to work?"

"Lead the way, boss." She followed him as he crossed the yard to get to the house, but her mind was still stuck on that day.

"You knew she didn't want to be dumped! What the fuck were you thinking? She could have drowned. Fucking idiot," Lincoln snapped and turned away from his brother, incalculable rage flashing in his eyes, stiffening his jaw.

Sara watched him storm to the back of the boat, ignoring Gracie when she tried to talk to him. She'd never seen him so furious before— never. Lincoln's red plaid swim trunks were stuck to his legs like another layer of skin, his broad back taut. She was stunned by his reaction. Looking at Cole, she knew he was too.

Cole turned to her, his features tight. "I'm so sorry. I didn't—I was just having some fun. You're okay?"

She wiped water from her face, nodding. The outdoor carpet of the boat prickled her soft flesh and she moved to stand. "I'm okay."

He helped her up, wrapping his arms around her. "If anything had happened to you—"

"It didn't," she broke in, eyes on Lincoln. He stared out at the endless water, profile carved from stone. He'd isolated himself from the rest of them, as though he didn't want their taint of irresponsibility near him, or maybe just his brother's.

"Because of Lincoln."

Something in his tone made her glance at him, the flatness of it maybe. "Are you mad that he saved me?" Incredulity made her voice higher than it usually was.

He scowled, dropping his arms from her. "No."

"Well, that's good, because the alternative was drowning."

The scowl deepened. "I know. It's just...I'm supposed to save you, not him. I'm supposed to be there for you, not him."

"You were too busy having fun driving the boat and trying to dump us," she snapped.

"I know. I'm an ass."

Her anger faded at the look on her husband's face. It was full of self-recrimination.

"And proud."

He nodded somberly. "That too."

She felt herself soften toward him, as she always did. He looked so young, so pitiful. "I still love you."

Cole looked up, flashing a grin brighter than the sun. "Good to know."

"But if I was dead, I wouldn't."

"I'd still love you even if I was dead," he retorted, trailing a hand along her hip and causing her to shiver.

"Okay, you two, it's fun watching you almost make out and everything, but can we get going?" Spencer asked from where he lounged on the seat, Gracie beside him.

Cole moved to captain the boat and Sara walked toward Lincoln. The boat lurched forward as it accelerated and she grabbed the ledge to steady herself. She adjusted the yellow swim shorts as she neared him, tightening the straps of the turquoise bikini top. He didn't look at her as she approached, his cool gaze trained ahead.

"Thank you," she said quietly, sitting in the seat next to him.

Lincoln glanced at her. "I was scared out of mind, when you went under and I couldn't see you. I—"

"Earth to Sara." She ran into Lincoln's chest, his hands steadying her as he set her back. "Sleepwalking again?"

She shrugged, her face burning. *I don't know what I would have done if anything had happened to you.* That's what he'd said. She hadn't wanted to think about what it could have or could not have meant at the time. She wasn't inclined to think about it that much now either. And yet...why had he brought up *that* day? Was he trying to tell her something without telling her something? Was she looking into it too much? Did he want her to remember what he'd said? Did *Lincoln* remember what he'd said?

"Why that day?" she pressed. An icy sharp wind started, tousling her hair around her face. Sara impatiently pushed it behind her ears, not letting him look away.

His neck convulsed as he swallowed. But he didn't look away. Lincoln's eyes were zeroed in on hers, looking at her in a way that made pressure form in her chest. "That was the day things changed for me."

"Meaning?"

He finally looked away, tapping a pad of paper against his thigh. "Do you remember what I said to you, after it happened?"

She wasn't prone to lying. She didn't like being lied to and she didn't like doing it to others. He was so intense, so still as he waited, like what she said mattered astronomically to him. *Lie, Sara. For him. For you. Lie.*

She opened her mouth.

"Yoo hoo! Mr. Walker!" a short, stout lady with graying blonde hair called, waving from the barn entrance. She had on paint-splattered jeans and a blue flannel jacket.

He sucked in a lungful of air, giving Sara a wry glance. "There's the possible client. Better say hello."

He strode toward the middle-aged woman and she followed, frowning at the realization that she didn't think she *could* lie to Lincoln. Not about something that seemed so important to him. Maybe not about anything.

CHAPTER 14

SHE FOUND HIM by the stream at the back of the house. It was still winter, but March was coming and that let Sara think maybe the snow wouldn't linger too much longer. Still, she was glad for her winter coat, gloves, and boots as she made her way through the foot of packed, dirty snow. Spindly trees surrounded them, caked with white. The sun was behind clouds, casting grayness to the air that Sara imagined would resemble her heart if it were to be cut open. Icy, gloomy, numb. Broken. Splintered. Oozing sorrow like a shallow wound oozed blood. Only her wound wasn't shallow—it was bone deep, right into the marrow.

Lincoln's head was uncovered and the gentle breeze played with his dark waves. He wore jeans and a black sweatshirt. His head was down and she wondered what he was thinking about. Her eyes drank in the sight of his strong frame.

"Did you get the job?" she asked his back.

He slowly turned, no surprise showing on his face at her presence. She was sure he'd known she was near—he always seemed to know when she was close. Lincoln's eyes went up the length of her until they connected with hers. Heat swept through her and Sara crossed her arms, looking at the slowly trickling stream of water. Most of it was frozen, but there were patches where water weaved through the ice. Water wasn't solid and yet it found a way around the wall of ice. The concept was interesting. She supposed it could be used as a metaphor for life—not hers, but someone else's.

"Of course I got the job." His tone wasn't arrogant, simply matter-of-fact.

"So...what are you doing?" she asked, not sure what to say. Just his nearness had put a crack in the numbness that was her. Maybe that was why she'd ended up at his place when she'd decided to go for an aimless drive. Lincoln was able to take the emotionlessness away. Maybe he was the water and she was the wall of ice and he was slowly breaking through the numbness to reach her.

"I'm wondering if I have it in me to swim across the massive body of water before me."

The stream was about six feet in width. Sara looked at it and couldn't help the snort of humor. He was taller than it was long. "I don't know. I'm not sure you're up to it."

"Are you saying you doubt my masculinity?"

"You could just lie across it and call it good."

It was his turn to snort. He glanced at her, a smile teasing his lips. "Now what would be the sport in that?"

She took a deep breath of frozen air, the air so cold it was hot inside her mouth and throat. "I remember what you said."

He stiffened beside her, his expression giving away nothing. "What do you mean?"

"On the river, two summers ago, what you said. A few weeks ago you asked me if I remembered. I did. I do."

He stared down at the ground. "It doesn't matter."

"But it must. I mean—you wouldn't have brought it up otherwise, right? *Is* it supposed to mean something? I don't understand the significance of it. Or maybe I do, but I don't want to. Or...not. I don't know what I'm trying to say." She sighed and faced the house.

"It was nothing."

He was lying to her. She turned her head so she could see his profile. He didn't move, he didn't blink, as her eyes perused the side of his face. "It was something," she clipped out.

"You're right. It was, but..." He sighed. "It doesn't matter now."

"Why doesn't it matter?" She waited for his answer, wondering why she was having such a hard time sucking air into her lungs.

His eyes fixated on her. There was something about the endless gray depths of them and the way they *smoldered* like smoke from a fire, mysterious and magnetic. "I'm trying...so hard...to do the honorable thing," Lincoln said, his voice harsh with emotion.

She frowned, moving back a step. "What do you mean?"

"I feel like Jekyll and Hyde most times I'm around you." He studied her face. "You must think I'm crazy."

"Right now, at this moment, yes, I do," she said.

He didn't laugh. He didn't even smile. "When you want something so bad, when you deny yourself it, day after day, for so long, after a while, you ask yourself why you're even doing it. You hope it will fade and die, you hope your secrets won't be revealed, because it wouldn't just kill you if they were, it would kill other people as well. You forsake yourself for the greater good, but sometimes, most times, it's too much of a burden. Do you know what I'm saying?" he asked slowly.

She backed up another step, shaking her head. "No. I don't," she said, her voice cracking.

"Sara." Lincoln moved for her.

She put a hand out. "Don't." She spun around, hurrying up the hill. He called after her in a ragged voice, but she didn't pause, didn't turn around. Tears, warm and unwanted, trickled down her face and her chest hurt so bad she wondered if she could pass out from it. Whatever he was trying to tell her, she didn't want to know it. She *couldn't* know it.

As soon as the door opened, she blurted, "I'm sorry."

He blinked tired eyes at her, moving away from the door to let her enter. "For what?"

"For the other day, when I left. I'm sorry. And also, for now, for showing up so late and unannounced. It's almost ten at night and you probably have to work tomorrow." She was shivering, partly from the cold, partly from the words that had haunted her since the minute Lincoln had spoken them.

He groaned, rubbing his eyes, making them redder than they already were. "Oh my *God*, Sara, I'm so sick of hearing you say that. I don't want your apologies." He turned away from her.

"Then what?" She swallowed, her eyes on his tense back. "What do you want?"

He swung around, locking her in place with his gaze. "Do you really want me to answer that?"

She backpedaled from the power of his gaze, from the ferocity of him. "I don't know what you mean." *Yes, you do.* She felt like she was playing a game and one false move and she would lose. But it wasn't a game—it was their lives.

"You always say that. But I think you do." He cocked his head. "Maybe you just don't want to." He stepped toward her. "I'm sick of this. I'm sick of you blaming yourself, I'm sick of seeing you hurt like you do. I'm sick of pretending, I'm sick of being your buddy when all I want to do is..." He pressed his lips together, shaking his head.

She sucked in fast breaths, her hands opening and closing at her sides. She showed Lincoln her back, his words incomprehensible, the look in his eyes undeniable. Sara closed her eyes against it, but it was burned into her retinas. She couldn't make it unseen. She couldn't remove it from her mind.

"I saw you first," whispered through the air.

She stiffened, her heart immediately beating too fast. She kept her back to him. "What?" came out sounding strangled.

"I saw you first. Only days before he did, but I still saw you first. I was walking in the woods and I saw you along the road. Your hair was in a ponytail and it bounced against your back as you walked. You had on jeans and a pink hooded sweatshirt. The sun made you glow like an angel and something happened in my stomach. It felt like the air was knocked out of me. You stopped to look at some purple flowers, picking one to tuck behind your ear."

He inhaled deeply, his voice ragged when he continued, "The next time I saw you, you were with Cole, and that was that. But I saw you first, Sara. And when I saw you, I knew you were meant for me. I'd never felt like that before and I've never felt like that since. I tried to deny it, I tried to forget you. I hoped every woman I dated would be the one to take the place of you in my heart. Only it never worked. Not even the fact that you were my brother's could make it stop.

"The guilt I felt, have always felt, it's torn me up inside. The anger and resentment I've fought against every day since that first day I saw you with him—at myself, at Cole, at fate. It hurt every time I saw you hug or kiss, because I wanted to be the one doing the hugging and kissing. The way you looked at him...I wanted that for me as well. Wanting my brother's girl, wanting my brother's wife...what kind of horrible person was I? Didn't matter. I kept wanting you."

She was struggling to breathe and nothing was happening. She wanted him to stop, to shut up, to quit saying the words he could never take back, the words that could never be erased once spoken.

"Then the wreck happened and the guilt became too much, because, sometimes, I'd thought about if Cole wasn't around, maybe it would have been you and me. Not that I'd ever wanted anything bad to happen to him, but just, like if he'd moved away, or was married to some other woman. I never would have wanted to happen what did, but sometimes, in the back of my mind, I wondered if I was to blame. Maybe it was my fault, somehow, for wanting the woman I could never have. And the pain of losing him was horrible, agonizing, but the thought of losing you was unbearable.

"The worst thing is...after everything...I still want you," Lincoln ended softly, his voice raw, pained. "I saw you first, but you never saw me. Never have. Not even now."

She closed her eyes. The air shifted behind her and she felt his heat seep into her back and knew he was close. "Don't. Lincoln, I can't hear this," she said, her voice cracking.

"It's already done. I can't stop. I *won't* stop," he said raggedly. She felt the feather light touch of his hand as it brushed hair away from her neck and she shivered. "I'm *done* stopping, Sara. *See* me. *Please.* Just once. Turn around and see me." His hand wrapped around her upper arm and slowly turned her around. She kept her eyes closed, not strong enough to accept what she knew she would see in his eyes.

"Look at me. *Look at me*, Sara," he commanded, his fingers digging into her shoulders.

She mutely shook her head, tears dropping from her eyes and falling down her face. Her heart hurt from the tightening in her chest.

"Look at me," he pleaded.

The entreating note in his voice was too much and she could no longer deny him his request. She finally did. Sara looked at Lincoln. Her eyes drifted over his lowered eyebrows, his intense gray eyes, his straight nose, and stopped on his full lips pressed together. The tightening in her chest and heart deepened. God, he was beautiful. Lincoln was wrong—she saw him. She had for a long time. She just hadn't been able to acknowledge it to herself.

"Cole had it all. Good looks, easy-going manner. He was the well-behaved one, the quiet one, the one that didn't blow a gasket at the slightest provocation. There was the slightly reckless side to him, but nothing too major. He got decent grades and didn't get into too much trouble. I was never jealous though. I never felt less than. He didn't let me. I never wanted what he had.

"Until you." Lincoln's fingers tightened on her arms. "You I wanted. And that was the first and only time I was jealous of Cole. I'm still jealous of him. I'm jealous of my brother, who's dead. How fucking sick is that? I can't stop it though. I can't stop the way I feel about it, about you. He still has you. The only thing, the only person, I ever really wanted, and you're his. Still. Always. You never see me, not even with him gone."

"I see you, Lincoln," she told him softly.

His features tightened, his laser gaze locked on her. "What do you see? Tell me. Tell me *something*."

She opened her mouth, but nothing would come out. Her pulse was racing and she knew if she voiced her thoughts, nothing could go back to the way it used to be. Maybe it couldn't already anyway. Maybe that was done—those people she and Lincoln used to be no longer existed. The way she was now, the person standing before her; that was who she and Lincoln were now, be it good or bad, wrong or right.

Her stomach dipped. "I...I have...feelings for you. I don't know how that happened or when exactly, but it did. I don't even know what they are, but I have them. Do you know how that makes me feel? *Horrible.* I feel like a horrible person. I just know...I can't turn them off and I wish I could and I don't even understand what they are, not really. It scares me. I'm scared." Her eyes burned and her throat tried to close.

He slammed his fingers through his hair, messing the waves up. His eyes were pained, his mouth turned down. "How do you think *I* feel? He is...he was...my *brother*. I've wanted you since the day I met you. *How do you think that makes me feel?* I'm torn up inside, Sara. My insides are ravaged and ruined and *I don't care*. I don't care. All I know is it hurts to look at you and it hurts even more not to. I *need* you. I need you.

"It doesn't matter that he's my brother, it doesn't matter that he is...was...your husband. It doesn't stop me from needing you. I see you when I wake up, I dream of you, I see you in every woman's face and I see you in the sky and even the grass. You're everywhere. You're everything. That's all that matters. You're all that matters. So hate me. Never speak to me again. Doesn't matter. I'll still need you. I'll need you till I take my last breath and I'll need you even after that," he panted, his chest heaving up and down.

"Stop, Lincoln, don't." He was making it worse. She couldn't hear anymore. It hurt. Her heart was breaking, hearing the words pouring from him, hearing the conviction in them. This was wrong—it *had to be* wrong.

But he wouldn't stop. Maybe he couldn't. Lincoln continued, relentless. "All those times I wanted to hold you, all those times I wanted to pull you into my arms and couldn't, not the way I wanted to, not the way you needed me to, but would never admit—it killed me, Sara. It's still killing me. I want you for mine. I want you always. I started to slip up. These last few months...I couldn't stay away. I couldn't pretend anymore. That's why I've been acting so—so *crazy*. It was too much, loving you and not being able to. Every time I saw you, I just wanted to hold you and take your pain away. And I know I did. I know you feel it too. But you don't want to."

"Please," she beseeched, wanting to shut off the sound of his voice, wanting to stop the sinking feeling taking over her. She was falling, fading, suffocating from it all. Her, him, *them*. Words she didn't want to hear, but couldn't *not* hear—it was destroying her. The way she felt, not knowing how she felt, and about her husband's *brother*, it was *agony*.

Lincoln reached for her, his hands cupping her cheeks. "I want you, Sara. I've always wanted you. Damaged, broken, irrevocably ruined, I still want you. It doesn't matter to me. *I don't care.* I'll always want you. No matter what. No matter where you are. If you're with me or not, I'll want you. It's not ever going away. Maybe Cole was it for you, maybe none of this matters, and I'm tearing out my soul for you for no reason, but...you were it for me. You're it for *me.* Always have been."

She stared at him, seeing how unhinged he was, her breath leaving her much too quickly when he raised his intense eyes to hers, not once removing his gaze from her face as the minutes slowly ticked by. His words washed over her, seeped into her, warmed her, and made the numbness go away. She blinked her eyes against tears, feeling so many conflicting emotions she had no control over. It didn't matter what she wanted to feel or not feel—she felt what she did, and what Sara felt scared her.

Look away. Leave. Before it's too late. She couldn't stop herself when she lifted a hand and traced the sharp angle of his cheekbone. He went still, inhaling sharply. For once his face didn't try to replace Lincoln's. It was just Lincoln she saw. He was all there was now. She let her hand drop and turned away.

"You're leaving." It wasn't a question.

Sara paused, eyes on the door. "I have to."

"Why?"

Her face tried to crumple and she locked her jaw to thwart it. "Because I finally see you," she whispered.

IN THE THREE weeks since the confrontation between them, Lincoln had kept his distance. They'd had stuttering phone conversations full of long pauses until eventually they'd not even bothered. There was a strain on Sara that had little to do with her husband's death and more to do with the chasm of confusing emotions between her and Lincoln. How had it all gotten so messed up? Everything had fit, everything had been complete before the wreck, before she'd lost her husband. Now there were just hundreds of puzzle pieces and nowhere to put them.

Lincoln was at her house now. He'd stopped on his way home from work. Her eyes kept going to him across the table, but words failed her. She didn't know what to say. Sara wanted to hug him, to touch her cheek to his, to feel his arms around her and she also wanted to never see him again.

He sighed, tapping his fingers on the table. "This is awkward."

"A little." She pushed the cold cup of coffee between her hands.

He ran his fingers through his hair, hanging his head. "We fought about it once."

"What?"

"You." He looked up, piercing her with his powerful gaze.

"What do you mean? I don't understand." *Liar, Sara.*

"I think you do. I think you know what I mean. We fought about you, right before the wedding. Cole suspected my feelings for you. He confronted me. I didn't admit it. I didn't deny it. He knew."

"What did he say?"

"He didn't *say* anything. He punched me. He punched me in the face and said you were his. He said he'd seen you first, like that was enough to claim you as his." Lincoln gave a bitter laugh. "Only he hadn't. I told him that too. I was so angry, so sick of acting like it didn't kill me every time I saw you together. I guess I told him that because I was hurting, knowing you were about to be married. I was desperate and I wanted Cole to hurt like I was hurting. It was a shitty thing to do.

"His eyes...they dimmed a little. He didn't say anything. He just left. I felt like an ass and I suppose I should have. We never talked about it again. I don't know why I'm even bringing it up. I guess, I don't know..." He shook his head. "I don't know why I'm telling you this."

"That was a mean thing to do," she choked out.

"I suppose I never should have said anything, but—" Lincoln rubbed his eyes, his face tense with strain. "It was the one thing I had over him. That I saw you first. It was all I had and when he hit me, I just, I had to retaliate. Immature. Childish. I know."

She stared at him, not really seeing him, but a memory.

Sara smiled at his reflection in the mirror as he came up behind her. "Ready to go?" She set the brush down, the smile leaving her lips as she took in his expression. She turned to face him. "What's wrong?"

Cole averted his face as he played with the brush on the bathroom sink. "Do you...do you have any doubts?"

"What do you mean?" she whispered, dread forming inside her.

He rubbed his jaw, still not looking at her. "About us. The wedding's coming up—"

"The wedding's in two days," she interrupted shrilly.

"Yeah. I just...do you? I have to know. Do you have any doubts?"

Her stomach dropped. "What? No. Never. Do you?" Her pulse tripped as she choked the words out. If he doubted his love for her, she wouldn't be able to take it.

"No. Of course not. I love you. I love you more than I've ever loved anything or anyone. I just...I wanna make sure I'm it for you too." He lifted his head, showing his distraught in the eyes that were a darker blue than they normally were. His jaw was tight, his lips pressed together.

"You're it for me too, Cole," she vowed, grabbing his dry, calloused hands and kissing the backs of them.

"Sure?"

"Positive."

The troubled look faded and a grin captured his lips. "Better be. We got a wedding coming up." He grabbed her and spun her around the small bathroom, knocking stuff over and making her laugh, which made him laugh.

Sara fisted her hands, staring at him. "You made him doubt himself. You made him doubt me. Why did you have to tell him that?"

Lincoln gritted his teeth. "I never gave him any reason to think I cared about you more than...more than I should have, but he thought it, knew it, anyway. I didn't say anything until he punched me. I told you that. And if he had doubts, I didn't put them there."

"What are you saying? That he had doubts on his own about marrying me?" she whispered, her chest squeezing painfully.

"You think that's what I'm doing?" His eyes flashed as he shot to his feet and advanced on her. "You think I'm trying to make you feel like shit? So what, I feel good or something? You really think I'd do that?"

"That's what you're doing."

"It's *not* what I'm doing!" He loomed over her, his face close to hers. "What I'm *doing*...what I'm doing...I don't know what I'm doing." He hung his head, his hair tickling her cheek.

She sucked in air through her lungs, but it was never enough. She was struggling. Her heart pounded with his proximity. Her body responded to him whether she wanted it to or not. She didn't *want* it to. She didn't want to feel about him the way she did. Especially now, at this moment, when he was saying what he was saying.

"I just want you to know that he wasn't your only chance at happiness, that he wasn't the only man you can love. I just want...I just want you to admit you care about me. *Something.* I want something from you, Sara, and I'm getting nothing."

You have more of me than you know. She couldn't tell him that. It was true, but she couldn't say the words. As he stared down at her, the pull of him was too powerful, hypnotic. She didn't understand why a yearning was forming inside her, pulsating with need, longing for something, for *Lincoln.* Sara's eyes remained locked with his as she angled her face up. His brows lowered, his breathing quickened.

What are you doing? something inside her screamed and she leaned back in her chair, shaking and unnerved. "I think...maybe..."

He straightened, his facial expression empty. He crossed to the front door. "Yeah. Take care, Sara," he said as he opened the door, but there was a hint of mockery to it.

HE HADN'T BEEN perfect. He'd been a little too prideful at times, and even somewhat selfish, but she had loved him anyway. He'd been her husband, her world, and she'd loved him. And now—She inhaled deeply, briefly closing her eyes—now there was pain and loss where the love had been. Lincoln had no right to point out his flaws to her, as if she hadn't already known them, as if she would forget them.

When Sara thought of Lincoln, her insides knotted uncomfortably and she felt a little sick. It made her think of him—her husband—less, and that brought relief and guilt with the realization. Most days she felt emotionless, especially when her thoughts went to him. There was just...a void where he was supposed to be and that hurt the most. It was as if all the grief she'd had stored up for him had evaporated or been buried with him to be replaced with nothing.

She wanted to hate Lincoln for making her feel when that was the last thing she wanted. The numbness faded when he was near. He brought life back to her, and it was painful and stinging like a limb coming awake after going to sleep from disuse. Sara hung her head as she leaned against the kitchen sink, her hands gripping the edges of it. If God was really around, she'd like to ask Him why. She'd like to ask Him why about a lot of things, but most prominent in her mind was: why her? She was ungrateful, unworthy of the life she had. If she could give it back to her husband she would. *Too late. It's too late for that.*

"Are you here?" someone asked. It took a moment for Sara to realize that the unfamiliar voice was hers—high and breathless and distorted.

She slowly turned around, wondering what she would see, wondering what she would hear. It was her kitchen, same as it should be. The air didn't shift, no image produced itself, and there was no disembodied voice. There was no one. It made her sad, which she realized was probably not a good sign. Pretty soon she'd be having full conversations with inanimate objects.

The pull to leave the house was profound. Sara quickly washed the plate and cup from her supper. The peanut butter and honey toast and milk had been tasteless, but it had reduced the gnawing sensation in her stomach. She tugged on a coat and stood before the closed front door, thinking of the painting of the blue door the color of his eyes. Her hand trembled as it reached for the doorknob. She already knew where she would go. Something in him called to her.

She opened the door, icy air brushing over her as she stepped outside. The month was April, but the nights said it was still January in temperature. It was dark out, sporadic streetlamps adding a hazy glow to the houses and not completely thawed ground, giving it a surreal look. She hurried to the car and started it up, quickly pulling the car out of the driveway.

Days, sometimes weeks, went by without them speaking, but it always became too much. There was a point, without fail, when it turned unbearable for Sara to continue to keep her distance from Lincoln, and she knew it was the same for him when he abruptly appeared at her house, surly and confrontational, but close-mouthed about that day he'd changed everything with his confession.

She didn't know what they were doing to each other. It was like they tried to stay away from each other, and then they couldn't stay away any longer. And his words—those words Lincoln had spoken to her—they haunted her, made her hot and cold at the same time, caused her heart to race, and filled her with fear so intense she tasted it in the bitterness on her tongue. Why had he *said* those things to her?

Because they're true. Sara swallowed painfully, eyes on the darkened house. It was obvious he wasn't home. The truck wasn't out front. Not a light was on in the house. She glanced at the clock on the dash. It was after eight.

She shivered in the cold car, ready to turn around and head back home when she saw something in the window. At first she thought it was merely the Christmas lights on the Charlie Brown Christmas tree twinkling, but no, it was a shape, large and masculine. And it was outside on the deck. That's what had caught her attention; the lights had blinked out for a moment when the figure shifted. She had the passing thought that it was odd that the Christmas tree was still up when it was April, but it disappeared as soon as it formed.

Apprehension followed her as she got out of the car, looming over her in a dark mass of unease. Why was he outside, in the dark? Had something happened to him? Pressure built in her chest at the thought, hurrying her steps.

"Lincoln?" she called as she walked up the deck stairs, her tennis shoes thudding on the wood as she went. She jerked to a stop, blinking at the murky form before her. Her voice was slightly breathless as she asked, "What are you doing? Are you okay?"

He lifted his head, his features in shadow. "Define okay."

"Are you injured? Do you need to go to the doctor?" Sara took a step closer to him, her heart beating a little too fast.

"Nope. Must be *okay*. What are your thoughts on alcohol?" he asked evenly.

"What?" she asked, dumbfounded by such a question.

He sat back in the chair, clanking something on the table next to him. She squinted her eyes at the clear bottle that looked disturbingly empty and then looked at him again. He wore a white tee shirt that glowed in the dark and jeans. He had to be cold, but he was strangely still.

"Are you *drunk*?"

"What does that mean? *Drunk?* What signifies one as drunk? Slurring of words? Imbalance? Large consumptions of alcohol? If so, I am one for three." He smirked. She didn't know how she knew he was smirking with it being so dark out, but she did. It was in his voice, slightly mocking and low. "You didn't answer me."

She frowned at him, crossing her arms. "What are my thoughts on alcohol? It's okay. In moderation. I think you overachieved on the whole moderation thing."

"I moderate. I moderate my hand going up to my mouth and my hand going back to my lap. Tell me that isn't moderation."

"Why are you doing this?"

"Doing what?"

She gestured toward the bottle. "This. Drinking. You don't drink."

"Clearly...I do." Lincoln grabbed the bottle and tipped it up to his lips, tilting his head back to finish it off.

She stared at him, knowing he was hurting and she was hurting because of it. "You don't have to do this."

He stood, carefully and slowly. "Yes. I do. I'm drinking my sorrows away. Isn't that what people do?"

"Not you."

"Not *usually*," he corrected, leaning his hips against the wood railing of the deck and crossing his arms.

Sara's arms dropped to her sides. A burning need began inside her—no, that wasn't true—the burning need *already* inside her grew. Her arms ached to wrap around him, her heart pounded at the thought of him being close to her. Lincoln was too far away; physically and mentally. She wanted to bring him back to her, but she didn't have the right.

"I never was a big drinker. I think I've found the error of my ways."

"Going to turn into an alcoholic now, are you?" she asked quietly, her stomach knotting. Everything was wrong—his words, his behavior. None of it was Lincoln.

"Why not? What have I got to lose?" His eyes, previously hidden in the dark, sparked with silver fire as they trailed up and down her face. *Not you*, those eyes said.

Her skin chilled more than it already was and she rubbed her arms. "Lincoln, this isn't you."

"Do you know the term 'broken record'?" he softly mocked.

Her face flushed. "Yes. I do," she said stiffly. "Are you implying something?"

"I don't think *implying* is necessary. It's pretty obvious. You've been saying the same things over and over since you got here. By the way, *why* are you here?"

"I wanted to check on you," she said, sounding lame and *feeling* lame. *I miss you. I need you.*

"Well, here I am." He lifted his arms out, his movement raising his shirt and exposing his hard stomach. "You did your civic duty. You're not obligated to hover. I'm a big boy."

"Lincoln, what you said—"

"Which time?" he interrupted.

She walked over to him, close enough to feel his heat, close enough to smell the undetectable vodka scent. It was sharp, like frozen air, or ice. Not really a scent of anything, but different from Lincoln's normal citrus scent. It didn't belong on him.

"About your feelings for me..." Sara trailed off, not knowing how to continue.

"I can't do this anymore," he said softly, halting her from taking another step or speaking another word. "I was an idiot to say anything. I was an idiot to think it would matter. I was an idiot to think it would change anything, make any difference. I was an idiot to think maybe you had the same feelings for me I have for you. It was wrong of me. Cole is my brother. I never should have—anyway...forget it. Pretend I never said it, any of it."

She tried to breathe, but it was stolen from her with the weight of his words. Pain pierced her heart, welled inside it, and broke it. "What?" she dumbly asked.

He turned his head away and she could see his jaw clench and unclench. "I don't know why I thought anything I said would matter.

You're still in love with my brother. Maybe you always will be. Maybe that's the way it's supposed to be. I'm going to leave you alone now, Sara." He looked at her then and her stomach dipped from the force of his gaze no darkness could hide. "My first mistake was thinking I could pretend I didn't feel the way I do about you, my second mistake was thinking things could go back to the way they were after I told you how I feel, but...they can't. I see you and I'm just, I'm so *angry* and I hurt and..."

Lincoln ran a hand through his hair, causing it to stick up in spots. Her fingers itched to smooth it down. "Or maybe my first mistake was letting myself fall in love with you. Not that I had any choice, not really." He exhaled loudly. "Forget about me. Forget what I said. I don't think you can move on with me bothering you, which is what you need to do. So I won't. I'll stay away." His throat worked and he said in a voice that sounded like gravel, "You should go."

She didn't want to go. Sara wanted to enfold him in her arms and make his sorrow go away, but what he wanted, what he was asking for; she couldn't give it to him. Not now. Maybe not ever. So she left, leaving a piece of her behind with Lincoln. The more time she spent with him, the more he took of her. Pretty soon there would be nothing left of her— it would all be with Lincoln. That thought scared her, hurried her feet as she made her way to the car.

CHAPTER 15

SARA PUT THE car in park and turned the key. The engine went silent. She stared at the log-sided building with apprehension. The house was a house that held memories and pain and love. It held Lincoln too. Her pulse tripped and her heart raced, making her dizzy.

It had been two weeks and one day since she'd last seen Lincoln, and every day she'd picked up the phone to call him and had instead hung it back up. Sara was a mess. Her thoughts, her feelings...she didn't even know if what she felt was real. That was what bothered her the most. What if he was the replacement brother? What if none of it was real and one day she would realize it? She'd end up hurting Lincoln and that thought killed her. It literally made her chest ache. She didn't even know what she felt for Lincoln. It was all jumbled together and indiscernible. She only knew she thought of him every day and there was hollowness inside her the sight of him could fill.

She quietly knocked on the door. His truck was parked in the driveway so she knew he was home. She waited and when he didn't answer, she let herself in. The scent of coffee lingered. It was silent in the house and no lights were on, casting grayness to everything in the house. Her stomach kept turning over. She didn't know if Lincoln would be happy to see her or not, but it had been too long. She needed to see him.

The straggly Christmas tree caught her eye. There was a twinge in her chest at the sight of it with the ornaments and white lights she and Lincoln had put on it. She couldn't believe he had left it up for so long or that it was still alive. Her stride was awkward, hesitant, as she made her way up the stairs. To the right was Lincoln's bedroom. The door was open. Her insides jumbled at the sight of him. Longing hit her and she briefly closed her eyes against it.

The room was medium-sized with wood floors and walls. A black comforter covered the bed and framed pictures of outdoor scenes covered the walls. There her painting was—above the bed like he's said—a forest of trees in browns and greens. She wondered how often Lincoln looked at it, wondered if he looked at it to feel closer to her.

The room carried Lincoln's scent and that of laundry detergent. She shivered though it was warm in the room. Sara stared at his broad back as he folded a shirt and put it in a dresser drawer, her stomach swirling as she waited for him to notice her. It didn't take long. She had never realized before how he always seemed to know when she was near before anyone else did.

He paused, glancing over his shoulder. "Why are you here?"

Those magnetic eyes locked on hers, causing her insides to quiver. They were dark with an unnamable emotion. Why was she there? Because she couldn't stay away. Sara opened her mouth, only the sound of her hurried breath leaving her, faint and raspy. Words failed her.

"What is it? What do you want?"

"I..." she trailed off, not sure how to voice what it was she wanted.

"You told me to leave you alone. So I am. Why are you here?" he repeated, enunciating each word slowly, as though to make sure they registered in her head.

What did she say? Sara didn't know what to say. She didn't know why she was there—she only knew she couldn't stay away any longer.

"I didn't—I didn't say that."

"You did. You said it when you didn't call me, when you didn't come here, when you said nothing. When you left without even a goodbye. You told me to leave you alone without saying a single word. So...what do you want?"

Their eyes connected and she couldn't breathe. Lincoln had made it easier for her to breathe since her world had fallen apart not once, but twice. This time, though, he made it impossible to. There was heat in his flint-colored eyes and in the tense set of his jaw. She pushed everything from her mind, all thoughts, anything that could remind her of the past, of what used to be, of all she'd lost and would never have again.

Instead she thought of what she had now.

"Make it go away. I need you. *Please*. Make it all go away," she whispered, her eyes pleading, but her head angled proudly.

Lincoln stared at her, a noticeable tick in his jaw. His shoulders were slightly hunched and his face went completely devoid of expression. She thought he was going to turn away, reject her. Her heart ached at the thought. She would die if he did. She wouldn't recover from the rebuff, not at this moment, not when she needed someone the most. Him—Sara needed *him*. She told him with her eyes what she would never be able to say with her lips.

With a soft curse he reached for her, his muscled body slamming into hers, shooting sensations through her, forcing her body to life. His grip was tight, suffocating, and she wanted it to smother it all away, kill the remorse and pain, make it no longer exist. Maybe for this one moment it was possible. Lincoln needed her as much as Sara needed him. She knew by the way his heart pounded against her chest, she could tell by his grip that clung to her as much as it held her. Who was saving whom? Maybe they were saving each other.

She entwined her fingers in his silky hair and jerked his head toward hers, his chest heaving against hers as their lips ensnared one another's. Her legs went weak when he moaned low in his throat. His hands on her, rough and warm, up and down her back, squeezing her outer thighs, made her weak with longing. Lincoln spun them around and the back of her legs hit the bed. They fell onto it, their lips still locked. His mouth was gifted, tugging and sucking and loving hers. So long. It had been so long.

His weight was heavy and welcomed. She sighed against his lips at the feel of it. His hardness fit with all the soft parts of her and she let go. Sara left her reality to cherish this moment, to revel in all that was Lincoln. His unshaven jaw chafed her neck as he teased her sensitive skin with his lips and teeth.

There was no room for her husband here and that's how it had to be. That's how she wanted it to be. She'd hate herself later. There was no time for it now. It felt *right* with Lincoln. How could it feel so right?

He pulled back just far enough to question her with his eyes. If he asked her if she wanted him to stop, if he looked at her like that too long, she'd lose her courage. She'd leave. Sara would forsake this moment of reprieve to wither away in the suffering that followed her everywhere.

"Don't do that," she whispered, shaking her head.

She reached for the hem of his shirt and tugged. Lincoln let her, helping to get it over his head. He tossed it aside. His gaze never left hers and the intensity in it made her stomach swoop and her mouth go dry. Her insides warmed and melted as she rubbed her palms down the front of his sculpted chest and defined abdomen, satisfaction and a sense of power surging through her when his skin pebbled and he sucked in a sharp breath. His body replaced the one committed to memory, his flint-colored eyes took over the blue, and Sara let it happen. She lost herself in him and found a piece of herself at the same time. It was only a tiny, small piece, but it was something she hadn't been sure would ever return to her.

"You're so beautiful," he whispered roughly, caressing the side of her face. She turned her face to his palm and kissed it, surprising herself at the tenderness she felt for Lincoln. When had it happened?

"Love me, Lincoln," she told him.

He gently pulled her top over her head and put his cheek to hers. "I already do."

Not what I meant, she thought as her chest constricted, but he was already moving them up the bed, into the middle of it, and Sara let his declaration fade from her mind as sensations took over. His eyes were so dark with feeling they almost looked black. All thought left her at the force of his expression. It was strong enough to debilitate any she may have had.

His fingers trailed along her skin, his lips following after them. Shivers went over her, goose bumps rising on her flesh. Sara's breathing turned fast, gasping, as he hurriedly removed the rest of her clothes, his actions jerky, frenzied. His next move was at complete odds with the previous. He went still, silent. He stared down at her, his eyes worshiping, his features tight with an emotion unnamable. It was hot, feral, and possessive. And something else.

Lincoln studied her body and face like he would die if he didn't, like she was his air and he was fighting for her, or maybe like he knew he'd never see her again after today and he'd forget what she looked like over time so he had to memorize each part of her and keep it alive in his mind forever. That look ruined her, altered her, and changed everything she'd thought she'd known. She was reborn in Lincoln's eyes, and if only for a short amount of time, at least it was hers to have.

He didn't have to say anything. Sara was burned, singed, from the way he looked at her. Then he spoke. "I need you," he panted, swallowing hard. She knew. She had seen it in his eyes. She needed him as well.

Her eyes must have said so. Lincoln groaned and gathered her against his chest. His heart thundered there, arousing her more. The feel of his skin on hers was euphoric. Sara was whole in his arms. He only released her to quickly shed his clothes, and when he knelt before her, proud and unapologetic, she was undone. She didn't care if it was right or wrong; she only knew it was necessary. For her, for him, for their souls.

Their bodies were slick with sweat, hot. Her heart pounded and she simultaneously felt weak and strong. Sara's and Lincoln's bodies met and connected in a way she had only experienced once before. *Don't think about it*, she told herself. She focused on him instead—the way his breath hitched, the fire in his eyes, the feel of him inside her, how his body moved with hers, and that fleeting interval when they both were enraptured and as one.

That moment was perfection—that moment when their human bodies worked magic. Sara wanted it to never go away. That moment when Lincoln looked at her like she was everything. Too soon reality came back, crashing around her, turning something meant to be beautiful into something ugly. Shame, fierce and inescapable, burned through her cheeks.

When she tried to pull away, Lincoln's arms stiffened around her. He turned them so his body covered hers, his arms bracing either side of her and raising himself up to be at eye level with her. His lips thinned when he took in her expression. "Don't look like that."

"Like what?" she whispered, turning hollow inside.

"Like that was a mistake," he ground out, his jaw clenched.

The life that had flared up in her disintegrated, leaving her lost and weak and shattered again. She closed her eyes, trying to forget what she'd just done. It reared up, black and glaring with accusation. An instant of completeness for endless regret. Had it been worth it? She began to cry; silent streams of grief fell from her eyes. Lincoln moved so that he was on his back with one arm holding her against him. Sara wanted to let him hold her, she wanted to let him take it all away, and because of that, she had to go.

"Let me go, Lincoln," she quietly told him, staring at the ceiling. Even as she told herself to pull away, Sara felt her fingers flex into his muscled side. It was an unconscious action, but not missed by her.

"Never," he vowed, tightening his hold on her.

The tears fell harder, sliding from her face to his chest. "I need to go."

Cursing, he released her. "Why?"

"Because..." She sat up, holding the blanket against her nakedness.

"Because this was wrong, a mistake, and you regret it? Is that why?" Lincoln pulled himself into a sitting position. "It wasn't, Sara. You know that. It was *right*. And that's why you're scared."

"I can't...I can't think about this right now." Sara moved from the bed, clutching the blanket to her as she searched for her discarded clothes. She'd betrayed him. She'd betrayed their love. Sara was hunched over, staring at her pale blue shirt, when the anguish mounted and became too much. She went to her knees, sobbing.

"Dammit, Sara, stop this," Lincoln pleaded, tugging on his boxers and going to his knees before her. "*Stop this*. When are you going to stop hating yourself so much?" He grabbed her forearms and held them tightly, forcing them down when she went to cover her face. "Don't hide from me, and don't run away. *Please*."

She stared at him, wishing his image would blur and disappear, but it didn't. Lincoln stared back, his features fierce and immovable. He wasn't going anywhere. But she'd thought the same of her husband, hadn't she? Her soul shriveled, died a little more, at the realization.

"I can't stand this emptiness inside me anymore when you're gone," he said raggedly.

"I need to go," she repeated, softly but firmly. That much she knew. Sara didn't know a lot of things at the moment, but she knew that.

She hurriedly gathered up her clothes and tugged them on, feeling his eyes burning into her the whole time, speaking so loudly her ears rang, telling her all his thoughts and feelings with just the heat of his gaze. It didn't matter what he was saying or thinking or feeling, or even not saying. Sara couldn't deal with it. In the quiet it was so loud.

When she was almost out the bedroom door, his words stopped her. "You're still living, Sara."

She took a shaky breath, her chest squeezing and squeezing until she thought it would explode. "Maybe I shouldn't be."

The air crackled with his angry strides and then he was yanking her around, glaring down into her face. "You don't get to die with him. *I won't let you.*"

"How do you know...I already didn't?" she choked out, spinning around and running down the stairs, trying to run from that stricken look she'd glimpsed on his face, trying to run from the past, from Lincoln, even from him.

THE PAST LIVED in the closed doors of the house, in the house itself. She knew that. She knew what she had to do, though the thought of it made her palms sweaty and her heart race. Sara stared at the door to the nursery, just looking at it making the air thick, stifling, making it hard for her to draw air into her lungs.

Sara opened the door, sorrow hitting her immediately at the lingering scent of a little life taken too soon. Baby powder and lotion. She trailed a hand along the dresser, touching a pale green stuffed horse. At first she'd thought it was a mistake. It had been impossible to go from one minute of joy with a soul blossoming inside her to unbelievable emptiness when it was taken away. It hadn't made sense. She'd forget at times, touching her slightly rounded stomach that hadn't yet returned to its normal flatness.

He'd watched her, hurting for her, for him, for their child. The pain in his eyes mirrored Sara's. It had been a dark time in their marriage; a time when if they hadn't fought to keep it, their marriage could have been lost. She gathered the toy in her arms and pressed her cheek to its softness. She'd wondered if God hated her. She'd wondered what she'd done to upset Him so much to take her baby's life. The sight of babies and children had caused grief so strong she couldn't function. Pregnant women repelled her; Sara had loathed the sight of them. She'd thought of all the children with parents that were cruel and abusive to them and wondered why they were allowed lives they didn't want, didn't appreciate, and she, who wanted nothing but to love a little piece of her and her husband, was denied.

They'd gotten through it. Eventually it didn't hurt so much; eventually she could operate without the horrible ache. She'd never gotten over it, not completely, but she'd had to accept it. Sara didn't think a mother ever did get over it. As soon as that life had been inside her, it had been a part of her and always would be. The hollowness never really went away; even now it was with her, reminding her of the life not given a chance to live.

Sara inhaled slowly, setting the toy down. She blinked her burning eyes and picked up the stack of boxes, crying as she boxed up all that was left of her baby she'd never been able to hold. Clothes, toys, knickknacks; those were what she had left of her baby and Sara had to part with them.

"People you love aren't defined by objects, Sara, but by the place they hold in your heart."

She absently nodded, a surge of courage pulsating through her, making her task a little more bearable. The voice sporadically popped up whenever she seemed to need to hear it the most. She almost didn't notice it anymore. It was ingrained in her; an unknown embodiment of strength, or maybe it was simply her conscience. Didn't matter.

The next room was the bedroom. It hurt to open the doors and let it all escape; all the emotions she'd wanted to keep bottled up to never forget, but she had to do it. She knew she did. If Sara didn't, she'd be stuck for the rest of her life; living in a past that would remain evasive. If she didn't, she would die on the inside, like she'd feared she already was. Lincoln had shown her she wasn't. A small part of her resented him for that, while the other rejoiced in it. She closed her eyes at the thought of him; her emotions a torrent of confusion and guilt and longing where he was concerned. She tried not to think of him, but even when she shoved him away, she still felt him—in her heart, on her skin, everywhere.

Sara grabbed the pillow and blanket from the couch and put them on a shelf in the bedroom closet. It was cleansing, cathartic, and sad all at the same time. She stared at the bed, dismayed to find herself thinking of

Lincoln and him both. They both couldn't be in her heart, could they? She covered her face, remembering the smell and feel of Lincoln against her, yearning for him. When she thought of her husband, it was with overwhelming grief and guilt. How could she let another man touch her, his *brother*, when she was supposed to love *him*?

She hesitantly sat on the bed, running a hand over the cool fabric of the blanket, despondency dragging her down. Sara didn't know what was right and wrong to feel; it felt like a betrayal to her husband at the same time it felt...right.

"Till death do us part. You know the drill."

"Is that supposed to make me feel better?" Sara whispered.

The air around her faintly laughed, gruff and masculine. "Nah. I'm just letting you know, in case you didn't, *I'm dead*."

Inhaling sharply, she looked around the room, seeing nothing unusual. It was just a room; a room alive with memories, but still, just a room. She rubbed her forehead, shaken. She dropped her hands, determination jutting her jaw. She stiffly lay down on the bed, clasping her hands over her stomach, and forced her eyes to close. She hadn't slept in the bed since he'd left. But she was going to now. Sara relaxed her breaths until they became deep, even, and she slept the dreamless sleep of an exhausted soul.

CHAPTER 16

THE GARAGE WAS exactly as he'd left it. The blue Dodge took up half the white-walled building. Tools littered the workbench. Sara's eyes were gritty, stinging, as they swept over the room he'd spent hours a day in, tinkering with his endless projects. His tool belt hung on the wall by the door. It was a cooler day out and it seeped into the garage and into her, causing her to shiver though she wore his hooded black sweatshirt.

She fiddled with the radio near the small refrigerator, finding a country station, her lips unconsciously curving up at the Tim McGraw song. He'd loved Tim McGraw. *Remember him before the accident. Remember him with joy, not tears.* That was her motto. Sara was trying to smile instead of cry.

Most times she failed, but sometimes, like now, she could remember the love they'd shared before he'd been taken from her instead of the pain she'd lived with in place of him since the accident. She could remember him and not crumble. The hardest feat, the one she hadn't been able to overcome yet, was saying his name, thinking his name. It was beyond her at this point.

You don't have to hurt *to mourn someone,* Mason had said. It made sense, it really did, but it was still too soon for her. She didn't think it was improbable and that was an improvement.

He'd been gone over half a year now, though really he'd been gone a lot longer. It had been close to two years since the wreck. It didn't seem possible that it had been so long ago, and yet, she'd only said goodbye a short six months ago.

Tim crooned about remembering him after he was gone, causing chills to go up and down Sara's arms. The tears came then and that was no surprise, but the surprise was it didn't hurt quite as much as it usually did. There was hollowness inside where her love for him had once been. It saddened her that that was what their love had been torn down to.

With a deep sigh, she wiped her eyes with the sleeve of her shirt and pushed the button to open the garage door. The garage door rumbled up, creaking as it went, allowing sunshine and a view of the street in. Sara jiggled the keys in her hand, hauling herself into the cab. It smelled like fresh linen and a fine layer of dust covered the dash. She inhaled and exhaled deeply as she sat in his truck, recollections swirling around her, sucking her into a happier time.

"We're gonna have a little white ranch-style house 'cause I'm too lazy to climb stairs. You're going to plant some pretty flowers."

"Really? You think so?" Sara grinned as she gazed at the pink and orange sunset from the passenger side window of the truck.

"I know so. We gotta make our residence presentable so we don't scare possible visitors off."

"Visitors." She shuddered.

He laughed, deep and low. "You're right. They'll interrupt our alone time."

"Our alone time or the time you're hoping we're spending having sex?"

"Same difference."

The summer day was turning into night, the heat slowly lowering as dusk approached. She smiled, enjoying the warm breeze fluttering through her hair from the partially opened window. "And then what?"

"Then, let's see, two kids?"

She shrugged. "Sure." Sara glanced at his profile, watching as a slow smile formed to his lips.

"We best get started on that ASAP. That is a prerogative."

She laughed, touching his lips with her index finger. "We can at least wait until after the wedding." He kissed the tip of her finger, his blue eyes flashing heat at her.

"Right. But there's no reason we can't practice our form until then."

She leaned across the console and planted her lips on his rough cheek, giving him a slobbery kiss. "Love you."

"Love ya, babe. Even your drool." He winked, turning his gaze back to the road.

The smile didn't immediately fade with the memory and Sara was glad of that. She inhaled deeply, almost feeling as if he was sitting beside her, smiling with her.

"IT'S NOT SUNDAY," she said as she opened the door, cool air rushing into the warmth of the house, causing Sara to shiver.

"I realize that." Mason's eyebrows lifted as he waited.

"Uncle Mason?" a little voice chimed and her gaze was pulled down.

"Sundays aren't really helping, are they?"

Sara shifted, her eyes never leaving the blond-haired boy with wine-colored eyes. The boy was a miniature Mason. "Who's this?" she asked, ignoring the question that really hadn't needed to be asked.

He smiled. "Can we come inside?"

She blinked, opening the door wider. "Oh. Yeah. Come in." She closed the door behind them, crossing her arms and leaning against it.

"It's obvious I'm not the one helping you," he said. "Lincoln, right?"

Sara looked away, again not answering. Lincoln—everything with him was a mess. There were so many emotions involved where he was concerned and she was unable to sort through them at all. At least, not yet. The longer she kept her distance, the bigger the chasm inside her grew. She wanted so badly to go to him, but she didn't know what to do after that.

"Uncle Mason, I'm hungry," the boy said, tugging his gray baseball cap lower on his head.

"I know, buddy. We'll leave in just a bit. I just wanted to say hi to my friend quick, remember?"

She offered the boy a smile. He had a serious face, his eyes watchful. "Hi. I'm Sara. What's your name?"

"Derek."

Her eyes flew to Mason's.

He shrugged, a small smile on his face. "I thought it was time you two met."

"Derek?" she repeated slowly. "This is Derek? The one you talk to?"

Mason put his arm around Derek, hugging him to his side. "Yep. The reason I had to get my head out of my butt."

Derek giggled, clapping little hands over his mouth. "You said butt!"

"He's your brother's son?" she asked, blinking her eyes against tears.

"Yeah. Annie was pregnant when..." He looked at his nephew, his throat working. Mason shrugged, not finishing his sentence. He took a deep breath and continued, "I took one look at this chubby, wide-eyed baby and I *wanted* to live. I wanted to be someone he could be proud of."

She knelt before the small boy. "You are one special little being, you know that?"

He smiled, nodding his head. "Yep. Uncle Mason tells me that all the time."

"And how old are you?"

"I'm four and a half and I go to 4K and Mrs. Matthews is my teacher and she smells like flowers, but they don't smell good. They stink." He wrinkled his nose up.

Sara laughed. "Oh, really?"

"Uh-huh. Uncle Mason is taking me to Pizza Hut today because my mom needs a break and she calls Uncle Mason when she needs a break. But that's okay because I like Uncle Mason. I don't like his girlfriend because—"

"Okay, buddy," Mason interrupted, "that's probably enough."

She glanced up at Mason, a grin on her lips. She looked at Derek. "What's wrong with your Uncle Mason's girlfriend?"

Derek shrugged, fidgeting. "She wears too much makeup and she's always trying to kiss him and it's gross."

"She must like him a lot."

"I guess. Can we go now?" he asked, looking at his uncle.

Sara straightened, catching the expression on Mason's face as he looked at his nephew. He was looking at his world. "Thank you, Mason, for everything," she said, meaning it.

He nodded. "If you ever want to talk or just want to stop to say hi, here's my card." He pulled a black business card from his jeans pocket.

She took it. "I will. So you're releasing me, huh?"

"It was never about me. It was about you and what or who helped you the most. It hurts my ego to admit it wasn't me."

She nodded, glancing away. "Right. Um...before you leave, can I show you something first?"

"Of course." He turned to his nephew. "One more minute, bud."

He sighed. "Okay."

"You got your book?"

The boy nodded, taking a tiny book from his pocket.

"You can sit at the table and look at it, all right?"

"All right."

Mason motioned for her to proceed. A chair to the table scraped the floor as Derek pulled it out, situating himself at the table with his book. She smiled faintly, turning away. Every step that took her closer to the paintings made it a little harder for her to breathe. She forced her footsteps closer to their destination. She grabbed the doorknob and tugged, opening the door to the studio. Two paintings stood against the wall, side by side. Sara stared at them, her heart giving a twinge. One was of a closed blue door, the other the same blue door opened to show gray eyes. It was haunting with a touch of mystery to it.

"What does it mean?" he asked from behind her.

She shook her head. "I don't know. It just...my mind wandered both times and this is what I came up with. Once before he died and the other time after."

"Who has gray eyes?"

She turned around. "Lincoln has gray eyes."

Mason smiled softly. "I thought so. It's okay."

"I don't think it is," she whispered.

"You know...holding on isn't holding on. It's letting go."

"I don't know what that means." She blinked and a tear dropped to her cheek.

"You will," he vowed, moving forward to hug her.

"It hasn't been long enough," she said into his shoulder, returning the hug. In the person she'd last thought she would, Sara had found a friend.

Mason pulled away. "Life isn't measured in time, but by moments. When you figure that out, you'll be golden."

She blinked her stinging eyes, turning away from his knowing ones.

"I think you have all your answers. You just have to see them. I got a hungry nephew to feed. Like I said, anytime you want to talk, look me up. I won't even charge you."

See me, Lincoln had pleaded. Sara briefly closed her eyes and more tears fell to her face. She opened her eyes, shaking the memory away. "That notebook you gave me?"

He paused at the doorway, looking over his shoulder at her. "Yeah?"

"It's full of sketches," Sara admitted.

Mason smiled. "I'm glad."

"Thank you, Mason," she said, her voice trembling with emotion.

"I didn't do anything, Sara."

"So I should thank you for nothing?" A small smile formed to her lips.

He laughed. "Yeah. You'd be surprised by how many times I'm told that, actually." He tapped his fingers on the doorframe. "See you around."

"'Bye, Sara!" Derek called and she called a goodbye in return as they walked out the door.

She inhaled deeply, closing her eyes. She missed Lincoln. The ache in her chest widened, became painful. That connection they'd had, before and after they'd explored one another's bodies in the most intimate way—she needed it. She needed him. Even if they couldn't be what he wanted them to be, Sara couldn't imagine her life without him in it. It was his voice she longed to hear, his arms she wanted to feel around her. When had it all changed?

THE RING THAT never left her finger, other than when it slid off, was heavy. It weighed her down, like the love she had yet to completely say goodbye to, like the past she had to move forward from. Was it as simple as removing a ring? Would the shedding of it take all she couldn't get over with it as well? She took it off her finger, raising it to eye level. It twinkled when the sunlight filtering in through the thin bedroom curtains caught it. It was a solitaire diamond. Simple.

Sara placed the cool metal to her lips and kissed it, clasping it tight within her hand for a moment. Closing her eyes, she bowed her head, willing the release to come, willing the ache to go away. It didn't. Neither happened. It was a silly thought. With a sigh, she opened the jewelry box on the dresser that housed rings and earrings and necklaces; all the things she used to wear and no longer did. There was a silver cross necklace her mother and father had given her as a graduation gift from high school. With a twinge, she pulled it out and clasped it around her neck, feeling closer to them merely by putting it on. They'd touched it once, they'd bought it for her—it was a link to them.

Sara set the wedding ring down on the cream-cushioned interior of the jewelry box, resisting the impulse to pick it back up, and with resolve stiffening her jaw, she picked out a pair of white crystal studs and a ring. Tucking her hair behind her ears, she put the earrings in her lobes and pushed the silver-leafed ring on the middle finger of her right hand.

She stared at the image looking back at her, noting the smudges under her eyes and the hollowed-out part below her cheekbones. She didn't recognize the face; it wasn't the one she remembered. The features were the same, but the look—that was something new. Continually beaten down, but still standing. That was the look in her eyes. That was Sara. *You* are *strong*, she thought, her brows lifting at the truth of it. She blinked, a little piece of herself given back to her with that realization.

SHE FOUND HIM in the woods, surrounded by blooming trees and newly born grass. The earth was back to life. Sara envied it. The air was cool, crisp. Birds flew past, singing their joy. It smelled like fresh grass and she inhaled deeply, feeling like maybe she was looking at a form of perfection.

Lincoln wore dark jeans and a gray tee shirt. Her heartbeats picked up at the same time her stomach swooped. Something inside her, maybe all of her, sighed at the sight of him. She dug her hands into the pockets of her light jacket and stopped beside him. He didn't look at her, but Sara knew he knew she was there. His body slightly shifted toward hers, unconsciously pulled to her.

"I love you, Sara."

The air was stolen from her lungs at that admission. "Lincoln—"

"I love you so much it hurts." He turned his head toward her, his eyes glaring the truth at her, demanding her to see it. "My heart literally *aches* when you're not around, even when you are. My throat tightens and there's this horrible pressure in my chest. Because you're not mine and I want you to be, and even if you were, I don't know that this fucked up feeling would go away. It's...it's...*part of me.*" He muttered something, wearily running a hand through his dark waves as he looked away.

Again she tried to speak and he cut her off with a steely look. "It shouldn't have happened, but it did. Or maybe it was supposed to happen. I don't know. But now..." His throat convulsed. "Now I just love you and it's all I can do and it's all I'll do. Forever. I'll just keep loving you." Lincoln turned shiny eyes from her to stare through the wooded forest.

Sara's eyes followed his and she saw her husband waiting for her in his black tuxedo, his eyes lit up with happiness, a grin on his lips. The vision of their wedding day faded and it was a forest of trees once more, but the sorrow stayed. It always did. Such a powerful thing—sadness. It had the power to wipe out happiness in the span of one second.

"He'd want you to be happy. Cole wouldn't want you to be pining after him for the rest of your life, scared to live, scared to love again."

"I know," she said quietly.

"But you're going to keep hiding, aren't you? You're going to keep denying yourself, denying us, until everything we have, or could have, is gone. Because you're scared." He faced her again, his eyes too bright. "You don't think I'm scared too? Every breath I take is full of fear, but I keep breathing. I keep hoping, even though it scares the *fuck* out of me. Because the thought of losing you, of not having you at all, scares me more."

It was happening. She was falling, being torn apart, and this time, it was in the anguish she witnessed in Lincoln's eyes. The pain *she'd* put there.

"I don't know what to tell you," she whispered. "I know I miss you when we're not together. But what it all means...I don't know. I have to learn how to move on without him and I'm stumbling right now. I have to learn how to accept that he's gone and even though it's not okay, *I* can still be okay. Somehow. I have to do this on my own. Otherwise..." She took a deep breath. "Otherwise I'll never be okay. Not for myself, not for you, not for anyone."

Lincoln exhaled noisily, squinting into the sun. "I know what you're saying, I do. But...it doesn't stop the way I'm feeling. Ya know, I always wanted to be like him. But not this time. I want you to look at me and see me, not him. I don't want to be a reminder. I want you to look at me and *forget* him." He faced her, the force of him overpowering.

"I want you to want me for *me*. But you have to let go of him to find me, Sara. So you have to figure that out. You have to decide what I am and you have to mean it. I'm yours. I just want to make sure, I have to know, that you're mine. So you go do what you have to do."

She blinked her tear-filled eyes, the chasm inside her lengthening. "Okay, Lincoln."

"Okay." He showed her his profile, his features stiff, unyielding.

Sara turned in the direction of her car, lost once more, and was immediately grabbed and whirled around. He threaded his fingers through her hair, pulling her face up, and assaulted her lips with his. Longing crashed over her and she responded to his fire with her own, her body thrumming with need. She grabbed his hair and twined it around her fingers. Lincoln moaned, moving them against a tree. The rough bark abraded her skin through the thin material of her jacket. He kissed her with a raw need, hunger in every touch of his lips to hers.

Lincoln tore his lips away, eliciting a whimper of yearning from her. His chest heaved up and down and his eyes blazed with passion as he stared down at her. "You think about this moment, right now, while you're out finding yourself, Sara. 'Cause you know what? I already found you. You're mine. I'm yours. I know it. You know it. You just have to see it."

THE NEED TO have a connection to him, even if only from her end, had been strong and Sara had walked into the garage before she'd known what she was doing. She'd stayed away for so long; not moving forward, but now it was time. She had to do it for herself, if she ever wanted to be at peace. If she ever wanted to be happy, even if she ever wanted to have a future with another man. Lincoln's gray eyes shimmered in her mind and she pushed them away. This was for her. He couldn't be a part of it, though he always was with her, no matter what she was doing or not doing. Imbedded into her heart and her being.

The boxes were endless, her past sprawled out around her in cards, letters, and photographs. Sara sat on the dirty floor of the garage, randomly plucking a faded piece of paper from the top of the box. She opened it, laughing shakily as she read the note.

Roses are red
Violets are blue
I got a boner
And it's because of you.
Happy Valentine's Day.

She wiped her damp eyes, staring at his messy handwriting. Sara had loved everything about him—even his warped sense of humor. She set the note back in the box. She sorted through her past, keeping remembrances of him she could never part with, setting aside all she could. She found a black baseball cap with a snowmobile logo on it and set it on her head. Halfway through she even grabbed a beer from the mini-fridge, but it was old and she didn't like Busch Light anyway. One drink and she tossed it out.

The doors of the house were open, as were the doors to the future. It was time. It hurt. But it was time. She couldn't live in the house anymore and she couldn't live in the past. Sara had finally come to terms with that, though knowing something didn't make it hurt any less.

She'd taken most of their belongings to be auctioned off. She had to start over fresh, and even the most generic of items were reminders of him. Not that she wanted to forget, never that, but Sara wouldn't be able to progress beyond what she now was if he was staring her in the face every place she looked. The house was so empty, but it didn't *feel* emptier. Everything that had meant anything to her had been gone for close to seven months now.

An offer had been made on the house and she was going to accept it. The truck was gone; the camper as well. Each time she parted with a piece of him, of *Cole*, she was brought that much closer to herself, whoever she was. Sara had to think his name, say his name, to make it real. She had to let go of him to find herself, to *live*. Sometimes she felt guilty about that, but most times she felt as though the restriction on her lungs had loosened a bit. He was with her, Cole would always be with her, but that didn't mean she couldn't move on as well.

And then there was Lincoln.

He was absent from her everyday living, but never far from her mind. Sara didn't know where they would go from here, what would become of them. He had been the one solidarity in the flowing river of her despair, a lifejacket to keep her from drowning. But did she love him? *Could* she love him without feeling remorse? It was hard to think about him without thinking of Cole. None of this would even be an issue if he was still alive. But he wasn't. And it was.

I saw you first, whispered through her, causing her to shiver. Lincoln saw her first, but she didn't see him, not really, not until now.

She finished up with the last box, adjusting her teal blue cotton shorts and purple top as she stood. It was done now—all of him designated to cardboard boxes. Not that he could ever truly be kept within a box. He was in her heart and that was the safest, soundest place for Cole to be. She took a deep breath, trying to center the contradiction that was her. The need to see Lincoln; the need to stay away. The need to never let Cole go; the need to let him go.

All that was left was to remove the belongings from the house, along with herself. That day would be upon her soon. In less than a week she was leaving, but she couldn't leave without saying goodbye to Lincoln. Sara looked at the neat boxes sitting around her legs, stacked in rows. She turned away from her past. Sorrow and relief hit her as she left the garage. The sun was warm, soothing as it heated her. She looked at the house they'd bought together, remembering the wilting flowers around it, remembering their first night in the house, remembering him. Sara brushed tears from her eyes and pointed herself in the direction that would take her to Lincoln.

She began to walk.

It was Sunday, which meant chances were good he wouldn't be working. Sara knew that wasn't always the case, especially with the weather nice as it was. Sunny days were working days for builders, no matter the day of the week. She had no words planned, nothing was forthcoming as far as what she should say or do when she saw him, if she saw him. *Please be there.*

With each step, her apprehension and anticipation built. Sweat began to trickle down her chest and Sara pulled the rubber band from her wrist and knotted her thick hair at the top of her head.

It took over an hour to reach the house in the woods. It loomed before her, her pulse speeding up as she took in the structure that epitomized all she loved. *All I love?* She froze, her hand pausing on her damp brow. Her hand slowly lowered to her side and she pushed the shock away, deciding now was not the time to think about that. But as she walked up the steps of the deck and knocked on the door, seeing that drooping Christmas tree in the window, emotions she couldn't ignore, not this time, slammed into her. Why hadn't he taken it down yet?

"What are you doing here?"

She whirled around, her pulse escalating as she took in his unclothed chest. It was bronzed from the sun, muscled from daily physical labor. She knew that chest. Sara had run her fingers over it, smelled it, kissed it, felt it pushed against hers. Her eyes went up, meeting his dark gray ones. Lincoln's hair was damp with perspiration and winged up around his ears and on the back of his neck, making him appear younger than he was. The black athletic shorts he wore hung low on his hips, showing the toned cords of his lower abdomen. Sara wanted Lincoln to hold her, kiss her, never let her go. When had the emotions shifted, turned into more, become love?

"Were you running?"

"Yeah," was Lincoln's curt response.

"Why'd you keep the tree?" she blurted.

His eyes shifted down as he slammed a hand on his hip. "I felt sorry for it." His pose was belligerent, like the set of his jaw.

Sara walked down a step. "You felt sorry for a tree?"

"Yeah. I did. It just...it looked so pitiful and tried so hard to survive and...yeah, I kept it. What do you care?" He scowled at her.

Another step.

"Why are you here anyway? I thought you needed time, space, whatever." His words were harsh, but his voice was strained, like he was struggling to stay in control, like he was hurting on the inside and trying to hide it on the outside.

"It reminded you of me, didn't it?"

"No," he quickly denied.

"Liar." She was almost to him.

"It has a much nicer disposition."

Sara stopped before him, smelling sunlight and sweat, and underneath that, Lincoln. Emotions welled up, threatened to burst through her and expose all she felt.

"Why are you here, Sara?" he repeated slowly, his eyes locked with hers. There was something in his expression, a vulnerability she'd never seen before. Her heart squeezed.

"I'm leaving."

He stiffened, his eyes, his face, everything shutting down. "What?"

She brushed hair from her face with a trembling hand. "I got a temporary place up north. I'm going to stay there for a month or so, maybe two. The house..." she trailed off, her throat tightening.

"What about the house?"

"I'm going to accept an offer on it tomorrow. I'm getting rid of everything. I'm..." She stopped when he showed her his back. It was taut, sculpted, and shaking. Her fingers yearned to touch him, to trace a pale thin scar on his left shoulder blade, to take the quiver from it.

"You're leaving," he said in a dead voice.

"Only for a little while. Just until...until I have things sorted out." She watched his back move with the force of his breaths.

He turned and glared at her. "What is there to sort out?"

You. I'm scared of what I feel for you. I don't know how to accept it yet. I'm scared of what you feel for me. The way you look at me; like I'm everything, it scares me. When I look at you, I'm lost in you. I'm trying to find myself and I can't do that with the distraction of you. You consume everything. But she couldn't say any of that.

She swallowed, glancing down. Her throat was dry. "Me, Lincoln. I need to sort me out."

"Up north *where?*"

"I don't know if—if I should tell you," she said, looking down at the ground.

"Afraid I'll follow you? Don't worry. I won't." His words were cold, final, and they hurt.

Her eyes jerked to his and he looked away from the pain on her face, his expression ashamed. "That was uncalled for."

"You leaving is uncalled for," he snapped back. Lincoln closed his eyes, taking a deep breath. "I'm saying all the wrong things." He rubbed a hand on the back of his head. "I feel like we're going around in a circle, you and I. If you know you don't feel the same as I do, if you know there's no chance for us, at least tell me. You don't have to escape Boscobel to escape me. I've kept my distance, for you. It kills me, but I've done it. I'll leave you alone, if that's what you want. Is that what you want?" His pain-filled eyes met hers.

It broke. Whatever had been keeping her emotions in check shattered and she reached for him, feeling complete, centered, only when she finally held him. His skin was hot and hard against hers, wet with sweat, and when his fingers gripped her waist, digging into her flesh, when the hardness of his body was flush with the softness of hers, Sara was lost again. Or found. Maybe she had to be lost in him to find herself.

"I love you, Sara, love you so much," he murmured into her ear, his hands holding her face steady as Lincoln studied her. "I love you," he repeated, his words thick with the truth of it.

She blinked her eyes and tears slid down her cheeks. She couldn't say it. She loved him, she loved Lincoln, and Sara couldn't say it. She'd always loved him—that hadn't changed, but the *way* she loved him—that had. So much.

He stepped away, dropping his hands from her. She fought the need to touch him again. Lincoln's face was blank, his eyes dim. Her heart cried at the devastation in the set of his shoulders, in the way he held his head. Sara wanted to ask him to wait for her, to not give up on her, but that wouldn't be fair to him.

"Have a nice trip," he muttered, striding for the house.

No. Don't leave like this. Don't let it be like this. Go to him! Run. Tell him you love him. Tell him! No matter how loudly or passionately her conscience shouted at her, she didn't have the power to do it. She couldn't. Instead she turned around to begin the long walk back to the house that would soon no longer be her home.

CHAPTER 17

SARA FIDDLED WITH the cellular phone, facing the car. She took a deep breath, staring at the phone number on the phone. It was time to go. Her belongings had been reduced to what was in the car and the rest had been put in a small storage unit until her return. She took a deep breath. He was fading from her and that was what was the most unbearable. The exact shade of his eyes eluded her, the certain timbre of his voice when he spoke—even his scent. It was all leaving her. Leaving her and filling her with a terrible loss, making a part of her hollow. Sara thought that was what hurt the most, more painful than his absence was the lack of everything that embodied him. She didn't want to forget him, not a single detail of him, and it was already happening.

The pull to call Lincoln was maddening, unavoidable, and so she hit the send button, listening to the ring of the phone. It took her back to all the countless times she'd called him after the car accident, when he'd been all that was between her and insanity from the depth of grief she could not bear. He had saved her from herself so many times. This time, though, she had to save herself. *I wish I knew how.*

"Sara," Lincoln said by way of greeting.

She closed her eyes at the sound of his voice, shocked by how much it affected her. It sent tingles from her scalp down to her fingertips. When he didn't say anymore, she floundered with, "Hi. I, uh…I…I'm leaving today." *Pathetic.*

A pause. "Be safe," was his gruff response.

"I will." She tapped her short nails against the roof of the car, the sun glaring down on the crown of her dark hair. "I just...I wanted to say goodbye." The distance between them was suffocating her and it was *because* of her.

"And so you did."

"Right. Goodbye, Lincoln." Dread pooled in her stomach, growing until it filled her with a sick feeling.

She began to move the phone from her ear when he said sharply, "Sara, *wait.*"

"Yes?" Her voice was breathless and her heart pounded in anticipation of Lincoln's words.

"I don't want you to go. I know you're going to go anyway, but I just want you to know that."

"I have to go," she whispered, clutching the phone tightly to her ear.

"I *know* that. I know." He let out a loud sigh. "Just..." He broke off and she could feel the hesitation from him even through the phone. "I'm going to say this and you don't have to say anything back, okay? *I love you.* Remember that."

I love you, she thought back as the line clicked off. With a heavy heart, Sara got into the car and began her journey. She didn't know if it was necessary for her to leave her life in Boscobel in order to find herself, but maybe it was. The house, the town, even Lincoln—they all reminded her of what she'd lost. This separation from all she knew was the one thing that without a doubt, felt *right.*

The hours she drove with only her thoughts to guide her were reflective and also inescapable. She had never really thought of herself as weak or strong before the accident, but since then, she'd convinced herself she was the weakest kind of person. The kind who couldn't say goodbye, the kind unable to function on their own, unable to accept loss and carry on. The kind of person who broke in the wake of tragedy instead of growing stronger because of it.

You're only human, a voice inside her head said. Was that really an excuse? She struggled with forgiveness for herself, for her inability to save him, even for being only human. Humans were flawed, so easy to die, so prone to be hurt and hurt the ones they loved, consciously or not. And yet forgiveness was not so easily given, not to herself.

WAUPUN, WISCONSIN HAD over 11,000 residents, but not much more than Boscobel as far as entertainment went. Actually, Boscobel had one up on Waupun. There was no movie theater, old or otherwise, in the town of Waupun. Sara thought the population being so high might have something to do with the two prisons in the city. She supposed in that regard Waupun *did* have one up on Boscobel, though it wasn't necessarily a *good* thing.

Her destination had been random. She'd gotten a map of Wisconsin, closed her eyes, and put her finger on a city. Her finger had actually landed on Beaver Dam; a trendier city about half an hour from Waupun, but as her parents had an old friend who owned a motel in Waupun, she'd contacted Dana Newman for an extended-stay room instead of sticking with Beaver Dam. It was more of an inn than a motel; too nice to be reduced to the title of motel. Sara wasn't really sure how Dana knew her parents, only that she'd seen her at occasional birthday parties and get-togethers throughout the years. She was charging her next to nothing because, as Dana had said, she'd always liked Sara and she was sorry she'd gotten so much rotten luck in her life.

Dana also didn't need the money. She was wealthy enough from being the wife and divorcee of rich men four times over. Short, platinum blonde, with leathery brown skin, Dana liked to be stylish, even when the look she was going for was much too young for her sixty-ish body and face and she should probably lay off the tanning bed. Sara had been there over two weeks and every day at eight in the morning, Dana brought over a cup of coffee and a doughnut because she was too thin and no boy wanted to lay down with bones. Her words. She wore tight capris in black and white and alternating flashy tops with headache-inducing designs and wobbled in six-inch heels no woman had any right wearing, least of all an elderly one.

The room was the size of a small apartment and located on the second floor of the motel, complete with a kitchenette with fun-sized appliances and furniture. The walls were creamy white with pale pink, white, and celery green accents for furniture and fabric. It was uncluttered with a bed, dresser, and a pale green chaise lounge with a neoclassic design. The bathroom had a garden tub with a skylight above it. Sara loved it. If she had to pick a room to live in, this would be it. *You are living in it, at least temporarily.*

A pamphlet in Sara's motel room boasted: "Waupun comes from the Indian name of "Waubun" which means "dawn of day." In fact, Waupun was originally supposed to be named "Waubun" but the State of Wisconsin made a spelling error, and Waupun never bothered to change it." She snorted when she read that.

She lay on the comfortable full-sized bed with the pink paisley comforter, staring at the white ceiling fan and light. Where did she belong? Not in this foreign city she'd escaped to, not in the past or in the house they'd bought together. Maybe Sara didn't belong any*where*, but with *someone*. She'd come to Waupun to find herself and instead she was finding Lincoln.

His eyes glared at her in their powerful way from the recesses of her mind, she felt his arms around her in the warmth of the sun. She longed to hear his deep voice that spoke so passionately and kissed just as passionately. *You're stupid for leaving.* She tried to make herself feel better by telling herself she wouldn't have realized that if she hadn't gone. It was little consolation. The point was she was wasting time she could be spending with Lincoln—the man who'd awoken the fire inside her she'd thought forever snuffed out. And still, she couldn't return, not yet.

She hadn't told him where she was going not because she was afraid he'd come after her, but because if she had she'd thought she'd be more likely to return before she was ready to, which really didn't make sense, but was true all the same. He didn't know she was only about three hours away, so it was as though she didn't know how close she was to him either.

As she looked at the light bulb for so long she began to see spots Sara finally accepted it. Somehow the light made her see all she hadn't wanted to. It was a literal epiphany. She'd been in limbo, unable to move on, unable to go back, while Cole had laid there, some part of him unable to let go as well. Sara would have kept waiting. He'd known that too. That was why he'd written that paper and that was why he'd given them a year to find a way back to each other.

She had pushed it past a year in hopes of his recovery, but their time had been up. At least, in this life. But never in her heart. He would always be in her heart, *always*. Sara just had to learn to think of him without it hurting so much. She had to learn it was okay for her to live even when he didn't. She had to say his name, think his name without falling into an abyss of despair. She had to do all he'd want her to do. She had to breathe. *Lincoln makes you breathe.* It was true. Lincoln made it possible for her breathe and took her breath away at the same time.

She closed her eyes and gray eyes in a sharply chiseled face greeted her in the darkness of her shut eyelids. Guilt tried to accompany the pang of longing that hit her hard and she breathed deeply to center herself. She sat up and rubbed her face, wondering what he would think of this, wondering if Cole would hate her for having feelings for his brother. *He would want to punch Lincoln in the face. He* would *punch Lincoln in the face.*

"True. I *did* punch him in the face once, didn't I? You deserve to be happy. That's all I ever wanted for you."

Her hands dropped from her face, the smile sliding off her lips. Why did she keep thinking she heard him? That hadn't ended when his life had. If anything, it seemed to happen more often. It came from out of nowhere, but seemed to come from within her as well. It was a little blessing, a small piece of him that hadn't disappeared with his life. Sara got to her feet and walked over to the easel awaiting her near the glass doors that led to a small deck, absently twisting her hair up into a ponytail as she stared at the empty canvas.

"Paint for me, Sara. Paint me and let me go."

She inhaled slowly, trying to find a calm that wanted to evade her, and did as commanded by a figment of her imagination, a ghost, or her unstable mind. She painted his profile in gray and black. She captured the powerful gaze, the straight nose, the thin lips. Portraits were capable of imprisoning a piece of the soul for all eternity and in her art, she was able to keep a piece of her husband close to her. Even when his voice left her for good, she'd still have this. Sara stared at Cole's silhouette, her eyes caressing his features. *So different from Lincoln's.* She turned from the easel, wiping her paint-splattered fingers on her old jean shorts.

What do you know as truth? she asked herself as she searched the counter in the kitchenette for her sunglasses. *You love Cole. Cole is gone. You love Lincoln. Lincoln is here. You blame yourself for Cole's death. You have to stop blaming yourself. You feel guilty of the feelings you have for Lincoln. You have to stop feeling guilty.* Sara found them on top of the refrigerator, shoving them onto her face. If only it was as easy as telling herself to stop doing one thing and to start doing another.

"Not easy, but worth it. It has to be worth it."

She rolled her eyes at Cole's voice, leaving the cool interior of her temporary home to face the humidity and sun of Waupun. It was going to be a scorcher of a day, even for June. As far as scenery went, it didn't differ that much from Boscobel. There were lots of leafy trees, swaying from the warm breeze, and green grass galore. There was even marshland near the town, another similarity to Boscobel. So basically she'd gone from Boscobel to a bigger Boscobel. Flowers scented the air and awed her eyes at the rainbow of colors as she walked along the sidewalk. Sara had always loved flowers—she just wasn't any good with them.

As she was crossing the street, her cell phone rang in her pocket, blaring out 'That's Not My Name' by The Ting Tings. Sara paused under the shade of a tree, quickly pulling it from her shorts, her breath hitching at the name and number. Her heart pounded harder in anticipation and her palms turned sweaty. He hadn't missed a day yet. She didn't want to think about what it meant when and if he did.

"Hello?" she said breathlessly. As was routine, he didn't say anything back.

Noting a public bench farther down the street, she walked to it. "I go for walks every day. Something I used to do and got out of the habit of doing. It's so quiet here. I mean, there *is* noise, of course, but it's like everything inside *me* is quieter. I don't know how to explain it. I'm calmer, I guess. Not so sad. I can think clearer and I see things in a different way than I used to. It's good for me. But I miss you like crazy."

She sat down on the bench, the metal branding the backs of her legs, but not uncomfortably. "It's strange to think of us. You, me, Cole, and how we're all connected." Sara watched a blonde-haired woman walk by pushing a stroller and swallowed, turning away. "You remember when I lost the baby? I was inconsolable. Cole and I were barely speaking. We were both hurting so bad and didn't know how to comfort each other. You told Cole you were going to kick his ass if he showed up to work one more day in a piss-ass mood. It was the first time he smiled in days."

She tucked a loose strand of hair behind her ear, eyes on the vehicles ambling up and down the road. A set of modest houses ran along the length of the street across from her. "You made us sit at a table and talk. You started by mentioning the weather. Then we had to say what our favorite colors were. Then you said something about how bad I was at sports and Cole agreed. Totally ridiculous stuff, but the point was, we were talking. You brought up funny memories and told some bad jokes. Before long, Cole and I were laughing and looking at each other as we talked. You saved us. You're always saving people, Lincoln. But what about you?" She took a deep breath.

"You've always been there for me and Cole. You were there, even then, shoving us back to life. You've always done that, but at what cost to you? It had to have been hard, loving Cole and loving me, and wanting us to be happy, even though it meant you couldn't be. You sacrificed your happiness, again and again, for mine, for your brother's. You are truly an exceptional person," Sara said, her throat thick. "Take care, Lincoln."

FRESHLY SHOWERED, SHE tugged on a pair of lightweight pink shorts and a yellow tank top, the emptiness of the motel room somehow soothing. She'd done some minor shopping at the local grocery store earlier in the day and had the preparations for a salad. She sat at the small table by the windowed doors, staring out at rolling skies of gray clouds the color of Lincoln's eyes. A storm was coming. She wondered if it was storming where he was.

It was strange how a difference in atmosphere had the power to alter her view on things, but that was life—full of ironies and impossibilities that happened. Like the wreck that had ultimately taken her husband; like the feelings she and Lincoln had for one another. Never, ever would Sara have thought she would love him the way she did, or that he'd loved her for so long without telling anyone. The burden that must have been, carrying that around for so long. She couldn't imagine what that must have felt like. *Like you feel now, only twenty times worse.* She feared she might burst from holding all her feelings inside. She wanted to shout to the world how much she loved Lincoln.

She took a sip of water, almost upturning the glass when her cell phone rang. The number was Lincoln's. Her nerves played havoc with her as she grabbed the phone. He continued to call every day. He called every day, but never said a single word. It was a mixture of respite and torture to partake of these silent conversations with him.

"Hello, Lincoln," she said, her voice rough. She cleared her throat, pushing the salad away. He didn't say anything, but that was what she'd expected. "It's storming here. I love thunderstorms. Cole did too. We would sit on our porch outside and watch the rain fall down, blanketing the earth in water, listening to the sound of it, listening to the thunder rumble. It was relaxing. Even the lightning cracking the sky was comforting. It made me realize how insignificant and small I was compared to the world. It made me feel sheltered, like I was in my own shell of safety. Then Cole would look at me and I'd realize how wrong I was about the first and how right I was about the second. I'd like..." Trailing off, Sara swallowed and continued, "I'd like to do that with you sometime...watch a storm, I mean...if you want."

She heard his breathing, closing her eyes to focus on that one small part of him she could have even with the distance between them. It was silly and illogical, but just hearing his even breaths made her feel at peace. Sara could imagine them lying side by side, sleeping in the same bed, their limbs intertwined, she falling asleep to the sound of his steady breathing.

"I'm glad you called, I'm always glad when you call, but I have to ask you something." When he didn't respond, and she'd known he wouldn't, Sara sighed. "How did you stand it? All those one-sided phone conversations? I guess I deserve your silence. Apparently you're better at this than I am, because really, I just want to reach through the phone and force your lips to open and words to come out of your mouth. Although, on the one hand, maybe it's best that you aren't speaking to me. I can't imagine you have anything particularly nice to say. Not that I blame you. I was kind of a mess before I left. I mean, I'm still a mess, but a slightly less psychotic one." She rubbed her face, suddenly tired, imagining him inwardly snorting at that.

"I painted him a few weeks ago. I painted Cole and I thought of you. I close my eyes and I see yours. I came here to find myself, but I'm finding you instead, Lincoln. How does that work?" Sara chewed the inside of her lower lip. She just wanted him to *say* something, anything. But maybe it was better he didn't. It had to be about Sara; she had to be the one to make the first move, the one to reach out, the one to talk.

"I miss you. I miss you so much," she said raggedly, blinking her eyes against tears. She heard the sharp inhalation of air on the other end of the phone, knew he ached for her as she did for him. "You know, I never really thought about your eyes that much before. I never realized how they followed me through a room, how they were always on me, how whenever I looked at you, you were already looking at me. Was it always like that? Of course it was.

"I was so blind about so many things. I suppose I needed to be then. I shouldn't have been noticing you when I had Cole. So I'm glad I didn't. But now, now I remember so many things, only in a different way. I remember how your eyes lightened to a paler shade of gray when you looked at me, like your whole being amplified when you saw me. I remember how you stood up for me, no matter what, even when there was nothing to stand up for me about. I remember your protectiveness. I remember how your smile had a certain tenderness for me alone. I remember you, Lincoln, the *real* you, finally. Take care, Lincoln," she said softly and ended the call, heavy with yearning.

She wanted so badly to return to him, to be with Lincoln, but something held her back, something kept her in Waupun when everything she wanted was in Boscobel. She knew what the problem was, or what part of the problem was, at least. Sara was scared. That was obvious. It wasn't just about Cole and moving on without the guilt and being able to say goodbye to him without it aching so much, although that was a great part of it. What she was scared of the most was that if she was open about her feelings for Lincoln, what was to stop him from being taken away from her? Her mother, father, Cole, and their unborn child— they'd all been taken from her. Maybe it was irrational, but it made all the logic in the world to Sara. The fear was part of her, looming over her every second of the day and even at night.

If You can hear me, if You're really here...I just want to know why. Why did they have to die? Sara's throat closed with emotion. *And what's to stop it from happening to Lincoln? He can be taken away too.*

"Stop thinking like that. It's not about that."

"Then what is it about?" she whispered, eyes closed, elbows on the table and hands on her face.

"Just hold on. Hold on to what you have and forget about all the rest. And...have a little faith."

She dropped her hands from her face, staring at the shadowed room with bleary eyes. Thunder rumbled outside, lightning cracked, and the sky cried a flood of tears of either joy or pain. *Give me strength, please. Give me strength to live, to love again.* Who was she asking? A shiver went down her spine as lightning struck her eyes, momentarily blinding her with white light, the only answer to her unspoken question.

THE KNOCK CAME at exactly eight in the morning. Sara finished braiding her hair and snapped a rubber band around it as she walked to the door. Sunlight and Dana greeted her. She was blinded more from the sight of Dana than the fiery light in the sky.

"Morning, sugar," she said in her brittle voice that was lilting at the same time it was abrasive. She held two steaming mugs of coffee and a white bakery bag was tucked under one arm.

"Hello, Dana." She blinked repeatedly to bring her eyes back into focus and stepped away, allowing Dana to enter.

Her hair was teased up around her head, a white-blonde Q-tip with a brown stick-like body beneath it. Her brown eyes were lined with black eyeliner and her eyelids were shadowed with midnight blue. Rouge cheeks and apple red lips completed the artwork that was her face. That wasn't what had made Sara see temporary spots though. That credit had to be given to her ensemble of a sequined top of red, white, and blue stars, red capris, and white heels.

"It's the Fourth of July," she informed Sara, sitting down at the small table by the doors.

She sat down across from her. "Oh?" It had completely escaped her what the day was. Cole and Lincoln had both always been big on the annual fireworks display put on at Kronshage Park in Boscobel. Sara had tagged along for something to do. She wondered if Lincoln would be going to it this year.

She accepted the coffee Dana pushed toward her, taking a careful sip. She made excellent coffee. It was strong, but not bitter. Smooth and flavorful. Dana removed two napkins from the bag and placed an oversized cinnamon roll on each, setting one in front of Sara. Her stomach growled as the smell of frosting and cinnamon and sugar hit her.

"'Bout time you got your appetite back," she commented after eyeing her for a beat. "You were all skin and bones when you got here." She sniffed, pulling a piece of her roll off and dipping it into her coffee before taking a bite.

"How did you end up in Waupun, Dana?" she asked, taking a bite of her roll. The sweet bread was heaven to her taste buds, somehow thick and fluffy at the same time.

"Fourth husband owned this Godforsaken motel," she said with a grimace.

She gave her a surprised look. "You don't like it? You take such good care of it. The housekeepers do an excellent job. The outside is clean and well-maintained and the flowerbeds are so pretty. It's a nice place, Dana. Truly."

Dana sat up straighter at the praise. "Of course it is. As you said, I take good care of it."

"Where is the fourth husband?" she asked, hiding a smile behind her coffee cup.

She snorted. "Don't know, don't care. He split, leaving me with this place."

"Oh. I'm sorry."

"Don't be. He was a liar and a cheater and I'm glad to be rid of him. Plus, I love this place."

Sara didn't point out that Dana had just contradicted herself. It wouldn't do any good. She was crabby and also refreshing at the same time. She thought her placement here, in this town, in this motel, near

Dana, was perfect. The ache for Lincoln was there, always, but she was doing okay.

"You're my date for the fireworks," she announced, finishing off her cinnamon roll.

"Your date?"

"I sit out on the deck and watch them. You can keep me company. Not like you have anything better to do anyway, here without your man like you are."

She stiffened, lowering her coffee cup. "What?"

Dana got to her feet, her knees cracking, and rolled her eyes. "Oh, you. It's obvious you're hurting. I know all there is to know. A look like that in your eyes—it's from a man. I've had it in my eyes many times. You love him," she stated bluntly.

She looked at the partially eaten cinnamon roll, fingers tightly clenched around the coffee mug. "I do."

"You love him, yet you're here. Why?"

"My husband—"

"Is dead," Dana interrupted, moving to the door. "I've kept tabs on you, dear, especially after your parents passed. You always intrigued me. Such a somber young child; not talking much, always observing. You were special, even as a child. And obviously there's a man out there that feels the same. Some people aren't lucky enough to find love once, and you've found it twice. Remember that."

WHO ARE YOU? Sara stared at her lightly tanned reflection, waiting for a response that only she could provide. Her brown eyes were brighter than they'd been in recent months, but a hint of sadness could still be deciphered, if one really looked. She swiped hair behind her ears and leaned toward the mirror, searching for a glimpse of the woman she'd been two years ago, before the wreck that had splintered her life apart into tiny pieces.

She couldn't find her. She couldn't remember who she used to be. That woman was lost, gone, never to be found again. Maybe she wasn't supposed to be found. Maybe finding herself wasn't about going back to who she used to be, but instead was about accepting everything and learning to live, not in spite of, but because of, all she'd gone through. Maybe this woman, looking back at her, was the Sara she was meant to be. Scarred in all ways, slightly ruined, imperfect, but alive.

The girl who'd lost her parents and found hope in a man when she'd worried it was all but gone—that wasn't her. The young woman broken by the loss of a child and repaired in the eyes of her love wasn't her either. And the woman weak and full of self-hate and regrets, grieving for all she could not change and was unable to live without, that was no longer Sara as well. This was her, whoever she was—this woman staring back at her. Remade, reborn, reconstructed into a woman able to hope and love once again.

She turned the light off and left the bathroom, the pull too strong to ignore. Sara scrolled through the saved names on the cell phone, pausing on *Cole*. Her thumb caressed the name and number, the pang in her heart bittersweet, but not overwhelming as it used to be. She hit send just to hear his rough voice drawl on the voicemail: *"I ain't here so call Sara. Don't leave a message. You know I won't listen to it."*

A smile stretched her lips and Sara let her head fall forward, her hair blanketing the sides of her face. She closed her eyes and memories and scents and touches enveloped her, peace coming with them for the first time. She hadn't had the heart to disconnect the service to Cole's phone, but it was something she would do when she returned to Boscobel.

The phone rang, startling her. She fumbled not to drop it and stared at the screen. It was Lincoln. She shouldn't be surprised, since he hadn't missed a day in the past five weeks since she'd been gone, but she always feared one day there wouldn't be a phone call from him. Sara was frightened that one day he'd realize loving her was too much trouble.

"It's so beautiful here, Lincoln. The scenery is green, lush, peaceful. You're probably wondering where *here* is, aren't you? About that...I didn't tell you not because I didn't want you to follow and I was afraid you would. That wasn't it at all. I didn't tell you because I was afraid if I did, *I'd* be the one to leave before I should, that *I'd* be the one to run back to you before I had healed enough.

"I do feel better. I do feel a peace I didn't before I left. The rest...I'm finding it as I go. I'm finding...me. I think. I still don't know who I am or who I'm supposed to be. Maybe I'm not supposed to figure that out and that's what I had to figure out." She sighed, rubbing her forehead.

"I suppose you're wondering *why* I had to travel all the way to where I did to figure things out. I don't know. To get away from everything that reminded me of him, to heal. I want to ask you to wait for me, to keep loving me, to not decide I'm a waste of time, but I don't feel like I have the place to tell you that. Do I? I can tell what you're thinking. Even now, when you're not talking, I can feel your anger. You're bristling with it, aren't you? So stubborn. Why have you loved me for so long?" she whispered. "I don't think I'm worthy of it. But I guess it's not for me to decide who loves me or doesn't."

Sara walked to the sliding glass doors and looked out at the pink and orange sunset, placing a hand on the cool glass, touching the sky. "I guess I should admit the obvious. I *didn't* find me. I failed in that quest. I came here to find me and found there wasn't anything to find. The person I used to be, the old Sara, she's gone. I can't find what no longer exists. But that's okay. It has to be.

"It doesn't hurt as much. I don't know if it's because I'm away from it all or if it's because I'm simply healing. But I can think of him without feeling like my heart is being ripped out. I can think his name. I can say his name. Slowly, painfully, my wounds are closing. I know it won't take weeks or months to be completely healed. I don't know if I ever will be. But at least I can breathe without feeling like my insides are being crushed.

"I..." She swallowed and turned away from the window. "You don't remind me of him, Lincoln; you *obliterate* him. That makes me sad and relieved all at once." Her throat tightened. "I'm losing him, the part of me that loves him; it's leaving, fading. I know it has to happen. He's gone. I finally accept that Cole's gone. It hurts. I know it will always hurt. But you...you make it stop hurting. I miss you. At first I told myself it was because I was lonely. I told myself a lot of things at first, but I do...I really do. I know...I know you can never replace him. I don't *want* that.

"I see you now, Lincoln. I think I always did, but I wouldn't let myself. I see you and I—" She bit her lip to keep the declaration in. The silence from Lincoln was thick and full of longing. She could feel it; hers mirrored his. "I see you. I know that, if nothing else," she said lamely. "I'm not making sense. Good night. Take care, Lincoln."

THE RAIN PELTED against the glass, blurring the darkened world outside of the room. She stared at the rivulets as they slid down the pane, each one a piece of her past washing away. She looked at her faint reflection in the glass, sucking in a sharp breath at the face looking back at her. It wasn't her own. A sad smile partially lifted his lips and his eyes stared all the love he had for her, would always have for her, back at her.

"Cole," she whispered, her tears mocking the raindrops on the window as they trailed down her cheeks. "I miss you." Sara's throat was tight and her chest ached. That part of her heart that would always belong to Cole mourned him. "It scares me that he's taking over your place in my heart."

"He's not taking it over. You're just making room for him. You do have the capability to love more than one person." She heard the grin in his voice, closed her eyes to better hear him.

"But I think of him instead of you. I want him like I used to want you."

"You should. He's alive. I'm not. I get it. I'm okay with it. You're the one who isn't and has to be." A pause. "Take care, Sara."

She lifted a palm to his face and it shifted away like sand in the wind, one tiny particle at a time until only her image could be seen. She couldn't see him, but his words stayed with her, whether actually heard or imagined. *Take care, Sara.*

"YOU'RE READY TO go."

She played with a dandelion in the grass, staining her fingers with yellow. She brushed her fingertips over the soft petals, thinking of Lincoln's lips and shivered in spite of the humid, hot day. Her clothes were already unpleasantly sticking to her and it wasn't even noon yet.

"How can you tell?" she asked Dana, glancing to where she sat cross-legged on the blanket, surprisingly sprite for one so old. She wore a purple and hot pink zigzagged shirt and silver capris. Sara wore a more muted outfit of a white tee shirt and black cotton shorts.

The tree they sat under afforded shade, but little respite from the heat. It had been close to eight weeks since Sara had made the trip to Waupun, lost and confused. She wasn't either of those things anymore, though she also wasn't exactly whole. She and Dana had gotten closer over the weeks, spending more than their habitual morning coffee and doughnut time together, going for walks and Dana playing the local tour guide to her, watching movies at night, sitting on her deck that was connected to the motel. She absolutely thought the world of Dana. They looked like grandmother and granddaughter, but that had little bearing on their kinship.

Dana drank from her glass of vegetable juice, the ice clinking against her teeth as she tipped her head back. "Your eyes. They aren't so sad. Your back is straighter. You don't hesitate with every action or word you say. You're ready."

It was all true. The oozing hole of agony was shrinking, deteriorating in size and power over her. She could finally breathe again, on her own. And that was what she'd needed before she could begin to absolve herself of responsibility over circumstances out of her control.

Sara pushed her sunglasses to the top of her head and gave Dana her full attention. "How did you meet my parents?"

A smile stretched her red lips. "My second husband was distantly related to them. Very distantly. I met them at a family reunion many, many years ago, before your time. There was something about your mother that drew me to her, much like I was drawn to you—an inner spark, a flame that wouldn't be snuffed out. A quiet strength that seemed frail, but was stronger than steel. People like that get underestimated a lot, I've found. Sometimes *they* even underestimate themselves."

"You'll get no denial from me," she replied, inhaling slowly and deeply of the fragranced air of newly mowed grass, so thankful she'd found the strength she hadn't been aware she had.

Dana turned her brown eyes to Sara. They were warm and bright. "You look like her, but you also have your father's chin and eyes and his quiet manner. I've always found the ones that are the quietest make the most of their words when they *do* talk."

She smiled, touching the cross necklace she wore around her neck, thinking of her parents and her husband. "Cole was like that. He didn't have to say much to get his point across."

"I met him."

She blinked, surprised. "You did?"

"At your wedding. I'm not surprised you don't remember. You only had eyes for him. But his brother, I remember, only had eyes for you. Cole was the embodiment of happiness and his brother was a perfect imitation of brooding. Except when you looked at him. *Then* he lit up."

Sara shifted, suddenly hotter than she'd been a moment before. She hated knowing Lincoln had been loving her and hurting because of it, for *so long*. It made her feel guilty, though she'd had no idea of his feelings for her at the time. But Cole had known. That must have twisted him up inside. She hung her head and rubbed her forehead, weary of the past.

"Don't feel remorseful. We don't choose who we love. Love chooses us. You love him now. That's all that matters."

She reached over and took her leathery hand, squeezing it. "I'm not ready to go, not yet. I want to spend a little more time with you, if that's okay?"

Dana's eyes watered and she hastily swiped a hand across them, scowling. "If you really think you need to. What's an old lady got that a young strapping man doesn't?"

A smile teased Sara's lips. "Well, for the moment...*me*. If you'll let me stay."

"Of course I'll let you stay," she replied gruffly. "I expect you to bring your man friend around sometime too so I can drool over him. I don't get much action these days."

"Deal." Laughing, she got to her feet and helped Dana up, then reached down to fold up the blanket. She tucked it under her arm, saying, "*Much* action?"

"Never you mind. Come on. You can help me oversee the cleaning ladies. I think one of them has been snitching soap and I aim to catch the thief." Her eyes sparkled in anticipation and Sara laughed again, wrapping her arm around Dana's thin shoulders as they walked back to the red and brown brick rambling structure called Newman Motel.

CHAPTER 18

"I EXPECT YOU to visit within the next few months. I've gotten used to you being around. I also need my eye candy fix and your Lincoln will do."

Sara put the last of her bags in the trunk of the Pontiac and closed it, turning to lean her hips against it. She crossed her arms, squinting under the glare of the August sun. A smile on her lips, she met the fluorescent pink and orange clothed Dana head on. Her hair was teased exceptionally high today in honor of Sara's departure.

"My Lincoln?"

"Well, he isn't mine and I know he isn't anyone else's. Boy calls every day and says nothing. Crazy lovesick fool." She shook her head, but a smile curved her lips. "He's yours," she said definitively.

Warmth trickled through her at the thought. She hoped he was. The phone calls hadn't ceased as the time had drawn out, giving her encouragement that maybe, even though it wasn't right of her to expect or want him to, he was waiting for her. She felt like she'd been waiting for him for so long as well.

"I promise I will be here within *one* month, not two. I'll miss seeing you too much if I go any longer than that. Maybe you could come visit me in Boscobel as well."

Dana dabbed at her eyes with a wadded up tissue, smearing her makeup. "Well. If you insist."

She reached over to wrap her in a tight hug. Her flowery scent amplified with her nearness and caused a small twinge of homesickness for her in Sara's chest even though she hadn't left yet. She vowed, "I do."

The wind blew, scattering fallen leaves and waving tree limbs as though Waupun was saying its own farewell to her. She smiled, feeling a closure she hadn't known was possible.

"I'm old, Sara. I've known a lot of people. I've loved a lot. Hell, I've married a lot. But you," Dana patted her cheek, "you're my girl. I'm glad you picked up the phone and decided to call me. I think I got as much out of our time together as you did, if not more. I always wanted a daughter. You'll do."

"Only I'm more like a granddaughter," she teased around the tears burning her eyes.

"Hush," she said, reaching up to kiss Sara's cheek, her lips papery thin and cool. "I didn't say *how* old I was."

"I'll call you," she promised, unable to resist the pull to hug her friend once more. She kissed her tight cheek, already missing her.

"You better." Dana gave her back a pat as she turned to get into the car.

Hands on the steering wheel, her gaze went to the second floor room that had been her home the past few months. Dana walked past the front of the car on her way to the office, waving as she went. She smiled and waved back, inhaling slowly around the churning sensation in her stomach. Her nerves were jittery with excitement and fear. It was time to say goodbye to another piece of her life and began a new one. Beginnings and endings—that's what life was made of. Sara turned the key in the ignition and turned the car in the direction of Boscobel.

SHE SAW WITH a clarity she hadn't been able to before the time spent in Waupun. She knew she could love Lincoln without betraying Cole. Some things, like the blame she'd placed on herself for the loss of her husband's life, weren't so easily accepted. But she was trying and that was all she could do. Forgiveness, even for oneself, was earned. Sara was earning it with each thought of Cole that was happy instead of sad, with each smile she allowed herself, with every sunrise and sunset she gazed at with thankfulness, and with every breath she felt worthy of instead of unworthy.

She'd been gone a little under three months and she'd been back over a week. It was unusually hot for September in Wisconsin, making her think even the weather could be confused at times. There had been no calls from Lincoln since her return and she wondered why that was. Had he known the exact day she'd come back to Boscobel or was it a coincidence that that was the day he'd decided she wasn't worth waiting for? The thought made her heart painfully squeeze. Or maybe he was simply waiting for her.

Sara talked to Dana every other day. She made her laugh with her recollections of her marriage fiascos and her continuing search to find the thieving housekeeper at the motel. They both knew there wasn't one. Dana's employees were honest and trustworthy; it was just something to talk about and she was certainly a good storyteller. Even with the distance between them, they still had their coffee and doughnuts at eight on Mondays, Wednesdays, and Fridays as they chatted about nothing of importance. The conversations were important; not the words spoken during them.

The house she'd found to rent was red with tan trim, small, and filled with unpacked boxes and new furniture. It fit her and Sara felt a relief upon entering it she hadn't known whether she'd feel or not. It was time to get back to herself—the new self that was living without Cole and able to do so. She would make this home hers and only hers, leaving the ghosts of the past where they needed to be, in the past, in the place in her heart designated to Cole and her parents and their unborn baby; to love and not mourn.

Painting was easier and her finished art had more depth to it than it used to carry. The colors were bolder and the peace she found didn't fade as soon as she set the paintbrush down. Sara painted with her soul now. Every stroke of the paintbrush on canvas was a gift to those not with her; every painting a piece of her she would share with the world with joy and not sorrow or fear. Business was slow with her artwork at the moment, having been out of practice and contact with the art world for so long, but she was confident it would be steady again in time. Like her.

On one such day, as she painted, her mind drifted to the day she'd seen the 'C' in the blue paint and thought it an omen from Cole. Maybe it had been, but maybe it had been in a different way from what she'd thought. Sara set the paintbrush down and tried to recollect the exact shape of the splatter on the floor. Could it have been an 'L'? Even then, had he been telling her something? Had she seen a 'C' at the time because she'd had to see that or because it truly had been? Did she know it to be an 'L' now because she wanted it to be or because it always had been? An interesting concept. The letter 'C' and the letter 'L' could be quite similar, depending on the hand that wrote them. Or it could have simply been a splotch of paint.

She'd bumped into Mason and his nephew one day at the park and had spent the afternoon swinging and playing with Derek; regaling Mason with tales of her Waupun adventure and Dana. He'd looked at her with contentment, knowing she was on the right path. It was because of him and Lincoln and so many other people, but most of all, it was because of Sara.

As she now left the house, a warm breeze played with her hair. She gazed at the leafy green trees and grass as she walked, her destination filling her with apprehension and purpose. Lawnmowers whirred along in various yards, tossing the scent of freshly mowed grass in the air. Kids shouted and squealed as they played. The sun was hot, warming her lightly suntanned skin. She'd loved Waupun, but she didn't want to live there. Her home was here, in Boscobel. Her home was wherever was closest to Lincoln, even if not *with* Lincoln. Even if they couldn't be together, even if he no longer wanted her, Sara wanted a part of him, she *needed* a part of him—even if it was only his friendship and nothing more. .

She hadn't heard Cole or seen anything unusual since she'd been in Waupun and had heard his final words of "Take care, Sara" in her mind. So maybe he was truly gone and that had been his final goodbye. That saddened her, but it also set her free in a way. Of course, maybe he'd never really been with her at all. But her mind, at least, she had needed him to be, for a while anyway.

She walked through the rusted gate of the equally rusted fence, her skin prickling as she gazed at the land littered with tombstones. Giving a slight shudder, she walked toward his headstone. She had never liked cemeteries. They were filled with the dead and no matter where she stepped, she feared she was walking on a body. Graveyards made her feel like she was in another world—where the dead were never really dead. Winds were cool and harsher here, shadows lengthened and darkened, and even when it was warm out, it was colder here. Sara didn't want to think of Cole being in such a place, but this was where he was now, and so this was where she would talk to him. She knew it was only his body and not his soul buried beneath the ground—it wasn't really *Cole*—but it was the closest she could physically get to him.

It was the anniversary of the car wreck and also his birthday. September 1st. In a way he was born on the same day he died.

The tombstone was rectangular and gray, as simple as the man had been. It read 'Cole Walker – Beloved Son, Brother, and Husband' with his date of birth and date of death. *Where are you, Cole? Where are you now?* She glanced around the empty cemetery, uneasily realizing she was the only living being here. It made her skin break out in goose bumps. She knelt on the uneven ground, searching for words to say, but nothing came to her. She'd made her peace with herself and now she was trying to make her peace with God as well. And Cole.

"I don't know what to say. I know you're not really here. I have to believe you're somewhere better, or I won't be able to do this. I won't be okay unless I think that." Her knees became stiff the longer she crouched down beside the tombstone, but it didn't matter. "I guess the reason I'm here...I guess what I came to say is..." Her eyes burned with unshed tears and the wind picked up, tousling her hair around her face as she stared at the stone she knew would be cold and smooth. "Goodbye. I came to say goodbye. Not to you, never to you, but to—" Sara blinked and unlocked the tears. "To the life we had together," she whispered, brushing the tears away with a trembling hand.

The cold breeze abruptly stopped, a warm stillness taking its place. She smiled in spite of the tears, love and sorrow welling in her heart for the man she'd been blessed to have. She had to remember that—she had to be thankful for the time they'd had together, instead of thinking of the time they hadn't gotten.

"Goodbye, Cole," she whispered, slowly standing. A collage of images, thoughts, and emotions pierced her as she stood—blue eyes, gruff laughter, warm hands, coffee and cherry-flavored Carmex, passion, tenderness, sadness, *love*. Sara took a deep breath and turned, all of it fading away at the sight that met her.

Down the gravel path, standing just inside the fence, was Lincoln.

Sara's pulse jumped as her eyes caressed him. It had been almost three months since she'd seen him and it had been far too long. A day was too long. She wanted to run to him. Her feet even moved forward in anticipation. Hunger propelled her, though she had no idea what kind of reciprocation she would receive. His dark locks were disheveled and wavy, the way they should be, and his gray were eyes riveted to her. She now knew they always were and always had been. Lincoln wore a black tee shirt that was tight against his toned frame and khaki shorts, his stance wary as she approached.

Her stomach was swirling, her heart pounded at a scary rate, and she thought she'd pass out or go insane if she didn't touch him. But he seemed so far away. Her fingers longed to smooth his furrowed brow, her lips wanted to feel the firm softness of his on them. She *ached* for him. Sara's eyes devoured the sight of him. If it was all she had, if it was all she was allowed, then she would let her eyes take their fill and then some. She would stare at him until he faded from her view, and even then, she'd see him in her mind. Forever.

"How did you know I would be here?" she gasped out, trying to catch her breath that was evading her. Sara self-consciously touched her dirt-smudged pink shorts and tugged at the white shirt she wore, knowing she looked horrid. She tried to smooth her thick hair down and then gave up. This was *not* how she'd wanted to look for their reunion. It was also not the place she'd had in mind for it either.

"I didn't."

"Oh." Something inside her deflated and she tore her gaze from his, feeling immediately empty. "Did you—did you know I was back? From...where I was?" She glanced at his unreadable expression.

"You know Boscobel. Everyone knows your business before you even do," he said dryly. "I knew where you were, Sara," he added softly.

She frowned. "You did? How?"

Lincoln sighed. "Do you really think I wouldn't find out where you were going so that I knew you'd be safe? So I knew you'd be okay?"

"But...Spencer," she said, realization dawning on her.

"Having a cop for a friend can be good at times," was all he said.

"You two are okay? You and Spencer? You talked and everything?"

He snorted. "Guys, talking? Guys don't *talk*. We ridicule each other, toss back a couple beers, sometimes even throw a few punches, and move on."

"So did you then? Move on?"

"Yep," he replied shortly.

"Good." She exhaled. "I'm glad." Sara studied his gray eyes.

Lincoln shifted his jaw and looked over her head, not letting her see in his face what he didn't want her to. "Did you come to say hello or did you come to say goodbye?" He nodded toward the hill where Cole's headstone resided.

"I don't..." She frowned. "What do you mean?"

He shook his head. "Nothing. You need a ride?"

For the first time she noticed the Dodge truck alongside the road, parked haphazardly, as though he'd been in a hurry to park it. "Sure. I live on—"

"I know where you live," he interrupted darkly, turning and stalking to his vehicle.

She followed, confused. It felt like her gut was shredded into millions of irreplaceable pieces. Like she was swallowing glass, or had had all the air stolen from her lungs. Even it was better than not being near him, not being able to gaze at his flawed perfection.

The ride was tense, silent. She was only minutely surprised when he pulled the truck up to the right house. Lincoln's body was wound tight, like a taut string. There was so much strength in that body, so much power. A tick in his jaw captured her attention and held it as she struggled for the right words to say. In the end, there were none.

His voice was gravel when he said slowly, evenly, "Do you know...I wanted to tie you up so you couldn't go? I seriously thought about it. Or I was going to kidnap you and lock you in my room until you saw reason. Only I figured Spencer might frown on that. Bad thing about having a cop for a friend," he muttered.

Sara inhaled sharply, knowing she should be disturbed by that declaration but finding she was oddly pleased instead.

"And then the phone calls. Those were torture. I wanted to shout at you, plead with you, tell you how much I loved you. I wanted to get in my truck and go to Waupun and bring you home with me. I even thought about just going there and watching you—just to see you, just to know you were really okay. I have serious issues where you are concerned." Lincoln let his head thump against the steering wheel, his shoulders slumping.

"I wanted to leave. I wanted to turn the car around before I even left Boscobel," she quietly admitted. "But I had to go, otherwise I would have never known if I truly felt for you what I thought I did or if you were just a crutch I leaned on in my time of need. I wouldn't have known the depth of my feelings for you. I wouldn't have been able to heal. I wouldn't have known—" she broke off, unable to continue.

"*What?* What wouldn't you have known?" he demanded, still not looking at her.

"Do you hate me?" Sara blurted, mentally kicking herself at how weak she sounded, like she would die if he did. A part of her would, she knew that much.

His head swung around, his features twisted in incredulity. "*What?*"

She played with the hem of her shorts, her leg warm against her hand. "Do you hate me?"

"Of all the stupid—*no*, I don't *hate* you. Some days I wish I did. It would make all of this a hell of a lot easier. You think I can just turn my feelings for you off and on, like a switch? You think *months* are sufficient enough time to forget you, to move on, to get you out of my system?" Lincoln leaned across the console, locking her in place with his stormy eyes. "I will *never* get over you, Sara, *never*."

"But I left you. I'm sorry. You didn't want me to go and I did anyway. I just...I had to." Her expression pleaded with him to understand.

"I know, I do." His tone was weary, resigned.

"I love you," she whispered brokenly.

He froze, his expression turning to granite. Lincoln slowly turned his gaze away to stare out the windshield. His jaw shifted as he inhaled deeply. "Do you mean that?" he asked roughly, eyes still trained straight ahead.

Sara wordlessly nodded, and then realizing he wasn't looking at her, she reached for him. Her hand grasped his hard bicep and squeezed, needing him closer. With a groan, he grabbed her and pulled her onto his lap so that she straddled him. "Tell me again," he begged, burying his face into the crook of her neck, his fingers digging into her thighs, holding her like he feared she'd vanish if he released his grip on her. His body trembled and tenderness rushed through her.

"I love you, Lincoln," she said, her voice clear and strong. She cupped his sharp jawline in her hands, the rough texture of his unshaven skin tingling against her palms, their eyes so close she saw the gold in them, so close she saw the raw need in them. "I think I love your eyes the most. The color, the shape, even your long, thick eyelashes. They're silver and gold and I see your soul in them and I see myself in them as well. I love the way they spark to life in anger and humor, the way they're always locked on me, wherever I am. Like you're afraid if you look away I'll disappear or you'll lose me. You won't, you know," she added softly.

Lincoln swallowed. "Do you know how long I've waited to hear you say that?"

"That I love your eyes?" she teased.

"Yeah, that too. But that you love *me*?" He studied her face.

"A long time?"

He took a shuddering breath. "You have no idea, Sara. *None.*"

"You're right. I don't. But I'm here now. And I'm yours."

Their eyes locked. She felt the heat and hardness of his body beneath hers, the way the fiery warmth rolled off him and onto her, connecting them, intertwining them with desire and love, invisible tendrils sweeping through her and him, branding them as each other's.

The opened windows of the truck let balmy air blanket them, marginally cooling the heat of their skin. She fit perfectly to him, her body the missing puzzle piece to make Lincoln whole and vice versa. Sara placed her hands on his firm chest and felt his heart thunder beneath her palm, focusing on that. So many times she'd listen to Lincoln's heart and centered herself in the steady thrum of it.

He threaded his fingers through hers, those smoky eyes never leaving hers as he declared, "You're not leaving my sight for a very long time, not until I can convince myself you're really here and mine. And I don't know if I'll ever be able to fully convince myself of those things, so get used to seeing me. A lot."

Lincoln's lips captured hers before she could respond, possessing them, possessing her, telling her that she was his, telling her what she already knew. He tasted like sweetly tart lemons and sunshine and her future. The emotions coursed through her veins, pulsed through her heart, and slammed out of her with all the passion of her being. It was right; they were *right*. She and Cole had been right, but she and Lincoln were right as well. Cole was her past—a past she would never forget, would always hold on to—but Lincoln was her present, her future, and she would hold on to that just as tightly.

DAYS AND NIGHTS went by, turning into weeks. It was mid-September and it was still in the seventies during the day in Wisconsin. The nights cooled off considerably, letting Wisconsinites know the heat wouldn't last much longer and to enjoy it while they could. Sara and Lincoln had decided to do so by taking the pontoon boat out on the Mississippi river. Sand bars full of green foliage and trees littered either side of the vast, brown water with boats anchored near them, people milling in the water and sand, looking like colorful specs as they boated past.

Lincoln's eyes glinted silver in the sunlight as he shut the engine off in the middle of the river, jumping to his feet and reaching for her. He grabbed her hands, spinning her up and around as 'Ho Hey' by The Lumineers blasted from the boat radio. The pontoon boat gently swayed in the Mississippi river, the sun glared down at them. Sara laughed, feeling free in his arms. The scent of sunscreen lingered on her skin and his. His body was hot and hard against hers, desire flaring inside Sara with the smallest of touches from him.

No matter how long she stared at him, how often she touched him, or how long she was in his presence, it wasn't enough. She was learning to rejoice in each minute spent with him, to live them to the fullest, because no one ever knew when it would be the last. Instead of being sad about it, she was blessed by each smile he gave her, each hug that was hers, each night spent in his arms. Sara would hold each moment close to her heart and treasure it, like this moment.

He sang to her, his voice deep, slightly rough, and beautiful. Their faces were inches apart, brown eyes locked with gray. She smiled as he smiled, his fingers entangled with hers.

"I love you," she told him.

Lincoln leaned his head down to kiss her. "I love you. Sometimes it's hard to believe you love me back, finally. I've loved you for so long, so impossibly long. I thought that's the way it would always be—me loving you, you being clueless."

"Hey." She jabbed his hard stomach. "I'm not always clueless."

"Sometimes you are."

Sara nodded. "I suppose I can admit that."

He grinned, saying, "This feels like a dream, a really good dream." Lincoln caressed her face, stroked her hair, and pressed a kiss to her temple.

"If it's a dream, let's hope we never wake up."

"If it was a dream we'd be having a lot more sex."

She snorted, looking up at the fiery ball that was the sun and quickly looking down, spots in her eyes. "Why do you love me?"

"*Why* do I love you?" he repeated, a frown between his brows. "I know *what* I love about you. I love your hair, I love the way your brown eyes light up when you're excited about something. Your nose, your lips. Even that small scar above your lip. The way you eat chocolate—"

Lincoln closed his eyes, inhaling slowly. "I could watch you devour a chocolate bar forever. Really. I could. There's something so sensual about your lips kissing it, tugging the chocolate into your mouth, the way your eyes close—" He swallowed, running a shaking hand through his hair. "It's hot," he ended abruptly.

Her lips parted at the mixture of pleasure and pain on his face. That's—" She swallowed, tried again. "That's not what I asked."

He grinned. "I know. But I'm on a roll. Just go with it. I love your laugh, your smile, your sense of humor, your strength. I love the look on your face when you're painting—you look completely lost, consumed. It's the same look you have when I'm inside you. Like you're shattered and whole at the same time. I love that look," he said, his eyes darkening.

Abnormally hot, even with the sun shining, she said, "Stop talking like that. And don't look at me like that either."

"Why? Am I turning you on?"

"No," she lied. "You're getting off subject."

"Okay, okay." He exhaled noisily as he visibly fought for composure. "Why do I love you," he mused.

She nodded, her hands clasped loosely on his narrow hips. "What made you love me?"

"Do you remember the first thing you said to me, the first time we talked?" he asked slowly, twirling a lock of her hair around his finger, gently tugging it.

She searched her brain, seeing a baby-faced young man with laughing gray eyes and a mocking grin. "You said something about serial killers. It wasn't funny."

He laughed. "You're right. It wasn't. I said my brother wasn't one, but you didn't know if I was or not. Something stupid and lame like that. I couldn't think straight when I saw you, when I realized you were the girl I'd seen walking. It was the first thing that came to mind, what Cole had told me about your encounter with him. Your comeback was something like how I didn't know about you either."

Sara crinkled her nose. "That's what made you love me?"

"Nah. But you always had quick-witted retorts to counter mine. I liked that." He grinned, dazzling her with the beauty of it. "That day on the river, when I realized you could be taken away from this world, that's when I realized how *much* I loved you. It killed me that you belonged to Cole, but at least you were living and breathing and that was enough, it had to be enough, but the thought of you not being alive—that I couldn't deal with."

"Hence the punching of Cole in the face."

"He deserved it," he said with a scowl.

She laughed. "No argument from me. He kind of did, yeah."

The grin was back in place, along with the shine in his eyes. "You always understood me. I think that was it. I didn't have to pretend with you, I didn't have to not say what I wanted to. If I was being rude or grumpy, you called me on it. You *got* me. I felt alive when I was around you, Sara. I felt like I belonged when I'd never felt that before, not even with my own family. Not that anything was horribly bad or anything growing up, really. I just felt..." Lincoln shrugged. "Misunderstood."

"Don't forget Grandma Lena. She was pretty horrible." She touched his cheek, kissing the faint smile from his lips.

"You can't kiss me while talking about Grandma Lena," he said with a cringe, pulling away. "It totally kills the mood."

"I doubt that," she said, laughing as his eyes flashed the truth of her words at her.

"I think it's time to go back." He turned the boat on, steering them along the river. "You completely turned me off talking about Grandma Lena. That's almost as bad as when I met Dana last week and she eyed me up like I was her last meal."

The wind played with Sara's hair as she laughed, brushing it out of her eyes. It was true. Dana had enjoyed their impromptu visit immensely, maybe even a little *too* much if the slap she'd landed to Lincoln's behind was anything to go by.

He glanced back at her, grinning, and everything went still for a period of time no longer than a minute, but astounding and endless in its clearness. Cole had been hers to love first, but Lincoln, Lincoln was hers to love last.

"Why do *you* love *me*?" he called above the noise of the motor.

Sara looked down at the brown waves crashing against the side of the boat as it raced along the river. Why did she love him? He'd never given up on her, he'd forced her to live, to feel. He'd taken the darkness away with his lightness. Lincoln had always been there for her, even when she hadn't wanted him to be. His arms were home to her, his touch cherished. He was passionate and strong and good. He made her laugh. In him she found herself. Sara wanted to spend every day with him and even if she couldn't, she'd take him everywhere with her, in her heart. Every hour of every day was not enough, would never be enough with him. Sara was stronger because of him and she was *better*. It wasn't even a question, why she loved him. A better one would be a question of—

"How could I not?" she called back, telling Lincoln with her eyes all he meant to her and it was endless in its entirety.

EPILOGUE

THE LEAVES WERE dropping. Browns, reds, yellows, and oranges. They fell from the trees, floating back and forth as they descended. The sky was overcast and gray. Sara stood on a bluff at Wyalusing State Park, feeling a peace she hadn't been allowed to feel the last time she'd stood on the same exact cliff so many months ago. How very different her life was now from then. She was *living* and she was *thankful* to be alive. How ashamed she was to admit that she'd once thought so carelessly of the life she'd been gifted. That was over now. She'd come around full circle and was finally, blissfully, in one whole piece. Sara had had to do it on her own and she had.

The wind was cool, tousling her long hair behind her, invisible fingers tenderly caressing it. The trees swayed with it and she unconsciously rocked side to side as well. Sara closed her eyes and felt him all around her. It was strange how she saw him in the leaves, heard him in a song, felt him in the air. Cole was everywhere, but it didn't hurt anymore. She'd never really lost him, only a part of him. He was still with her in her heart and memories, where it mattered, and he always would be. The loss was there and sometimes there were the thoughts of what might have been, but in them, there was also what *was*, and that was Lincoln. She could never regret him. The what ifs and what might have beens crumbled in the wake of Lincoln. He had the power to eradicate them and eradicate them he did with a simple look or touch.

There was a special, carved-out part of her that belonged to Cole. Lincoln knew and understood; it was the same for him. It was hard not to think what the years would have been like, what Cole would have been like, if he still lived, and so, they talked of him often. They talked of his quirks and habits and endearments, and in that way, they kept him alive. Cole still lived, would always live, within those who remembered and loved him. No one ever really died that way; no one ever really had to say goodbye as well.

She inhaled deeply. The air smelled like years of happiness, eyes the color of stormy skies and promises kept, and everlasting love. Cinnamon and lemons and Lincoln. A leaf, crinkly and brittle, brushed her cheek as it fell, like the tender touch of a loved one long gone saying hellow. Sara smiled and opened her eyes, listening as the wind tossed the leaves about, finding peace in the song of them.

Warm arms wrapped around her from behind, centering her as they always did, loving her however damaged or imperfect she was. All Sara had to do, all she could do, was love Lincoln back. They stood like that, listening to the music of the leaves, rejoicing in their love and lives, both of which could be fleeting and at the same time never-ending.

"I love you," Lincoln murmured into her hair, cocooning her in his warmth and scent.

No one could control the length of their life, but they could control how they lived it.

She was choosing to live it not in sorrow and pain, but with hope and love. She was choosing to be strong; she was choosing to be happy. She was choosing Lincoln. She would always find herself in Lincoln's eyes. Love was forever, love was not lost when a life was. Love did not fall away or weaken a person. Love was strong and people were stronger because of it. Love continued, in all forms, in every way, until the end of time and even after that. It was in the glance of gray eyes, it was in the caress of a fallen leaf, a steady heartbeat. It was wholeness, peace and sacrifice, and even tragedy.

"I love you," she said, a smile on her lips as she gazed down at his arms locked firmly around her.

It was all of that and as little as that.

BONUS

LINCOLN'S EULOGY

I KNOW EULOGIES are supposed to highlight all the things we love about the people we've lost, but I can't do that, not with Cole. We all know everyone loved Cole. We all know all the many ways and forms he was awesome, and yes, we all know he will be insanely missed. So I'm not going to get into any of that. Instead I'm going to highlight all the ways he was annoying, all the ways he drove me crazy, all the ways he pissed me off, because honestly, that is what I will miss the most about him—all the ways he aggravated me. I'd give anything to have him punch me in the arm one last time or try to trip me as I walk past, and most especially, be handed a cup of that awful gas station coffee he knew I loathed and still brought me every day we worked together.

I compiled a list of the ten most irritating Cole-isms. I'm sure a lot of you will agree with me on these:

1. He always took the last helping of mashed potatoes. That really irritated me. I mean, he was smaller than me, so he shouldn't have needed to eat more than me.

2. His singing. It was terrible. I think he purposely sang off-key just because he knew how much it bothered me. No one can sing that bad without trying to.

3. His love of Peeps. I mean, really? Those are the most disgusting things I've ever tasted. How could he enjoy those? It's like shoving a wad

of sugar in your mouth and letting it dissolve on your tongue. It makes me shudder thinking about it.

4. *The movie Titanic. I apologize to those of you who like the movie, but Cole just ruined it for me, he really did. He watched that movie every single time it was on TV. He said it was because of the ship, but really, I know it was the love story that had him hooked. And I know this 'cause I saw him tear up a time or two, even though he tried to hide it. Guy was a closet sap.*

5. *Snowmobiling. Don't get me wrong, I love snowmobiling. Just not with Cole. He had to race against everyone, which isn't all that bad, but damn, the guy never lost. Can I say damn? No matter how many times I raced him, I lost. As did all of you unfortunate enough to decide to go against him.*

6. *His laugh. Cole was gifted with the laugh of a horse. No lie. It sounded like he was whinnying every time he thought something was funny.*

7. *Cole's lack of cavities. This brings me back to the Peeps thing. How can someone eat so much unhealthy food and never get a cavity? I was going to say good genetics, but then where does that leave me? Shafted, like usual.*

8. *How he always stood up for me growing up. Sure, he let me fight my own battles, but when I couldn't, he was there, and even when I didn't want him to be, he was still there. Always watching. Always making sure I didn't get my ass kicked. Can I say ass? Anyway, sometimes I didn't want him around because I thought it made me less of a man to have my older brother hovering, even though I was glad he was there, which also made me mad. Apparently I was a confused kid.*

9. *Grandma Lena. No matter what I did, didn't do, said or didn't say, Cole was her favorite. She told everyone it was because he wasn't loud like me, but really, I think she was just a sucker for his baby blues. Those eyes got him out of trouble more times than they should have. Whatever it was, yep—shafted again.*

10. *And what I really hate the most about Cole is that he's gone, and I can't tell him any of this. He was my brother, my best friend, the one I looked up to more than anyone else, the person I strove to be the most like, and now there's this void where his light should be. So, yeah, most*

annoying thing about Cole is him not being here. Not in the literal sense anyway. He'll always be here, in my heart. Pain in the ass, pain in the heart; both of which I gladly endure. Sorry about the ass thing again.

Love you, bro.

ABOUT LINDY—

 USA Today bestselling author Lindy Zart writes in a multitude of fictional genres because, well, her brain requires it so she stays somewhat sane. She has been writing since she was a child, but luckily for readers, her writing has improved since then. She lives in Wisconsin with her husband, two sons, and one cat. Lindy loves hearing from people who enjoy her work. She also has a completely healthy obsession with the following: coffee, wine, pizza, peanut butter, and bloody marys.

You can connect with her online at:
twitter.com/lindyzart
facebook.com/lindyzart
lindyzart.com
amazon.com/author/lindyzart

Listen to the playlists for Lindy's books on spotify.com
Get an eBook autograph from Lindy at authorgraph.com

Made in the USA
Lexington, KY
29 September 2016